Without You

Reylynn Purdue

For my husband, who has loved me through thick and thin.
Thank you for being my hero and the reason I believe in happily ever after.
I love you always and forever plus one day.

CONTENTS

Chapter 1 1
Chapter 2 17
Chapter 3 35
Chapter 4 53
Chapter 5 75
Chapter 6 87
Chapter 7 97
Chapter 8 109
Chapter 9 119
Chapter 10 125
Chapter 11 135
Chapter 12 151
Chapter 13 163
Chapter 14 173
Chapter 15 181
Chapter 16 191
Chapter 17 199
Chapter 18 207
Chapter 19 213
Chapter 20 223
Chapter 21 233
Chapter 22 239
Chapter 23 247
Chapter 24 251
Chapter 25 259
Chapter 26 265
Chapter 27 273
Chapter 28 281
Chapter 29 289
Chapter 30 295

Chapter 31 305
Chapter 32 315
Chapter 33 323
Chapter 34 329
Chapter 35 333
Chapter 36 347
Acknowledgments 355
About the Author 357

1

I blinked my eyes, and I looked up at the ceiling. Music from downstairs had come into my room and woken me up. I looked at my alarm clock. It was twenty after six. I rolled onto my side and opened my nightstand drawer. I retrieved the orange medication bottle and sat up. I dumped out the contents into a small pile on my pastel pink comforter.

One, two, three, four, five, six...

I counted the white pills as I put them back into the bottle.

Seven, eight, nine, ten...

I wondered if I belonged at one of those meetings for people with addiction problems.

I imagined myself standing in front of a room of strangers.

"Hi, I'm Roxanne, and I..."

I...what?

"And I'm a..."

The room I was standing in suddenly got a lot smaller. As I looked out at all the faces staring back at me, my stomach twisted. Those weren't the faces of complete strangers. Every face now belonged to my mom.

The word addict *stuck in my throat, choking me.*

But I wasn't an addict. I could stop at any time.

I beheld my mom's face. Her beautiful blue eyes that had once shined with pride for me were now full of disappointment. I hated seeing her looking at me like that.

"You know me. I didn't used to be this way. I have a good reason for using your pills. I need them. It's the only thing that eases the pain." I was begging for her to understand.

But her expression of disappointment stayed with me, even as each one of her disappeared.

The sound of a slamming door downstairs pulled me back to reality. I glanced around my room, feeling empty. I shook my head, trying to forget the image of my mom's face.

Eleven, twelve, thirteen...

I dropped the last pill back into the bottle and twisted the cap on. My heart raced at the thought of running out of pills. I couldn't run out. I needed them.

The pills were crucial because I wasn't the girl I used to be. That girl had been destroyed the night of graduation—when I'd walked into my home and found my mom's lifeless body on the kitchen floor. Apparently, I hadn't had enough heartache because the day after I'd put my mom in the ground, I'd walked in on my boyfriend of the past four years in bed with Miss Slutbag.

Who knew a person could endure such heart-shattering pain and survive?

I certainly didn't want to survive, but it'd turned out that someone couldn't die from heartache alone. If that were possible, I'd be six feet under with my mom right now.

I wished I wasn't the girl who needed pills, who welcomed the pain-dulling haze they would bring. I wanted to be the girl I once was. My mom had been proud of that girl. It wasn't fair. I used to be happy. I used to be a whole person. Now, I was just a broken mess.

My mom's lifeless face flashed in my mind. My chest tightened.

I turned the bottle in circles between my fingers. The pills had belonged to my mom. She used to get terrible migraines. She had called them her angel pills, stating that each pill would give her a tiny miracle by taking away her pain. The pills hadn't taken away my hurt. I could feel the agony in every single ounce of my body. It was the kind of pain that had been woven into my soul. However, the pills would dull the pain even if just for a while. Any kind of relief was better than none.

My mom's face was in my head again. This time, she was full of life, sporting her look of disapproval.

I tried to forget about what my mom would have probably thought of my new life and how I was spending my time. But I couldn't, and it was the reason I was now contemplating whether or not to get out of bed. This had become a daily event. I wasn't sure if most people had to convince themselves to get out of bed and continue with life, but once again, I didn't used to be this way.

I used to wake up at five in the morning just to get a few hours of dancing in before school. My mom had always gotten up with me, coaching me and pushing me to dance my best. She'd constantly reminded me that Juilliard only took the best, and she'd believed I was the best.

I looked at my alarm clock through tear-filled eyes. Only five minutes had passed since I last looked at it. It would be dark in a few hours.

Music and laughter wafted into my room.

My brother must be getting ready for one of his epic parties.

Oh, yay.

I wiped my eyes and sighed with annoyance at the thought of my brother having another party this week.

Brent shouted, "The kegs are here!"

My assumption had been confirmed.

It made me sick that this was Ryan's way of dealing with his grief. It was absurd. I clutched the bottle of painkillers. Then again, I guessed we all had our own ways of dealing.

I rolled myself out of bed and tossed the bottle into my nightstand drawer. I made my way into the bathroom and found myself looking at a hideous sight.

Beyond the disaster that was my reflection, I could still see all the ways I looked like my mother. The ache in my chest intensified as I took in my aristocratic nose, high cheekbones, and pouty mouth. My mouth would even turn up into the same smile as hers. At least, it had when I used to smile, back before she had died and my world had fallen completely apart. My most distinctive feature that stood out as proof that I was my mother's daughter was by far my eyes. They were the same sapphire blue as hers.

My hair was the only thing that had separated me from being my mother's mini me. Hers had been a fiery red that most women would pay thousands to replicate. Mine, on the other hand, was a boring chestnut brown that I'd gotten from my father. On a good day, my long hair was full of life with wavy curls—yet another thing I'd gotten from my mother.

Today was not one of those good days. Today, my hair was a frizzy giant rat's nest. My skin was a shade of white that it had never been. Seriously, I could pass for a ghost in a bad horror movie. But I guessed that staying inside for weeks on end would do that. The dark circles under my eyes did surprise me, seeing as I had been in a self-prescribed drug-induced sleep for pretty much the last four days. Adding to the disgusting factor, I hadn't showered during that time. I continued to look at myself as the tears fell.

This is what I've become—a forlorn disaster.

"You look like shit!" I spit at my reflection.

I turned away from the mirror, repulsed by the girl looking back at me.

After undressing, I got into the shower. The water was too hot, but I didn't bother to cool it down. The sting from the hot water searing my skin was almost a relief from the throbbing painful ache deep inside me. The ache was always there, threatening to come up and rip out of my chest.

I sat down on the marble-tiled shower floor. I pulled my knees up to my chest and held them there. I put my head down and cried. This wasn't anything new. I'd been crying every day since she died. I lacked any hope of this pain ever dissipating.

The water eventually went cold, and I was shivering. I stood up, pushing the pain deep inside me, and I finished my shower.

After the shower, I got dressed, and then I brushed my hair and teeth. I smothered lip balm on my dry lips and headed downstairs to get water that my body desperately needed.

Pausing in the hallway outside of my parents' room, every part of me wanted to run in there and hide in the closet. It was the only place where I could still feel her. That was probably because her scent lingered and was strong in there. As my body shook with its need to crumble to pieces, I knew going in there now would completely unravel me. I forced myself to continue down the stairs.

I caught sight of my brother outside. He was loading a keg into a trash can. Past him, a group of girls in bikinis were sitting with their feet in the pool. The sight of them out there, laughing and carefree, made me want to scream. Granted, if everything were different, I'd be out there with them, not caring that the sun was about to set and it was getting cold. But everything was different. My mom was dead, and I pretty much hated everyone who didn't care.

Ryan saw me and gave me a head nod.

My brother was the complete opposite from me. In all the ways I took after our mother, he took after our father. He was also way taller than me, standing at six-three. I was five-eight. He had wavy auburn hair, not that anyone besides his family would ever know. When his hair wasn't buzzed, it was usually hidden under a cap or beanie. He also had our father's strong jawline and broad shoulders. The only thing Ryan and I had in common was our blue eyes.

I gave him a small wave and then went to the fridge for a bottle of water.

Brent strolled in from the living room, greeting me with that God's-gift-to-women smile. He'd been my brother's best friend for as long as I could remember. Through the years, Brent had gone from good-looking to drop-dead gorgeous. His body was as dangerously close to perfection as one's body could get. As if that weren't enough, he also had sun-kissed skin and hypnotic hazel eyes.

It should be illegal for one person to be that gorgeous.

I used to spend hours in the sun trying to get my skin as tan as his. I would be outside, battling the sun's cancer rays, fighting my Irish genes that tried to keep my skin as white as possible.

After spending a couple of weeks in my house, I was already as pale as a ghost. Brent could go outside for five minutes and instantly become a walking advertisement for tanning. To say I was envious would be an understatement. He'd claimed it was his Italian genes, but I'd called bull. My father was Italian, and Ryan and I hadn't been blessed with the year-round tan.

But those things didn't matter to me anymore.

"Hey there, Princess. You finally decided to wake up?" His voice was deep and sexy, like the rest of him.

Of course, I was standing at the open fridge, gawking at him like a crazy stalker. It wasn't my fault that he was ridiculously easy to look at. His jet-black hair was sticking up in all its excellence.

A man's hair shouldn't shimmer like that.

It wasn't hard to see why I had been obsessed with him for part of my life. He had been my first crush when I was eight. By thirteen, I had been positive that he was the one. I had planned our wedding and named our future children. Of course, he hadn't known about it, and neither had my brother, but it was perfect. My brother, the killer of true love, was the reason my fantasy hadn't come to life. He had an outrageous rule that made his friends absolutely off-limits to me. I knew it, and they knew it.

It was embarrassing to think of how obsessed I used to be over Brent. I'd never had feelings like that for any other guy—well, until Kevin.

Ugh! Stupid, stupid Kevin.

Just thinking about him made my stomach cramp up, leaving me feeling sick.

I opened my bottle of water and took a few small sips, trying to ease my queasiness.

Brent laughed. "Or you can just stand there and ignore me. It's cool."

I held up my bottle of water as if showing it to him would take away the fact that I had been staring at him like an idiot. "I figured I'd get up and drink something before I died from dehydration." It was a bad joke on my part. Just speaking about death caused the twisting pain in my chest.

The memory of my mom's body lying on the floor just a few feet away from where I now stood made me dizzy. I clenched the fridge's door handle to steady myself as I shut it.

He smiled. "We can't have that. Drink up, Princess."

"I hate it when you call me that," I reminded him.

Brent had been calling me Princess since I was ten years old. He'd never told me why he called me that. I always just figured it was because from age three to now, I'd dressed up as one of the Disney princesses for Halloween. Granted, the costumes had gone from cute and adorable to sexy, bordering on slutty, as I got older. But I was always a princess. In retrospect, I'd kind of asked for it.

He chuckled. "Old habits die hard. You will forever be Princess to me."

I let out an annoyed sigh and changed the subject. "Correct me if I'm wrong, but didn't you and Ry just have a party a few days ago?"

He shrugged. "You know Ry. He loves to host a good shindig. Besides, it keeps him distracted and out of his own head. Everyone has their own way of coping."

Shindig? Really, Brent? Who says that anymore?

"I get that, but don't you think it's getting a bit excessive? I'm kind of tired of the endless amounts of people coming in and out of our home."

Ryan came in from out back. "Hey." He smiled. "I'm glad you are finally out of bed."

Yesterday, he'd spent most of the day trying to wake me up, but I had been too tired from the pills, so he'd finally given up.

"I see you also showered. You're just full of surprises today, aren't you?" Ryan teased.

I rolled my eyes at him.

"Maybe you will surprise us even more by eating something," Ryan added.

"Not hungry, so I guess I'm all out of surprises." I walked past him and toward the stairs.

"Hold up, Roxy. I need to talk to you." Ryan stopped me.

I whipped around to face him. "What? You want to tear me down some more?" I didn't know where my hostility was coming from, but it was there.

"Whoa, sis. Chill the dramatics. I wasn't tearing you down."

I huffed and crossed my arms over my chest. "What then?"

"Dad will be home tomorrow night. We're going to stick with tradition and go to the beach for the Fourth."

"Great. Have fun. I'm not going." I stared past him at the wall. Pain was pulsing through my body after hearing the plans.

"Yes, you are," he countered.

"No, I'm not!"

"Come on, Princess, it will be fun, and you should get out of the house," Brent chimed in.

"You"—I pointed at Brent—"stay out of it." I looked at Ryan. "I'm not going!" I didn't know how much clearer I could make it.

The beach on the Fourth of July was something we had done with Mom. There was no way I would go. I didn't get why Ryan wanted me to either.

"God, Roxanne, stop being selfish. It's going to be a day about honoring her memory. Mom would want us to do this. Think about what she would want. Go for her," Ryan said.

I thought about it for a moment. Of course he had pulled the Mom card. I hated that he was right. Our mom had loved the rare chance when we got to have family time. Our father was one of the top plastic surgeons in the world. He had decided that it didn't matter if he worked four hours away. So, family time had been extremely important to Mom. Growing up, I hadn't understood why we didn't just live in Southern California with Dad.

Whenever I'd asked, Mom would just say, *This is home. Always has been, always will be.*

From what she used to tell me, Dad had taken her on vacation to the Central Coast, the coastal cities from Santa Barbara to Monterey. That was all it had taken. Mom had fallen in love with the beautiful little city that was smack dab in the middle of California's coastline. They had built a house in San Luis Obispo after getting married.

I would never understand why Mom had put up with him working so far away. It wasn't like he couldn't have a practice here. But having his practice in Beverly Hills had been more important to him than eating dinner with his family every night. It hadn't mattered though. Our mother had loved him fiercely, no matter the distance or his faults. That was just who she had been. She had been amazing.

"Fine, Ry. You win. I'll go—for Mom," I said, defeated.

"I also thought we could try spending more time with Dad." He cleared his throat. "I think Mom would want us to, you know, do more family stuff."

I shook my head in disbelief. What had made Ryan even think that our dad would want to spend time with us was beyond me. Mom, Ryan, and I used to spend our summers down in Southern California with him. Even with his family right there, he'd never really had time for us.

When I was ten, I'd begged him to let me work in his office. I would stuff and address envelopes, sharpen pencils, and stock supplies. I'd thought that if I was with him more, maybe he would love me. I'd wanted the same kind of relationship that he had with Ryan. That summer, I'd realized that my dad was never going to treat me the same as he treated Ryan. In fact, the only way I'd ever gotten his attention was when I frustrated him. This was often even when I'd tried my best not to. The next summer, I'd begged my mom to just stay home. Ryan had wanted to be with his friends, and I'd wanted to focus on dance. We never spent another summer down south. If Dad had missed us being around full time, he never showed it.

The one time my father had told me that he was proud of me was when I'd been accepted into Juilliard.

After Mom had died, I'd stopped dancing. I'd loved to dance, but Juilliard had been her dream for me. I couldn't imagine doing it without her. The day of her funeral, I'd decided that I wanted to go to the University of Southern California like she had. It was one of the many backup schools that I had applied to in case I didn't get into Juilliard. I had been accepted to the USC. I hadn't thought that choosing the USC over Juilliard would be a big deal, but for my father, it had been. Any pride he'd once felt toward me was destroyed the moment I'd told him I changed my mind.

"I'll go on the Fourth, but don't you dare try to make me spend any extra time with that man."

That man was the one who would only make it home every other weekend and on some holidays. He hadn't bothered to make it to my graduation. He also hadn't been here with her. Our mother had died alone. If he had been here, maybe, just maybe, he could have saved her. As usual though, he hadn't been here. I could forgive my father for a lot of things, but not being here for her was something I would never forgive.

Ryan let out a deep breath. "We will talk about it later."

"No, Ryan, we won't talk about it later." I turned and headed up the stairs.

"Roxanne, I wasn't done talking to you," he called after me.

"Too bad. I'm done talking to you!" I was being moody, but I couldn't help it. I was furious and sad all at once. I couldn't contain my emotions, and I didn't want to be around anyone.

Once in my room, I found my cell phone and fell onto my bed. I looked at my phone to see I had three missed calls from my best friend. I selected Tonya's name and called her back.

"Hello?" she answered.

"Hey."

"How are you doing today?"

"My mom is still dead, and I still hate life. I did manage to take a shower today, so that's a good sign."

It wasn't really that good of a sign. I'd woken up only a few hours ago, and already, I no longer wanted to be awake. Actually, sleeping for another four days straight sounded blissful.

"Showering is always good. Did you know I came by yesterday?"

Hopefully, she hadn't seen me in all my drugged-up glory. "No. Did Ryan tell you I was sleeping?"

"Um…Ryan let me come up and see you. You were more than just sleeping, Rox. You were completely dead to the world. It scared me."

I hated that I'd scared her. I wished she could understand that the only time I got any sort of relief from the treacherous pain was when I was sleeping. Then again, that was only if I wouldn't have the nightmares of the night I'd found my mother. Most of the time, the pills would help keep those at bay.

"I've just been exhausted," I lied. It wasn't that big of a lie though. I had been exhausted. It was just self-inflicted exhaustion.

"I know you're dealing with a lot right now, and I won't even pretend to understand your pain. I just think that maybe it's time you talk to someone."

The concern in her voice was hard to hear. I didn't want Tonya worrying about me. I was fine—well, maybe not fine, but I had been dealing the best I could. She was my best friend, and I loved her, but I didn't need this right now.

"Seriously, Ton, I don't need to see a therapist who is going to sit there and tell me that it is okay to be sad about my mom's death."

"Rox, I saw the bottle of pills. As your best friend, I'm not going to judge you, but I wouldn't be a good friend if I didn't tell you that I think you should talk to someone."

"I am talking to someone, Ton. I'm talking to you. You're better than any therapist out there."

"Sucking up to me won't make me change my opinion on the matter."

I heaved a sigh of annoyance. "Yeah, yeah. Let's just drop the subject altogether and agree to disagree." I was starting to regret calling her, and I hated that I felt that way. I knew she meant well. I just didn't care to hear it.

"Fine," she groaned.

"So, Ry's hosting another party tonight." I pinched the bridge of my nose. I was starting to get a headache.

"Really? Didn't he just have one? I swear, he is turning your house into his own at-home frat house."

I truly hoped my house wasn't going to become a permanent place for Phi Kappa Psi. I was already living with two Phi Psi brothers, and that was more than enough.

"Brent says Ry is doing it as a distraction. I just wish he would deal with her death in some other way. I'm sick of always having people here."

"You both need to see a therapist."

"Tonya!"

"Just saying. I'm closing my mouth about it—for now. Do you want me to come over and keep you company?"

I didn't really want to be around anyone, but I also didn't want to deal with another one of Ry's parties alone. It was messing with my psyche. I might have imposed my new sheltered life on myself, but I was depressed enough, and I hated being an outcast loser, hiding up in my room. I could always go downstairs and join in the festivities, but I'd rather pull out every hair on my body, one by one, before participating in Ryan's nonsense. So, up here I stayed, feeling like the loser that I was.

I was about to agree to her coming over, but I knew there would be more talk of therapists and not using pills, and I didn't want to have those conversations.

"As much as I love you, I think I'm going to head back to bed. I hope you understand."

There was a long pause, and I knew I'd hurt her feelings.

"Oh, um...yeah, I get that. You should just rest. I'm being dragged to San Diego in the morning anyway. Annual Miller's family reunion!" she mocked in excitement. "Then again, if you want me to stay in town and be here for you, you know I can totally stay, so you have someone to talk to or sit in silence with."

I knew she would stay in a second without regrets if I asked, but the last thing I wanted was to make her feel like my personal babysitter.

"No, really, it's fine. I don't want you to skip your family vacation to sit around with me while I cry. I want you to go and have fun. Besides, this is important to your parents. It's the last summer they have with you before you run off to college. You have to go."

I knew how much my mom had been looking forward to having our last summer together before I would leave for college. *Our mother-daughter adventures would have just been getting started.* I couldn't fathom being the reason for Tonya missing that time with her mom. At least one of us should enjoy having a mother.

I could hear the noise level rising downstairs as people arrived.

Stupid, stupid Ryan.

"Are you sure?" Her voice was full of doubt.

"I'm positive."

"I'm worried about you."

"That's because you are a great friend, but you have nothing to worry about."

I wasn't lying about her being a great friend. I just wasn't exactly telling her the truth about not having anything to worry about. Hell, a blind man would be able to tell that I was a wreck.

"Remember, I'm only a phone call away. Just call, and I'll come running," she stated.

I wanted to smile, but it just wouldn't happen. It was so screwed up that I was incapable of smiling anymore.

"I'll miss you." *I already do.*

"I'll be missing you more."

I could tell from her voice that she was still contemplating whether or not to just come over.

"Night." I ended the call and tossed my phone on the bed.

I thought about taking some Tylenol for my headache, but I decided that I was done with being awake. It was highly overrated. I retrieved the pill bottle from my nightstand and cracked it open. Sliding three pills out, I tried to convince myself that I needed them. My head was already pounding, and I didn't need a full-blown migraine.

I thought of my mom.

"Roxy, I pray you don't get my migraines." She combed her fingers through my hair as I lay next to her.

"I'm sorry you're in pain."

She closed her eyes and held my hand. "Thanks to my little angels, I'll be feeling better in no time. Just lie here with me until I do." She squeezed my hand three times. It was her way of saying, "I love you," without words. Three squeezes said it all.

One pill would be enough for my headache. I didn't need the other two. But more than my head was hurting. I just wanted the pain to be gone, so taking three pills was a necessary action. Maybe they would be my angels and take away all my pain this time.

Miracles occur all the time, right?

The definition of *insanity* was doing the same thing over and over and hoping for a different result. At least that was what Albert Einstein had been quoted as saying.

Maybe I am going insane?

While I was busy going back and forth with my conscience, there was a knock on my door.

If that's another jackass wondering if my room can be used to have sex in, heads are going to roll.

"Hold on." I grabbed my water and quickly swallowed the pills. *So much for the mental debate.* "Come in."

Brent opened the door and came in. "Hey, Princess." He smiled.

I shook my head and rolled my eyes at him.

He held out a plate of food. "I know you said you weren't hungry, but you really should try to eat something." He grinned at me.

That smile always gave him his way.

I took the plate of food. "Thanks. I'll eat it later."

He sat down on the end of my bed.

I raised an eyebrow in confusion. "What are you doing?"

He gestured toward the plate. "Waiting for you to eat."

"I told you that I would eat later."

"I heard you. The sooner you start, the quicker I'll leave you alone."

I let out an exasperated breath. "Fine."

I took the fork and started stabbing the macaroni salad. I made a point to show him my fork before shoving it into my mouth. I chewed my food and then repeated the overly dramatic actions. After three bites, his smile widened. I hated that he was enjoying this. I didn't find it funny at all. I finished the helping of salad and set the plate to the side.

"There. Now, you can go." I gestured to the door.

He laughed and got up. "You can't survive on macaroni salad alone, but it's a good start. Try to eat some more, all right?" He walked toward the door.

"Maybe I don't care if I survive." The words had come out of my mouth before I even noticed what I had said.

Brent turned to face me. His eyes widened, and his body visibly tensed. He moved to stand on the side of my bed. "You'd better care, Roxanne."

I'd known he was upset before he spoke, but the fact that he'd used my name was proof that he was pissed.

"Yeah, okay," I breathed, looking away from him. I just wanted him to leave.

He exhaled a sigh of frustration. "You're not the only one who lost her." His voice deepened with anger. He walked back to the door.

I looked at him again. "I didn't mean anything by it, okay? I'm sorry I said it!" I yelled at him.

I didn't want to have this conversation with him. I didn't want to have it with anyone. I could feel the painful ache inside me growing as my chest tightened.

"Do me a favor. Don't ever let Ryan hear you say that. I don't think he could handle it." He slammed the door behind him.

I hurled the plate at the door. It was a bratty move, but it was all I could do. It wasn't like I hadn't known I wasn't the only one who had lost her. It just felt like everyone else had already let her go and moved on. Dad had gone back to work, and Ryan and Brent had started partying. The world had kept spinning even though she was gone. It was as if her death hadn't changed everything. It wasn't right. For me, it had changed everything. The night she'd died, my life had shattered into billions of tiny pieces that I would never be able to put back together.

I closed my eyes and pictured her laughing. All the pain I had been forcing down before pushed its way back up. I felt as though I was being torn apart from the inside out. I curled up into a ball, squeezing myself tight, and cried. I cried for my mom. I cried for the life she hadn't gotten to finish. I cried for the things we would never do. I cried for all the things she would miss. I also cried for myself. I cried because there was a small part of me that wished I could be like my brother. I wished I could continue living without feeling guilty that she wasn't. Deep down, I knew that she would want me to go on and live my life. I just didn't know how to do that. I hated myself for not being there for her.

When I'd found her, it was nothing like I had seen on TV. She had been cold but not stiff. There had been no blood. Her body hadn't even appeared pale or discolored. I'd never, ever forget her eyes. The way they'd looked would permanently haunt me. They had been open but void of life, like they hadn't even belonged to her. It hadn't mattered how much I screamed or shook her. It had looked like my mom but not my mom. She had died.

Later, we'd found out that she'd died from a brain aneurysm. Days after her death, Ryan had tried to comfort me by telling me what Dad had told him. Dad had said that it had happened quickly and that mom hadn't felt any pain. I hadn't cared that Dad was a doctor. He'd never died from an aneurysm. Even if it was quick, I couldn't stop thinking that there must have been a moment, even if only a brief one, when Mom had known what was happening to her. She had been all alone, and she must have been scared.

I opened my eyes and stared out the window at the darkened sky as the tears continued to fall. I felt like I was staring into a black hole of sadness that would forever consume my future.

"I miss you," I sobbed.

I couldn't take it anymore. I needed to feel her again. I needed to be close to her.

I got out of bed and ran down the hall to my parents' room. I went into the gigantic walk-in closet and shut the door behind me. I turned off the lights and lay down in the middle of the floor. I folded my hands together and pressed down on my chest, trying to stop the pain. My hands were trembling. I took deep breaths in through my nose to calm myself. I inhaled the honey and vanilla fragrance lingering in the closet. My mom had smelled like honey and vanilla from all the baking she had done.

I noticed the scent of my mother wasn't as prominent as it had been the days after she died. It was starting to fade, and I felt as if I was losing her all over again. I needed her to stop fading away. I wasn't ready for her to disappear completely. I curled up on my side, squeezing myself tight again, as if my arms were the only things keeping me from falling apart into a billion pieces the way my life had. Loud sobs racked through my body. I closed my eyes and bawled uncontrollably.

I didn't know how long I'd been crying for when strong arms lifted me from the ground, tightly holding me.

"Shh…shh…just breathe," Ryan whispered into my hair.

Ryan had seen me fall apart like this more than once, so when I finally looked up at him, I was surprised to see fear in his eyes. I tried to steady my breathing, but it was impossible. I was now doing the breathing-hiccuping thing that would happen when I cried too hard.

"It's okay. I've got you," he reassured me.

"I-I m-miss her s-so much." I couldn't help the stuttering.

"Shh…I know. I miss her, too."

My entire body was trembling. My brother set me on our parents' bed and held me against him, resting his chin on my head while he rubbed my back. I leaned into him. He reeked of beer and smoke from the fire pit.

"She'll always be with us," he said, trying to console me.

Maybe he truly believed it, and that was how he had been able to move on without her.

I didn't say anything. I just continued to sniffle.

"Think about it, sis. You'll realize that there is no way she wouldn't be watching over us. Come on, it's Mom we are talking about. Not even God has the balls to tell her no."

That almost brought a smile to my face—*almost*.

He squeezed me tighter. "She doesn't want to see you like this. I hate seeing you like this. I've been trying to give you space and let you deal with this in your own way, but you've hardly left your room. Roxanne, you barely ever eat, and you sleep all the time. It's not healthy. Mom would be pissed at me if I didn't do something."

"Ry-Ryan, I'll b-be fine."

"Someday, you will, but as of right now, you're not."

"I-I don't know wh-what you wa-want from me," I said, pulling away to look at him.

"I want you to live your life, not just let it go on without you. If you need a reason, make it her. You think I don't want to stay in bed every day and bawl my eyes out? I get up for her. Her life ended too soon. It's not fair to her if we don't live ours. She wouldn't want that."

"I-I don't know h-how to let her go," I cried.

"You don't have to let her go. I haven't. Hold on to Mom with everything you have. With that said, you can't keep letting every day pass you by."

"Ry—"

"No excuses, sis. Just say okay."

I stayed silent.

"Mom would want you to at least try. Remember, 'Tomorrow is a new day with no mistakes,'" he said, reciting a quote Mom had always used.

"Okay, I'll try," I conceded.

"Good. Now, are you coming downstairs? Or are you going to bed?" he asked, getting up.

"For tonight, I'm going to choose to go to bed. I have a full day of life to live tomorrow, and I need to get plenty of rest," I said, trying to lighten the mood so that he wouldn't be as worried about me.

"All right, you get some rest." He smiled. Then, he gave me another hug, and he kissed the top of my head. "I love you."

"I love you, too." I scooted back on the bed and lay down on my mom's side.

Ryan walked to the door and then paused. "I know this is going to be hard, but I know you can do it. You're stronger than you think." His voice was full of sadness.

It hurt me to hear him unhappy, knowing that I was the cause. "Thanks, Ry. Good night."

"Night, Roxy." He closed the door.

My body felt heavy from the crying and the pills I had taken earlier. Ryan was right. Mom would hate the way I'd been dealing with my pain.

"Tomorrow is a new day with no mistakes," I said to the darkness.

Maybe I would be stronger tomorrow. Maybe I would even be strong enough not to use pills anymore.

I closed my eyes. They burned from all the crying. I rolled over, burying my face into my mother's pillow. Her scent was starting to fade from here, too.

Maybe I'm not that strong after all.

I cried silently as I let the effects of the pills take over and put me to sleep.

2

I woke up to a pillow being slammed into my head.

"What the hell?" I screamed. I was half awake and mostly dazed.

I rolled over as Tonya plopped herself down on the bed next to me.

Tonya beamed down at me. "Good morning."

I rolled my eyes and pulled the pillow from under my head before placing it on top of my face.

"Don't tempt me with the chance to smother that pretty face. I'll do it!" Tonya threatened with playful sarcasm.

I pulled the pillow off my face and looked at her. She stuck out her tongue. I threw the pillow at her, only to have her catch it.

Damn it!

"Nice try." She laughed.

"I'm up, Ton. What do you want?" I asked.

She crossed her arms. "I want you to know that it's almost noon," she informed me, looking irritated.

I stared at her, not knowing what to say. She rotated her body to lie down next to me. She was quiet for a moment as we both just lay there. She let out an exasperated long breath. Then, she took my hand and laced her fingers through mine.

"I want my best friend back," she pleaded.

"I know. I'm trying," I said, barely a whisper.

She sat up and turned to look down at me. "Bullshit! You're not trying at all. You have shut out all your friends but me. You even keep me at a distance. Everyone is worried about you. I keep telling people that you just need time. But, Roxy, you can't spend the rest of your life in this damn house!"

I sat up. *Has she been practicing speeches with Ryan?*

Wait—shouldn't she be with her family?

"Shouldn't you be in San Diego?" I asked.

"I'm driving down tomorrow. This is more important. You are more important."

"You're right. I haven't been trying. But, starting today, I will."

I didn't really want to, but I saw how much my depression-induced seclusion was affecting everyone else. I didn't want them to worry about me. I was broken, and they couldn't change that. There was no reason for them to be pulled into my misery.

It's time to move on. Just thinking those words made my heart feel like it was being smashed with a sledgehammer.

I inhaled deeply and told Tonya the truth, "I don't really know where to start. Losing my mom was terrible enough, but after what Kevin and Slutty McSlutty did—God, I get sick from just thinking about those two. I don't know how to be around everyone again. Everyone knows what happened. It's humiliating, Ton."

"We can still kill them." She grinned. "Just saying!"

I wished it were only that easy. Knowing how crazy Tonya could get, I knew better than to even entertain the idea. "Um…no. We both know orange isn't your color." I tried to smile but just couldn't.

"Whatever. You're just scared because you're too pretty for prison," she retorted.

I wanted to laugh, but that didn't happen either. "It's true. I'd wind up being someone's bitch."

She laughed hard. Again, I wanted to laugh with her, but I had no such luck.

"Doubtful. You would probably get shanked first just for talking back," she quipped.

I shrugged. "Meh…probably."

She gave me her most serious look. "Roxy, you have been thrown into a tornado of emotionally damaging life events. There's no perfect way to go back to your life. Just know that, as far as our friends are concerned, you have nothing to worry about. Everyone has sided with you. You don't have to be embarrassed. Kevin was a tool, and Sara—well, she has always been a whore. You're the one who people miss and care about. They just want to see your beautiful face again. So, get up, get dressed, and get back out to the land of the living. Even though it still hurts like hell, fake it till you make it. Pretend everything is fine with a fake smile and fake laugh. Hopefully, one day, you'll notice that you're not faking it anymore."

I was thinking that same thing. The last thing anyone really wanted to know was that I wasn't holding it together. Even the people who loved me didn't want to deal with the sadness.

Last night, I had decided to just pretend that I was doing better. I didn't know if I would be able to pull it off, but I sure as hell was going to give it a shot. I never again wanted to see Ryan look at me the way he had last night. He had his own pain, and I couldn't continue to cause him more.

"Oh, wise one, please tell me more," I jested. I managed a fake small smile. I got up from my parents' bed and headed down the hall to my room.

Tonya followed behind me. "Don't worry. I will! In fact, we're going out tonight. No excuses. As your best friend, it's my job to help you get back out there. Besides, what better way to say fuck you to Kevin than to find some super steamy sex machine to take his place?"

She laughed, and I imagined her thrusting her pelvis. I turned to see her doing exactly that. She was ridiculous.

I collapsed onto my bed. I looked at my nightstand and thought about the bottle of pills inside. Today would be the first day in weeks that I wouldn't be using them. My heartbeat quickened as I tried to push all my worries from my mind. I could do this.

I looked up at Tonya, who was playing with her hair at my vanity. "I think I'm going to be accepting applications for a new BFF," I joshed. The huge smile that I gave her was as real as Pamela Anderson's breasts.

"As if." She swung around to look at me. "Besides, it would take too long to break someone else in. Also, I know all your secrets," she said smugly. "Deal with it. You're stuck with me—forever!" She laughed manically for comedic effect.

"Ton, I'm not ready to be around everyone—not today!" I whined.

"Then, my gift for you is perfect," she said, digging through the Chanel bag that I'd bought her for her birthday.

She handed me an ID card, and I looked at it. My face was smiling back at me. I couldn't place when that picture had been taken.

I peered up at Tonya in bewilderment.

"I got a copy of your passport photo," she answered without me asking. "As you can see, you and your brother are now twins. How does it feel to be twenty-one? I gave you Ryan's birthday, so it would be easy for you to remember. What do you think?" She was bouncing with excitement.

My eyes widened in astonishment. "I can't believe you got me a fake ID."

She handed over her own for me to check out.

"Tonya, these are good, like really good," I proclaimed.

"I know, right? They're awesome," she said in a singsong voice. "My cousin, Joey, is friends with the guy, Shane, who did them. He is like some counterfeiting genius. He's most likely going to end up in prison at some point. As you can see, his work speaks for itself."

"You're crazy, and I love you, but you shouldn't have spent money on these."

She laughed. "I didn't. He wanted to charge me five hundred for each, but then I took him to bed, and he gave them to me for free." She radiated with pride.

I was momentarily stunned. "You hookered yourself out for fake IDs? My eyes felt as though they might pop out of my head.

Sure, Tonya was promiscuous at times, but this was a whole new level. Maybe me being a hermit was bad for her, too.

She turned back around and smiled at me through the mirror. Then, she perused my lip glosses until she found her favorite red one.

"Calm down. It wasn't like that." She glossed her lips and turned to face me again. "He is crazy sexy. I wanted him. After I had him, he just happened not to want my money. That's what I call a win-win."

She has no shame.

"Please tell me the two of you are not an item now," I grumbled.

The last thing she needed was to start hanging around future prison inmates.

"Yeah, right! Most likely to be in prison at some point, remember? We just had fun together." She winked at me.

I rolled my eyes at her ridiculousness.

"Don't look at me like that! You're just jealous. I'm getting laid while you're sitting here, drying up."

"What?" My eyes widened in disbelief. *How could she say that to me? I'm emotionally scarred, remember?*

"You heard me!"

"I'm jealous that you hooked up with a future convict? Hmm…not so much." I stuck my tongue out at her.

Tonya laughed. "I think the lack of sex you haven't been getting has made you cranky," she teased as she headed for my closet.

"Okay…with that said, I want to make something crystal clear. Are you listening?" I asked loudly.

"Yep. Continue," she called from inside my closet.

"I'm done with guys," I told her.

She popped her head out of the closet. "Are you telling me that you're a lesbian?"

"Oh my God! No! I don't want a boyfriend," I stated.

"I've been telling you for years that having a boyfriend is overrated. But Mr. Douche Bag made you crazy in love, and you wouldn't listen." She disappeared into the closet again.

"Seriously, Tonya!" I yelled, annoyed.

I didn't want to think about Kevin or how I felt. If I could just forget him altogether, I would—well, probably not. I couldn't deny that we'd once been happy. It was too bad that there was no happy ending for Kevin and me.

She leaned out of my closet to look at me. "Sorry. Too soon," she apologized. "Let's get back to no boyfriends. Yay!" She cheered, trying to lighten the mood. "Welcome to the slutty side. We have hot boys and condoms galore," she said in a failed attempt to mimic *Dracula's accent.*

Crazy girl.

"I didn't say I wanted to be a slut, Ton. I just don't want to give someone the power to hurt me."

"Which one do you want to wear?" she asked, holding up two dresses. "CK or A&F?"

"I don't care. You choose." I was already rethinking my decision to go out. It was a horrible idea.

"All right, I pick this one," she said, tossing my white Calvin Klein mini dress on my bed. Then, back in my closet she went. "What you need is a boy toy. It's summer. You need to just have fun with no serious relationships." She came out with my open-toed hot-pink Jimmy Choo shoes. She was having too much fun with this. "The saying, 'The best way to get over someone is to get under someone else,' is true. Trust me. It's how I got over Blaine, Kyle, Tom, Derrick—well, you get the point. I'm saying that it works. You will be over Kevin in no time. Plus, you will have no problem getting guys to help you with that."

As much as I loved Tonya, there was a small problem with what she had said. She hadn't actually gotten over Blaine. I knew this, but I didn't have the heart to remind her of that fact. Blaine and Tonya had been together from eighth grade until the summer before sophomore year. He had been all of her firsts. After Blaine had broken her heart, she never stayed with the same guy for more than a month. Luckily for her, Blaine's family had moved to Montana halfway through sophomore year. She no longer had to deal with the pain of seeing him.

But I was willing to try her method even if it was flawed. It wasn't like I could feel any worse than I did now.

Hot guy plus no emotional attachment—what could go wrong?

I got up and looked at myself in the mirror, instantly feeling discouraged. "I have the I'm-a-heartbroken-train-wreck-and-still-hung-up-on-my-ex-while-grieving-for-my-dead-mother look written all over me." I frowned. "I doubt guys will be chasing me down."

"Oh, sweetie, that's why you have me," she said.

I took a deep breath. I could do this—or at least I had to try. I thought about how I'd decided to move on for everyone else's sake, but I knew I would be doing *this* for me.

The ache in my chest was back. I exhaled my breath and then clapped my hands together. "Okay, let's do this!" I said enthusiastically.

"Woot, woot! Roxy's gonna get laid. Roxy's gonna get laid," Tonya sang.

I walked into the bathroom. "Shut up, Ton, or I'm going back to bed!" I yelled.

I had no intention of having sex tonight, but the thought of making out with a random guy did send a shiver of excitement through my body. Now, if I could just get rid of this awful ache in my chest, life would be great. Okay, life would still suck, but at least I wouldn't hurt as badly.

"Fine. I'll be downstairs while you shower. I left yoga pants and a tank top on your bed. Throw that on when you get out. I'm going to make an appointment at the salon."

"That's not necessary," I said.

"Trust me. Yes, it is. Tonight is about you getting back out there. We're going all out."

I groaned, "If you insist."

There was no use in arguing. She had already made up her mind. I was just going to have to suck it up and go along with it. It was the least that I could do after all she'd done for me lately, which was already above and beyond what any friend should have to do.

"I do. Don't forget to shave your armpits, legs, and vag. I don't even want to know about the forest you've grown down there." She laughed.

Okay, maybe I overstated how amazing she is. "Will you just go away already? Apparently, I have a forest to cut down. Turn on my stereo on your way out!"

"You'll thank me later!" she hollered before turning on my stereo.

I doubt that.

The All-American Rejects blasted into the bathroom. I didn't believe that I would survive the night without a complete meltdown. My heartbeat picked up pace once again. I tried to push away the anxiety building on top of the ache that already lived in my chest. I closed my eyes and attempted to get lost in the music.

I can do this.

If all else failed, at least I could say that I had given it my all.

"Mom, please don't let me fall apart," I begged.

It might be ridiculous asking my mom for help, but I needed something to hold on to.

Tonya's quest to get me back out there started with retail therapy. While we were in Abercrombie & Fitch, I noticed how shaky I was. My chest throbbed with pain, and waves of nausea had me regretting that I'd ever left my house. I had to keep reminding myself to breathe.

In the dressing room at Express, I was trying on a red leather mini skirt when I realized how often I'd kept thinking about the bottle of pills in my nightstand. My stomach twisted as I thought about what my mom would think of my way of dealing. I was disgusted with how weak I was feeling.

Tonya didn't get upset when I had to take a moment to keep myself together. She helped me through it.

Hours later, in American Eagle, I was sick of being disgusted with myself, and I decided I was done with being weak. I had to stop thinking about the stupid bottle of pills. I couldn't be that person. I paid for the blue jean jacket that Tonya had said I just had to get, and I smiled for the first time all day. It was ridiculous, but as we left the store, I felt as though my mom might actually be proud of the fact that I was trying to be strong.

Tonya and I went to get massages and mani-pedis. Then, we got our hair done. I decided to lighten my dark hair with some blonde highlights. Tonya, already a platinum blonde, went more drastic with plum-colored streaks. Not many people could rock that color, but Tonya totally owned it. Of course, she had her hair curled for the night while I had mine straightened.

I smiled at Tonya. She looked fantastic. She was wearing a strapless black mini dress that she'd bought today along with purple ballet flats. She had refused to wear heels since tenth grade because Andy Parks had asked her where he could get a pair of stilts. He was a short-ass prick, but the damage had been done. She was five-eleven and a bit self-conscious about it, not that I would ever understand why. She was beyond beautiful.

I twisted my hair around my finger as we stood in line to get into The Flying Pig. It was a popular bar with the college crowd. Tonight, I was feeling a bit more upbeat. I wasn't full-blown excited, but I wasn't completely dreading it either. I looked ahead to see how far we were from the entrance. I twisted my hair some more and bit down on my bottom lip.

Tonya elbowed me in the side. "Stop fidgeting," she hissed.

We were standing in a line. *Who the hell is going to care if I am fidgeting?*

"Look at this line. It's taking forever to get in. We've already been standing here for thirty minutes. I'm not a patient person, Ton," I reminded her.

A group of girls in front of us were smoking. I absolutely detested smokers. It was such a disgusting habit. I was already annoyed by the wait, and I wasn't going to breathe their toxic fumes, too.

"Rox, don't you dare say anything. If they want to kill themselves, that's their choice. We're outside. Don't start a fight, and get us banned from this place before we even get in." Tonya scowled me. She knew me way too well.

"This is absurd," I said, trying not to breathe in the smoke wafting my way. I really wasn't sure I could go much longer without saying something. I pulled Tonya out of line by her arm.

"Are you crazy, Rox? The end of the line is another two blocks down." Aggravated, she pulled her arm from my grip.

"We're not going to the end of the line, dumbass. We're going to the front," I announced, walking up the line.

She caught up to me. "I swear, if this doesn't work, you're walking home."

"Oh, ye of little faith. Have you forgotten who I am?" I gave her a fake smile. But I was the one who seemed to have forgotten. I didn't know if I would even be able to pull this off. I wasn't this girl anymore. *Fake it till you make it, right?*

"Yeah, okay, hot stuff. Work your magic 'cause we're almost at the front."

I stopped and inspected the line. I just needed the right guy. Most of the men seemed to be coupled off. Then, I saw two of Ryan's fraternity brothers. I recognized them from a party Ryan had let me go to at his fraternity house months ago. I thought that the blond one's name was Chase—or maybe Chance. It didn't matter what his name was. I just needed him to get us through the door.

I nudged Tonya. "Follow my lead, and don't forget to thank me later," I said.

We made our way over to them.

I bumped into Chase—or Chance. "Oh my God! I'm so sorry. I wasn't paying attention," I lied, smiling sweetly.

I prayed that he wouldn't see through this sham. I was about to bat my eyelashes, but I thought that would be overkill.

He smiled at me, and I breathed a sigh of relief.

"Don't worry about it. You okay?" His eyes showed true concern.

Aw, how sweet is he? And extremely cute, too.

"Yeah, I'm fine." I looked down at the ground and then back up. "Wait...I know you. Ch-Chase, right?" I asked. *Please let this act be convincing, and please let that be the right name.*

He smirked at me. "Yeah, you're, um...Roxanne. Ry-Man's sister, right?"

Well, at least I said the right name.

Tonya jabbed her elbow into my side.

I shot her a look. *Please don't ruin this, Tonya.*

I took a deep breath. I could handle this. We would have a kick-ass night, and then I would just ask Chase not to say anything to my brother. Everything was going to be fine.

"Everyone just calls me Roxy. Sorry again for bumping into you." I placed my hand on his forearm and seductively bit my bottom lip.

Chase looked me up and down. "Roxy, you can bump into me anytime." He showed off his pearly whites.

"I like the sound of that."

The line was moving up, and they were almost in. The girls behind them kept giving Tonya and me the stink eye.

Chase gestured to the door. "Are you two coming in?"

"We were going to, but the line is obnoxious, so we're going to find somewhere else to party."

He pouted. "Don't do that. Come in with us. I'll buy you a drink."

Mission completed. It took everything I had not to jump for joy.

I turned to Tonya and smiled. "What do you think, Ton? Want to go in?"

"Will I be getting a free drink, too?" she asked Chase with a smile of her own.

"For sure. We've got you ladies covered." Chase nodded at the guy next to him. "This is Luke," Chase introduced us.

"Hey!" Tonya and I said at the same time.

Luke gave us a head nod of his own. I had pulled it off, and we were about to go in. I thought about my brother and how he would react if he found out about this. The thought made me nervous. I reminded myself that he wanted me to live my life, and that was what I was doing.

The guy checking IDs at the door nodded at Chase.

"Hey, man." Chase did some special handshake with him that I had seen Ryan do with his other frat brothers.

"What up, bro?" the door guy asked Chase.

"Nothing much, man. Just out for some fun."

Chase continued to talk while Tonya and I held out our IDs. The guy barely even glanced at them before stamping the inside of our left wrists.

Wow! That was easy.

Tonya walked in with Luke, and he slung his arm around her shoulders. Luke was not only good-looking, but he was also very tall. In other words, he was perfect for her. I smiled to myself, knowing that she had to be happy.

Chase placed his hand on my lower back and guided me into the bar. The place was packed. He pulled me in front of him and held on to my hips. I had missed the feeling of having a guy's hands on me. His touch burned my skin through the thin fabric of my dress. I was almost embarrassed by the way my body was reacting.

We followed Luke and Tonya to a spiral staircase at the back of the bar. At the bottom of the stairs, a bouncer nodded at Luke and then unhooked the red velvet rope to let us through. We climbed the stairs to the second floor. It was less crowded up there. On this floor, a number of black leather couches and chairs were placed sporadically, and there was another bar. Unlike the bar downstairs, this bar was behind a wall of glass.

The bartenders were putting on a show while mixing drinks. They were throwing bottles high in the air and catching them behind their backs. It was incredible.

Chase's breath was hot on my neck. "Pretty sick, huh? Welcome to the VIP lounge."

My stomach twisted nervously. I twirled my hair around my finger and smiled. He put his arm around my waist and pulled me closer. I knew that I shouldn't be letting him touch me this way, but it felt too good to make him stop.

We found an empty couch with a glass table in front of it and made ourselves comfortable. I sank back into the couch. This was fantastic and exactly what I'd needed. The atmosphere was perfect. The music was too loud to even concentrate on painful thoughts. The aching in my chest had been replaced by the uneasy twisting in my stomach from full-blown guilt. I knew how my brother felt about me hanging out with his friends, so he wouldn't be happy about one touching me the way Chase was. But I would take feeling guilty over grief any day.

Chase put his hand on my thigh and leaned in. "So, where's your brother tonight?"

I shrugged and gave him a devilish smile. Tonight wasn't about Ryan. It was about me. I moved in closer to Chase and ran my hand up his thigh. "I'll tell you where he's not," I said into his ear.

A waitress brought out bottles of top-shelf liquor and champagne along with a bucket of bottled beers and cans of soda.

Luke handed money to the waitress. "I took the liberty of ordering bottle service. That way, you girls can have whatever you want without the wait," he said as he pulled Tonya into him.

Chase mixed cherry-lime soda and vodka in a glass with ice and handed it to me. I took a huge gulp and felt it burn all the way down my throat. My eyes watered, and I was trying my hardest not to start coughing. I didn't want him to think that I was a loser who couldn't handle a little vodka. Trying to prove this fact to him, I took a long drink from my straw.

Big mistake. I shook from the intensity. *Damn, that's strong.*

Chase leaned in. "Make sure you stir it before you take a drink."

Great. He officially knew I was a newbie at drinking—well, drinking like this at least.

I could do a keg stand and throw back shots with the best of them. Apparently, mixed drinks were my kryptonite.

I didn't know why I was feeling so embarrassed, but I was determined to show Chase that I could handle his little drink.

I looked over at Tonya to see that she had made herself comfortable on Luke's lap. I stifled a laugh.

Chase put his arm around my waist and pulled me into him. "Can I tell you how glad I am that you bumped into me?" He took a drink of his beer.

"Would you still be glad if I admitted that I had done it on purpose?" I questioned.

"I'd feel honored that you went to the trouble." He grinned.

"In that case, I'm glad that I bumped into you, too."

Even though I was trying hard to ignore it, the guilt of breaking my brother's rule was clawing at me. Being in a bar was one thing, but hanging out with Chase was another. I knew he was off-limits.

I downed my drink. My body shook again. *Ryan might kill me, but I can't be held responsible for what I don't remember. Go big, or go home.*

"Who's up for shots?" I lined up the glasses. I could conquer shots.

Tonya squealed, "Me, me, me!"

Chase poured the shots and then winked at me. Everyone took a glass.

I held mine up. "Here is to a night we won't remember," I toasted.

Tonya cheered, and we all threw back our shots. Tonya then pulled Luke toward the dance floor. I was happy that she was having fun. She deserved a good time. I felt like I had held her social life hostage while I locked myself away to grieve the loss of my mother and the loss of a relationship that I'd thought would be forever.

My body was starting to warm from the alcohol. I enjoyed this feeling.

I scooted back and looked at Chase. "Thanks for letting us come in with you guys." I kissed him on the cheek.

Chase leaned into me. "Do you not know how hot you are? I would have been a fool not to ask."

"Another?" I gestured to the shot glasses.

Chase and I downed three more shots. I looked over at Tonya to find her dancing with her backside against Luke, her ass grinding into him.

I laughed and shook my head. *That's my Tonya.*

That warm feeling transformed into a tingling one. It was a sure sign that I should slow my intake of alcohol before I would have to be carried out of here.

Chase pulled me onto his lap, and I giggled. Then, I turned and straddled him, causing my dress to ride up. His hands worked their way up my bare thighs.

Chase moved his right hand off my ass. He pulled out his iPhone from his pants pocket and aimed it at us. "To making memories we won't remember," he stated.

I smiled at the camera. I was feeling good. I never wanted this feeling to end.

"Do you wanna dance?" Chase asked.

My body stiffened. Although I was in a bar where dancing was common and only for fun, I still couldn't bring myself to do it. I was scared of how much dancing, of any kind, would hurt. Dancing reminded me of my mom, and I didn't want to fall apart from thinking about her.

Damn it. I was not about to let tonight be ruined over my hang-ups.

I pushed my body down on him, hoping he would drop the dancing subject. "I'm more than happy right where I am." I smiled at him.

Chase quirked his brow at me and smiled. "You know, I swear, Ry-Man said that you were his younger sister. I didn't know you two were twins."

I laughed and rocked my hips against Chase. "We're not twins. I am his younger sister," I admitted.

Chase gave me an inquisitive look. I bit my lower lip and performed my best innocent look. Then, I pressed myself down harder on him.

He squeezed his fingers into my flesh. "Roxy, are you telling me that I snuck you into a bar?" He moved his hands on my hips and rubbed his thumb over my skin where the dress had cutouts.

I was really feeling the alcohol, and he was looking extra yummy.

"Of course not!" I mocked in shock. "We have IDs," I stated matter-of-factly.

"You know, your brother—"

"Shh…" I pressed my finger to his mouth and then leaned into him. "He never needs to know. I won't tell if you won't." I then vaulted over the line my brother had drawn years ago. I grazed Chase's earlobe with the tip of my tongue.

He groaned. "You're a naughty girl, aren't you?" His breath was hot on my neck.

I sucked his earlobe between my lips. "Very, very naughty," I moaned.

Chase groaned again as he moved his hands to my ass. He kissed down my neck. I could feel how turned-on he was through his pants. Knowing that he wanted me right now was making me throb between my legs.

I pulled back and looked at him. *No reason to stop now.*

I pressed my mouth to his, showing him that I wanted this. I parted my lips, allowing him to explore my mouth. I moved my hands up into his hair and tugged playfully. His hands squeezed my ass as he pushed himself into me, making sure I knew exactly what he wanted.

I didn't know how long we'd been kissing before we both needed to pull away for air.

"You're too fucking hot," he breathed against my neck.

I leaned in to kiss him again just as Tonya plopped down next to him.

"Don't mean to interrupt, but I have to pee, so I'm stealing her," she chimed in.

I gave Chase an apologetic look and a quick kiss before sliding off his lap. I pulled down my dress and walked to the restroom with Tonya.

"What the hell, Ton?" I asked as we stood in line for the restroom.

"What the hell nothing. You were about to make him come in his pants, Rox. Pace yourself. We have all night for that." She laughed.

I didn't have a comeback. I simply shrugged, and we stood in silence.

Finally, it came to me. "Like you weren't doing the same thing?" I shot at her.

"Huh?" She looked confused.

"You were all over Luke," I specified.

She laughed. "Delayed much, Rox? Geez, are you drunk already?"

I smiled sheepishly at Tonya and shrugged again. "Meh?"

Yet again, we were in a line that wasn't moving, and I now also had to pee really badly. I took Tonya's hand, walked to the front of the line, and then crossed the hallway to the men's room. I tried the handle.

Look at that.

It opened, and Tonya and I went in.

"You know, this is why you're my best friend." Tonya smiled.

"Why? Because I'm impatient?" I joked.

She chuckled and squatted over the toilet. "So, Miss Sex on a Stick, do you think you will sleep with him?" she asked.

"I don't know. I think I want to, but it's weird to think about being with someone who's not Kevin." I went pee while she washed her hands.

"I get it. The first guy I was with after Blaine was bizarre. I felt like I was doing something wrong."

It was comforting to know she understood my feelings.

"Exactly!" I flushed the toilet with my foot, almost falling over in the process.

Tonya busted up as she watched me regain my bearings. I washed my hands and thought about if I really wanted to have sex with Chase. I didn't even know the guy, and I didn't think my brother would ever let me live it down if he found out. I was thinking it might not be worth the trouble.

"You need a good one-night stand to get you back on the horse. Although, the choice of guy could have been better." She smirked. "Don't get me wrong. He's hot, but if Ryan ever finds out"—she tsked—"he is going to kill you both."

She had read my mind.

I couldn't stand my brother's ridiculous rules, but I understood them. As much as I wanted to hate my brother for his outrageous overprotectiveness, I couldn't. Ryan had his reasons.

When I was five, Ryan was supposed to hold my hand and watch me while our mom had paid for groceries. Ryan and I had walked over to the candy machines at the front of the store. He'd let go of my hand at some point, and I'd walked off and made my way outside. I couldn't see my brother anymore, and I had been lost and alone. I might have only been a few feet away from him, but at five years old, that hadn't registered.

I'd made my way back into the store and walked around, looking for my mom. I had been missing for a whopping fifteen minutes. My mom used to say those were the worst fifteen minutes of her life. As terrified as I had been in the time away from my family, I'd gotten over it as soon as I saw my mom. My brother, on the other hand, never got over that day. He'd blamed himself for not watching me, and even as an eight year old, he had been hard on himself. He'd crawled into my bed that night and promised never to let anything bad happen to me and that he would always protect me. Well, he had taken that promise to the extreme. I loved my brother, but he could be a pain in the ass.

I shook my head, not wanting to think about what would happen if my brother found out. I forced a laugh and threw up my hands. "Great. Thanks a lot. Now, I'm in need of more alcohol."

"You girls are smart," said the next girl waiting for the girls' restroom as we exited the bathroom.

"Aw, Ton, look at us. We're total trendsetters."

We erupted with laughter.

When we got back to the guys, Chase looked uneasy.

"What's wrong?" I asked.

"Your brother is on his way here," Chase informed me.

Panic washed over me. I couldn't have Ryan find out that I was here.

"Well, not to be rude, but Tonya and I should go before he gets here and sees us." I smiled at Chase, hoping he would understand.

The serious look on Chase's face only got more intense. "He already knows that you're here. That's why he's on his way."

I was stunned sober. *This is not happening.* "Are you kidding me? How did he find out?" I screamed and pushed past him to retrieve Tonya's and my purses.

Chase grabbed my arm. "I uploaded our photo to Instagram without thinking."

I yanked my arm out of his grasp. "Seriously?" I shouted.

I shoved Tonya's purse into her arms. "Tonya, we have to go now."

"Roxy, I'm sorry. I didn't realize that he was going to flip out like that. He called and was going nuts. He demanded that I tell him where we were," Chase apologized.

"I'm his baby sister! What did you think he was going to do? Hand you a condom, and say, 'Here you go. Have fun.'" *How moronic is this guy?*

I took Tonya's hand and headed out of the bar. By the time Tonya and I were outside, I could hardly breathe. I could hear the thumping of my heart pounding in my ears. This was bad, so freaking bad. All day, I had worked at holding myself together. Now, I was on the cusp of falling apart.

I felt the signs of a panic attack coming on, and it was one that had nothing to do with my mother.

Tonya was rubbing my back, trying to calm me down. "Rox, just breathe. You didn't do anything wrong. You don't even know how upset he is. In fact, he's probably just mad at Chase. Breathe, dollface, just breathe."

Breathing was not helping. I pulled out my phone and called Ryan. It only rang once before he answered.

"Don't you dare think about leaving," he seethed.

"Ry, calm down. It's not what you think."

"Don't lie to me, Roxanne! You know better! One rule! One goddamn rule! Leave my friends alone! That's all I've ever asked!" he yelled.

Thinking that Ryan could calm down had been a delusion. My whole body started to tremble. My brother scared me when he got mad like this, but it wasn't because I thought he would ever hurt me. I was scared for whoever else was the target of his rage. Right now, that was Chase.

Poor unsuspecting Chase.

Oh God, what have I done?

"Ry—"

He cut me off, "And what are you doing in a bar? Who do you think you are? Yesterday, you were inconsolable. Today, you're trying to fuck my fraternity brother. What the hell's wrong with you?"

He was still yelling, and I was having a hard time breathing. I couldn't handle his rage.

I gave my phone to Tonya. Then, I sat on the curb and dropped my head on my knees. This was such a mess. I had known better than to hook up with his friends.

What the hell is wrong with me?

"Hey—hello? Shut up! She's not on the phone anymore, Ryan. No, I won't be putting her back on! Call me that again, and we won't be waiting around. I'll chance a DUI!"

Tonya could handle my brother much better than I could, but her brave front was just an act. She feared Ryan in the same way that I did. He was crazy.

"No, Ryan, fuck you!" Tonya yelled into the phone before hanging up. "Come on. We should go before he gets here," she said.

"No, Ton. That will just make things worse." I stood up and dusted myself off.

Chase and Luke walked out of the bar and over to us. Chase wrapped his arms around me and pulled me into him. I stood stiff against him.

"Roxy, I had no idea he would be that upset. Let me talk to him, okay? I'll tell him that it was entirely my fault and that you didn't even remember who I was."

I pulled away and looked up at him. "No, I don't want you to lie for me. I'll handle my brother, but you should go," I urged.

"I'm not scared of your brother." He pulled me into him again.

God, I wish he would stop being so touchy.

He was most likely going to get his ass beat because I'd wanted to feel something other than pain. I was selfish. I had known better.

The squealing of tires made me quickly step away from Chase. He turned and stood protectively in front of me. He might have thought that he wasn't scared of Ryan, but he didn't know how crazy Ryan could get.

"Get the fuck away from my sister!" Ryan thundered as he hopped out of his car.

Brent got out of the passenger side.

Just when I thought this night couldn't get any worse.

Chase put his hands up. "Look, bro, take it easy."

Chase had no idea what he had gotten himself into, and I felt terrible.

"I will tear you to pieces. Get away from her!" Ryan's voice was murderous.

"Ryan, it was my fault," I said, stepping in front of Chase.

"Shut up, Roxy! You and Tonya need to get in the car now!" he screamed.

I looked at Tonya. She rolled her eyes but headed to the car with me.

Before I closed the door, I looked at Chase and mouthed, *Sorry.* I rolled down my window and took in the fresh air like it would magically make everything better.

Ryan got in Chase's face. "You knew that she was my sister."

Brent was pulling Ryan back, trying to get him back in the car.

Chase tried again to defend me. "I screwed up, bro. I came on to her. She didn't do anything, man."

Stupid boy. Why didn't he just agree to stay away?

Chase was not the first guy who had crossed the line where Ryan was concerned. My freshman year, one of Ryan's fellow teammates, Adam, had tried hitting on me at a team barbeque. I'd shot him down right away. Plus, I'd had no interest in him. He hadn't stopped though. Later, during a party that I had gone to with my brother, Adam had taken his pursuit of me to another level. He'd pushed me into a corner and kissed me. It had only been a kiss. Granted, it was an unwanted one but still just a kiss. Ryan had seen it, and he'd pulled Adam away from me, but my brother hadn't just pulled him off of me. Ryan had beat up Adam badly enough that he had ended up in the hospital for two weeks. Adam never said it was my brother who had put him there, and neither had anyone else who witnessed it.

That was the last time any of Ryan's friends had ever hit on me. In fact, most would just treat me like a little sister. It was safer for them that way.

Ryan had made it very clear that his friends were off-limits to me. They knew it, and I knew it.

Luke stepped in closer, ready to defend Chase. "Let's just call it a night, and forget this crap ever happened. All right, man?"

Brent and Ryan were finally backing up. I let out the breath I had been holding.

"You ever think about touching her again, and I'll kill you," Ryan threatened.

I was humiliated and couldn't even look at Chase.

Ryan and Brent got in the car.

"Ry—"

"Don't even speak," Ryan warned as he sped away from the curb.

I leaned into Tonya and held her hand. I felt sick. All that I wanted to do was go back to staying at home and popping pills. *Who would have thought that would seem like heaven?*

3

"Rox…" Tonya was shaking me awake. "Roxy!"

"Huh?" I mumbled.

"Hey, dollface. I have to get going," she informed me.

I sat up. My head was pounding, not that I was all that surprised. Between the alcohol and crying, last night had done me in. "Give me a sec, and I'll get ready." I yawned.

"No, it's fine. Brent's going to take me to my car."

"Oh. Are you sure? I can take you."

She smiled. "Yeah, I'm positive. I just wanted to say bye before I headed out."

I pouted. "I'm sorry that last night was ruined."

Tonya frowned. "Oh, no. Don't start apologizing again. Last night was great. I was out with my best friend, having fun. Seeing you smile last night was worth all the Ryan drama."

I snorted. "God, that was embarrassing. I'm so disowning him."

She snickered. "Good luck with that."

I tightly hugged her. "I'm gonna miss you very, very much."

"I'll be back before you know it." She kissed my cheek.

"Drive safe! And call me when you get there."

"I will. Happy Fourth, girlie. Please try to have fun today," she said from my bedroom door.

I rolled my eyes. "Yeah, I'm so sure that Ryan and I will have loads of fun."

"I'll call you later," she promised.

"Love you, bitch."

"Love you, slut," she said before closing the door behind her.

I fell back onto my pillow and glanced at my alarm. *Good God, it's only six.* As I stared up at the ceiling, the room seemed to be spinning. It was most likely because of all the alcohol I had drunk. I looked at my nightstand. I hadn't used the pills though, and that was a step in the right direction. I decided to reward myself with a few more hours of sleep. I closed my eyes and fell back asleep.

I woke up again to bloodcurdling screaming, and I realized it was coming from me. I was screaming as if I were being stabbed to death. Apparently, my dickhead brother had decided to pour a bucket of ice water on me.

Good fucking morning to you, too.

It was a horrible way to wake up.

"What the…" I jumped out of bed. "What the hell is wrong with you?"

"That was for hooking up with Chase. There are billions of people in this world, Roxanne. Billions! Asking you not to hook up with my friends isn't that insane of a request."

I stormed into my bathroom. "You're a fucking lunatic!" I yelled before slamming the door.

"You haven't seen lunatic, sister of mine, but you will, if you don't leave my friends alone," he threatened.

"Go to hell, Ryan!" I screamed at him through the door.

I took off my wet clothes, put on my robe, and returned to my room. Ryan was standing in the same place with his arms crossed, looking smug.

I stomped my foot like a three-year-old who hadn't gotten her way. "Get out of my room!" I demanded.

He just started laughing.

"What? What is so funny?"

"You. You're absolutely hilarious when you're mad. I can almost imagine smoke coming from your ears," he cracked.

"Just so you know, I hate you," I fumed.

He was still laughing. "Like that's even possible."

"Trust me. It's possible!" I went to my bed and started taking off the bedding. *How is it possible that I got the world's biggest asshole for a brother?*

"Seriously, you can get out now!" I reminded him.

"Get dressed. Dad already left the house for the hotel. I told him that we'd meet him there."

I had forgotten that our dad was due to come home last night. I was praying that Ryan hadn't told him about last night's events.

I sat on a dry edge of my bare bed and defiantly crossed my arms. "You owe me an apology."

Ryan chuckled and walked to the door. "Not gonna happen. Hurry up, and get ready."

"I'm not going with you!" I snapped.

"Suit yourself, but remember, today isn't about us. Today is about Mom," he said before leaving my room.

I got up and slammed my bedroom door. This was going to be a fan-fucking-tastic day for sure.

I put on my blinker and turned right at the corner to make another loop around the block. I really should have left the house earlier. *Who am I kidding?* Had my brother not made me feel guilty by saying that today was about Mom, I wouldn't have come at all.

Ryan had been a complete ass today. The last thing that I wanted to do was spend the day with him.

Knowing that I'd have to be around my father today wasn't helping either.

As if those things alone weren't bad enough, trying to find a parking space in jam-packed Pismo Beach on the Fourth of July was proving impossible. Even the valet guy at the hotel had laughed when I asked him to park my car. I had been extremely wrong in thinking that the hotel would park my car no matter when I showed up just because we had a suite at the grandest hotel on the beachfront. Evidently, they had stopped valeting cars at ten this morning. There was no parking for miles.

This was awful. My bright idea of driving around the block until someone left wasn't working out so well. Living on the coast, smack dab in the middle of California, most certainly had its perks. It was absolutely beautiful here. I lived where other people came to vacation. It was holidays, like the Fourth of July, that were a terrible reminder of that fact.

Too many people, too little space.

"Fuck!" I slammed on my brakes to avoid hitting the silver Honda Civic that had just cut me off. I flipped off the driver. "Learn to drive, dickhead."

That was it. I was done looking. I would deal with Ryan and his disappointment speech later. He was the only person who could rival our father in disappointment speeches. I could already hear him saying how Mom was looking down on us, and I'd let her down. As far as my father was concerned, it wouldn't have mattered if I had shown up yesterday. He would still find something to be disappointed in me about. If there was one thing I could count on, it was that if my father wasn't ignoring me, I must have done something wrong because that always got his attention.

Miraculously, a red sports car pulled away from the curb right in front of me.

"Thanks, Mom. I'm sure that was all you," I said aloud. I then cursed again when I realized that I was going to have to parallel park. "You couldn't have made it easy, could you?" I hated parallel parking but not enough to search for another spot even though the thought was tempting.

Thankfully, I managed to park without incident.

I turned off the car and sank into my seat. *Why is it important to Ryan and Dad to go through with today?*

Mom was gone. This had always been her thing. There was no reason to pretend like we were a happy family. We weren't. This was just ridiculous. We could have honored her and still stayed home. I was sure she wouldn't have minded.

I stared out the window to see a guy standing at the back of a red GMC truck in front of me. He unzipped his black wet suit and peeled off the top half, letting it hang at his waist. He was tall and tan with dark brown hair—well, I thought it was dark brown. It was still wet from the ocean, so I couldn't be sure. His back and arms were well defined, and I couldn't help but watch him as he loaded his surfboard into the back of his truck.

I bit down on my bottom lip as I continued watching the sexy surfer. He had a set of abs to die for, and those pecs were…wow! He was all kinds of panty-dropping sexy. He wrapped a towel around his waist and removed the rest of the wet suit.

I would be lying if I said that I wasn't wishing his towel would drop and give me a show. I watched him walk to the cab of his truck and take out a bag. I looked him up and down. I might have actually started to drool. His dark hair glistened in the sun, showing he had some blond highlights. I felt like a stalker, but I couldn't stop staring. I couldn't get over how perfectly sculpted his body was.

God have mercy.

He even had those yummy jaw-dropping back dimples that turned me on to no end. Just as I was mentally deciding what he could possibly have going on under his towel, he turned and looked at me.

I quickly spun around and pretended to grab something from the backseat. I readjusted my oversized Coach sunglasses. *They're dark enough to hide the fact that I was ogling him, right?* I felt the heat in my cheeks and prayed he didn't know that I had just been checking him out. I needed to get to the hotel. I didn't have time to be embarrassed.

I twisted to see if he was still looking toward me. Thankfully, he wasn't. Mr. Eye Candy was busy pulling up a pair of board shorts with white-and-blue checkers. He threw the towel in the back of the truck. His shorts hung low, showing his sexy V on his lower abdomen.

Whoa…

I needed to snap out of it and quit gawking. I was ashamed to be around myself. I gathered my beach bag and purse before I got out of my car. I made a point of not looking at him again, and I walked toward the hotel.

I wasn't even ten feet away from my car when I saw Kevin and Hookerella walking, hand in hand. They were just down the block and coming my way. I stopped moving, I stopped breathing, and my heart stopped beating. I turned into a statue.

Fuck, this is not happening.

This was one of the reasons I had shut myself away in my home where I could avoid horrible situations like this from ever happening. My stomach knotted up, and I felt sick. Astonishingly, I forced my body to move, but I was still having a hard time with the whole breathing thing.

I turned and headed back to my car. I wasn't sure if Kevin had seen me. I didn't want it to look like I was running away even if that was exactly what I had done. I walked over to Surfer Boy, who was now talking on his cell phone while sitting on the tailgate of his truck. I could just talk to him. Hopefully, Kevin and Hookerella would just stride right by and not even notice me. I set my bags down.

"Hey." I waved, and I knew I was being rude.

"Sure, man. Um…can I call you right back?" Surfer Boy said to the person on the phone. He hung up and then gave me his attention. "Hi." He smiled.

Damn. Even his smile was perfect.

I wiggled my finger for him to come over to me. He walked over to the curb.

"Hi," I said again. I wasn't sure what to say next. I had no choice but to just ask him what I needed from him. It wasn't like this moment could get any worse. I was facing humiliation no matter what. I exhaled. "I know that we don't know each other, but could you just pretend like we do and talk to me?" My request had come out as desperate as I felt.

He looked at me, completely confused. At that moment, I wished the earth would just open up and swallow me. I bit down on my lip and twirled my finger around a ringlet of hair. My chest was starting to feel tight around my racing heart.

Why didn't I just get back in my car and hide? It might not be too late.

I glanced over my shoulder.

Kevin's eyes met mine.

If I got in my car now, he would know that I was in fact trying to hide. I had no choice.

Who cares if this guy thinks I'm crazy?

I wasn't about to let Kevin see me run. This was DEFCON 1.

"Okay, there is a huge chance that I'm coming off as a crazy person. Please understand that I'm desperate."

The look on Surfer Boy's face said it all. He thought I was crazy.

Honesty is always the best policy, right?

"Full disclosure—my ex-boyfriend, who wrecked my world, is about to walk by. I'm begging you to please pretend to know me." I knew how pathetic I'd sounded, but I would kick myself for that later.

He slightly tilted his head to the right and gave me a confused smile. Then, he just stood there and gaped at me. I was now seriously doubting the whole honesty-is-always-the-best-policy idea. It sure as hell wasn't helping me.

"Roxy?" Kevin called out from a few feet away.

My insides twisted into knots at the sound of Kevin's voice.

Please just kill me now.

I didn't know what I was thinking.

Oh, right, I wasn't.

I stepped forward, wrapped my arms around the sexy stranger's neck, and pressed my lips to his.

Yeah, so this is way more than I asked from him.

Please don't push me away.

I was trying to will this guy not to call me out. Surprise and relief flooded my body as I felt his arms wrap around my waist, and he returned the kiss. His tongue grazed my lips, and I parted them, allowing him access.

Wow...

People shouldn't just grab strangers off the street and kiss them, but damn, this guy could kiss.

Kevin cleared his throat behind me. I reluctantly pulled away from the amazing kissing stranger and turned to face Kevin and his whore.

"I thought that was you." Kevin smirked.

I wanted to smack that smirk right off his face. I hated him for what he had done to me. The raw ache I always got when I thought of him was once again burning in my chest. It was a hideous reminder of how much I had cared for him.

I pressed my back against—oh fuck, I didn't know his name.

"Kevin." I feigned surprised. Yep, I was getting an Oscar for this performance. I then looked at Hookerella. Unfortunately, I couldn't hide my disgust. Okay, so maybe there wouldn't be an Oscar in my future. It wasn't my fault that my nose instantly crinkled up at repulsive things or people. "Wow. Crazy seeing you here," I lied, giving my best fake smile. It wasn't crazy. This was my own personal hell.

Surfer Boy wrapped his arms around my waist. I found myself smiling an honest smile, which amazed me. I was going to have to pay him or something after this hell ended. He was impeccably playing his part. Kevin's eyes darted between my savior and me. I thought I saw jealousy cross his face, but that couldn't be. He didn't want me or love me. He'd left me, and he now had a fucking skankbag hanging on his arm.

I rolled my eyes.

"Who's your friend, Roxy?" Kevin asked, sizing Surfer Boy up.

Can this day possibly get any worse?

I didn't fucking know his name. I couldn't very well introduce him as Surfer Boy or Mr. Hot and Sexy.

Before I had a chance to say anything, my hero moved beside me with one arm still around my waist. He stuck out his hand toward Kevin. "Hey, man. I'm Jordan, the boyfriend."

My hero has a name—Jordan. Hmm…I like it.

"Kevin." He shook Jordan's hand. "This is my girlfriend, Sara." He swung his arm around Sara's shoulders and pulled her closer.

I wanted to correct him. Her name was no longer Sara. It was Whore, Skankbag, or Hookerella.

That walking STD would never be Sara to me again. Sara had been my friend—actually, one of my best friends. Other than Tonya, Sara had been the only other close girlfriend I had. I was acquaintances with lots of other girls, but I'd confided in only Sara and Tonya. Tonya and I had welcomed and become friends with her in sixth grade after Sara's family had moved here from Boston. She'd meshed well with us—until she'd started screwing my boyfriend.

Seriously, what kind of friend does that? Oh, right, Sara does.

She was no longer my friend. She was Hookerella, and I hated her.

She looked annoyed with the whole situation, but she managed a small smile at Jordan. I just wanted to gag. I rolled my eyes again.

Kevin gave Sara an apologetic look. "Why don't you go ahead to my uncle's place? I'll be there soon," he told her.

"You sure?" she asked him.

He hugged her and said something in her ear before she smirked and walked away.

Is it wrong that I have fantasies of feeding that skank to sharks?

"I didn't know you were seeing someone," Kevin said as soon as Hookerella walked away.

"That's because it's none of your business." I glared at him.

"Rocket, don't be like that. I know we haven't talked since everything went down, but I think that we should," Kevin said.

My body tensed so much that I thought I might turn into a rock. *How could he stand there and use his pet name on me? How does he think anything about this situation is okay?*

"Kevin, don't ever call me that again. As for talking, don't count on it," I said. It was all I could do not to start crying.

Jordan's thumb started making a circular motion on top of my stomach. I focused on it and pushed away the sadness.

"I'm not trying to upset you, Rock—Roxy."

I almost felt like laughing. He had already hurt me beyond repair, but he was worried about upsetting me. I felt the tears building. I could not let myself cry in front of him. I dug my nails into my palms.

Before I had a chance to say anything else, Jordan stepped forward. "Kevin, right? Roxy doesn't seem interested in talking to you. You should go."

Kevin glared at Jordan. Kevin wasn't a fighter. He would act tough, but when it came down to it, he was a coward.

Kevin stepped back. "I'm sure that she has told you about what happened. We have a lot to discuss, but if now isn't the time, it's cool, man." He looked at me again. "We will talk about everything later."

"There's nothing to talk about. It's over. We're over." I snapped. "You should catch up to your girlfriend." Just saying those words left a dirty taste in my mouth.

Kevin snorted. "Whatever you say. I will see you around, Rocket."

My blood was boiling. He had some nerve, continuing to call me that.

"Let's hope not." I glared at him.

"Just think about having that conversation with me." He turned and walked away. He glanced back at us a few times.

In order to avoid watching him, I turned my body into Jordan's. I let out a deep breath.

I will not cry. I will not cry. I will not cry.

I pushed back the tears that were on the verge of spilling over. I didn't understand how I could be both sad and furious at the same time. I just knew that it was taking all my strength to keep from bawling.

Jordan's arms squeezed me tighter as he held me close. It was comforting and just what I'd needed. I sank into him. Being held against his chest made my stomach flutter. His body was solid, and his skin felt warm. He had a cool ocean smell, and it was intoxicating.

Suddenly, his arms dropped, and he took a step back. "He's gone."

He moved so quickly that I almost fell forward. I straightened myself and then looked down at the ground. I didn't know what to say.

How is it that this complete stranger just helped me get through the moment every girl who's had her heart broken dreads?

Now that we were alone, the realization of what had happened hit me.

Oh my God! I kissed him.

My cheeks heated up. I was beyond mortified. People always talked about desperate times calling for desperate measures, but no one talked about the horrid moment right after taking those measures.

Maybe I can just run away. I mean, he already thinks I'm crazy, right? If I just sprinted off, it wouldn't be that huge of a shock.

I looked up at him, and he was gazing down at me. I quickly glanced away and started gnawing on my bottom lip.

How the hell am I supposed to thank him for what he just did? Maybe I can send him a gift basket. Mom always said that it was the best way to say thank you. The card could read, Thanks for pretending to be my boyfriend and for helping me save face with my ex. Oh, and sorry I raped your mouth with my tongue. Enjoy this wine and extremely expensive disgusting cheese.

No, this isn't the type of thing I can send a gift basket for.

I looked at him again. I'd pretty much stared him down earlier, but I was now getting the up close view. Completely gorgeous was an understatement. He looked to be about the same height as Ryan, so I would say he was around six-one. His hair was messy, but if I hadn't seen it earlier, I wouldn't have been able to tell if he'd spent hours making it look like that. Evidently, all he had to do was run his fingers through it. His face was perfect with full and kissable lips—I could vouch for that—a chiseled jawline, and teal-green eyes with flecks of gold throughout.

My stomach fluttered in the most intense way, surprising me. I felt the heat rising in my cheeks, and I forced myself to look away from him. I stood up a little straighter. I decided that I could just fake being normal and act like this kind of craziness happened to people all the time.

"I-I…" *Wow, I have no clue what to say.* I might have been able to pretend happiness, but I had no idea how to fake my way out of this mess. I chose to stick with my earlier method, full-blown honesty. "All right, I don't really know what to tell you. What you just did…I-I don't even know how to begin thanking you," I told him.

Jordan laughed. "Don't worry about it. It was interesting, to say the least." He smiled.

I rocked back on my heels. "Well…" *What to say? What to say?* "I give you a ten on your acting skills and a nine and a half on kissing. If you want me to pay you for your trouble, I will." I couldn't believe that had just come out of my mouth. I officially wanted to jump off a cliff, not that I could ruin my relationship with him any more at this point.

Who the hell am I kidding?

We don't even have a relationship. We're still strangers—who just happened to kiss while pretending to be together. He probably thinks I'm some psycho girl, and he took pity on me. I bet he never wants to see me again. Oh, yeah, I'm making sure he has a great story to tell.

Great, now, I'm rambling to myself. I am hands-down certifiable.

I stuck out my hand. "I'm Roxanne Daniels. My friends usually call me Roxy. I'm not saying that we're friends. I mean, it's not that I don't want to be your friend. I'm sure you're a great friend. What I mean is—" This was just splendid. I was now rambling out loud. *Fuck me!*

He gave a small chuckle with a huge smile. That perfect beautiful smile made my breath catch.

Jordan shook my hand. "It's nice to meet you, Roxy. I'm Jordan Carter. My friends call me Jordan." He grinned.

Aw, not only is he sweet but funny, too.

I found myself smiling once again.

He does know that he can stop with the act, right? I'm the crazy girl here. He doesn't have to pretend he's enjoying this.

"I'm sure meeting me has been anything but nice. I know we met under unusual circumstances, but I'm glad you were around. Thank you again for everything." I let out a deep breath.

He stepped closer to me. "Unusual for sure but entertaining nonetheless."

Awesome. Just awesome. He has enjoyed my painful humiliation.

"Well, I owe you one." *Not that I'll ever see you again.*

His eyes turned playful. "I'll keep that in mind."

He tucked my hair behind my ear and ran the backs of his fingers down my cheek. His touch made my skin tingle, and my heart rate picked up.

Why is he touching me? And what is up with the butterflies?

I hadn't been ready for butterflies. I didn't want them. Butterflies would lead to feelings, feelings would lead to caring, and all caring would lead to was heartache. I'd had enough of that for a lifetime. Although I had just met Jordan, I knew that he would be trouble if I got too close to him.

I stepped back and looked away from him. It was time for me to go.

"I really need to go. My brother and my dad are probably freaking out. Have a great Fourth." I picked up my bags, turned, and walked away.

I had taken two steps when Jordan stopped me.

"Rox, wait."

I turned back to look at him.

"I would like to see you again."

"Did you just call me Rox?"

He smiled "Yeah, but not like rocks from the ground. Just Rox. You know, instead of Roxy."

"Yeah, I get it. It just surprised me. The only person who ever calls me that is my best friend."

"Seeing as I'm hoping to become your friend, I say that it fits perfectly then."

I had a feeling that his smile always got him anything that he wanted, much in the same way that Brent's charming grin did. I despised how much I adored Jordan's smile. I also hated how much I liked him calling me Rox.

Yep, he's getting to me. That's just a reminder that it is time to walk away.

"After today, I think it might be better if we didn't do the whole friends thing."

That wasn't exactly the truth. The truth was, he was someone that I could easily like, but I couldn't have that. I had too many butterflies fluttering inside me as it was. I was an emotional mess with serious issues. I wasn't ready for someone like him, and I probably never would be.

"I disagree. Give me a chance to get to know you better," he said.

I was already shaking my head, but before the words came out, he interrupted me.

"Please," he said.

Really? He has to say please? How am I supposed to just walk away, especially after what he just did for me? Fiddlesticks.

"What the hell? Sure." I smiled, and I was back to faking.

I pushed away my guilt and did what I had to do. I gave him a fake number.

I left him and made my way back to the hotel. I forced myself not to look back at him. I knew that it was wrong to trick him after all he'd done for me. I just couldn't take the chance of getting to know him better.

When I got to the hotel suite, everyone was already there. In the Daniels family, the Fourth of July always called for a big celebration.

My papa owned a successful winery about an hour away. He and my grandmother had bought this suite from the hotel when it was built. My grandma had wanted a place on the beach for their family to enjoy. We had been coming here every year since I was six.

My mother had loved planning the traditional Fourth of July party. She hadn't believed in hiring an event planner or catering service. She had done everything all on her own. She would spend days in the kitchen, making something special for everyone. For my dad, it was brownies, and Ryan and Brent couldn't get enough of her Oreo Bark. She would make lemon bars for my grandparents and chocolate-dipped pretzels for Uncle Zack. For me, she always made strawberry cupcakes with cream-cheese frosting. She would produce everything from scratch. She'd laugh when I'd ask why she hadn't just bought the stuff. She'd believed all the hard work and love she'd put into her food really made a difference.

She always told me, *"There's emotion in the food I make for others, and they can feel it. You can't buy emotion in the grocery store. Don't you ever forget that, Roxanne. You always cook for the special people in your life, no matter how long it might take."*

Every year, I would be amazed at how she'd pulled it all off. For our family, it was as big of a holiday as Thanksgiving or Christmas—at least, it used to be.

This year, my father had hired an event planner and a catering company. Whoever was in charge of this mess had failed miserably. With extreme overkill on the red, white, and blue, the suite looked like America had thrown up on it. Along with the patriotic décor, pictures of my mother's smiling face were everywhere. She would have hated this.

The suite had its own full-sized bar along with two bedrooms, a huge living room with two comfy hideaway-bed couches, three baths, and a large kitchen. The floor-to-ceiling windows overlooking the ocean were my favorite part about this suite. I really loved the view of the water, especially at sunset.

My father was standing at the bar with Papa and Uncle Zack.

I inhaled and made my way over to my dad. *Time for fake smiles.*

"Hello, Daddy, Uncle Zack, and Papa." I set my bags on the ground next to a barstool. I tried to ignore the tightness starting in my chest. *I can do this. It's just one day.*

My dad drew in a deep breath. "I see you finally decided to grace us with your presence."

Great.

Dad had been drinking, and he was unmistakably annoyed with me.

"I'm sorry that I'm so late," I apologized. "Parking was a bit, um…it was horrible."

Dad snorted, clearly unimpressed with my reason for being late. "You should have come with your brother. He managed to get here on time."

This was my father. In his mind, Ryan could do no wrong. Even if I did something right, Ryan would still do it better.

Well, had he not been such a prick to me, I probably would have.

I wasn't about to tell my dad what an ass his son was because I would then have to explain what had happened last night. So, I stayed quiet.

"Rich, give the poor girl a break. It's in her genes to be late. She gets it from her grandmother. That woman was never on time for anything." Papa smiled at me.

Grandma had died last year from lung cancer. Her death had been hard on all of us. Unlike with my mom though, we'd at least gotten to make peace with her dying and say our good-byes.

"Now, Dad, don't make excuses for her. Roxanne's been showing up later and later every year," Dad said to Papa.

I attempted to apologize again, "I'm really sorry, Daddy. You're right. I should have left sooner."

"For once, Roxanne, try making your family a priority." He shook his head with disapproval.

Make my family a priority? I was late, for fuck's sake. There are worse things I could have done, like not come at all.

This was ridiculous coming from the man who always put work before his family. That was my father though. Nothing he did was ever wrong. To say we were not close would be an understatement. I didn't get him, and he didn't get me.

My mom used to tell me that having a girl scared him. She'd found this humorous. She would tell me about how my dad had taught me how to ride a bike and how it had been harder for him to let go and let me ride on my own than it was for me. I had been fearless, and she'd claimed that it terrified him. My mom used to tell me stories like that all the time. She'd constantly remind me how much my dad loved me. I'd once believed her, but now, I wasn't so sure. Deep down, I loved the man, but it was hard to love someone I could barely tolerate. Maybe my dad felt the same about me.

"I said that I was sorry for being late," I sassed.

"It seems like you've been saying sorry a lot lately. I guess we should at least be grateful that it wasn't because you were arrested again."

He had to go there.

"She was never officially arrested, Rich. She was just cuffed," Uncle Zack reminded him.

The night I had gone to Kevin's and found him in bed with the skank, I had understandably been upset. I had just walked in on my boyfriend fucking one of my best friends. I'd freaked out. I had taken the baseball bat from behind Kevin's bedroom door and busted everything in his room that I could. I'd smashed his flat screen TV, his computer, and his trophies. Then, I had gone outside with the bat to work on his car, a '69 Mustang that he had restored himself. He had just finished it before we'd graduated. It was his prized possession, so it had only seemed fair.

One of them had called the cops. I would have been arrested, but my uncle, the chief of police, had handled the situation. My father hadn't cared about how much I was hurting. He'd just told me what a disappointment I was. He'd called Kevin that night and promised to pay for all the damages, and then he'd left for Los Angeles right after. After he had left, I'd started using my mom's pills.

Just thinking about it all now made my chest constrict and burn with pain.

"Zack, don't downplay her actions. She put you in a terrible position that night," Dad reminded his brother.

I crossed my arms and squeezed myself. I was on the verge of losing it. I needed to get away. I couldn't deal with this.

"Uncle Zack, Papa, it was really great seeing you." I hugged and kissed them both.

"Keep your chin up, buttercup," Papa whispered in my ear.

He had been telling me that since I was a little girl. It usually eased my worries and brought a smile to my face. Today, that smile was fake.

I turned to my dad. "Happy Fourth, Daddy."

He looked past me and took another drink of his scotch.

I picked up my bags. The ache in my torso started to throb harder. I couldn't handle pretending to be happy for all the people who had shown up to remember my mother. I didn't want to see their sympathetic looks or hear their promises of how it would all get better. It would never get better. I felt as though I would explode from the sadness that I was pushing down.

I needed time to myself before I could continue to pretend to be okay. I rushed to the room that I always used and threw my bags onto the bed. Then, I made my way through the room to the balcony. I stepped through the sliding glass door and released the tears that I had been holding in.

I was startled when arms wrapped around me from behind.

In a gentle voice, Ryan asked, "Are you okay?"

I didn't understand why he'd even bothered to ask. I was broken. I would never be okay. I thought that he'd already known that. I wiped away the tears and tried to regain control over my emotions.

I turned to face him. *So much for making sure my brother never saw me sad again.* "I'm just peachy," I lied.

"All right, that was a stupid question." He grinned.

"You think?"

He pulled me into another hug. "I'm sorry about this morning."

I was flabbergasted. Ryan *never* apologized.

He stepped back, took my hand, and squeezed it three times. Considering that he never apologized for anything, this was huge.

I owed him an apology of my own. "I'm sorry for last night. I should have never crossed that line. It won't happen again."

"It'd better not." Ryan smiled but his tone was deadly serious.

I looked over his shoulder and saw Brent sitting at the patio table, watching us.

Great. He also got to see my mini breakdown.

I hadn't even noticed that they were out here. This day was turning out to be all kinds of crappy. I wiped my eyes again and walked over to the table. I pulled my sunglasses down to my face from on top of my head and I sat in the chair next to Brent.

"I see that you managed to make it on time," I said to Brent.

He smirked. "Nah. I showed up about an hour before you did."

"Where the hell did you find parking?" I questioned.

"Way out in Bumfuk, Egypt. It took me an hour to walk here. I figured Ryan could drive me back to my car."

I was now extremely glad that I had found a spot where I did even if it had come with seeing those two wretched people.

"By the way, thanks, you know, for taking Ton to her car this morning," I said.

"No problem, Princess. I was headed that way. My cousin is staying at my condo for the summer. I stopped in to make sure he wasn't wrecking the place."

"Well, at least someone is getting use out of the place."

Brent had lived with us since he was fifteen. Before then, he had stayed the night so often that my mom made the downstairs bedroom for him. No one had ever discussed Brent moving in with us. It'd just happened.

Brent's parents had never been the hands-on type, not like my mother was.

His mom, a former fashion model, was usually on some vacation or too drunk to even notice Brent. As for Brent's dad, the last time I'd seen Mr. Barnett was when I was thirteen, and my mom had hosted Brent's sixteenth birthday party. His dad had made an appearance after the party was over, and he'd handed Brent the keys to a Porsche. Then, he'd said he had a flight to catch and left.

Brent never talked about how mad his father's actions had made him, but it wasn't hard to figure out after he'd pushed that Porsche off a cliff that night. His parents hadn't seemed to care about how Brent felt. Instead, they'd just bought him a condo after he'd graduated from high school because actually showing up to watch him walk would have been too much to ask of them. It was no wonder Brent and Ryan were best friends. They both had absent fathers to complain about.

After Brent and Ryan had started college, I'd thought they would move into Brent's new condo. My mom had been spending long weekends away with my dad, and I couldn't wait to have the house to myself. Kevin and I had started getting to the point in our relationship where we wanted more quality alone time. Annoyingly enough, Ryan and Brent hadn't left. They had chosen to go to college close to home, and it didn't get any closer than going to college in our home city.

I'd detested them for staying at home, especially when they'd caught Kevin and me practically tearing each other's clothes off as they came through the front door. In my own defense, no one was supposed to be home. Ryan had gone berserk at seeing his baby sister like that, and he'd made Kevin leave. In my utter embarrassment, I had blown up at Brent as Ryan had walked Kevin to his car. Rudely, I'd reminded Brent that he had his very own home and that Ryan and he could live there and stop ruining my life. My comment had clearly hurt Brent. He'd just told me that this was the only place that had ever felt like home to him. Then, he had gone outside to make sure Ryan wouldn't kill my boyfriend. I'd felt dreadful for hurting Brent. It hadn't been his fault that my brother was a bit crazy.

Brent shrugged. "I already have a home. My parents should never have bought that place for me. I'm happy right where I'm at." He smiled.

"I'm so glad that you're happy," I stated sarcastically.

Ryan snorted. "Don't start with the attitude, Roxy. Remember why we are here today. I don't want any whining out of you. What the hell took you so long anyway?" He poured the contents of his flask into his iced tea.

I gave Ryan an evil sneer. "Oh, shut it. You're lucky that I even came here at all after your stunt this morning."

"Do I even want to know?" Brent asked.

"No!" Ryan and I said in unison.

Ryan passed the flask to Brent. I sat up, snatched it from his hand, and took a swig. It was vodka. I shook from the intensity of the alcohol and then took another long drink.

"Easy there, killer," teased Brent.

"Trust me. I need this more than you do." I took one more drink and then handed it back.

He had no idea how awful this day had already been, not that there was much hope for it getting better.

"Besides, there is a fully stocked bar inside. Why are you guys drinking from a flask?"

Ryan laughed. "As you said, the bar is inside. We were trying to hide out here, and then you found us. Besides, Dad has been drinking all day. I don't think people need to see anyone else from the family drinking, too. He'll be lucky if no one starts thinking that he has a problem."

"Oh, no! The prestigious Dr. Daniels is a drunk?" I gasped and clasped my hand over my mouth in horror.

They both chuckled.

I stood up and looked out at the beach. I wanted to get away from here. Sunbathing would be a good excuse. Besides, I needed to work on my tan—or lack of one. "Do you two want to head down to the beach?"

"Sure." Brent stood up.

"We can't, man. Sorry, Rox. Dad set up a meeting for Brent and me with the CFO of Ad Corp, and he should be here soon. This could get us a short-term internship this summer," Ryan pointed out.

Ryan and Brent were both majoring in advertising. Of course, my dad would set up something for Ryan. He actually loved him.

Brent shrugged. "Sorry, Princess. Maybe later." He winked at me.

"Whatevs." I walked into the room. I found a piece of gum in my purse and popped it into my mouth.

I grabbed my beach bag and headed back into the living room. I tried to slip out without being noticed, but I was unsuccessful. My dad saw me right as I was headed for the door, and he was staring me down, so I walked over to him.

"Where do you think you're going?" he asked.

"Down to the beach for a while," I answered.

"Do me a favor, Roxanne, and try not to get lost. Be back for dinner. Your brother is giving a speech," he said.

"I will."

He snorted in disbelief. "We'll see."

I walked backward toward the door. "Not like you would miss me anyway," I sniped before blowing him a kiss. I turned and walked out the door.

I knew my attitude would just give my dad another reason to be annoyed with me, but it wasn't like that wouldn't happen anyway.

After heading down the stairway, I made my way through the hotel lobby. I couldn't get outside fast enough. I didn't know why I always let that man's approval, or lack thereof, get to me like nothing else.

Why can't I just be a normal girl with a normal father who loves me? Why can't my mom still be here? Why does life have to be this difficult?

Once again, I pushed my pain deep down inside me, and I stepped outside into the golden sunlight. There was a hum of excitement floating in the air. People were bustling around enjoying the beautiful day. I may not be happy right now but at least I was free from the suite of sadness.

4

The beach was packed. Down by the water, children of all ages were running around and splashing in the ocean while parents stood nearby with watchful eyes. I remembered when I had been one of those happy kids. I wished I could go back to those times when fairy tales had been my example of true love. That was back when I'd still had my mother, and I'd never even known Kevin existed. I had been carefree with no clue about what true heartache felt like.

I didn't want to feel all the sadness right now. I wanted to be someone else, someone who didn't cry every day, who wasn't constantly shoving the hurt down, who was happy again. I just wanted a couple of hours of blissful ignorance. I guessed faking normal wasn't too far from faking happy. So, I decided that was exactly what I would do. Today, I would pretend to be a normal girl, who was lying out on the beach and having fun.

I spread my towel out. Today was the perfect beach day. The temperature was in the high seventies with a light breeze. The sun felt amazing on my skin. I shimmied out of my Daisy Dukes, and then I took off my black halter top, revealing my favorite pink bikini from Victoria's Secret. I lay down on my stomach and pulled out a book from my bag. I could do this. I could pretend that I didn't have a never-ending ache in my chest and that I didn't feel like I would fall apart at any moment. Today, I was going to be normal, and normal people didn't have to hold themselves together.

I started reading, and I tried to get lost in my book. Unfortunately, I found myself reading the same paragraph over and over. My mind drifted, and I started thinking about seeing Kevin. He'd still looked decent.

Okay, who am I kidding?

He was as hot as ever, but he wasn't the astounding guy that I'd thought he was over the years. I used to think Kevin was the sexiest man on earth. Well, he'd seemed to be a close second behind Brent. Today, I no longer glorified Kevin. Maybe it was his ugly, hurtful act that had made him less appealing, or maybe it was Jordan.

Now, that boy could give Brent a run for his money.

I touched my lips as I thought about his kiss.

God, I have to get these guys out of my head.

I didn't want Kevin. I could never have Brent. As for Jordan, I didn't need butterflies. What I needed was what Chase had given me—all heat and no butterflies. I shook my head, trying to forget about all of them. I needed a new guy—one who wouldn't give me butterflies but would help me to forget, a guy who wasn't on my brother's off-limits list.

Suddenly, someone plopped down next to me, causing me to squeal. I looked up to see that it was Jordan. I was pretty sure that I had just decided that I needed a guy who didn't give me butterflies. Jordan wasn't an acceptable candidate.

"What the fuck? You scared the shit out of me," I shrieked.

"Has anyone ever told you that you have quite the mouth?" he asked.

I shook my head and rolled my eyes. "Has anyone ever told you that it's rude to scare people?" I shot back.

He laughed. "I wasn't trying to scare you, I swear." He put his hand up in innocence.

I smirked. "Sure you weren't."

"It's the truth. I was just headed down the beach to meet up with friends. I was checking out your ass, and then I noticed that it was you. I really didn't mean to scare you. Forgive me?" he asked with puppy-dog eyes.

"Did you just tell me that you were checking out my ass?" I snickered. A tingly feeling flickered low in my belly.

"Yes, ma'am, I did. You have a great ass, by the way." He smiled his amazing smile.

"I'll forgive you for scaring me and for checking me out if you promise never to call me ma'am again. It's just rude. I'm not old or married, and most importantly, I don't have saggy tits," I explained.

He laughed hard. "I've never heard someone be so opposed to being called ma'am. I am sorry. As for checking you out, I didn't ask for your forgiveness. You're gorgeous, and you know it. If you didn't, you wouldn't be wearing that tiny bikini. It screams, 'All men, look at me now.'" He lay down next to me on his side. "And about those tits of yours—I think I should be the judge of whether or not you're a ma'am. What do you say?"

I blushed intensely. I couldn't believe that he was being so presumptuous. Then again, he'd kissed a stranger and pretended to be her boyfriend. Maybe this wasn't so far-fetched. I didn't actually know him.

"Um…yeah, I don't think so. You can just take my word for it. My tits are amazing," I replied smugly. I went back to my book, hoping he would just go away. I was supposed to be forgetting all about him.

Jordan poked me in the side, making me jump.

"What are you doing?" I squealed in annoyance.

"I think you should come with me." He grinned.

"Look, I know that I said we would hang out again, but I don't think right now is the best time. You see, I'm really into this book." I didn't know why I was being such a bitch. Okay, yeah, I did. This guy filled me with emotions that I was trying to stay away from.

"Oh, is that right?" he asked, sitting back up and snatching the book from my hand.

"Hey!" I hollered, rolling over to my side.

"Come on, Rox. Come hang out with me for a bit. I promise you, your book will still have the same ending when you get back." He smirked.

I almost smiled but stopped myself. *Why is it easy to smile around him?*

He stood up, holding his hand out for me. "Come on. Come hang out with your boyfriend for a while."

His statement made me sit up.

"You're not my boyfriend," I objected.

"What? Now, I'm just your boyfriend when it's convenient for you?" he teased.

I groaned. "Stop with the boyfriend thing, okay?"

He laughed. "Are you always this uptight?"

I was about to snap at him, but I thought that might prove that I was being uptight. However, I couldn't halt the eye roll.

Jordan laughed. "Just come with me. I promise that it will be fun." He stepped closer. "Please?" He pouted, holding his hand out to help me up.

Again with the please? Really?

Every part of me knew that I should say no, but I didn't know how I could. He was adorable with that pouty face. Besides, I had just decided that I would fake being normal for the day.

What is more normal than a girl going off with a hot boy? This is exactly what I needed.

I could handle being around Jordan and all his perfection for a little while even if he did have a habit of giving me butterflies.

"Fine, but just for a little bit."

I took his hand and stood up. I picked up my shorts and shimmied into them. I watched as his eyes worked over my body. I couldn't deny that I was enjoying the way he was looking at me. A tingle ran up my spine as I pulled my phone out of my bag and shoved it into my back pocket.

"All right, let's go." I gestured down the beach.

A few feet away from the wet sand Jordan took hold of my hand.

"I think we should play a game," he stated.

I looked down at our clasped hands and considered ripping mine away, but the comfort I felt from holding his hand made me smile. "What kind of game?"

"It's a get-to-know-you game," he answered.

I couldn't understand why he wanted to know me better. If anything, he should be running away. I had given him more than enough reasons to want to keep his distance from me.

"Trust me. You don't want to get to know me. In case you've forgotten, I'm the crazy girl who kissed a complete stranger today," I reminded him.

"I haven't forgotten about the kiss, but I'm not sold on the crazy part. Who knows? Maybe you will change my mind."

"Just so you know, you were warned, so no complaining when you decide that I'm in fact crazy. How do you play this little game of yours?" I smiled.

"It's easy. I tell you two truths and one lie about myself, and you have to pick out the lie. Then, you do the same. We have three rounds, and then we enter into the five-questions portion of this game. That involves us going back and forth, honestly answering any question we're asked. If you refuse to answer said question, then you, um…" He looked out at the water and then back at me as he smiled. "You get thrown into the water."

I laughed. "I physically can't throw you anywhere. I'm at a disadvantage. I don't think I can play."

"No, you can play. I swear to throw myself in the water if I lie."

"But what if you don't throw yourself in?" I asked.

"I guess you will just have to trust me." Jordan smiled.

"Trust you? I don't even know you."

"Looks like you really should play the game then," Jordan said smugly.

I was waiting for an anxiety attack to take over and ruin my persona of normalcy. I took a deep breath. *I can do this. It's just a stupid little game.*

"Oh my God, fine. You go first," I said.

Jordan swung our hands back and forth and smiled his glorious smile. "All right, hmm…I'm an only child. I hate cats. Oh, and I'm an escaped convict on the run."

"So, you love cats," I joked.

Jordan shook his head. "Not even a little. They are fur balls of pure evil. Now, it's your turn."

I was surprised that I still didn't feel the anxiety I'd been sure was going to overcome me. For some reason, being with Jordan was not only easy but also fun. It was nice not to have to fake my smiles.

"I absolutely hate skinny jeans on guys, my best friend's name is Tonya, and I rob banks on Tuesdays just for the hell of it."

"I'm going to have to remember that you love a guy in skinny jeans." Jordan smirked.

"Ew…please tell me that you don't wear them." I laughed.

Jordan laughed with me. "Never."

"That's good. If you said you did, we couldn't be friends." I rocked into him. "Your turn."

Jordan suddenly swept me into his arms. I was confused, but before I could even ask what he was doing, he told me, "You were about to walk through a pile of seaweed."

I looked down at the ground in disbelief, but sure enough, there was a huge pile of seaweed with flies swarming around it.

Jordan set me down on the cool wet sand. A chill worked its way through my body.

I'm just adjusting to the change in temperatures.

I failed at convincing myself that Jordan wasn't having a serious effect on me.

I swallowed hard. "You could have just pulled me away from it. You didn't have to pick me up," I told him.

Jordan smiled down at me. "I could have."

Butterflies swarmed in my stomach, and that irritated me. I didn't want butterflies. I turned away from him and started walking down the beach again. I tightly crossed my arms against myself, so there would be no more hand-holding.

Jordan was striding next to me again. If he'd noticed my sudden change in attitude, he didn't let on.

"Your turn," he said.

"No, it's your turn," I corrected him.

Jordan grinned with amusement. "I know. I was just making sure you were paying attention."

I rolled my eyes. "Sure you were."

"I tripped over a cat when I was five and broke my arm. I have a pet dinosaur. I couldn't stop thinking about you after you rushed off earlier," Jordan said.

I slowed down as I looked at Jordan. *Did he really just say that?* Here I was, acting like a bitch, and he had to go and be sweet.

"What kind of dinosaur? And do you feed it cats?" I asked with a smile.

Jordan laughed as he wrapped his arm around my shoulders and pulled me into him. "You can ask your questions later. It's your turn."

As we continued down the beach, I tried to focus on the cold seawater hitting my feet when a wave came in while I ignored the warmth of his arm around me.

"I'm a vampire who loves the sun, I've always wanted a dog, and I hate that you give me butterflies." I looked down at the sand.

Jordan got in front of me and stopped me from walking. When I looked up at him, he smiled.

"I like that I give you butterflies. My best friend is a zombie, and I really want to kiss you again."

I didn't shoot back with a funny comment this time. I just stared at him. He wouldn't want to kiss me if he knew what a broken mess I really was.

I decided that the only way to make him see that was to tell him the truth. "I'm a superhero, my mom died last month, and I'm not someone you want to waste your time on."

Jordan placed his hands on my hips. "My dad died when I was ten. I understand your pain. I have a talking monkey."

I saw the sadness in his eyes. I hated that I'd caused him to reveal something about himself that he probably didn't even want to think about. I felt terrible. I didn't have the words to explain how sorry I was.

I stepped forward and wrapped my arms around him. "You took too many turns," I said against his chest.

Jordan tightly held me. "It's my game, so I can do what I want." He then took a step back and smiled at me. "Do you want to ask the first question, or should I?"

I couldn't believe that he still wanted to continue the game, let alone continue talking to me.

"I'll ask the first question," I answered.

I knew exactly what I wanted to ask, and this might be the only chance I would have.

"Ask away. I'm an open book." Jordan took my hand again, and we started walking.

"All right, Mr. Open Book. Why did you help me today instead of calling me out?" I asked.

"I told you, I was glad to help," he answered.

The cold ocean water played with my feet. "I know. But why?" I pushed.

He gave me a serious look and then stopped walking. "Seeing as we've already kissed and I am your boyfriend"—his eyes twinkled—"I'll give you—how did you put it? Full disclosure?"

I nodded and smiled even though I hated him teasing me about being my boyfriend.

"I followed my high school girlfriend to college. Don't judge. We were together for two years before that. A month into the new school year, everything went downhill." Jordan looked down at the sand. "Our relationship was dysfunctional, and neither one of us was happy anymore. Still, the first time that I saw her after the breakup, she was with a guy, the one who had been the cause of our final fight." He looked out at the ocean. "I must have looked like a psycho standing there, watching them kiss. Even though I didn't want to be with her anymore, it still bothered me to see her happy with someone else. It probably makes me an ass, but we were together for a long time, you know?" His grip tightened on my hand. He noticed and let go. "What I'm trying to say is, if I could have had some girl to pretend to be my girlfriend at that moment, I would have. I was glad that I could help you out today." He grinned at me.

"I'm extremely thankful for your help." I smiled. "Has anyone ever told you that you should be an actor?"

"Nope, you don't get to ask another question. It's my turn." He laughed and took my hand again.

We continued walking.

"I told you the story of my ex. What's your story?" he asked.

It was nice of him to share, but I didn't want to, so I went with the less-is-more approach. "Not much of a story. We were together, and then we weren't."

"Oh, no, you have to be honest, or you are getting thrown in the water. You told me that he wrecked your world. I was there today, remember? He assumed that I already knew the story. Now, I want to."

I decided telling the truth wouldn't make the day any more embarrassing than it already had been. Maybe it would even explain why I'd acted insane today.

"Okay, fine," I sighed. My pulse started to quicken but without the tightening of my chest that usually followed. I dropped Jordan's hand and folded my arms across my chest, preparing for when the pain would come.

"I guess the best place to start is at the beginning. Don't worry. I'll give you the Cliffs Notes version." I somehow managed to smile at him. "Kevin and I started dating our freshman year. I loved him more than I even knew was possible. I was ridiculously happy." My heart hurt as I thought about how happy I had once been.

"Senior year, he started to change. The daily I-love-you-beautiful comments had stopped, and he became distant. Then, when I told him that I got into Juilliard, he wasn't excited or even happy for me. All he said was, 'Cool.' I mean, you would think that after finding out his girlfriend had gotten into the college she had worked her ass off for, he would have said more than *cool*, right?

"Oh, and then during the last few months before graduation, we were fighting all the time. It seemed that, no matter what I did, I somehow always pissed him off. When I suggested that we should break up, he begged me not to. He said that we could make it through anything. He told me that he loved me and wanted us to be together forever. I believed him."

I stopped walking. I blinked back the tears that had started to gather.

"My mom died the night of graduation. Kevin was with me that night. He kept telling me that it would be okay, and we would get through everything together. After that night, I didn't hear from him again. He just disappeared. I thought that maybe he was just freaked out about us finding my mom's body. I tried to make up any excuse for why he would possibly leave me to deal with everything on my own.

"Finally, I was sick of making up excuses, and I went to his house the day after my mom's funeral." Bile rose in my throat, and I swallowed hard. "I always just let myself in. That was when I found him in his room, fucking one of my best friends. You had the disgusting pleasure of meeting her today." I took a deep breath. "The worst part was that he should have just dumped me. I could have handled that." I looked away and wiped a few tears that had escaped.

Jordan pulled me into his chest. "I'm sorry, Rox. I'm so sorry. I shouldn't have asked."

I stepped back, out of his hold. I was totally embarrassed. "I'm the one who's sorry. Between my craziness earlier today and me crying now, I'm sure you have realized that I'm nuts, but in my defense, I did warn you."

"Come here." He pulled me back into his chest. "Don't ever apologize for crying, okay? I'm sorry about the loss of your mom. I was never the same after I lost my dad. I'm not trying to compare losing my dad to you losing your mom. I just want you to know that I understand your pain."

I'd had a lot of people tell me how sorry they were for my loss. From most of them, it had just felt like words, but when Jordan had said it, I'd believed him. This caused a few more tears to spill over.

He took my face in his hands and made me look up at him. "For the record, had I known what that guy did to you, I would have beaten his face in." He wiped away the remaining moisture off my cheeks.

His gaze held mine for a long silent moment. His thumb brushed across my bottom lip, causing my breath to falter. He saw my reaction, and a small smile appeared before he slowly leaned in and kissed me. That tender kiss made my heart skip a beat, and my knees weakened. Then, it ended.

Two things happened in that moment. One, I wanted more of him. Two, I appreciated that talking about my mom and Kevin hadn't caused me to have a horrible ache in my chest like it usually did.

Jordan took a step back. "Sorry. I probably shouldn't have done that. It's just that I've wanted to kiss you again since this afternoon."

"I'm not complaining." *Oh, but I should be.* I pulled the edge of my bottom lip in between my teeth. *What the hell am I doing? Oh, right. I'm faking normal.* "Do you mind if I ask what happened to your father?"

Jordan intently stared at me for a moment. I could see the pain in his eyes, and it almost made me want to look away, but I didn't. He had listened to me talk about my mother. I wanted to show him that I was here for him if he wanted to talk about his dad.

"Is it one of your questions?" he asked.

"It doesn't have to be if you don't want to talk about it. I'll understand," I told him.

"Open book, remember?"

"Then, yes, it's one of my questions."

"He was a firefighter. He worked a lot, but somehow, he always found time for my mom and me. There were days when I knew that he was exhausted, but he would still throw the football around with me, or we'd play game after game of basketball." Jordan cleared his throat and looked out at the ocean. "He died in a building fire." Anger crossed his face when he glanced back at me. "He went back in to save the cat of a little girl who he had just rescued. I'm not sure I'll ever truly understand why he ever thought that cat was worth risking his life for. I try to remind myself that was just who my dad was. He gave all of himself to others, but in the end, it cost him his life."

Jordan was right. I understood his pain, but there was no comparing our situations. We'd both lost someone who we shouldn't have. That kind of sorrow couldn't be compared. It could only be understood.

"I'm so sorry." Honestly, I knew there was no more that I could say.

Nothing was going to take away his pain or make him feel better about his dad being gone. I would never understand why anyone ever tried to say more.

I closed the space between us. I knew he was done talking about his father. It had to be hard for him to open up about it at all, and I was moved that he had done so. I wrapped my arms around his waist and pressed my cheek to his chest. I hugged him and let the heartache that we were both feeling be felt in silence. He encircled me in his arms and rested his chin on my head. I focused on the rise and fall of his chest as he breathed, and I lost myself in the strong connection between us.

After just holding one another for I didn't know how long, Jordan finally dropped his arms, and I took that as my cue to step back.

He gave a small chuckle. "Well, aren't we two balls of joy? I understand if you want to just head back, but if you think you can handle more time with me, we're almost there."

"I'll be okay." I let out a deep breath. "That is, if you still want to be around me?"

He took my hand. "Good luck getting rid of me."

We walked a short distance farther before we got to the part of the beach where vehicles were allowed.

"Jordan!" yelled some guy from the large group of people to our left.

Jordan gave a wave and headed in that direction.

He squeezed my hand a little and leaned in to whisper in my ear, "I'm sorry in advance."

I gave him a confused look, but then I understood when a guy came toward us. This guy was tall with jet-black hair spiked wildly in every direction, and he had tattoos covering his chest and arms, but his most distinctive features were his ripped muscles.

"Nice to see you finally made it," the guy boomed.

He grabbed Jordan into a guy hug and gave him a fist bump. "What up?"

Jordan shrugged his shoulders. "Not much, man. Travis, this is Roxy." Jordan smiled at me. "Roxy, this is Travis."

"Oh…she's what took you so long. Nice, man, very nice." Travis grinned as he looked me up and down like I was a tasty piece of meat. He licked his lips, causing a nervous shiver to run through me.

I now regretted not grabbing my shirt. I wasn't enjoying his stares.

"What up, girl? Nice to meet ya." He winked at me.

Jordan cleared his throat. "Back off there, buddy." He gave Travis a strange look.

"Ah, I'm just teasing the girl." Travis smiled at me again.

Remarkably, I wasn't as creeped out by him this time.

"Hey," I uttered nonchalantly, giving a tiny wave.

I looked past Travis to see two blondes running toward us.

What's the point of even wearing a bikini top if it only covers your nipples?

The two blondes could definitely pass for porn stars.

"Jordan!" they squealed at the same time. They engulfed him in a hug and then stood, hanging on to him.

I had to step away to keep from getting knocked over.

Wow, maybe I should have stayed with my book.

I rolled my eyes at the blondes, and Jordan caught me. He smiled at me and untangled himself from them to stand right next to me again.

"Katie and Monica, this is Roxy," he introduced me to them, lacing his fingers through mine.

Their mouths hung open as they eyed Jordan's hand wrapped in mine. "Hi," they said flatly in unison.

Nope, they were not nearly as happy as they had been a moment ago. It almost made me laugh.

"Aw, ladies, don't pout. You can share me tonight," Travis said, swinging his arms around both girls' shoulders.

One of the blondes shot me an evil look before snuggling into Travis.

Guess she won't be joining my fan club.

"I'll catch up with you later, man." Travis gave Jordan a head nod. He looked at me and then back at Jordan. Then, he smiled a devilish grin and shook his head. "You two have fun." He chuckled, and then the three of them turned and headed back to the group of people by the fire pit. Travis looked over his shoulder as he pointed to the huge lifted black truck. "The good stuff is in the bed of my truck. Kegs are on the side. Enjoy."

"Want a beer?" Jordan asked, tugging me toward the beast of a truck.

I nodded. "Please."

On the way over to the truck, another guy came up to us. "What's up, bro?" He bumped fists with Jordan.

"What up?" Jordan seemed happier about seeing this guy. He placed his hand on the small of my back. "Roxy, this is Scott. Scott, Roxy." He seemed more enthusiastic about introducing me to Scott than he had been with Travis. "Scott and I shared a dorm last year," Jordan informed me.

Scott actually held out his hand, and I shook it.

"It's great to meet you, Roxy." Scott smiled.

"Thanks. You, too." I grinned at Scott.

He wasn't as tall as Jordan, and he had a baby face, but he was good-looking nonetheless. He also had tattoos covering his arms, but he wasn't all beefed-out like Travis. Scott also didn't come off as creepy like Travis had. He just seemed nice.

"I'm gonna grab us some beers. Be right back." Jordan headed toward the kegs.

"So, how did you and Jordan meet?" Scott asked me after taking a drink from his cup.

Oh, you know, I kissed him without asking, and then he pretended to be my boyfriend in front of my ex. Isn't that how everyone meets?

"We just met today. I parked behind him." I smiled wide, like a pageant girl, and then I thought I might be coming off as weird, so I nervously pulled my bottom lip between my teeth.

"No shit?" Scott laughed. "You two seem like you're an item."

"Oh, um…no, we're not," I corrected him.

I couldn't believe that Jordan and I had given off an air of togetherness. Part of me was giddy at the thought, but I quickly shoved that part down. I was just supposed to be faking normal, not wanting to actually be with Jordan.

Scott eyed me like he knew there was more to the story.

"Here, babe," Jordan said, handing me a red cup.

I took the cup and smiled. I hadn't missed the fact that he'd called me babe. The butterflies were dancing in excitement.

Taking another drink from his cup, Scott looked at Jordan and then back to me. "Roxy was telling me that you two just met?" Scott said, but it sounded more like a question.

"Yeah, we met this afternoon. She was parked behind me, and I caught her checking me out while I changed out of my wet suit."

I almost choked on my drink. I couldn't believe he knew that I had been gawking at him. I felt my cheeks get warm.

"I wanted to talk to her, but she was gone as soon as she got out of her car. I didn't think I'd ever see her again." Jordan looked at me. "It must be my lucky day because I just found her on the beach. I wasn't about to let her get away again."

He draped his arm over my shoulder and pulled me into him. His touch wasn't helping me not want him.

Scott nodded at him. "Sweet. Hey, man, I have to get back to the grill. You're staying around though, right?"

"Yeah, we'll be around," Jordan said.

I had already drained my cup. *Way to keep it cool, Roxy.*

"Awesome, I'll find you later." Scott jogged off to the grill in the center of the human circle.

Thinking about food made my stomach growl, and I placed my hand over my abdomen.

"You hungry, babe?"

I knew I should tell him to stop calling me babe, but I was a girl, and truthfully, I adored it. *This is just for today.*

"Yeah, a bit."

Jordan led me over to a white truck with the tailgate down. All kinds of snacks were on it. He headed back to the keg to refill my cup while I loaded a plate with fruits, veggies, and a handful of chips. I walked a few feet away from the truck and sat down on the sand. I was eating cantaloupe and watching Jordan as he made his way back to me. He kept getting stopped by people, and I thought it was cute that he almost never took his eyes off me. It made me feel special.

My stomach was doing somersaults. I shouldn't be feeling this way. I knew Jordan was going to be trouble.

He handed me my cup and sat down next to me. His smile was captivating and pushed away my need to get up and leave.

"I hope some of that is for me?" He pointed toward the plate that I had put together.

"Maybe?" I smirked.

He nabbed a chip and popped it into his mouth.

Damn…

He even made eating chips seem sensual. The fluttering in my tummy continued.

His eyes locked on mine. "All right, Rox, tell me more about yourself."

"I believe you need to ask a question. It's your turn." I smiled.

"You're right. It is my turn. What are three random facts about you?"

"Three random facts, huh? Okay…one, I don't like chocolate. Two, I hate baseball. Three, I'm right-handed."

Jordan laughed. "Well, those were some random facts. I'm not much of a baseball fan either. But how can you possibly not like chocolate?"

"Is that your official question?" I asked with a smirk.

"No. Besides, it's your turn, but we will get back to the chocolate thing."

Jordan pushed his foot into the sand and tickled the bottom of my foot, causing me to giggle.

"Have you come up with a question yet?" he asked.

I didn't know what to ask him, but I didn't like the fact that I wanted to know everything. I had to remember carefree Roxy was on limited time, and soon enough, I would have to go back to the nightmare that was my life.

"What's your favorite color?" I asked.

"Hmm…this morning, it was green, but after seeing your eyes, I can honestly say that's my new favorite color. They are the most brilliant shade of blue. We will call it Roxy blue." He brushed his fingers down my cheek.

Flippity-flop went my stomach. *Oh, boy…*

"Sounds like a good color." I tried to slow the beating of my heart but to no avail.

"Trust me. It's the best color."

His gaze was intense, and I had to force myself to look away.

"It's your turn," I said as I stared down at the sand. "What do you want to know?"

"Everything," he said.

I quickly looked up at him in surprise.

He smiled at me. "But let's start with the small stuff. What's your favorite color?"

I glanced down at my hot-pink bikini top and then back at him. "Pink." I smiled.

"I should have guessed." He laughed.

I observed the crowd of people by the grill. My eyes found Scott, and I let out a sigh. "Thanks for not telling your friend about how we really met. I don't think he believed my edited version."

"Ah, Scott. He's harmless. Like I said, he was my dorm mate. He knows me better than most people. He's not the judgmental type."

"So, is that how you know everyone here—through college?"

"Is that your question?" Jordan smirked. "I'm just kidding. I know everyone here through Travis. Travis is Scott's older brother. Most of the people here are Travis's friends."

"Hmm…I wouldn't have pegged them for brothers."

In fact, besides the tattoos, they were polar opposites, even down to the eyes. Where Travis's eyes were dark and sinister, Scott's were a pale shade of green and kind.

Jordan laughed. "You have to meet their parents. They each take after one."

"I get that. That's how my brother and I are. In every way that I look like our mom, Ry looks like our dad."

"Who's the oldest?"

I crinkled my nose. "Unfortunately, him."

Jordan grinned. "Earlier, you said something about getting accepted into Juilliard. That's an impressive school. What did you get in for?"

"Dance, but after my mom…" I focused on the sand and pushed my toes deeper into it. "Well, I just can't imagine going there anymore."

I was afraid to glance at him. I didn't want to see pity in his eyes.

"I get that. You must have real talent though, if you got in?"

I felt a smile pull at my lips. I couldn't believe how easy he made it to talk about my mom. I shrugged. "I'm all right."

"I wouldn't have guessed you to be the modest type. How about you show me how *all right* you are sometime?" He wiggled his eyebrows.

I chuckled and shook my head at him. *Time to change the subject.* "What college do you go to?"

"University of Southern California." He smiled.

"No way," I gasped.

"Yeah, way. Why are you so shocked? Don't tell me that you are a UCLA fan?"

I couldn't believe that he went to the same college that I was going to be attending. *What a freaking coincidence.* If I happened to believe in fate, I might consider this as just that.

"No, not a UCLA fan. It's just a small world, I guess. That's where I'm headed in the fall."

"It must really be my lucky day." He smirked.

"I guess so." I playfully rocked into him.

"It's your question," he said.

I had totally forgotten about our little game. "What are three random facts about you?"

"One, my birthmark is on my left butt cheek. Two, I like the smell of gasoline. Three, I hate Twitter almost as much as I hate cats."

I smirked at Jordan. "Hashtag you lie."

Jordan's eyes widened. "No, no, no. Don't you even start!"

My smile widened. "Hashtag you know you love it."

"Oh God, you have to stop. Please stop." He laughed.

I was having too much fun with him to stop. "Hashtag make me."

Jordan stared at me, his eyes burning into mine. My pulse quickened with excitement.

"You're incredibly beautiful, but you already know that, don't you?" He gave me a glowing smile that warmed my heart.

"Is that your question?" I bit my bottom lip and twirled some hair around my finger. My nerves were getting the better of me.

He took his thumb and eased my lip out from my teeth. Then, he leaned in and kissed me. Electricity went through my body. At first, his kiss was soft, but unlike earlier, he didn't pull away. I knew that I should probably stop it, but I just couldn't.

I let him kiss me because I wanted to feel something, anything, other than broken. I wanted to be the normal teenage girl without a care in the world, who ran off with a hot guy on the Fourth of July. I wanted to be the girl I had been before my mom died and I had to fake being happy. I let him kiss me because I wanted it, and it felt insanely good.

I almost felt better. I almost felt normal. I almost felt whole.

Almost.

He grazed my bottom lip with his tongue, and I parted my lips, allowing his tongue to enter my mouth. He tasted salty from the chips, and it mixed with the sweetness from my watermelon. It was intoxicating.

I ran my fingers through his hair, pulling him closer. I didn't just want more of him. I craved more of him. My other hand clutched his shirt, and I pulled him even closer.

The kiss became more intense.

His hands were in my hair as he cradled my head and laid me back onto the sand. I wanted him more than I needed air. He was making everything else just fade away. There was no more pain and no more sadness. The world around us ceased to exist.

My hand slipped under his shirt, and I ran my nails across his firm lower stomach. He pressed down onto me as a growl came from his throat. I felt his erection through his shorts against my thigh. The effect I was having on him made the throbbing between my thighs deepen. A moan escaped my lips.

"Get a room!" someone yelled.

With that, the world came back to me, and I froze. I couldn't believe that I had lost myself in him like that. I couldn't believe how much I wanted him.

What the hell is happening?

I had to cool things down.

Jordan spun toward the guy who had yelled and flipped him off. He rotated back and kissed me again, but I tensed up. This was too much, too fast. I had just met the guy.

This is bad, oh-so bad.

My emotions were getting away from me. I was starting to like him. I couldn't let this happen.

Jordan realized our kissing session was over without me ever saying a word. He kissed my nose and then helped me sit up. He sat right next to me, our arms barely touching. My heart was pounding unbelievably hard in my chest, and I swore that he could hear it.

"Do I get a ten for that kiss?" He nudged into me.

I laughed nervously and apparently too loud because people turned to look at us.

"Yeah, you get a ten." I leaned my head on his shoulder, trying to calm my heart. *It was just a little kissing. Why is my heart beating like I just ran a marathon? Stupid, stupid heart.*

"Is it your question or mine?" Jordan asked.

I honestly didn't have a clue whose turn it was, but I had a question I just had to know the answer to.

"I'm not sure, but I do have a question for you," I told Jordan.

"Ask away, babe." He smiled.

I knew what I was about to ask wasn't any of my business, and it shouldn't have mattered to me, but it did. It mattered more than anything.

"I know it's none of my business, but earlier you said that you and your ex had a dysfunctional relationship. What did you mean by that?"

Jordan took a drink of his beer and looked intently into my eyes. "We hurt each other a lot, over and over. Instead of just calling it quits and walking away from one another, we stayed together and then continued to hurt each other."

"What do you mean by hurt? Did you cheat on each other?" Even after the question was out, I didn't want to hear the answer.

Jordan stayed silent for a moment. I prayed that he couldn't see the fear in my eyes. Whatever he might say shouldn't matter to me. It wasn't like he and I would even talk to each other after today. I guessed I just wanted him to stay perfect a little bit longer.

"That's when all the games and hurt started. She cheated on me a year after we started dating. We were in high school. It should have been easy to just drop her and move on, but I loved her. I took her back. We applied to a lot of the same colleges, and when I found out we both had been accepted to the University of Southern California, I was stoked. USC wasn't my top choice, but it was hers. I was ready to get out of Oregon and be in California with my girl. A little over a month before we were supposed to drive out here together, I found out that she had cheated on me again. Everyone told me I should leave her."

He picked up a small piece of dried seaweed and started tearing it apart. "We actually did break up. But then, she begged me to forgive her and promised it would never happen again. I forgave her and stayed with her, but the truth was, I never trusted her again. We fought all the time. During that last month of us being home, we broke up and got back together more times than I can remember."

He dropped the bit of seaweed left in his hands onto the sand and looked at me. "I contemplated not coming out here, picking another school, and moving on with my life, but I just couldn't. I thought going to college together would show her that I was ready to start fresh, but things were just too far gone."

"But you never cheated on her, right?" *What the hell is wrong with me?*

Jordan's silence while he sat there, staring at me, made my stomach tighten.

"I'm sorry. I shouldn't have pried. It's none of my business," I said quickly.

"Rox, it's fine. No, I didn't." He smiled.

My stomach untightened as relief washed over me.

He laced his fingers through mine. "Let me take you out tomorrow night."

I wanted to say yes and then go back to kissing him and never stop. Thankfully, the warning flags were on parade, and I came to my senses. Jordan was not someone that I could continue to be around. He already had me feeling things that I didn't want to feel. More time with him was the last thing I needed.

"I don't date," I blurted out.

Jordan chuckled. "What?"

"I don't want a boyfriend, and the whole point of dating is to see where things might go. With me, the answer is nowhere." I pulled my hand from his. "I don't want to waste any more of your time." I stood up. "Today was fun, but I have to go." I turned and walked off.

"Roxy!" he called after me. "Hey!" He grabbed my hand, stopping me. "Where's the fire?"

"I just have to go. I've been here too long." I couldn't even bring myself to look at him.

"You're not a waste of my time. There is something special about you. I would hate for today to be the last time that I ever saw of you." He pulled my chin up, making me look at him. "I think it would be cool to hang out. Maybe we can try being friends?" he asked.

I quirked my brow. "Friends?" *Is he serious?*

I wasn't exactly looking for new friends. My life was a catastrophe. I didn't want to bring new people into it when I could hardly be around the people I had grown up with. Every part of me knew he would be trouble for me.

"Yeah. What do you say? Can we hang out tomorrow?"

He gave me his gorgeous smile, and the butterflies began flapping their wings. I knew what my answer had to be.

"No!" I stated firmly.

Shock crossed his face. Apparently, *no* wasn't something that he'd heard very often. I didn't want to be mean, but seeing Kevin today was a strong reminder of why I never wanted to chance getting that close to someone again.

I started to walk away again.

"Roxy, wait. What do you mean, no?"

"I mean, no. What part didn't you understand—the N or the O?"

"All of it. Is there a reason you don't want to be around me? I mean, I thought we were having fun."

I couldn't deny that the time I had spent with him was fun. That was also the problem. Jordan was hot as hell, funny, and caring. All of his perfection was only going to lead to me falling for him and getting hurt. Just thinking about it made my heart hurt.

I sighed, feeling deflated. "Today was fun, but I'm not looking for a new friend, especially not one who I want to kiss." *Good Lord. Did I really just say that? What the hell is wrong with me?*

He stepped closer and looked down at me with a huge grin on his face. "Hmm…you want to kiss me, huh?"

I rolled my eyes and stepped back.

Jordan chuckled. "Look, Rox, I just want to spend more time with you. I like kissing you, too, and I would like to keep doing it. If you think I'm looking for something serious, I'm not. I don't do serious. I think we are actually looking for the same thing—fun. We could try being friends with kissing benefits," he answered.

And here I was, getting all worked up over nothing. Jordan wasn't looking for anything serious either. He just wanted to have fun. After all, I was trying to be normal again.

What's more normal than a teenage girl having a summer fling?

He might not be the perfect guy for the job, but I was having a hard time persuading myself to say no again.

What could it hurt to spend some time with him? I mean, sure, I like him. Shouldn't I like the person I'm kissing?

That didn't mean I was going to fall for him. I just had to make sure that things didn't go beyond casual, not that it would. He'd just made it clear that he absolutely didn't want that.

In a matter of seconds, I had convinced myself that this situation would be perfect.

"It does sound appealing. I guess we could hang out again sometime," I accepted.

The smile that crossed his face made my knees feel weak. *Okay, that's not normal.* A smile should not do that to a person's knees. Feelings of uncertainty fluttered through me. Maybe *perfect* had been the wrong word. *Huge mistake* was sounding more appropriate.

What am I getting myself into? Even though I'd never actually done the casual-with-no-strings-attached thing, in theory, it sounded easy. *What if I can't do it?*

I was contemplating this as he pulled me into him, pressing his mouth to mine. I wanted to push him away, but all my body managed to do was wrap my arms around his neck and kiss him back.

Stupid, stupid body.

He pulled back. The kiss was once again too short, and I wanted more.

Damn, this is going to be bad. I bit my lip, embarrassed by how much my body had responded to him. *Remember, you're not looking for a new boyfriend.*

"Sorry. Should I not have done that?" He grinned.

I playfully smacked his arm. "Shut up!"

"I'm gonna take that as a sign that you're okay with the kissing." His eyes were eager, and his thumbs were making circles on my hips.

I laughed. "It's nice to know that you take a girl smacking you as a sign of attraction."

"Hey, some girls are into that. Who am I to judge?" He smiled.

I felt my cheeks warm. "Well, I'm not one of those girls, and I would judge the crap out of you if you were into that."

He gave a hearty laugh. "I said *some* girls are into that. I'm not a girl, and I'm definitely not into that. Just because I wouldn't be participating doesn't mean I should judge."

"You are a better person than I am," I admitted.

"I doubt that."

Why does he have to be so sweet?

Every part of my body wanted to be pressed up against his—with both of us naked. Once again, I was wondering what was wrong with me. Maybe it was just the fact that I had gone from getting laid on a regular basis to cold-turkey nothingness. *Yep, that has to be what's going on.*

"Okay, if we are going to do this whole casual thing, I think we should probably lay down some rules."

"Rules?" He raised a questioning eyebrow.

Was that really such an outrageous suggestion?

I didn't know how this worked. I had never done anything like this, but the idea of having some simple rules made me feel better about everything. "Yes, rules."

Jordan tilted his head to the left. "I don't know. I have always been a huge believer in the sentiment that rules are meant to be broken."

"If you don't want to have rules, then maybe this just shouldn't happen." I smugly crossed my arms.

"You have quite a feisty side to you." Another knee-weakening smile crossed his face. He ran the pad of his thumb over his bottom lip and eyed me with scrutiny. "All right. What kind of rules do you want?"

I swallowed hard and nervously twisted my fingers together. I hadn't actually come up with them yet. I'd thought it was something we would do together, but seeing as he didn't want any rules, I guessed I would be on my own.

"Um…I guess…" I paused, trying to figure out what to say. "No sleepovers," I blurted out. *Wow, that was lame, but it seemed fair. Boyfriends stay the night. Flings shouldn't. He's probably not even the stay-the-night kind of guy anyway.*

I received a devilish smirk from him.

"I see. You're a use-them-and-toss-them-out kind of girl." He laughed.

I didn't bother to inform him that I hadn't used and tossed anyone out. I was trying to appear in control even if I didn't have a freaking clue what I was doing.

"Whatever. My other rule is no falling in love."

"You want to have a no-falling-in-love rule?" He eyed me.

I didn't like that he was making fun of my rules. I felt that they were very important.

"Yes!" I didn't mean to snap, but I couldn't hold back the embarrassment wheeling up inside me.

"Sorry, I didn't mean to make fun. I promise not to spend the night or fall in love with you." He gave me a lopsided grin.

"This is just a temporary thing. Either one of us can walk away at any time. There are no strings attached."

"Okay. What else you got?"

"Nothing I guess." I chewed on my lip.

"All right then. With rules that easy, I don't think we should have any problems."

"Good." I turned to leave again.

He caught my hand. "You're still leaving?"

I let out a contrite sigh. "I don't want to, but I really do need to get back."

"If you insist, I'll walk you back." He laced his fingers through mine.

"No, it's fine, really. Go be with your friends. I've monopolized enough of your time already." I gave him a quick kiss. "Thank you again for everything today."

"Can I call you later?" he asked.

I suddenly remembered that I had given him the wrong number earlier. This made me cringe with regret. "You could, but you won't reach me. I sort of gave you a fake number."

"What?" he mocked, looking hurt. "And after all we've been through…" He smiled.

He took out his phone, and I gave him my real number.

"I don't know if I can trust you now." He smiled.

I pulled out my phone. "Call me," I told him.

He did, and I answered.

"Trust me now?"

"I guess." He winked at me and hung up his phone.

After the call ended, I noticed that I had a crap-ton of missed calls from Ryan and Brent and then one from Tonya.

"I'm sorry, but I really, really have to go. My brother has called at least a dozen times."

Jordan pulled me into him and kissed me again.

After kissing for a few minutes longer, I pulled away. "I really have to go."

"I know." Jordan kissed my forehead.

I smiled and turned to walk away, but before even taking a step, Jordan pulled me back into him and kissed me again.

Moments later, breathless and slightly dizzy, I finally started walking back to the hotel.

5

Halfway back to where I'd left my things, I was pulled out of my thoughts of Jordan when I heard Brent calling my name.

He jogged over to me. "Where have you been?" he asked with a hint of worry in his eyes.

"We are on a beach. I went for a walk."

He shook his head and pulled out his phone. "Your brother is freaking out."

I rolled my eyes. I wasn't a baby. Ryan needed to stop being overprotective.

I walked away from Brent as soon as he got Ryan on the phone.

"Wait up, Princess," Brent called, catching up with me after he'd gotten off the phone with Ryan. "Where are you going?"

"I'm going to get my things?"

"Ryan already brought your stuff up to the room."

"Of course he did!"

I was annoyed with my brother. I shouldn't have to check in with him every time I went somewhere. Brent wasn't any better at this point. They were both overbearing guard dogs that needed to be thrown into the pound.

I glared at Brent.

"Don't be like that. We found your bag when we came to join you on the beach, but you weren't anywhere around. After you didn't pick up his phone calls, Ryan started to worry."

"My phone was on silent, and I wasn't even gone that long," I snapped.

He shrugged his shoulders and smiled. "You know Ry."

I did know Ryan. I huffed out my annoyance and went back to thinking about Jordan. Instantly, I smiled.

After walking in silence for a while, Brent nudged me. "What's got you all smiley?"

"Um…no one," I answered

His laugh was forced. "You mean, someone? Who's the guy?"

I grinned. "Just some stranger."

Brent shook his head. "What am I going to do with you, Princess?" He slung his arm around my shoulders.

I snickered. "You don't have to do anything with me. I have Surfer Boy for that." I wiggled my eyebrows.

"Oh, really?"

"Yep." I stuck my tongue out at him.

"Stick that tongue out again, Princess, and you won't like what happens."

Is Brent flirting with me?

No. He's never crossed that line.

Wait—is he?

I ran ahead of him and turned around. I stuck out my tongue again, challenging him.

"That's it, Princess." He came barreling toward me.

I shrieked as his arms wrapped around my waist, and he hoisted me over his shoulder. I flailed my legs as Brent ran down toward the water.

"I warned you, Princess."

"I'm sorry, I'm sorry, I'm sorry!" I cried out. "Please don't. I'm sorry." I might have been cracking up, but I really didn't want to be thrown in the water.

Brent slid me down his body, and my feet hit the cold wet sand, sending a shiver through my body. I kept my arms wrapped around his neck. If he were still going to try to throw me in, I wouldn't go in without a fight.

Brent gazed down at me. There was something different about the way he was looking at me, causing my mind to go places it shouldn't. With only inches separating us, I couldn't help but wonder if it would really be that wrong to kiss him. I swallowed hard at the ridiculous thought.

Yes, it would be wrong!

I'd just had my tongue in another guy's mouth. As if that wasn't bad enough, this was Brent, the so off-limits Brent.

I unlocked my arms from around his neck and stepped back. "Thanks for not throwing me in." I turned my head down to watch my feet slowly sink into the sand.

"You have no idea how badly I wanted to, but seeing as your brother is freaking out and you still have to get ready for dinner, you got lucky."

I bit my lip. I might be pushing my luck, but I was feeling mischievous. I placed my hand on his firm pec. "I did get lucky." I stuck out my tongue and twisted his nipple simultaneously before sprinting off to the hotel as if my life depended on it.

Brent caught up, and we entered the hotel, laughing hysterically, as I tried to beg him to stay away from me. We attempted to stifle our laughter after we noticed all the attention we were getting from onlookers. This was easier said than done.

I was grateful no one was in the elevator—well, until I realized that it was just Brent and me, and I had nowhere to run to. After Brent pressed our floor number, he playfully pinned me in the corner and started relentlessly tickling me.

By the time the elevator dinged and the doors opened again, I was on the floor, begging him to stop. "Okay, you win. Stop, stop, stop." I gasped for breath and felt as though I might pee myself.

He helped me up and gestured for me to exit first. I walked backward, so I could watch him, and then I ran a few feet ahead. I had missed this feeling of being happy and carefree. I looked back at Brent to see happiness just radiating off him.

Is it wrong for me to want to hold on to this feeling a bit longer? I let out a deep breath. *Who am I kidding?* I wasn't this happy, carefree girl anymore. *Pretend time is officially over.* The thought made me want to break.

We were almost back to the room when Brent took my hand and stopped me.

"So, are you going to tell me this guy's name?" he asked.

I was about to gush about Jordan, but then I decided that I wanted to keep him to myself. I wanted to have something that Ryan and Brent had no control over. I let go of Brent's hand and smiled. "Nope," I said, going into the room.

I wasn't even through the door when Ryan started yelling, "What the fuck, Roxanne?"

I pushed past him into the room. Besides us three, the suite was thankfully empty. Everyone must have made their way to the banquet hall for dinner. I was already going to have to rush to get ready for dinner. I didn't need to deal with Ryan screaming at me, too.

"Shut up, Ryan!" I yelled back. Then, I looked at Brent. "Where did he put my things from the beach?"

Brent pointed at the room that I was using.

"I'm not going to shut up! You can't go disappearing like that and expect it to be cool. And put some clothes on. I don't know why you wear shit like that!" he shouted.

How delusional is he that he thinks he can control what I wear?

"I went for a walk. Stop treating me like a baby! I'm eighteen, Ryan. I can do whatever the hell I want. And there is nothing wrong with what I'm wearing. It's a bathing suit. I'm even wearing shorts. Stop being such an asshole." I made my way into the room.

Ryan was right behind me. "No one knew where you were, Roxy. You didn't pick up my calls. How do you expect me to react?"

"Not like a goddamn psycho! Besides, I'm here now. So, how about you get out of the room and let me change for dinner?" I yelled back at him.

"This conversation isn't close to being over." He walked out of the room before slamming the door behind him.

"It never is with you." I let out an aggravated scream and fell back onto the king-sized bed. All I wanted to do was crawl under the covers and disappear. Happy time was officially gone.

I looked around the oversized room and thought about my mom. Today, when I'd come to the hotel, I had been too caught up in other stuff to realize what being here actually meant. *How did I not take more time to think about her?* In this room, right now, I could see her.

"Come over here, and let me fix your hair." Mom patted the end of the bed.

I sat down and looked at her through the mirror on the wall in front of us. "You know Ryan will just mess it up as soon as he sees it," I reminded her.

"Maybe, but that doesn't mean we can't enjoy this time together and hope that your brother won't pester you today." She started braiding my hair.

"Do you have another son? Because Ryan lives to make my life hell." I laughed.

"Oh, don't say that. Your brother loves you more than you realize," she told me.

"Sure he does." I chuckled.

"Tell me about how your date went last night." She changed the subject.

I bit my lip. Last night's date with Kevin was life-changing.

"Roxanne, are you blushing?" My mom smiled at me in the mirror.

I was turning bright red. "Kevin and I had sex last night," I blurted out. I closed my eyes, too embarrassed to see the look on my mom's face.

She rubbed my shoulders. Then, she sat down next to me and wrapped her arms around me. "Oh, honey, you don't need to be embarrassed. You're sixteen. I knew this day would come eventually."

I looked at her. "So, you're not mad at me?"

"Oh heavens, no. As a parent, I wish my kids didn't know what sex was, but seeing as you do, I'm just happy you told me. All I care about is your happiness. We are going to have to discuss you going on birth control though."

I smiled. "I figured. Just so you know, we were safe…and it was perfect."

"My baby girl is growing up. You can stop at any time." She smirked and blinked back tears.

"I love you, Mom."

"I love you more. Now, let's finish your hair." She smiled.

My chest split open with the memory. *How is it possible for me to be pain-free less than an hour ago to now bawling like a baby?* I tried to stop the flow of tears, but it was no use. I missed her.

There was a knock on the bedroom door.

"Go away!" I shouted between sobs.

Ryan opened the door and came straight to the bed. He never was one to listen to me. He pulled me into a tight hug that I welcomed. I couldn't hold myself together. Maybe he could.

"I miss her," I cried.

"I know. I miss her, too." He hugged me tighter.

It was these moments when I remembered how remarkable my brother could be. He was my hero, the strong one. He always took care of me. Even when I pissed him off to no end, he would be there for me.

"I'm sorry that I didn't tell you I was going for a walk," I cried.

He let out a deep sigh. "I'm sorry that I overreacted. I shouldn't have yelled at you like that."

I was astonished. That was two apologies from him in one day.

Wow, I must really look pathetic.

He squeezed me three times and then kissed the top of my head. "Are you going to be okay for dinner?" he asked.

I reluctantly pulled out of his hug that seemed to be holding me together. "Yeah, I just need to wash my face and change really quick. You guys can go ahead."

"Nah, we'll wait." He ruffled my hair before standing up.

"Love you, Ry," I said as he headed for the door.

He smiled. "Love you, too, Roxy."

I really had to stop falling apart. I knew how much it killed my brother to see me that way.

Pull it together, Roxy.

After I calmed down and got ready, we headed down to the banquet room. The elevator was quiet until the fourth floor when two bikini-clad girls entered the elevator. Compared to their bikinis, my sundress felt like pants and a turtleneck.

By the third floor, the four of them had undressed each other with their eyes. Passing the second floor, the guys had the girls' numbers, and by the time the elevator doors opened again, the girls were spouting about how they couldn't wait to meet up later.

I rolled my eyes, disgusted.

Ryan threw his arm around my shoulders on the way to the banquet room. "Ah, sis, don't give me that look. This entire night doesn't have to suck!" he teased.

Brent laughed. "Ryan, don't worry about Princess. She hung out with her own stranger today."

I shot Brent a death glare, hoping it would evaporate him on the spot. Yes, his pretty face and godly perfect body would be missed, but him selling me out to my brother wouldn't be.

Ryan suddenly stopped dead in his tracks and dropped his arm, all humor gone from his face. "What? Is that where you were earlier, hanging out with some guy? I thought you said you went for a walk."

I huffed loudly. "We're not talking about this right now." I marched off, away from them both.

"You'd better believe we will be talking about it later," he warned.

With their long legs, Ryan and Brent were next to me by the time we entered the room.

"I'm starved. Let's all be happy and get stuffed," Brent joked.

Ryan and I both glared at him.

Brent shrugged his shoulders. "Or we can just eat. I need some food."

Ryan managed to laugh, but I was still too pissed off at Brent to find him remotely funny.

Did they forget what this dinner was about? How can either of them be happy right now?

I looked around the room. My heart ached at seeing all the pictures of my mom's smiling face. I had thought there were too many pictures in the suite, but that was nothing compared to this. There was also more people here now than in the suite.

I was having a hard time catching my breath. This was too much like her funeral, except for the part where everyone was laughing and smiling. Everything was wrong with this picture. My mom wasn't here. People shouldn't be happy without her.

If I'm not happy, how are they?

Bile rose in my throat.

I thought back to the afternoon with Jordan. I'd let myself get lost in him. I had been happy with him. It'd felt good at the time, but now, I was mad at myself. Today was supposed to be about my mom. But I'd chosen to spend time pretending like I was normal. I was a terrible daughter.

My father went to the microphone on the stage at the back of the room. "It looks like my children have finally arrived. If you can all take your seats, dinner will be served shortly," he announced.

Ryan took my hand and squeezed it three times.

I love you, too, Ry. I returned the squeezes.

We made our way to the table with all eyes watching us. I hated it and wanted more than anything to run upstairs and hide. I cursed myself for not bringing the bottle of painkillers. Right now, I could really use the dulling nothingness they would bring on.

I sat down between Brent and Ryan.

Brent leaned over. "If you need to go, just let me know. I'll leave with you," he whispered in my ear.

It was hard to stay mad at him when he always found a way to be sweet.

The room quieted down while eating as people started to eat.

Papa sat across from me. I could see the sadness in his eyes, but he still managed to give me a heartwarming smile. I smiled back even though it wasn't a real one. I knew how badly he wanted to see me holding it together.

I looked down the table at my father. In that moment, for the first time, I noticed that he looked exhausted and frail. I felt bad for being mad at him this whole time. After all, he'd lost her, too. Tears welled up in my eyes. All I wanted to do was run to my daddy and tell him how much I loved him. But I could never do that. We weren't close that way. I wasn't even sure if Ryan could get away with that. Then again, Ryan got away with everything.

Brent gave me a reassuring squeeze on my knee under the table. It startled me, but what stunned me even more was when he didn't remove his hand. Brent never let his touches linger. I was about to call him out on it, but then I decided against it. His warm hand on my bare skin had the calming effect I'd needed. I pushed down the sadness that was on the verge of pouring out. I could get through this. I could do it for her.

After everyone was finished eating, my dad stood. "I would like to first thank everyone for coming today. My wife would have been overjoyed to see each one of you here." His voice faltered for a second. "In fact, I'm sure she would have sent you all a gift basket tomorrow. But that was her thing, not mine, so don't expect one." He attempted to joke.

Everyone gave a small chuckle.

"All I can say is, thank you. It means a great deal to my children and me to share the Fourth of July with all of you." He paused, and I saw he was holding back tears. "Now, if you don't mind, my son would like to say a few words about his mother." He nodded at my brother.

Ryan stood, and his hands were shaking. He made his way to the stage. He was much stronger than me. He started a slideshow of pictures. I had thought all the pictures in this room were too much, but his slideshow was even more personal. I squeezed my arms across my chest. I was no longer sure I would be able to hold myself together.

Brent's thumb made circles on my knee, and I tried to focus on the warmth of his touch.

Ryan cleared his throat after saying hello. I knew this was hard for him.

"A lot of you here today knew my mother very well. I'm sure you all have your own memories of her and reasons for loving her. You all knew her as Rebecca Daniels—PTA member, book club host, event planner extraordinaire, and the best cookie maker in California.

"To me, she was just Mom, which was everything. When I was younger, I believed my mom had to be some kind of superhero. She was there for every game, Boy Scout meeting, bake sale, and car wash. Of course, as I got older, I realized she wasn't an actual superhero, but in my eyes, she was still my hero. My mom did it all, and she always had a smile on her face."

I couldn't hold my tears back any longer, and they flowed freely.

My brother continued, "My sister and I were always on the go. She had dance, gymnastics, and cheer, and I had all my sports. Our mom never missed one game, recital, match, or competition. Even with all of that, she always made us dinner every night. It didn't matter if we had to eat it in the car. She baked for the bake sales, went from business to business to look for team sponsors, sewed dresses, and made tutus. When I said she did it all, I meant it.

"I always knew I was lucky to have such a great mom. I just never realized how many other lives she touched outside of our home. I would like to know how she changed or touched each of your lives. A couple of books will be passed around. If you could take a few moments to write down something about my mom and how she touched your life, our family would really appreciate it. My mother was incredible, and our family is grateful that you all came to share this day with us. Thank you."

The applause was deafening as my brother left the stage. There wasn't a dry eye in the house.

I couldn't hold myself together any longer. I'd wanted to be strong enough to stay here, but I just wasn't.

As Ryan sat down, I stood up.

"I can't," was all that came from my mouth.

The pain was overwhelming, and the room felt as if it were closing in on me. I had to get out of there. I didn't care who was looking or how much of an embarrassment I was.

I ran through the lobby, outside to the beach, and all the way to the water's edge. I wanted to hurl myself into the waves and let them drag me under. Maybe then all this pain would stop. I crumpled to my knees and cried. The water washed over my knees and soaked my dress. I thought the hardest I'd ever cried was the day she died. Tonight, I bawled much harder. She was never coming back. I knew this. I didn't understand why it was hitting me like a brick wall all over again. My body throbbed with grief, every sob more painful than the last.

Two arms folded around me. I looked up, expecting to see Ryan, but it wasn't him. It was Brent.

"I got you, Princess. I got you."

I turned around, crawled onto his lap, and let him hold me. The waves splashed around us, but he never tried to move. He just sat in the water with me and let me cry. He rocked me back and forth, humming a lullaby I couldn't place. I cried until I felt I would get sick.

Finally, I was able to take steady breaths. The pain rocketing through my body wasn't as fierce as when I'd run out here, but Brent kept his tight hold on me.

I stared up at him. He had been crying, too. I wiped the teardrops from his cheek. My body started to shiver instead of the uncontrollable shaking it had done while I was crying.

Brent noticed the difference. "You're freezing cold. We should get you inside."

All I could do was nod. I stood, letting Brent get up. He pulled me into another hug as the fireworks started near the pier. The boom of each explosion rocked through my body, but it wasn't from the blast itself. It was more from the memory that pounded with it. My mom had loved watching the fireworks, and they were another agonizing reminder of something else she would never get to experience again.

I'd told Ryan I would start trying to live for Mom, but it was too hard. I didn't want to experience everything she'd loved if it meant feeling all this pain. I knew how selfish it sounded, but I just wasn't that strong.

I stepped back and looked up at Brent. I wanted to thank him, but the words didn't seem like enough.

I wrapped my arms around myself, trying to press back the pain. "I'm sorry I'm broken," I apologized.

He smiled down at me before pulling me in for another hug. "You're not broken, Princess. You're just a little bent. With time, you'll straighten back out. I promise," he said before releasing me.

We started to walk toward the hotel, but my body was weak, and my legs faltered. Brent caught me before I fell, and then he swept me up into his arms. I laid my head on his chest and let him carry me to the hotel. I thought he would put me down once we got inside, but he didn't. While we were in the elevator, I listened to his heartbeat. It was pounding faster than mine was. I assumed that was because he was carrying me. When we reached or floor, I wanted to tell him he could put me down, but the words never came out of my mouth. He brought me all the way to the suite door before he finally set me down and pulled out the key from his wallet. I slowly walked into the dark room after him. Brent flicked on the lights. The room was empty. Everyone must be on the roof, watching the fireworks.

In the light of the room, I felt embarrassment wash over me. I wanted to hide in the dark near the beach.

I twirled my hair around my finger. I couldn't look at Brent.

"I should probably change," I stated.

Brent cleared his throat. "Yeah, me, too."

Brent walked off to the room he was using while I went to mine. I changed my clothes and lay on the bed. My body had the familiar ache I would get from crying too hard. Tonight, the throbbing in my chest was extremely intense. I placed my hands over my heart. I prayed for the excruciating pain to go away. I didn't have Mom's pills to dull it, and I really needed some relief.

There was a knock on my door.

"Come in," I called.

Brent stuck his head in. "I just wanted to say good night."

"Oh." I sat up and fumbled for the words I was looking for. "About tonight—"

"Don't worry about it, Princess. I'll always be here for you. Try to get some rest." He smiled.

I nodded my head. He was about to shut the door.

"Brent!" I called.

"Yeah?" he asked, sticking his head back through the door.

I knew it wouldn't be enough for what he had just done, but I said it anyway, "Thank you."

He smiled again and then shut the door. It seemed like I had been saying thank-you a lot today.

My thoughts floated to Jordan and then back to Brent. I wanted to think over the day's events in more depth, but I just couldn't. My body and mind were both exhausted.

I closed my eyes and pictured Jordan. Amazingly enough, my prayers for relief of the pain were answered. The throbbing in my chest lessened, and I quickly fell asleep.

It sadly wasn't a restful sleep. The glow of sunlight lit the room as I was awoken by another nightmare about the night when I'd found my mom. I grabbed my phone to see it was only seven. I growled, hating that I was up so early. I wiped away the sweat beading on my forehead. Flashes of my mom's dead body were still in my head. I took a deep breath and reminded myself that it was just a dream.

Stupid nightmares. Is a dreamless night too much to ask for?

Oh, how I miss the bottle of pills back at home.

I could hear Brent and Ryan arguing over some football thing in the living room. I hoped that Ryan wasn't mad at me for running out last night.

The last thing I'd wanted was to fall apart in front of all those people. Having Brent see me in that state had been bad enough.

I groaned as I got out of bed. I dressed and brushed my teeth. I would shower later.

I looked around the room. The memories of my mom were pungent in here, and this caused the pain to throb wildly in my chest. I crossed my arms and squeezed. I breathed out the hurt until I could handle it. I swiped at the few tears that had escaped. I felt like crap, and I just wanted to go home and back to bed. Maybe just taking the pills for sleep wouldn't be that bad.

As much as I'd intended to go on living for her, after last night, I just wanted to go back to popping pills and sleeping. Even though it was what I really desired, I instantly felt guilty from knowing how disappointed that would make my mom. I let out a sad sigh and allowed a few more tears to fall.

I said a small good-bye to my mom. It seemed like that was all I did anymore. Saying good-bye to her in every place she no longer was. Each time would be just as painful as the last.

I gathered my things and threw them into my bags. I just needed to get out of here. I put on my sunglasses, and I headed out of the room.

"Look who's up bright and early," Ryan teased, looking absolutely shocked.

I raised an eyebrow at him. "Like anyone could sleep with the racket you two are making."

"Sorry, Princess. We'll try to keep it down if you want to get some more rest."

Brent's apology was sweet, but I really wanted to get out of here.

"Dude, don't tell her to sleep. It's a miracle that she's up right now. This is good," Ryan said to Brent before sending a spiraling football at his face.

It was no surprise that Brent effortlessly caught it.

I gave a small smile to Brent. It felt as awkward as I was afraid it would. "I'm just gonna head home. I'm sure I'll see you guys later." I moved for the door.

"Hey, sis, be quiet when you get home. I had to drive Dad back last night. He was drunk and demanded I take him home. He will probably still be asleep. As for sleep, don't you dare go back to bed," he warned.

"Yeah, totally. Whatever you say, Ry." Sarcasm rolled off my tongue.

He was still yelling something when I went out the door.

By the time I got to my car, my mind was no longer on my dad or Ryan. At this point, I wasn't even thinking of Brent anymore. Yesterday's events with Jordan were vigorously looping through my mind.

Once again, I was thinking about how wonderful he'd been to help me. Just thinking about him made me smile. Considering that smiling didn't usually come easily to me anymore, this surprised me. But whenever I had been around Jordan or thought of him, I just couldn't help but smile.

Where most people would consider this a good thing, I only saw all the different flashing warning signs. *How am I supposed to hang out with him when I already like him as much as I do?*

This was not a safe situation for my heart. Even though I knew that, every part of me longed to see him again—well, every part except for my heart. It knew better.

This made me think of seeing Kevin. *Stupid, stupid horrible Kevin.* Just remembering him made me sick. I hated that he was capable of hurting me as badly as he could. I despised the fact that the pain he'd caused was still lingering. I would never let someone get that close to me again. I might be allowing Jordan into my life, but there was no way I would let him into my heart.

6

When I got home, I showered and then put on some gym clothes. I hated to admit it, but Ryan was right. I needed to stay out of bed. I made my way over to the other side of our house, heading to the gym Ryan had gotten our parents to put in for his fifteenth birthday.

I started stretching to loosen up my body. My time of inactivity had made my muscles tight.

As I stretched, I thought about Brent's sadness last night.

He was still grieving for my mother, too. I hadn't realized just how much losing her had affected him.

I got on the treadmill and tried to run the thoughts of Brent out of my head. They weren't going away. I remembered the way he'd held and rocked me in the water while I cried and how he'd carried me to the suite.

I turned up the treadmill and ran faster. I had to stop thinking of Brent. He was my brother's best friend, the biggest no-no of all. No matter what had happened last night, Ryan considered Brent to be his brother. My mom and dad had treated him like a son. I should probably think of Brent more as a brother than some guy that I wanted to wrap myself around and never let go. Besides, Brent had no shortage of women in his life. I was and always would be the little sister of his best friend.

My phone rang, taking me out of my disturbing thoughts. I slowed down the treadmill and looked at the screen. It wasn't a programmed number.

"Hello?" I answered.

"Roxy?" asked a deep male voice.

Even though I had turned down the speed on the treadmill, just hearing Kevin's voice almost made me trip over my own feet and fly off. I quickly hit the Stop button.

"Roxy?" Kevin said again.

I was having trouble remembering how to speak. *How did I not remember his number? How did he have mine?*

Ryan had gotten me a new iPhone after I had thrown the old one against Kevin's wall during my freak-out. Ryan had also had my number changed for me. He'd somehow known that I wouldn't want to talk to anyone. My new number was the greatest perk of the new phone.

Kevin exhaled into the phone. "Rocket, I know you're there. Say something."

"How did you get my number?" I seethed.

"Hello to you, too, Rocket."

I could just imagine the smirk on his face.

"Stop calling me that," I snapped. "Why are you calling me? And who gave you my number?" I was trying to calm my pounding heart.

He laughed.

My stomach twisted. *Laughing? He's seriously laughing? What the fuck?*

"Ah, Roxy, you know I have my ways. I'm not about to sell out my source. As for why I'm calling you, that should be obvious. I want to talk."

"Look, Kevin, I don't know who gave you my number, but you didn't have it in the first place for a reason. I don't want to talk to you," I spit.

"Calm down, Roxy. Just talk to me." He tried to reason with me.

"This is me being calm. Go to hell, Kevin!" I screamed before hanging up.

Before I could overthink it, I blocked his number. I got off the treadmill and leaned against the wall. I sank down and hugged my knees.

A month ago, I had thought Kevin actually loved me.

A month ago...

Tomorrow, she will have been gone for one month.

I put my head down and cried. I was beyond sick of crying, but I had no idea how to make the pain or tears go away. My chest felt as though it were being ripped open. I hadn't realized how hard or loud I was crying until I saw my dad in the doorway. I tried to calm myself down, but it was no use. I was broken. I knew it, and from the look in my dad's eyes, he knew it, too. I needed to accept that I would never be all right. All this pain was never going to go away.

My dad walked closer. He looked as horrible as I felt. He seemed as though he had aged years in the past month.

How did I not notice this before?

The sparkle that used to be in his eyes was gone.

He sat down next to me. Unlike Ryan, he didn't pull me into a hug and hold me. He just sat there while I fell apart.

After I calmed down a bit, he asked, "Do you want to talk about it?"

I hiccuped from crying. "No." It was the truth.

Dad and I had never had serious conversations.

Why start now?

He exhaled. "I'm not your mom. I don't know how to speak to you like she did. I probably never will. If you need to discuss something, I'm here, but just remember that I'm not her." He stood up and stared down at me.

All the anger that I had toward my dad disappeared in that moment. Our relationship wasn't close to being fixed, but I wasn't angry with him like I had been. Right then, I just saw my dad, not the award-winning plastic surgeon who changed lives on a daily basis. I saw him as a man who had lost his wife, his better half, and his best friend. He was also the only parent I had left.

I stood up and hugged him. It was something I hadn't done in years. Dad had never been the affectionate type. I wasn't even sure if he would hug me back. It was just something I needed to do. I was about to release him when he finally returned the hug.

"I love you, Daddy," I whispered.

I didn't wait to hear him say it back before I let him go and left the room. I went to my bedroom and shut the door. I might be broken, but there was something comforting in realizing that I wasn't the only one.

My dad was lost without my mom, and even if we never became close, we had today and the one moment when he'd tried to be there for me. Knowing that somehow eased the throbbing agony I felt throughout my body. It didn't disappear, but I would take any kind of relief I could get.

Amazingly, yesterday had gone by without any more tears. My dad and I hadn't talked about what happened in the gym, but we hadn't avoided each other either. He hadn't belittled me or mentioned things that I should be doing differently. Actually, we hadn't done much talking at all, but the silence hadn't felt strained.

Ryan had come home later in the day. He had seemed relieved to see that Dad and I hadn't killed each other. Ryan couldn't hide his astonishment when I'd joined my dad on the couch and watched TV. Again, it had felt weird but comfortable.

Last night, I'd tossed and turned, having nightmare after nightmare. I'd kept seeing my mom's dead body lying on the kitchen floor. I had begged her to come back to me, not to die, but she had already left. I'd been having the same nightmare since I found her.

I'd grabbed my mom's bottle of pills more times than I could even count. I'd wanted them. I'd needed the pain-numbing haze that they provided. But each time, the thought of her had reminded me that I couldn't use them any longer. It sucked, but I couldn't numb myself into oblivion again. I would have to suffer through the pain, the memories, and the nightmares.

By four in the morning, I had gotten over trying to sleep. I'd gotten in my car and driven to the cemetery.

Now in front of my mom's gravestone, I knelt down.

REBECCA DANIELS

LOVING WIFE

AND MOTHER

I traced the engraving on her gravestone. "These words don't really grasp all that you were," I whispered to her grave.

I hadn't been here since the day that we buried her. I didn't remember a lot about that day. I had been out of it, walking through a fog of pain.

"I'm sorry that I haven't come to visit. I'm just starting to get out of the house again. Let me tell you, it's been harder than I ever thought."

It was weird talking to a stone, but I didn't want to stop. The grass was still wet from the night before, and the dew soaked through the thin material of my yoga pants, making me shiver.

I plucked a blade of grass and tore it apart as I spoke, "We all got together on the Fourth in your honor." My voice cracked. "A bunch of people came. You would have been impressed. Ryan gave a speech and talked about you." Tears slid down my cheeks. "It was very beautiful. You would have been proud."

I let out a sad long sigh. In this moment, I missed her more than I'd known was possible. I dug my nails into my palms to try to ease the pain suffocating my heart. I wrapped my arms across my chest and squeezed. I didn't know what I was doing. I didn't even know if I should be speaking these things aloud.

No matter how hard I pressed my fingernails in my skin, I couldn't stop the flow of tears. I couldn't stop the agony.

"I can't stop it. I can't stop hurting or crying. I can't stop missing you."

I was crying harder now. I shoved my knuckles into my mouth and bit down on them, trying to end the god-awful sounds gushing from my mouth. It didn't help. The muffling of my cries just made them more wretched. I fell forward and pounded my fists into the grass.

"Why?" I screamed. "Why did you have to die?" I was yelling at my mother as if it were her fault, as if she'd had some choice in the matter, or as if she could have possibly stopped herself from dying.

I knew it wasn't true, but it didn't matter. I continued to shout and pound on the grass anyway. My body was quaking as I collapsed onto my side, and I curled up into a ball. I hated what I had become. I hated that this was my life. I hated that she was gone.

I woke up to the sun beating down on me, and I couldn't believe that I had cried myself to sleep.

Great. Now, I'm not only the girl who screamed at her mother's grave, but I'm also the girl who slept in a cemetery.

I stood up. Every muscle in my body was sore, not that it mattered. The pain was just another reminder that I was here and she wasn't.

I half-expected the tears to start falling again. I waited for them, but they never came. I felt like I should say something else to her. So, I mumbled an apology for my freak-out, like it somehow mattered.

I walked away from her grave. As I did, I left a part of me behind, a small piece of my soul that was now waiting for the rest of me to shatter into pieces and join it.

"Are you okay?" Tonya asked when she answered the phone.

"I miss you," I told her. After I'd gotten back to my house from the cemetery, she was the only one I'd wanted to talk to.

She laughed. "I miss you, too." Then, her voice got serious. "But you're okay, right?"

I pressed down on my chest. I knew it wouldn't stop the ache, but I had to at least try.

"Yeah, Ton, I'm okay," I lied.

The line went quiet, and I could tell she was contemplating what to say.

"I feel like you're lying to me," she finally said.

"I visited my mom today," I admitted.

"And…how did it go? If you need me to, I can come back home. Never mind. You don't even have to answer. I'm coming home," she rambled.

"Ton, breathe. You don't need to come home. I just wanted to hear your voice. I just need my best friend to talk to me and make me forget how horrible life really is."

"Roxy, I'm coming home. I can talk to you when I get there. We can go out and have fun."

"Seriously, Tonya, I don't want you to come home. In fact, if you do, I will lock myself in my room and never come out. I just need someone to talk to. That's all I called for."

"If I didn't believe you would actually do that, I would already be in the car. I know you well enough that I will sit here and talk to you about whatever you want for however long you need, but don't think I will enjoy one second of it."

"You are an amazing best friend," I reminded her.

"Okay, you keep saying that stuff, and I might enjoy this conversation just a little bit."

I could hear her smile, and I wanted to smile with her, but I couldn't.

Tonya tried to talk about my visit to my mom's grave, but it was too hard for me.

Instead, I told Tonya about meeting Jordan. After she stopped screaming for joy that I was gabbing about a guy, I filled her in on how he'd helped me save face with Kevin. After a slew of oh-my-gods and calling Kevin and Sara every bad word, Tonya started demanding that I call Jordan.

"No, Ton. I can't," I objected.

"You have to, Rox. The only time that you didn't seem sad during this whole conversation was when you were speaking about him. You like him."

"That's exactly why I can't. I do like him. On the Fourth, he convinced me to hang out with him again. But every day that passes without talking to him is a reality check. He makes my stomach flutter. I don't want that."

"A fluttering stomach is not a death wish, Roxy. Do what he said. Spend time with him. Enjoy the kissing part and a whole lot more hopefully," she teased.

I groaned, hating what I had to admit. "I don't want to fall for him. I can't chance getting hurt. I won't be able to handle that kind of hurt again."

"Hmm...I say that you should still call him, and before you object, hear me out. You already said that you like him, right?"

"Yes, and that is the problem! Are you not listening?" I yelled.

"No, that makes it better. You can like him without falling in love with him. He can be everything that you need, but at the same time, he can be safe. I mean, it's obvious that he likes you, too. Don't you see how this is perfect?"

"Nope, not even a little."

"Think outside the box, Roxy. You need someone to get you over Kevin—all the way over him. You can move on from Kevin and test out controlling your feelings. You also need someone to keep you occupied and to fill your head with things not dripping with sadness. This Jordan guy can help you. Use him for what you need, but don't get attached. Keep things physical. He will help you get out of your head and forget for a while."

The thought of being with Jordan like that made my skin flush and my pulse quicken. He did have a way of making me forget.

"Oh, Ton, how would I get through life without you?"

"You wouldn't."

"Okay, I'll think about it. I'm not making you any promises, but I will think about it."

"Good, and do me a favor. Don't feel bad about using him. Remember, this is just a summer fling. He's getting the better deal. He gets you."

I was a broken, crazy, and depressed girl. I didn't really think he would be getting the better deal, but I didn't bother telling her this. "Again, I'll think about it."

We said our good-byes, and I decided to head downstairs.

Brent and my brother were high-fiving as I walked into the kitchen.

"What are you two so enthusiastic about?" I asked on my way to the fridge.

Ryan was shaking with excitement. "Roxy, do you remember the man Brent and I had to meet with on the Fourth?"

I gave him a questioning look. "The Ad Corp guy?"

"Yes. Well, he just called. He wants Brent and me down there next week for a formal interview. He wants to see some of our ideas." Ryan high-fived Brent again.

"This is tremendous, Princess. If we get this internship, it would look killer on our resumes." Brent was just as happy as Ry.

I realized that I hadn't seen Brent since I left the hotel. I was glad he was here now even if I still felt a bit weird around him.

"That's cool. I'm excited for you both."

After getting a soda out of the fridge, I walked out to the living room. Not seeing what I was looking for, I went back into the kitchen.

"Where's Dad?" I asked.

Ryan looked at Brent and then at the ground. He scratched the back of his head and then looked at me. "Dad went back to Los Angeles after he woke up this morning. He said something about someone needing surgery."

"He couldn't even call me to say good-bye?"

My hope of a better relationship with my dad flew out the window. *Why did I even delude myself into thinking it was possible?* This day was turning out to be crap.

"He didn't know that you were gone. He thought you were still sleeping," Ryan informed me.

Now, I was furious. "You mean, he didn't even know I was gone, and he still couldn't take the time to try to tell me good-bye!" I yelled.

"In his defense, I didn't know you were gone till around ten when I went to check on you."

I threw my hands up. "Great! That's fucking nice of you. Thanks for checking on me, Ryan, and thanks for once again making excuses for Dad. No wonder you're his favorite." I stormed off toward the stairs.

"Where were you, Roxy?" Ryan asked.

I spun around to look at him. "I was visiting Mom. It's been one month since she died, Ryan, not that you or anyone else is keeping track." I ran upstairs and slammed my door.

I felt that twisting pain in my stomach. I was being sucked back into the sinkhole of anguish.

Why doesn't Dad love me? Why does he always say good-bye to Ryan but not care about me?

I'd thought that we might have been on a better track after yesterday's conversation. It was clear that yesterday had been a fluke. We might have had a tiny moment, but that was all it had been.

I wiped away the tears that had started to fall. I dug my nails into my palms. I would not cry over that man. If he hadn't thought that I even deserved a good-bye, he sure as hell didn't deserve my tears.

My phone vibrated on my dresser. I looked at the screen and saw Jordan was calling.

My heart stopped. I answered as fast as I could, "Hi." I tried to hide the fact that I had just been crying.

"Hey." His voice was sexier over the phone than I remembered it being in person. "I'm glad you picked up."

I took a deep breath as his voice put me at ease. "You say that like you've been calling over and over."

"What I mean is that I was worried you wouldn't."

"Well, you shouldn't have worried. Remember, I'm the crazy one out of the two of us. I'm surprised that you called at all."

He laughed. "Are you kidding? I wanted to call you right after you walked away. I just told myself that I had to wait three days."

"But it's only been two?"

"Exactly! I spent all day checking my phone, hoping that maybe you would call me, but you didn't. I can't seem to get you out of my head."

"I'm sorry. I…" I didn't know what to say.

Luckily, Jordan didn't notice and continued to talk, "I want to take you out tonight. I thought we could grab dinner and a movie?"

Today had been full of terrible emotions. I didn't feel like going out and pretending to enjoy myself. I just didn't have the energy for it tonight.

"I don't think tonight is a good night."

"Are you busy?" he asked with a hint of disappointment in his voice.

"No, nothing like that. It's just that watching a movie isn't something I'd really be into tonight. Actually, you probably don't want to be around me at all tonight. I won't be much fun."

"We don't have to watch a movie. We could just hang out. All I know is I want to see you again. You could spend the night picking your nose, and I would still enjoy myself."

I laughed, and it shocked the hell out of me. It felt good. It amazed me how Jordan had a way of making the gloom and pain go away.

I suddenly wanted to see him. "Can we make a deal?"

"What? Anything," he answered.

"We can hang out tonight but no talking. It wouldn't be a date. It would—"

Jordan cut me off, "That sounds perfect! Let me get your address, and I'll pick you up."

I laughed again. "Not a date, remember? How about you meet me on the street where we were parked on the Fourth?"

Since he wanted to be around me as much as I wanted him to take away my pain, I had nothing to feel guilty for.

"I can do that. When should we meet?" he asked.

"Nine?" I stated, sounding unsure.

"That's perfect. I'll be there." I could hear the eagerness in his voice.

"Perfect!"

After I hung up with Jordan, my body filled with excitement of my own.

When I had been with Jordan on the Fourth, I had gotten lost in him. The rest of the world had seemed to disappear.

I had no idea what I was doing, and I didn't care. All I knew was that I didn't want to think about my dad or his lack of love for me. I didn't want to think about Brent or how badly I wanted him to hold me again. I didn't want to think about Kevin and how he'd thrown our relationship away to be with some whore. I most certainly didn't want to think about my dead mother.

I didn't know how, but Jordan made me forget. I needed him and his sad-thought-blocking abilities. I pushed down the pain threatening to consume me, and I did something that I hadn't done since before my mom died.

I docked my iPod and started dancing around my room. As I danced, I tried to let go of the day. It felt good to get lost in the music. I let the tingle of anticipation make its way through my body. I didn't know what I was more thrilled about—seeing Jordan again or the chance of feeling something other than pain.

7

I drove down the street, scanning the area for Jordan's truck. Tonight, unlike the Fourth, the street was nearly deserted. I saw his truck parked in the same spot where it had been before.

Butterflies danced in my stomach.

I got out of my car just as he was getting out of his truck. He walked toward me, and I completely lost my breath.

Good Lord, this man is gorgeous.

He was wearing dark blue jeans and a gray Volcom T-shirt that hugged his chest and shoulders. Even the way he strolled over to me was hot.

I swallowed hard. I had to control myself. *Control, control, control.*

"Hey," he said, looking down at me.

Once again, he smelled delicious, like the ocean mixed with mint. All I wanted to do was pounce on him, but I reminded myself that I needed to stay in control.

Damn, this is going to be hard.

I smiled at him, trying to push away my dirty thoughts. "Hi."

"You look gorgeous." He pulled me into a hug.

For heaven's sake, his sexy scent took over my senses.

Control, control!

I pulled away from him quicker than I wanted to.

"I have to say, you clean up rather nicely yourself."

I wasn't about to gush about how he looked extraordinarily stunning. He probably already knew this about himself. I was sure plenty of women had told him so.

"Where would you like to go from here?" he asked.

I smiled. "This way!" I took his hand, and we made our way down to the beach.

"Are you gonna tell me where we are going?" he asked.

"I'll give you three guesses, and the first two don't count." I smirked.

He laughed. "I know where we're going. I'm just trying to make small talk."

"Don't worry about small talk. It's not necessary."

"I don't want you to think that I just came here to hook up with you, Rox. I just felt like I needed to see you again, and on the phone, you sounded like you could use someone to talk to."

"In case you've forgotten, I stated that the one thing that I didn't want to do was talk."

We stepped onto the beach. Cool sand devoured my feet with each step. I stopped to take off my flip-flops.

"Roxanne, are you telling me that you brought me here to seduce me?" he mocked in astonishment.

We walked a few feet closer to the water. It was dark enough tonight that I didn't have to worry about him seeing me blush. I stopped walking and pulled him to stand in front of me. I dropped my flip-flops next to my feet in the sand.

"That's exactly why I brought you here. How am I doing so far?" I asked as seductively as I could.

He brushed my hair off my face. "I don't think that I ever stood a chance. Please understand though, if all you want to do is talk, I'll be fine with that, too." He was staring in my eyes.

The butterflies in my stomach felt like they were on the roller coaster ride of a lifetime. I smiled and shook my head to let him know that I didn't want to talk. I got a devilish smile in return as he brought his head down and kissed me.

Sayonara, control.

I wrapped my arms around his neck and kissed him deeper. His arms pulled me in even closer before his hands moved up and down my body. I wanted him more than I wanted my next breath of air. We lowered ourselves down into the sand, never taking our lips from one another. He cradled my head as he had done once before and laid it on the sand. I was grateful the beach was deserted tonight.

I parted my knees as he positioned himself on top of me. A small moan passed my lips, making a shudder rack through his body as a growl came from the back of his throat. I dragged my nails down his back over his shirt, and he groaned again as he pressed his lower half into me. My body rocked up against his, begging him to hit the spot where I wanted to feel him the most. He didn't disappoint as he ground into me. I moaned louder this time.

My body was burning with need from the inside out. The throbbing between my legs was pleading for more. Each time he pushed his hardness into me, I could feel my panties getting wet.

Then, Jordan pulled away.

"What are you doing? Don't stop!" My breathing was ragged.

I leaned up to kiss him again, but he stopped me.

"Hold on. I need to take a breather before I can't stop. I didn't expect you to get to me like this. I just need a minute," he warned me.

I smiled at how adorable he was being. "I'm not asking you to stop."

He looked beyond shocked. His eyes were questioning me, but beyond the questions, they were still burning with lust.

I cupped his face in my hands. "I'm not asking you to stop. I want this," I told him.

I pulled him down to kiss me. I needed this more than I could explain. The way he made me feel was like nothing I'd ever felt before. Kevin and I had had an active sex life, but my body never felt like this with him.

Jordan's kiss wasn't as intense as I preferred it to be. I fisted the hair at the back of his head and tugged while my other hand ran down the front of his jeans and gripped on to his hardness.

"Oh God, Rox," he groaned.

He stopped holding back. He kissed my mouth harder, so hard that it almost hurt. I loved it, and I couldn't get enough. His left hand traveled under my shirt before cupping one breast and squeezing it. His thumb circled my nipple through the lace of my bra.

I grabbed the bottom of his shirt and pulled it up. He moved back from me long enough to take it all the way off. His body was magnificent. I ran my fingers up his rock-hard abs, over his sculpted chest, to his shoulders, and then his neck. I combed my fingers through his hair before luring him back down to my mouth.

He paused after a quick kiss. He pushed up my shirt and then pulled it off. In the next moment, he unclasped my bra before laying my head back down. He sat back on his knees as he slowly removed my bra. I wanted to jerk him back down and kiss him more, but the way that he was looking me over stopped me from rushing this moment. I wasn't sure if it was the coolness of the sand or his eyes that gave me the chills. He slowly moved his hands up from my waist to the bottom of my rib cage.

"You're amazing," he said as he cupped both of my breasts.

He rolled his thumbs over my nipples, causing them to harden even more. I arched my back and whimpered at how good it felt.

I started tugging at the button on his pants. I needed him inside me. He caught hold of both my wrists and gently moved them to the sand above my head. He held my hands in place with one hand as he kissed my forehead, my temple, my nose, and my cheek. He pressed his lips to mine, letting his tongue explore my mouth. Then, his lips moved to my chin, my neck, and my collarbone, leaving a trail of soft kisses. He grazed each shoulder with his teeth, causing goose bumps to cover my body. He dragged the tip of his tongue down the curve of my right breast before devouring my nipple into his mouth. As he sucked and teased one with his tongue, he used his fingers to pinch and squeeze the other. My nipples were so hard that they hurt. I never knew that pain like this could feel fantastic.

"Please, Jordan," I begged for him to take me.

"Yeah, baby, that's it. Tell me what you want."

"I want you. Please I need this," I continued to beg.

Jordan's body suddenly went still, and he pulled back from me. He was intently staring down at me. I pushed up to kiss him and get things moving again, but he let go of my hands and sat across from me.

"I can't do this," he said.

"What?" I just lay there, stunned. *What the hell?*

With the heat of the moment now officially gone, I felt exposed. I reached for my shirt, pulled it over my head, and looked at him.

"It doesn't feel right," he told me.

"Were you not enjoying yourself? Because I was! I thought that we were having fun." I stared at him.

He ran his fingers through his hair and looked up at the sky. He seemed upset.

Maybe he's regretting his stupid move of stopping things.

He finally glanced at me again. "Trust me. I want the fun. You have no idea how badly I want you. I have also used enough girls to get over my own pain, so I'm not blind. I know you're using me, Roxy. I want to be with you. I just want you to want to be with me for the right reasons. I'd rather sit and talk and help you feel better that way than fuck you. That probably makes me sound lame, but I think you deserve more than this."

I don't want more than this.

I smiled a fake smile. "We aren't supposed to be talking, so you don't need to worry about that. What you were doing was perfect," I joked, trying to lighten the mood.

Jordan wasn't having it. "Using me for sex won't make your problems go away. Your problems will still be there when we're done."

I had been trying to forget my problems, but I hadn't thought he would make them go away. I'd needed him to take away all the pain that my problems had brought, and he had. Even now, the pain that I had carried in my chest wasn't there. I hadn't brought him here to use him for sex. Maybe I'd wanted to get lost in kissing him, but I hadn't expected things to escalate to this level.

"No! That wasn't what I was doing. I didn't come out, intending to have sex with you tonight. I thought we were having fun. Things between us just got intense. It felt good, and I didn't want to stop," I told him.

"You knew exactly what you wanted me for. It isn't just because this is fun for you, is it? You can talk to me. I want to help."

"I needed this, okay?" I was starting to get upset. The last thing I'd wanted to do was talk to him about my problems.

"Just tell me what's wrong." He was pushing it.

"What is up with you and all these damn questions? I told you earlier, no questions!" I yelled.

"I want to help you."

I grumbled in frustration and stood up. I started searching for my flip-flops. They were not where I'd thought I had dropped them.

"Why do you have to be such a girl right now? Most guys would kill for this. It's not a big deal."

Jordan stood. "Not a big deal? This wasn't just a hot night of kissing. You were about to completely give yourself to me. You barely know me. That is a big deal. I've been with more than enough nameless, faceless girls to know that I don't want you to be one, and I don't want to be one of the many guys that you use for a night and then forget about. I've done the one-night stand phase, Roxy, and I'm over it."

His statement hurt.

First, I wasn't dumb enough to think that he hadn't been with other girls, but he'd made it sound like it was tons of other girls. I didn't like knowing there had been so many other girls. But what really bugged me was the fact that I was freakishly jealous that they had gotten to be with him in a way that he was clearly rejecting me.

Second, how dare he think of me like that! I hadn't been with tons of guys.

I scanned the ground again for my flip-flops. I didn't see them, but I found my bra. I snatched it off the sand. I was growing madder by the second. I didn't care if I embarrassed myself. He wasn't going to stand there and call me some slut who used guys.

"I was with Kevin all four years of high school. He was my first and only. I am not some whore who uses guys for sex. It sounds like you know a lot about whores. Not only have you fucked a bunch of them, but evidently, you are one," I seethed.

That was it. I was done looking for my flip-flops. I could live without them. I just wanted to get away from him before I had a meltdown.

I took off toward my car. I wanted to go home and wash every bit of Jordan off of me.

How stupid was I to think that I could hook up with this guy? Sure, he made all my other pain fade away, but he just replaced it with a new one.

"Roxy, don't run off. Damn it. Just stop and talk to me!" he yelled.

I whipped around. "Why? Do you wanna call me a whore again?"

"Babe, I'm sorry. That didn't come out the way that I'd wanted it to. I wasn't calling you a whore. Please just help me understand. Why this? Why wouldn't you let me take you out?"

"You don't get to treat me like you just did and then call me *babe*. Actually, you don't get to call me *babe* at all. I told you that I had a bad day. I didn't want to go out and pretend to have fun. I needed this tonight. I wanted to feel good and not think about anything. Forgive me for wanting time with you. Trust me. It won't ever happen again." I turned away and headed to my car.

"Roxy, I'm sorry!" he apologized, catching up with me.

I gave him my best fuck-off look and kept walking.

He huffed loudly. "After my ex broke up with me, I swore off relationships, too. I know what you're doing. It doesn't work."

Just as I reached the sidewalk, he grabbed my hand to stop me.

"Don't do this. Don't make me chase after you."

"I'm not asking you to. I'm leaving because I don't want to be around you."

I tried to pull out of his grip, but he wouldn't let go.

"Please don't leave things like this. I'm really sorry. I messed up—big time!"

I attempted to jerk my hand away again but with no luck.

I did what I knew would work, and I was as mean as possible. "So did I! I thought you were actually worth my time. Big mistake! No wonder your ex dropped you for another guy!" I yelled.

It worked. He loosened his hold as sadness crossed his face, but I couldn't focus on that. I pulled out of his grasp and stepped backward. In that moment, something sharp tore into the bottom of my foot. An intense throbbing sting from my foot shot up my entire leg. I stumbled and almost fell to the ground, but Jordan caught me.

"Son of a fucking bitch! Fucker! Goddamn it!" I screamed out in agony.

Jordan scooped me up into his arms. My foot was burning with pain.

He laughed. "That's quite a mouth you've got there," he teased.

This was not a time for laughing. This was all kinds of horrible, and I didn't want him holding me. I was furious with him.

He carried me to his truck. "Let's have a look at what you did." He effortlessly held me with one arm as he opened the passenger door.

I was trying hard not to cry from the pain. The last thing that I needed was for him to see me cry. He set me on the passenger seat and lifted my foot to the car light.

After he inspected it, he said, "It looks like you stepped on glass."

I made the massive error of looking at it. My foot was dripping blood. I blinked furiously, trying to stop the spinning in my head. I knew this feeling. I knew what was coming. The blackness was taking over.

"Jordan…Jordan."

Coming out of the darkness, I saw a steering wheel and Jordan's chest. I attempted to sit up.

"Don't move. You passed out, fell off the seat, and hit your head." He put his hand on my arm, rubbing it.

My head was lying in his lap. My foot was still throbbing with pain. I tried to move away from him.

"Roxy, just wait! We will be at Travis and Scott's in a few minutes. They live a few blocks from the beach. Then, I can take care of you," he ordered sternly.

"The blood," I mumbled. "I don't do well with blood." Just thinking about how my foot had looked made me feel queasy.

"I kind of figured that out when you passed out on me. You scared the hell out of me." He looked down at me. His eyes were a new kind of intense. "You know, none of this would have happened if you had just taken the time to find your flip-flops instead of running off," he scolded me.

"I didn't want to be around you." I wanted it to come out louder and ruder than it had, but my voice wasn't cooperating.

He shook his head in disbelief. I closed my eyes to avoid looking at his beautiful face. I wanted to stay mad. My anger was crumbling with each passing moment.

How am I supposed to stay angry when he came to my rescue—again?

The car ride was silent.

I couldn't believe I'd passed out. *Ugh! Why couldn't I have just stayed passed out?*

Actually, slipping into a lifelong coma sounded much better.

Is it even possible to go into a coma from passing out?

Probably not.

Jordan made one more turn before stopping the truck. "We're here. Whatever you do, please don't look at your foot again. I couldn't get the glass out, and it's still bleeding." He was stern but trying to comfort me at the same time.

I nodded my head and then lifted it up from his lap, so he could get out.

He went around to the passenger side and opened the door. "Look up, okay? Don't look down at all. There is blood on the seat and floor. Up. Keep looking up," he directed.

He cradled my leg and guided me as I scooted out. I kept my eyes locked on him. I didn't want to chance seeing the blood.

Just great. I bled all over his truck. Seriously, world, you can swallow me up at any time.

Jordan picked me up out of the truck and carried me into the small house. It was a light-yellow beach-style home with a chain-link fence around the yard. He opened the gate, walked through it, and headed to the front door.

He knocked on the door, and a dog started barking.

Then, a male voice yelled, "Stop! Quiet!"

The dog continued to bark.

Scott opened the door. "Hey, man, that was quick. Damn, she is bleeding."

I wanted to look down at my foot and assess the damage, but I forced myself to look elsewhere.

"Dude, let me get you a towel," Scott said before running off down the hallway.

Jordan smiled down at me, which only made me feel worse.

Stupid, stupid Jordan and his perfect smile. How am I supposed to stay mad?

Remember, Roxy, he called you a whore.

Oh, yeah.

Hello, anger.

Jordan brought me through the door as Scott came jogging back to the living room with a towel.

"Wrap it loosely. She's staying tough, but it has to hurt," Jordan warned Scott.

Scott placed the towel around my foot.

My body stiffened as he did it, and I let out a small whimper. *Fuck, it hurts!* "Maybe I should just go to the hospital?" I suggested.

"Roxy, it's just glass. You don't need a hospital. If I can't get it out on the first try, then I will take you. Deal?" Jordan was attempting to compromise with me.

It's just glass. It's not like I was shot.

"Wait—but you already tried once."

At least in a hospital, I would be free to bawl like a pathetic baby without him seeing me.

Jordan looked into my eyes. "Trust me."

He carried me down the hall into the bathroom. He set me down on the toilet and sat on the edge of the tub. Then, he gently set my leg across his lap. "Remember, don't look!"

I nodded, but I felt an overwhelming need to start crying. My eyes began filling with tears. I squeezed my arms around myself and balled my hands into fists. I dug my nails into my palms. Not only did it keep me from crying, but it also helped to dull the pain in my foot.

Across from me, Scott stood next to Jordan's side. Trying to distract myself, I focused on Scott's face. He really was good-looking. He wasn't hot like Jordan, but his boyish looks worked for him. His blond hair was curly. Actually, if he straightened his blond locks, he could pass for Niall Horan from One Direction.

Okay, maybe not Niall exactly, but possibly his brother or cousin.

Jordan removed the towel, and I winced.

"I'm sorry, babe."

I wanted to remind him not to call me that, but right now didn't seem like the time.

"Scott, get me a pair of tweezers."

"Man, I don't even know if we have any. Let me go look." Scott left the bathroom.

Jordan noticed that I was struggling not to look at my foot, so he pulled the shower curtain far enough over to block my view.

"I'll have you all fixed up in no time," he reassured me.

I gave a weak smile. "I have some tweezers, but they are in my purse, which is in my car. Sorry. I'm a whole lot of no help."

Jordan let out a small laugh. "You're pretty tough, you know that? Any other girl in your situation would have turned into a blubbering fool."

Considering I was on the verge of tears, his comment didn't make me feel any better.

I glared at him. "You would know. You're the one who has all the experience with tons of other girls." I rolled my eyes at him.

The pain seemed to get worse with each passing minute. After Jordan's comment, the last thing I could do was cry. I dug my nails deeper into my palm. If I pushed any harder, I would draw blood. Then again, it might be worth it as long as I wouldn't see it or cry in front of him.

Jordan shook his head and turned his attention back to my foot. "I shouldn't have said that earlier. It's a part of my past that I wish you didn't know about. My ex really messed me up. I dealt with it the best way I knew. I know it was the wrong way, but I can't change the past."

I studied the little white seashells on the wallpaper to keep from looking at him. I didn't want to feel bad for what I'd said to him, but I did. I shouldn't have been mean. The need to hug him and comfort him was back, but it was unwanted.

Stupid, stupid emotions.

Scott came back into the room. "Here, man." He gave Jordan the tweezers. "I found them in Travis's room. At first, I couldn't wait to bash him for having a pair, but seeing as they are needed, it kind of took the joy away from making fun of him." He looked past the curtain at my foot. "Man! She's still bleeding!"

Jordan gave him a stern look. "Dude, shut up! Go see if you have any Band-Aids."

Scott snapped his fingers "Now, I know we have those." He left the room again.

Jordan looked at me. "I'm sorry ahead of time. This is gonna hurt. You have two pieces of glass in your foot, and one is pretty deep. Please stay as still as you can."

I felt nauseous. I didn't want them out anymore, not if it would hurt even more. I could live with one foot and constant pain. People did it every day.

I was shaking my head as Scott came back in with the Band-Aids and rubbing alcohol.

"Scott, hold her hand or something," Jordan ordered him. "This is going to hurt her." His eyes were full of concern.

Scott knelt down and put a hand on my knee. "You can use me for whatever you need—squeeze me, bite me, lick me, kiss me. Whatever will help you get through this." He chuckled.

Jordan glared at him. "I'm killing you when I'm done," he threatened Scott, who just smiled.

Jordan turned on the bathtub, which made me jump.

Scott rubbed my leg. "You got this," he assured me.

I wrapped my arms around Scott and buried my face in the crook of his neck. Scott's arms went around me, and he patted my back. He smelled good—not like Jordan but still nice.

Jordan ran my foot under the water, and I yelped in discomfort. I squeezed Scott harder. Once Jordan started digging for the glass, I didn't think I would be able to handle the pain. It made my foot burn and throb in the worst way possible. The discomfort shot all the way up my leg to my hip. I bit down on Scott's shoulder and felt him wince. I dug my nails deeper into my palms, but it was no use as tears escaped from my eyes.

"Ow!" I cried out, no longer able to hold it back.

Scott seemed relieved that I was no longer biting him.

"I almost got it, baby. Stay still," Jordan said.

I took a deep breath, ready to bite down on Scott's shoulder again, when Jordan said, "There. They're both out."

Even though the glass was out, my foot still throbbed in agony. Scott let me go and handed Jordan the rubbing alcohol and Band-Aids. Jordan dumped the rubbing alcohol on my foot, causing searing torture.

"Son of a shit! Fuck!" I screamed.

Scott laughed while Jordan just shook his head.

"You and your mouth," he mumbled.

Jordan bandaged my foot and gently set it on the floor. He stood up and smiled. Then, he punched Scott hard in the shoulder.

"What was that for, man?" Scott asked, rubbing his shoulder.

"Stop gawking at her like that, you dickwad."

Scott just laughed. "Sorry, bro. But she bit me"—he looked down at me—"and I'm kind of turned on."

The way he stared at me caused me to blush. Jordan raised his fist again.

Scott retreated through the door. "All right," he said, holding up his hands. "I'll go get some ice for her foot. You can lay her on my bed. My blankets are clean, but I can't say the same for my brother's." He then disappeared down the hallway.

Jordan picked me up and carried me out of the bathroom.

"You don't have to carry me," I told him.

He looked at me with incredulity. "Do you really want to walk?"

I shut up and shook my head.

A moment later, he laid me down on Scott's queen-sized bed. It was soft with deep-blue fluffy blankets that felt heavenly.

"You know, I might have a filthy mouth, but you have anger issues."

Jordan ran his fingers down my cheek. "Only when it concerns what I care about."

My heart skipped a beat.

So much for being mad.

I pulled him down and brushed my lips across his. "Thank you for taking care of me." As much as removing the glass from my foot had hurt, I was glad that he was here.

"Always," he said, rubbing his nose against mine.

Always? What the hell does that mean?

Scott came into his room and threw the ice pack and towel to Jordan. "I'd come closer, Roxy, but just looking at you gets me worked up," Scott teased me.

My cheeks heated up once again.

"Out!" Jordan raised his voice at Scott.

He walked back out, laughing, before shutting the door behind him.

"I'm going to go clean up the bathroom," Jordan said, placing the ice pack against my foot.

It stung for a second, but then it started to ease the burning pain.

He kissed my forehead. "I'll be right back."

After he left the room, the day seemed to crash down on me. I was absolutely drained, emotionally and physically. While waiting for him to return, I fell asleep.

8

I woke up the next morning with Jordan holding me, his hand clasping my breast. I might have snuggled up against him while I had been asleep, but I was awake now and pissed.

How dare he crawl into bed with me!

I tried to remove his body from mine, but this only caused him to hold me tighter.

I shoved Jordan's shoulder. "Wake up!" I ordered.

Jordan smiled sheepishly. "Good morning, beautiful."

"No"—I untangled myself from him—"it's not a good morning. Why didn't you wake me up?" I winced from the pain of moving my foot.

Jordan noticed, and then he reached over to the nightstand and grabbed a bottle of ibuprofen. He handed me two pills and a bottle of water. I took them without argument.

"You looked so peaceful. I didn't want to wake you." He flashed his movie-star smile.

He was right. I had slept peacefully—and nightmare free. I was thanking yesterday's emotionally draining events for the sleep. It had nothing to do with Jordan.

Nothing.

I rolled my eyes and tried not to let his charm get to me. "And you got into bed with me? Why? What happened to no sleepovers?" I was more upset with myself for having fallen asleep, not that he needed to know that.

Jordan laughed. "I was cold," he mused.

I huffed and tried to stand without showing how much pain I felt. I was unsuccessful.

"Slow down there, Mighty Mouse. There was nothing wrong with last night. Don't overthink it. Besides, you were cuddling with me. I thought that you didn't mind having me in bed with you."

"I was asleep. Did you just call me Mighty Mouse?"

"I did. You're this tiny person, but you're fierce when you're pissed. It seems fitting. I'm sorry that you're upset, but I won't apologize for sleeping in here with you. Besides, I wasn't about to leave you alone with horn-dog Scott hard up for you."

I grunted and threw a pillow at him. "You're infuriating."

He laughed. "Does this mean I don't get a good-morning kiss?"

My eyes bugged. *Seriously?* "Take me to my car!" I snapped, crossing my arms in annoyance.

He gave me a pouty lip and then unwillingly got up. I hobbled across the room. Jordan just shook his head at me and scooped me up into his arms.

"You don't have to carry me."

"I know, but I have things to do today. If I wait for you to gimp your way to my truck, the day will be over. I'm doing it more for me than you." He grinned.

"Well, when you put it that way…"

In the living room, I saw Scott passed out on the couch with his hand down his boxers.

I shook my head. *Men.*

"Should we tell him that we're leaving?" I asked.

Jordan opened the door. "I think he will figure it out when he wakes up, and we're not here."

During the drive to my car, I thought about how Jordan had taken care of me last night. He'd even made sure that his truck was free of blood before letting me in.

I was trying extremely hard to stay mad at him, but with each passing moment, my anger was dissipating. I probably could have held on to a bit of anger if he hadn't started singing along to "Wrecking Ball" by Miley Cyrus that had come on the radio. His singing was atrocious. He sang off-key and way too loud, and he added in words that in no way belonged. It was horrible, and I couldn't stop laughing. What made it a million times funnier was the fact that the boy could actually sing extremely well. He proved this when the next song came on. It wasn't a fluke either. He continued to sing perfectly the rest of the ride.

He had gone out of his way to embarrass himself just to make me smile, and I definitely wasn't mad anymore. Actually, I couldn't wait to spend more time with him. Sure, we'd had a fight, and one rule had been broken. Neither of us wanted something serious. I would just have to forget about the embarrassment of last night and start again with him. I promised myself that I would just enjoy Jordan. He was exactly what I'd needed.

After I got into my car and saw the list of missed calls and texts on my phone, my happiness vanished. I felt sick during the whole drive home. I considered staying out all day, but I knew it would just make things worse. Plus, I had no shoes.

I opened the front door of my house and tiptoed in. Considering my foot was injured, it was more like I wobbled quietly.

Before I could make it to the stairs, Ryan was barreling down them. "Where the fuck have you been?"

I felt myself cringe at the anger in his voice. I hated when he yelled at me. My brother would never physically hurt me, but he could make my life a living hell if he wanted.

"Answer me!" he screamed.

Brent ran out of his room and over to me. He pulled me into a hug. Ryan gave him a death glare, but Brent didn't release me.

"Are you okay? We were going crazy, worrying about you," Brent said.

Ryan was yelling again, "Where were you? Why didn't you answer my calls? Where are your shoes? What the fuck happened to you?"

I might have hated having Ryan yell at me, but I hated being babied even more. Now, I was pissed off.

"Oh my God, shut up! I'm fine! Stop treating me like a baby!" I screamed, pulling away from Brent.

This was obnoxious. Sure, I hadn't come home last night, but I was an adult. I shouldn't have to always check in with my brother.

"You'd better answer me, Roxanne!" Ryan shouted.

I didn't flinch away like I usually would. Instead, I gave it right back to him. "Or what, Ryan? What are you going to do? Tell Dad? FYI, he doesn't even care about me. So, go ahead!"

Ryan turned and punched the wall. "I fucking care, Roxanne. What if something happened to you? I'm supposed to be protecting you. I can't do that when you pull this shit."

I saw the fear in Ryan's eyes, and it hit me like a semi going downhill without any brakes. Feeling full-blown guilt, my shoulders hunched over. I felt like crap.

"She's here, Ry. She's okay," Brent said, trying to calm Ryan.

"I was with a friend, okay? I lost my shoes, and I cut my foot, so he patched me up. Then, I fell asleep," I explained. "I'm sorry, but I wasn't ignoring you. I didn't have my phone."

Brent's and Ryan's eyes shot daggers of questions at me.

Oh, crap. I'd slipped up. *Why did I say that to him? Let the interrogation begin.*

Ryan asked, "Who were you with? Why didn't you have your phone?"

I took a deep breath. "I left my phone in my car. Again, I'm sorry you were worried."

"Who were you with?" Brent's voice was edged with anger now.

I hadn't aspired to make either of them upset, but I wanted to keep Jordan a secret. I didn't need to share last night's events and get the third degree. Besides, Jordan was just temporary.

"It doesn't matter who I was with," I answered.

"The hell it doesn't!" Brent and Ryan shouted in unison.

I limped around them. "All that's important is that I'm fine—well, except for my foot. But that was entirely my fault. I'm going to shower now. You two have a great day."

Ryan huffed. "Rox—"

I cut him off, "I know, Ry. This conversation isn't over. I'm in need of a time-out. Go put another hole in the wall or something." I wobbled upstairs.

"Princess, were you with the same guy from the beach?" Brent called up the stairs.

I looked back and smiled. "Maybe?" I shrugged and made my way to my room.

After my shower, I lay in bed and thought about Jordan.

This morning, when we'd gotten back to my car, he'd apologized again for last night. He'd jumped to conclusions about me, figuring I had been handling my pain the same way he had. I might not have been whoring it up to the extent that he apparently had, but his presumptions hadn't been too far off.

I had been using him as I would have used any other guy who might want to help me get over Kevin.

I'd let go of my stubbornness and apologized for the horrible things I had said to him as well. We'd both agreed to a do-over for last night. But I hadn't dared to tell him how happy it made me.

Truth was, I was drawn to him like a moth to a light. It might be disastrous in the end, but for now, I was hooked. It was crazy how we still barely knew one another, but for whatever reason, he could make me forget. When I was with him, the constant pain in my chest wouldn't threaten to overcome me. Dealing with my mom being gone had become bearable. Painful thoughts of Kevin had disappeared. Jordan made me feel like I wasn't carrying a world full of sadness on my shoulders. He was some kind of magic.

I brushed my fingers across my lips and thought about Jordan some more. Just then my phone rang. I rolled over to retrieve it from my nightstand. I blushed when I saw Jordan's name. He was in need of his own ringtone.

"Hi!" I was way too cheerful.

"Hey, babe."

I could hear him smiling, which caused me to smile harder. "I was just thinking about you," I confessed.

He laughed. "I hope they were good thoughts."

"Oh, trust me. They were," I flirted.

"Oh, baby, tell me more!" he teased seductively.

"Not a chance." I laughed. "What did you call for?"

"I haven't been able to stop thinking about you. I thought I could use your injury as an excuse for calling you," he admitted.

"Aw, you're sweet, but you don't need an excuse for calling me," I said amorously.

Someone knocked on my door.

"What?" I called out.

"We need to talk." Ryan's voice deflated my happy time with Jordan. *What an asshat.*

"I'm sorry to cut this short. My brother wants to talk." I groaned. "I'll call you back."

"Sure. I'll talk to you later, babe."

I flung myself back on my bed. "Come in!" I hollered.

"We need to talk," Ryan stated as he sat down at my desk.

I rolled my eyes. "Yep, you said that."

"Drop the attitude, Rox. It's taking all my strength to control my temper," he warned.

I sat up. "What then? What do you want to talk about?"

He wasn't the only one with a temper, and I was sick of him treating me like a child.

He gave me a stern look. "You're my little sister. It's my job to watch over you."

"No, it's not. You're too overprotective, Ryan. I was gone for one night. What are you gonna do when I'm at college? Follow me?"

"I am dreading you going to college. If I could keep you closer, I would. I'm glad you chose USC over Juilliard, but I wish you would go to college here. I know you feel like I'm overbearing, but I think you'd be used to it by now. You are my little sister, I made a promise to you when we were kids, I'd watch over you. It is my job, Roxy. It always has been."

"That's not fair," I objected.

"Too bad. I was born first."

"But—"

"No buts, Roxy. This is how it is. With that said, what happened last night can't happen again." He stood up and raked his fingers through his hair, frustrated. "With Mom gone, I feel even more protective of you. Do you understand?"

I was downhearted. "Yeah, Ryan. Whatever you say," I mumbled.

"Rox, just work with me here. I'll try not to behave like a warden if you promise to keep me in the loop. I need to know that you're safe. I need to know where you are and whom you're with. You don't have to be home every night. I know that you're an adult, but for now, you have to understand that this is the way things have to be. I'll go crazy if I have to worry about you like I did last night."

He sounded exhausted, and I once again felt enormous guilt for making him worry.

I dropped the hostility. "Okay, Ry. I'll keep you in the loop."

He got up and walked over to my bed. He sat down and hugged me. "I love you, sis."

"I love you," I grumbled.

"Now, are you ready to tell me everything that happened last night?" He looked down at my bandaged foot.

I shook my head. "I promised to keep you in the loop from now on, but last night is all mine. I'm not sharing."

"You won't even tell me who the guy is?"

"Nope. All you need to know is that you don't know him. You get nothing else."

"He didn't hurt you? You were being honest about that?"

"I swear, he didn't hurt me."

Ryan had left town right after our mom's funeral ended. He had said that he just needed to get away. He still hadn't forgiven himself for not being around the night I found Kevin and Sara together. He'd wanted to kill Kevin when he found out everything that happened, but after a long phone conversation with our dad, he'd sworn to keep his distance. I might almost feel sorry for Kevin if my brother ever happened to run into him.

Almost.

"You can keep him a secret for now, Roxy, but I expect to meet him soon." Ryan gave me an imperious look.

I smirked. "Yeah, yeah, I know. Don't ruin our brother-sister bonding moment, warden."

As for him ever meeting Jordan, that wasn't going to happen. After all, Jordan was a temporary thing. There was no reason to have him meet the family.

"It's the burden of being the oldest. Don't blame me because you were born second." He messed my hair up and then stood. "Brent and I were thinking about Thai food for lunch. Do you wanna come?"

I gave him a dirty look for messing up my hair and then smiled. "Make it sushi, and I'm in!"

"I guess. Get ready. We leave in thirty." He smiled.

I saluted him. "Yes, sir!"

My brother was controlling and a pain in my ass, but I couldn't deny that he loved me.

I texted Jordan, telling him that I'd call him later tonight, and then I got ready.

When I got home after lunch, my body ached to head out back to my dance studio. I could hardly believe that I actually felt like dancing again—not just goofing-off-in-my-room dancing either, but putting-it-all-out-on-the-floor dancing. I needed the kind of dancing where something inside me would change, giving me the clarity I hadn't had before. I had a storm of emotions rolling through me, and dancing was always my best way to settle things down. But thanks to my bum foot, that wouldn't happen.

So much for clarity.

I hit Play on my iPod and turned my stereo up way too loud. I lay on my bed, listening to the music, as I tried to drown out my thoughts full of Jordan. I couldn't get his kisses out of my head. No matter how hard I'd tried, Jordan had invaded my mind and wouldn't leave. I rolled over and grabbed my purse off the ground. I pulled my cell phone out and sent him a text.

I can't stop thinking about your lips.

I should have had more restraint, but I hadn't. He was like a gravity force, and there was no staying away. I waited impatiently for him to text me back. I kept reminding myself that I wasn't doing anything wrong. I could enjoy him as long as I didn't get attached—or even worse, fall in love.

I checked my phone every ten seconds. After two minutes, I laid it facedown and cursed myself for wanting Jordan as much as I did.

"Catch My Breath" by Kelly Clarkson started playing from my phone and made my heart stop. It was the ringtone I had set for Jordan. I grinned obnoxiously.

"Hi."

"Hey, babe. How's the foot?" he asked.

"I'll survive."

"That's good. You know your text almost made me wreck. I thought you were going to just call me later tonight?"

He was driving. That explained why he hadn't texted back.

"I was, but you have this annoying way of interfering with my thoughts, and it caused me to miss you."

Oh God, why did I tell him that I missed him?

"Well, babe, I miss you, too. I would have texted back, but I'm driving. I thought calling would be safer. Now, tell me more about how you can't stop thinking about my lips."

Just the sound of his voice caused a warm tingle to form in my lower stomach. I couldn't deny the effect that he was having on my body.

"Where are you driving to? Do you want to just call me back when you get there?" I asked, trying to change the subject and tease him a bit.

"I'm actually headed to the airport."

What? I shot up. "The airport? Why?"

"I'm flying home for a couple of days to see my mom. I'll be back on Sunday if you want to hang out."

My heart sank, knowing he was leaving. At least I knew how to hide how I was feeling. "Sure, that sounds great. I guess I'll just talk to you when you get back."

He laughed. "Don't think you're getting rid of me that easily. The flight won't be long. I'm just going to Portland."

"If you're from Oregon, why not just go home for the summer?" I inquired.

The line was silent for a few seconds.

"It's complicated," he said.

His voice was low, and I hated hearing it like that.

"Complicated, huh? Good thing I'm the queen of complicated. Spill it."

"I don't want to unload my baggage on you, Rox."

"Jordan, I want to know about it. After all the emotional baggage I've laid at your feet, I actually think I need to hear yours."

"Fair enough, but you'd still better hang out with me. I will not accept you ignoring me after I tell you."

I didn't think there was anything that he could tell me that would stop me from wanting to see him.

All right, maybe if he tells me he's a serial killer, but that's about it.

"Promise," I answered.

"I told you that my dad died when I was ten. After that, it was just my mom and me against the world. She never brought guys around, or if she even dated, I never knew about it. She worked full-time as a nurse and took care of everything by herself. She's an extraordinary woman, Rox. You'd like her." He let out a heavy sigh. "Are you still there, Rox?"

"Of course. I'm listening."

"When I was fifteen, I stayed out more. Between sports, friends, and girls, my mom was always alone. I hated seeing her like that, so I pushed her to start dating again."

"That was sweet of you. You love your mom. You're a good son." *Why does he sound sad?*

"She started seeing this guy, Paul. He was always really good to her. He made her happy. A year later, they got married."

"Jordan, are you okay?"

"I hate him, Rox. I always have. I can't even tell you why because…hell, I don't even know why. Don't get me wrong. He is really good to my mother, but I've never liked the guy, and he doesn't like me. He and I always bump heads.

"Last summer, before I went off to college, he and I got into a massive fight. He wanted to put all my stuff in storage and turn my room into his office. I felt like he was trying to delete me from my mother's life. I flipped. My mom, of course, sided with me and told Paul to leave. She kicked out her husband for me. She has always put me first.

"During the week that he was gone, I saw how hurt she was and how much she missed him. I told her to have him come back. I convinced her that it was just a misunderstanding and that I was being childish. I was going to school soon, and I didn't want her to be lonely.

"When I came home for winter break, he and I got into another huge argument. He thought I should have a job and not be living off my mother. It was ridiculous. My mom wasn't even giving me money. My college was already paid for by my father's life insurance policy. Every penny I have to my name is from a trust that she had set up for me when my dad died. But here was Paul, saying I didn't even deserve that.

"I couldn't stand to be around Paul anymore. He talked about things he didn't understand. He didn't even have the right to discuss those things with me. I didn't want my mom to have to choose between him and me, so I chose to leave early, and I went back to school.

"He loves my mom, Roxy. He just doesn't love me. Therefore, I stay away. She is happy with him. I don't want to ruin that for her. I'm lucky to have family nearby, who are willing to let me stay at their places. I go and see my mom whenever Paul is out of town. He just left today. That's why I'm headed home."

Every part of me ached for Jordan. I just wanted to hold him and make him feel better.

"Paul sounds like a dick. You're a wonderful man, Jordan."

He laughed. "Paul is a dick. As for how wonderful I am, we will have to discuss that later because, right now, I am a man who's getting pulled over."

"Oh no! Is it because you're talking to me? I'm so sorry."

"Don't be. It will be the best ticket I've ever gotten. You'd better be ready to talk to me all night, babe, because you have a way of interfering with my thoughts, too, and I need Roxy time. I'll call you when I land, okay?"

My whole body tingled at his words, and I couldn't stop the Cheshire Cat grin that was plastered on my face. "It's a date!" I exclaimed.

"Talk to you later."

"Bye." I hung up the phone.

I hated that he was getting pulled over, but I couldn't wait to talk to him again.

9

It was Friday, and Tonya was finally home.

I hadn't realized just how much I missed her until she came over. She was happily surprised that I looked as good as I did. Apparently, I was glowing. If I were truly glowing, it was Jordan-applied.

Since he'd left, we had talked nonstop. It'd almost felt like he wasn't even gone. It absolutely went against my keep-things-physical-with-no-emotions plan, but I couldn't stop. Jordan and I had spent our days texting and our nights talking on the phone for hours. I had fallen into a dreamless state every night. I'd woken up happy with Jordan on the brain.

In just a matter of days, my life had turned around. I almost felt like my former self—almost.

Tonya dropped back onto my bed. I had been gushing about Jordan since she got here.

"Roxy, I'm thrilled to see you happy. But don't you think you should pull back a bit? I thought you didn't want a boyfriend."

"Jordan's not my boyfriend, Ton. I mean, he's not even around right now. We've just been talking."

A lot.

I hadn't told Ton that Jordan and I had also spent our nights having the most incredible phone sex.

"I think you should be careful. I mean, you said it yourself. He's not looking for anything serious. I don't want you to fall for this guy when he's only having fun."

In that moment, my blissful contentment crumbled. She was right.

What am I doing, getting attached to a guy who is supposed to be temporary? How did I forget my reasons for not wanting a boyfriend to begin with?

Oh, yeah, because Jordan is kind of mind-consuming.

I had to get a grip over my emotions. I had to hold my walls up and keep things casual.

"You're right, Ton. I am letting myself get attached. I'll dial it back."

"Don't get me wrong, Rox. If he is what you want, then go for it. But if you still want to stick to your former plan, then yes, you should dial it back."

"He doesn't want anything serious either, Ton. He's made that clear. I think we both just got caught up in the fun that we were having from getting to know each other."

"Please make sure your emotions are in check. I don't wanna see you get hurt again, girl."

I gave her a huge hug. "Thanks for always looking out for me." I kissed her on the cheek. "I'm in need of a smoothie pick-me-up. Let's go."

"Yum! That sounds perfect."

Tonya and I entered Jamba Juice, laughing. She was telling me stories about her cousins and their ridiculous behavior in San Diego. I laughed in all the right places and kept a smile on my face. For some reason, I was back to faking it. Tonya hadn't seemed to notice though, so I must have gotten really good at it.

The truth was, my chest was aching as I thought about pulling away from Jordan. I wondered if he would even notice or care. Well, he would probably realize. He had texted me three times since Ton came over, and I hadn't answered once. I'd wanted to, but Tonya was right. I was getting attached, and I wouldn't be able to handle it if I got hurt again.

Tonya and I got in line. Chase, of all people, was in front of us.

"Hey, hot stuff!" He smiled.

Wow, this is awkward. I didn't really know what to say.

"Hey!" I stated, overly surprised. I hoped it wasn't obvious how weird I was acting.

I looked at Tonya to see her eyebrow raised in amusement.

Apparently, it is noticeable.

He gave a head nod to Tonya, and she politely smiled back.

"You two aren't trying to get a better spot in line, are you?" He snickered at his own joke.

What was it about that night that made Chase seem fascinating? Sure, he's steamy, but why the hell was I willing to break my brother's rules for him? I mentally chastised myself.

"No. We're prepared to wait this time." I smiled to be nice.

Chase was next to order. After he ordered, he turned to me. "What do you girls want?"

"No, really, it's fine. You don't have—"

"I insist," he interrupted.

I shrugged at Tonya, and we gave our orders to the lady behind the counter. Then, we walked over to the corner to stand with Chase. We stood in silence for what seemed like forever.

Finally, Tonya asked Chase, "Hey, can I get Luke's number from you?"

"Absolutely." Chase gave Luke's number to her and then looked at me. "Speaking of numbers, I never got yours." He smiled.

This boy has big balls if he's willing to cross my brother, especially after being warned. I gave a small chuckle. "Um...yeah, that might be for the best."

"If you're worried about your brother—"

"Chase!" called out the guy behind the counter.

"That's us." I walked to the counter with Chase and got our smoothies.

I handed Tonya hers, and we walked out with Chase behind us.

I turned around to look at him. "Thanks for the smoothies. It was very nice of you." I was hoping he would just drop the subject and realize that nothing would ever happen between us.

"Anytime, Roxy." He looked at Tonya. "If you want to see Luke again, you two should come by our apartment tonight. We're having a small get-together for our friend's birthday."

Tonya was beaming, and I knew how much she wanted to hang out with Luke.

"Sure," she answered before I could give her the we-will-talk-about-it-later look.

"Sweet. How about you give me your number and then I can text you the address?"

"Um...actually, I don't think I can even make it. You should just give your number to Tonya."

His face dropped for a second before he gave his number to Tonya. Tonya gave me a quick questioning look before smiling at Chase like everything was perfect.

Chase turned to face me. "Roxy, if you're worried about your brother, I promise you that he won't find out about anything this time."

"I was wrong the other night. I know how my brother feels about me being with his friends. I'm sorry about all the trouble," I apologized, hoping he would just let the other night go.

Tonya picked up on the fact that I wanted to leave. "Thanks again for the drinks, Chase. I hate to have to take Roxy and run, but we're already late to meet my family," she lied.

"Just a minute," he said, stepping closer to me. "I'd really like to talk more about this. I mean, your brother and I are hardly friends. We're just in the same fraternity. I think he was just blowing things out of proportion that night."

I was starting to get annoyed that he wouldn't just drop it already. "Sorry, Chase. I really have to go."

Tonya and I headed to the car, leaving Chase behind. Part of me felt bad. The other part of me was thoroughly pissed off that he hadn't let it go. We had only spent a couple of hours together, so he should have gotten over it already.

Once Tonya and I were in the car, I was no longer feeling bad. I was just pissed.

"What the hell was that?" Tonya asked, reading my mind.

"Seriously, is he looking to get his ass beat?" I let out an irritated sigh and threw my purse in the back. I pressed play on the LCD display screen. The Script flooded the car. "You should still go tonight, Ton."

"No way. I'm not going without you," she stated.

"What about Luke?"

"I'll text him tomorrow or something." She smiled at me.

We headed out of the parking garage. I felt bad. She was giving up a chance to hang out with a guy she liked because of me.

"All right, what are we doing this weekend? Your choice." I hoped if I let her pick what we were doing this weekend, it would make up for not getting to see Luke tonight.

"Really? In that case, I think we should throw a party tomorrow. Or will Mr. Overbearing not let that happen?" She laughed.

"Yes, a party sounds perfect, and we don't have to worry about Ryan. He and Brent are headed down to Los Angeles right now. They have an interview with the CFO of Ad Corp tomorrow for some life-changing internship or something. The only thing life-changing about it is that if they do get it, they'll be gone for the rest of the summer," I told her.

"How did they manage to get that interview?"

"My dad, duh! He reconstructed the face of the CFO's kid last year, and that was after he'd pulled the kid from a burning car and saved his life. Dad was in the right place at the right time, and Ryan and Brent are reaping the benefits." I rolled my eyes.

"Okay, I know this is going to sound terrible because of what happened to that poor kid, but yay! A whole weekend without armed guards? Please tell me that you're planning on having sex with at least one guy this weekend." She was way too enthusiastic.

I shook my head. "You know you're like my own life-sized shoulder devil."

We both laughed as I drove back to my house. We had a party to plan.

After Tonya fell asleep that night, I called Jordan. It was late, and I had ignored him all day. I couldn't keep pretending I didn't miss him.

"Baby?" he answered.

It was three in the morning. *Why does he sound wide-awake?*

"Hey. Why are you still up?"

"I just got back home," he informed me.

What does he mean, he just got back home? Was he out? Was he with a girl—or girls?

I knew that we weren't together, but I was feeling crazy jealous at the thought of another girl being with Jordan.

What the fuck is wrong with me? I quickly tried to calm myself.

"Did you go out tonight?" I had no right to ask this.

"No, silly. I'm home, as in I flew back tonight," he answered.

"I thought you weren't coming back until Sunday?" I was sure that was what he'd told me because I had been counting down the days.

"My stepdad came home early." I could hear the disappointment in his voice.

I was sad for him. I hated that he'd had to leave his mom just because his stepdad was back. All I wanted to do was make Jordan feel better. I knew I was supposed to be pulling back, but as usual, when it came to Jordan, I didn't care about what I was supposed to be doing.

"Why didn't you call me?"

"I texted you earlier, but you never texted back. I knew your friend was coming home today, and I didn't want to bother you. It's not a big deal, babe."

I knew he had been trying to be nice, and I had been the one ignoring him, but I wanted him to want to call and tell me that he was coming home. I hated the new feelings inside of me.

"I'm glad you're home."

"Me, too." His voice was sad, and I could tell that he was lying about being happy to be back. "Do you want to do something tomorrow, Rox? I'd like to see you."

"I'm actually having a party tomorrow. Will you come?" The invite had come out before I could stop myself. I wanted to see him, and I didn't want to overthink it. Not talking to him today had been horrible.

"Yes, I will. I just want to see my beautiful girl."

His girl? When did I become his girl?

Did I want to be his?

The thought of being someone's girl again made my chest tighten.

Nope, I'm not ready for that—not yet…maybe not ever.

What happened to him not wanting anything serious?

Maybe I'm just overreacting to his words.

Yes, that has to be it.

I had to get off the phone before I said something stupid. "I will see you tomorrow then?"

"Does that mean we don't get to have a no-pants party before we say good-bye?" He sounded like he was pouting.

It was adorable. My body instantly reacted to what he had asked, but we couldn't go there, not tonight and not with all the insane thoughts going on in my head.

"I'm going to make you wait. Besides, you can have the real thing tomorrow. Best part about being friends with benefits are the benefits, right?"

"Right." There was a long pause, and then he sighed. "Friends with benefits, huh? I'll see you tomorrow, Roxy." He hung up.

Is he mad because we didn't have phone sex?

I'd told him that I would have sex with him tomorrow.

My mind was reeling, and I didn't fall asleep until after four, but I didn't sleep for long because the nightmares had returned. There I had been, kneeling on the ground and begging my mom to speak as I'd stared into the eyes that were void of life. When I'd awoken, I was shaking and covered in sweat.

Fuck me.

10

Tonya called Luke today. She told me that when she'd asked what he was doing, he'd said that he and Chase hadn't figured that out yet.

Did those guys do everything together?

Due to the awkwardness I still felt around Chase, Tonya had chosen not to invite Luke to our party. She was an amazing friend to put her wants aside for me. I was extremely lucky to have her in my life.

I was feeling guilty for ruining things for her with Luke, but Tonya made me feel better when she told me not to even worry about it. Before I could say another word about it, she was on the phone with Gavin, her booty-call extraordinaire. At least I wasn't messing with her sex life.

Tonya nudged me. She was rocking a plum-colored strapless dress that she had designed. It was beyond beautiful, but I felt that way about everything she'd made. The Fashion Institute of Design and Merchandising was lucky to be getting her talent in the fall. She had recolored the streaks in her hair a light purple, and she was looking fierce.

"This is going to be all kinds of outrageous fun. It is exactly what you needed." She beamed with excitement.

I swallowed hard. All I could do was nod. My chest was beginning to ache at the thought of all the people we had invited.

What if I break down in front of them?

Tonya kissed my cheek and muttered something about setting out chips and dips. It was nine o'clock, and people should start showing up around ten.

Hosting this party was probably a horrible idea, but there was no turning back now. I headed up to my room and tried to pull myself together. I put on a white summer dress that had big pink flowers printed on the lower half. It hung mid-thigh and showed off the right amount of cleavage. If I was going to lose it in front of everyone, at least I would look hot doing so. I fixed my makeup and hair, and then I headed back downstairs.

I stopped a few steps up from the bottom step and just stood there.

Tonya made her way over to me, wearing a huge smile. "You totally did not properly describe just how fucking gorgeous Jordan is."

"What?" I asked, confused.

"He and his friends showed up while you were upstairs. They are out back, tapping the keg for me."

"Oh, okay."

"It was awesome of them to pick up the keg for us."

"Uh-huh."

"Don't worry. I already paid them back."

My heart was pounding against my rib cage. "Good."

"Are you all right?" she asked.

No, I am completely freaking out!

"Yeah, I'm fine," I lied.

Tonya quizzically eyed me. "I don't believe you."

The doorbell chimed, and I flinched. I pressed my back up against the wall. I was scared to leave the stairway. "I will be fine. I promise. I just need a moment. Now, go let those people in."

I took in a deep breath as Tonya made her way to the front door.

I can do this.

I stepped down to the bottom step. I scanned the first floor of my house. Thanks to the open floor plan, I could see pretty much everywhere without moving. I saw everyone as they came inside and gathered in the living room and kitchen. Small groups people made their way out back. I had grown up with a lot of them. These were people who I had once considered friends.

Suddenly, it felt as though my large home was closing in on me. I held my breath and leaned against the wall. I wanted to disappear.

God, this is such a bad idea.

I couldn't be around everyone.

What if someone brings up my mom or asks about Kevin?

I couldn't deal with that yet. My chest throbbed with uncertainty. Every part of me wanted to retreat back to my room. I could just lock the door and stay in there forever.

Before I could turn and run, Jordan appeared in front of me. He smiled, melting away most of my anxiety.

"You're stunning." He stepped closer to me, wrapped his arms around my waist, and kissed me on the cheek.

"Thank you. And thank you for convincing Travis to pick up the keg."

Ryan had confiscated Tonya's and my fake IDs after our bar shenanigans, and I was grateful that Travis had saved the night.

"Thank you for the invite and for letting me bring those two fools."

I gave a small smile. I stepped off the bottom step to see more people coming in. My heart rate increased significantly. Just knowing that someone could ask the wrong question at any time had my anxiety spiking.

From behind, Jordan snaked his arms around my waist. "I missed you while I was gone."

I spun around and gazed deep into his eyes. "Really?"

I didn't know how it was possible that he'd missed me. We'd talked all the time.

But as I looked at him, I realized I'd missed him more than I thought. I'd missed touching him and feeling him close to me.

He nodded. I pressed my lips to his, praying he could take away the painful ache inside me. My hands fisted his shirt as I pulled him even closer. The ache didn't disappear completely, but I was feeling better.

He pulled back all too soon. I wanted more. I needed more.

"It's taking all the restraint I have not to carry you upstairs."

His eyes were full of need that I also felt.

I smirked at him and shrugged. "No one's stopping you. My room is at the end of the hall. You can't miss it. My door is covered with silly photos of me with my family and friends. Take me whenever you want. I'm all yours."

"I like hearing that you're all mine." His eyes were filled with an intensity I had never seen before.

I heard another cluster of people coming into the house. I turned my head to see that it was a group of guys and girls that I had gone to school with. I had cheered with most of the girls. The guys were all of the jock variety, meaning they had idolized my brother and Brent. Sadly, they were all friends with Kevin, too. These were the people who would most likely ask questions.

My heart beat even faster. I could hear it in my ears and feel it in my throat. I couldn't do this. Panicking, I headed upstairs.

Jordan was behind me and stopped me on the stairway. "Did I say something wrong, babe? Why are you running off?"

"It's not you. I just…I can't go back down there," I admitted. I folded my arms across my chest and tried to make the thumping stop.

"Why do you do that?" Jordan asked.

"Do what?" I asked, completely confused by his question.

"Why do you cross your arms and squeeze yourself?" he clarified.

I fumbled for the words. "I-I…I didn't know anyone noticed."

"I noticed, and I am curious as to why you do it." His hand rubbed my upper arm, sending comfort through my body.

"It will probably sound dumb to you, but I do it to keep my heart from beating out of my chest and to just make sure that I won't fall apart," I confessed.

"You do know that you won't actually fall apart, right?" He gave me a small smile.

I didn't know if what I was about to tell him would make him run away, but I felt like it was better that he know the truth now. "I do it because I'm broken. Don't bother saying that I'm not because I know how completely broken I am. So, when I start feeling this way, I fear that my broken pieces are going to start falling off until nothing is left of me. It doesn't matter if I know I'm not literally going to break. That's not how I feel on the inside. When my heart starts beating fast, I'm sure it's going to either explode or just come right out of my body. Again, I know neither will literally happen, but having a firm hold on myself sometimes calms me down."

Jordan pulled me into him. "I'll help hold you together. You shouldn't have to do it by yourself. I won't let you fall apart." He kissed my temple.

Even though I knew I shouldn't entertain the thought of him holding me together, I couldn't help it. Sure, our time might be limited, but there was nowhere in the world I'd rather be than in his arms.

Jordan firmly squeezed me. I felt like I could release the death grip I held on myself. I dropped my arms from around me and wrapped them around Jordan.

"See?" he whispered in my ear. "I got you. You're in one piece, and I plan on keeping you that way." He kissed my forehead. "And if you ever do happen to fall apart, know that I will always pick up the pieces. You're not alone."

Really?

He shouldn't say such things. I felt my stomach flutter. My mind wanted to trust him, and my body wanted to melt into him, so I could love the shit out of him. My heart, the smarter one of them all, knew better. Falling in love only led to heartache, and I couldn't handle any more pain.

I held him tighter. "Thanks for this." I sighed into his chest.

"For what?" he asked.

I pulled slightly away and looked up at him. "For this, right now. Even if it's not forever, I want you to know it means a lot."

His perfect mouth devoured mine. I once again found myself getting completely lost in him.

Sadly, he ended the kiss too soon. I snuggled into his chest.

I had to keep my emotions in check. They were getting away from me again. I felt myself falling deeper and deeper. I didn't want to even say what I was falling into.

This is temporary, I reminded myself.

We were friends with benefits, but I knew we would never be able to just be friends after this.

As much as people liked to say it could happen, I knew it never would. I wouldn't be able to be around him and not want to kiss him.

How could I ever be just his friend?

I hated that no part of me was ready to give him up. I needed to work on that.

I tilted my head back to stare up at the beautiful man holding me.

Damn…

We'd just started this—whatever it was—and I was already dreading saying good-bye to him.

He smiled down at me. "A penny for your thoughts?"

I smirked. "I was about to say, they're gonna cost you more than a penny. But seeing as my thoughts are about having you naked in my bed, I feel like I would have sounded like a prostitute."

He laughed. "I will never get tired of hearing the things that come out of that mouth of yours."

"I think you should let me show you what else this mouth can do. It's amazing!"

I didn't want to think about good-bye with him. Right now, all I wanted was to experience Jordan in the ways that we had fantasized about every night for the last week.

His eyes were smoldering. "You sure?"

I bit down on my bottom lip and nodded.

He smiled down at me. "Lead the way, baby."

We walked toward my bedroom. Jordan stopped just outside of my room to check out the collage of photos on my door. He pointed at a picture in the middle of my door. It was of my mom and me standing with Mickey Mouse.

"Is that your mom?" he asked.

"Yes. We went to Disneyland for a whole week last summer, and she insisted that we take a picture with every single character we saw. I thought it was ridiculous at first, but as the week continued, it became fun. It was like our own little game. We mapped out all the locations where the characters would be for meet-and-greets, and we ran to be the first in line when they finally came out. We even refused to let younger kids go in front of us." I laughed. "My brother thought we were crazy, and he was probably right. But my mom and I were on a mission."

Once again, I was amazed at how easy it was to talk about my mom with him. It still hurt to remember those incredible times, knowing I would never be able to make new memories with her again. The thought alone would usually have been enough to destroy me on the spot. But with Jordan next to me, I was able to survive it.

Jordan smiled at me and then continued to look at the photos on my door. Suddenly, he dropped my hand and pointed to a photo of Brent and me.

It was taken the day I'd turned eighteen. I was sitting on Brent's lap. We had just gotten into a cake fight, and we were covered in frosting. That picture captured another moment when I had been blissfully happy. It hurt to think that, just a few months later, my whole world had imploded, plaguing every memory with the black stamp of *before*—before she was gone, before I knew what heartbreaking pain felt like, before I hated the world.

"How do you know him?" he asked. His voice was tight, and he seemed to be getting upset.

Is he jealous at seeing me with another guy?

I laughed. "Brent? He has been my brother's best friend for, like, ever. He's lived with us for years," I explained.

Jordan stepped away from me and leaned against the wall. He let his head hit it, and I wasn't sure what was going on with him.

"What's wrong?" I asked, starting to worry about him.

He slid down the wall.

I knelt down next to him. "Jordan, talk to me," I begged.

He looked at me, his eyes full of regret.

What the fuck is going on?

"Out of all the people in the world, you have to be her?" He exhaled.

"What are you talking about? Jordan, you are freaking me out."

He let out a deep sigh. "Brent's my cousin, Rox. I'm staying at his house."

He pushed himself back up, but I was frozen, kneeling on the ground.

I felt as if the world had just shifted. Nothing made sense.

What? How the hell did I not know that Jordan was Brent's cousin? I mean, sure, family is a sensitive subject with Brent, and we avoided talking about it. But, seriously, how did I not even know his cousin's name?

It wouldn't have mattered since I probably wouldn't have ever connected the dots.

Jordan had said that he was staying with family. I'd assumed that meant with a family. We'd never talked about it again. All I knew of Brent's cousin was that he was staying, alone, in Brent's condo.

"How could I have been so foolish not to realize? He talks about you and your brother all the time. He's never actually called you Roxy though. He always refers to you as Princess. I once asked him what your name was, and he just laughed at me. He said I wasn't allowed around you, so I would never need it."

Brent didn't want Jordan around me. I was off-limits to him. My stomach turned, and I thought I might be sick.

"You're Brent's cousin," I whispered.

I felt like someone was standing on my chest.

This can't be happening. How is it possible that the one guy I want more than I should is now off-limits?

I wrapped my arms around myself. Jordan noticed and pulled me up to stand with him.

"Don't worry about this, babe. It doesn't matter."

I looked up at Jordan. He had no idea what he was talking about.

"It will to them. You don't know how crazy my brother is, and you said that Brent didn't want you around me. I'm off-limits. It matters."

"Fuck what he thinks, Roxy. I don't care. I didn't know who you were to him, but I *really* don't care. I'm not going anywhere."

"That's quite a mouth you have." I smiled.

He shrugged. "Yeah, that happens when I get worked up. I'm sorry."

He was apologizing to me for cussing. He had no idea how charming that was.

Nope, I'm not ready to give him up yet.

"Let's not tell him. I don't want to deal with the drama. I don't want what we have now to get screwed with. It's perfect." I beamed up at him.

Jordan cradled my face. "I don't want—"

Tonya came up the stairs. She interrupted Jordan, "Roxy! Get downstairs. People are asking for you." She held on to the wall to steady herself. Apparently, she had been enjoying the liquor.

"I'll be down in a minute, Ton," I reassured her.

"You'd better be," she warned before heading back downstairs.

Jordan chuckled. "She is quite the character."

"That's why I love her." I smiled. "Now, what were you going to say?"

"Nothing. You should get back to your party. We can talk about this later tonight."

"Seeing as it's my house and my party, I think we should just stay up here and have fun."

He kissed my forehead. "I don't think Tonya will let that happen."

"Good point. I guess I'll suck it up and go mingle."

"Good plan. I'm going to find Scott and Travis. If you need me to hold you together, remember I'm never too far away."

I kissed him again before heading downstairs.

I took in a deep breath. *I can do this. I will survive.*

As I made my way through the crowded house, I saw Tiffany and Scarlet pouring the rest of the bottle of Belvedere Vodka into their red cups. I walked over to the cupboard, pulled out the last two bottles of vodka we had, and put them on the counter. Ryan was going to kill me for going through all his liquor.

I waved at the giggling girls as I made a beeline for Tonya.

She draped her buzzed body over my shoulders. "I am so glad we decided to do this."

I shoved out a fake laugh. "Me, too. I can't believe how many people showed up on such short notice."

"Are you nuts? One, everyone has missed you. Two, it's a party. Three, free booze. Who wouldn't show?" She held up her red Solo cup and shrugged.

"All good points. Instead of becoming a fashion designer, maybe you should go into law," I teased.

She laughed and almost spilled her drink on me. "The only thing I would object to in a courtroom is the appalling clothing choices of most lawyers. I mean, come on. With all the money they make, you would think they could afford to dress better. OMG! I'm so tweeting that!" She pulled out her phone.

Yep, she's buzzed.

"Just don't let Jordan hear you say that he hates Twitter." I told her.

"Say what?" she asked.

"Nothing. Never mind." I laughed.

I felt the weight on my chest lift. No one was asking about my mom or Kevin—yet. Maybe no one would.

Gavin, Tonya's boy toy of the night, pulled her back into another kissing session.

Feeling like the awkward third wheel, I made my way over to a group of guys I knew. This would be my first real test. I might have gone to school with most of these guys since kindergarten, but they were all friends with Kevin now, too.

I playfully punched Ethan on the shoulder. "Hey, stranger!"

Ethan wrapped his arms around me, hugging me, and lifted me off the ground before spinning me. "Hey, stranger, yourself," he said, putting me back down. "Damn, Roxy, you need to eat. You're as light as a feather. Here, at least drink this." He handed me his drink cup.

"Thanks, jerkface. That's what every girl wants to hear. *Haven't seen you in a while. Why don't you eat something?*" I said sarcastically.

"Don't fret. You are still as beautiful as ever." He showed me his pearly whites.

I had to hand it to him. The boy had a great smile and some amazing blue eyes. Our senior year, he and I had won Best Peepers for the yearly contest in the yearbook.

He shook back his shaggy blond hair that had fallen into his eyes.

As I looked at Ethan, I couldn't stop wondering if he would make a good boy-toy candidate. I pushed away the thought. I liked having him in my life. I wouldn't want things to get weird. Plus, I had Jordan, and he was all I wanted right now.

I gave Ethan a huge grin. "That is why I keep you around. What girl wouldn't love those compliments?" I gave him another hug.

I joked around with him and the other guys for a while longer, and no one mentioned Kevin.

I peered across the room to where Jordan, Travis, and Scott were just entering from out back. My stomach fluttered at just seeing Jordan. I really had to get a handle on that. I had to remember that he wasn't mine. What we had would end. It had to end. With him being Brent's cousin, this couldn't last. The thought bothered me more than I wanted to admit.

A group of girls that I didn't even recognize stopped the boys. These girls had obviously never heard of a little thing called self-respect. I wasn't surprised by the attention they were trying to give Jordan and his buddies. Even in a roomful of attractive people, Jordan was still the most gorgeous guy there.

Jordan caught me staring and held my gaze. His eyes pierced right through me, and I swore that he could see straight into my soul. I wanted to look away, but I couldn't. The world seemed to stop as we stared at each other from across the room. I felt a shiver run through my body, and it shook me to the core. A part of the wall around my heart crumbled to pieces and floated to the ground.

Stupid, stupid weak wall.

Tonya nudged me. "Earth to Roxy!"

"Huh? What were you saying?" I asked, finally blinking and breaking the stare.

"I was telling you that we should do this every weekend."

I glanced back at Jordan. He was still watching me. He smiled and winked at me, causing me to radiate with desire.

Hands-down the best feeling ever.

"Yeah, Ton, that sounds great." I smiled dreamily.

"What's got you epically happy?" she asked.

I looked away from Jordan and smiled at Tonya. "Nothing. I'm just happy to be here with you." I shoulder-bumped her.

"Yeah, yeah. I know I'm fantastic, but that goofy grin isn't for me."

"Don't sell yourself short, sweets. I'm always happy with you."

"Okay, who are you? And what have you done with my best friend?" she joshed.

I stole one more glance at Jordan before turning my body and making myself engage in conversation with Tonya and the guys around us. After finishing off my beer, I felt myself relaxing and starting to have fun.

With Tonya, I walked around and mingled with other people who had come to our party. I no longer recognize most of the people, but everyone seemed to be having a blast, so I didn't care if I knew them or not.

So far, tonight was unquestionably a success. I was starting to understand why Ryan partied as much as he did. All the noise and booze helped ease the pain.

Tonya and I made our way outside and refilled our beers. A cluster of people were now in the pool. I took in a deep breath. As long as no one puked in it, it would be fine.

I scanned the patio and yard with my eyes, hoping to see Jordan. Suddenly, a disgusting thought of him being locked in a room with one of those bimbos ogling over him earlier popped into my head. I tried to push the image from my mind.

He's not my boyfriend. He will never be my boyfriend. He's free to hook up with whomever he wants.

I grabbed Tonya hand and pulled her into the middle of a cluster of people. "Come on. Let's dance."

11

Tonight had turned out to be way better than I'd ever thought possible. It was late, and more people had headed out. Tonya and I collapsed in a drunken heap on the grass.

"I think I'm trading Gavin in for Jordan's friend Travis. He's yummy."

"Oh, please no." I laughed. "Couldn't you go for Scott? I mean, he seems like the nicer douche bag of the two."

I wasn't trying to be mean. It was just that Jordan had told me all about how Scott and Travis were. They seemed to have a use-'em-and-lose-'em way of living when it came to girls. I guessed that was what Jordan used to be like, too.

My heart felt heavy. I didn't want to be one of those girls he just used. This, of course, made no sense because I was the one using him. But I wasn't just using him anymore. I actually liked him, and I thought he liked me, too.

Jordan had said that he didn't want me to be a one-night stand. The fact that I was different for him made me smile. He'd also said that he wasn't looking for anything serious. Suddenly, this bothered me, but once again, it made no sense. I didn't even want something serious.

Do I?

I was drunk and confusing myself.

Tonya belched really loud, which caused me to laugh and stop overthinking.

"He's pretty hot, but he's not as tall. Oh, brilliant idea. Maybe I can have them both?" she squealed. "What about you? Do you think you and Jordan will bow-chicka-wow-wow tonight?" she sang, thrusting her hips in the air.

"God, I hope so. In fact, let's go find them." I rolled over.

Tonya's head had been resting on my stomach, and it hit the ground. Laughing hysterically, we made our way back into the house. I walked into the living room and saw a girl with long brown hair sitting on Travis's lap, rubbing her fingers through his hair. I couldn't place how I knew her, but I knew that I didn't like her.

I looked at Jordan. He was sitting next to them while talking to a blonde whose face I couldn't see. But I did see that she couldn't keep her hands to herself. She kept touching Jordan's arm, and then she rested her hand on his knee. Suddenly, I remembered who the girl on Travis's lap was. It wasn't her that I didn't like. I hated her sister.

Shock rocked my body, and my stomach dropped. Before I even had a chance to contemplate what I was going to say to the whore talking to Jordan, Tonya bumped into my back. I felt the contents from her cup splash onto the backs of my legs.

"Sorry, Rox. I didn't see you stop." She giggled.

When I said nothing, Tonya looked up to see what I was staring at. The blonde whore finally turned her head and looked our way.

"Are you fucking kidding me?" Tonya screamed.

She made her way toward Sara the Whore and her sister, Stacy, who had made herself cozy on Travis's lap.

Jordan stood up. "Rox, why are you glaring at me that way?" he asked, walking over to me.

I could only imagine what my face must look like. I was beyond pissed off and disgusted with him. He knew who she was. He'd met her the same day he met me.

How could he sit there and talk to her like it was no big deal?

I couldn't even look at him. I walked by him and up to the whore sisters. "Get the fuck out!" I yelled.

"Oh, Roxy, did you really think you could throw a party and not invite me?" Sara stated grandly.

Is this skank serious? The only invite she would ever receive from me would be for a trip into a wood chipper.

"You must be confused, bitch. This isn't some free-for-all whore house," Tonya chimed in. "You heard my girl. Take your sister, and get the fuck out."

"You think you two can just cast me out. It says a lot about you both when you have to make everyone we were friends with ignore me," Sara hissed.

"It's really sweet that you think we have enough power to make people stop talking to you. Reality check—people stopped talking to you all on their own!" Tonya shot back.

I gave Tonya an amused smile.

"What the fuck is funny, Roxanne? You think I don't know that you're both telling everyone I'm a whore?" Sara spit.

"Just to clarify, we're not telling anyone you're a whore. We are simply stating that it would be safer to lick a disease-infested restroom floor than to sleep with you. There's a huge difference," I announced.

"That's funny because Kevin has no problem sleeping with me. So, don't pretend like you two aren't the reason people have been avoiding me. You bitches have been alerting everyone how much you hate me just because life didn't go the way little Miss Roxanne wanted. How about you stop throwing a bitch fit? Just admit, you lost. Really, jealousy doesn't look good on you."

My blood boiled, and I couldn't believe the nerve of this slut. Tonya was about to go off on a tangent, but I stopped her and stepped forward, getting into Sara's face.

"Don't flatter yourself and think that we were ever competing. We're not even in the same league! And jealous? Are you serious? You actually think I could ever be jealous of you? Please tell me you're kidding! I'm not the one who went after another girl's boyfriend. That was you. So, who's the jealous bitch now?" I seethed.

Sara laughed. "Kevin wanted to be with me. It turned out that he was as sick of you as I was. So, you can continue to play the she-stole-my-boyfriend card, but over time, no one will care. No one will care if you call me a whore. No one will care if you like me or not. No one will care about your opinion at all. Your reign as queen ended the day we graduated."

"Is that supposed to hurt me? Evidently, I gave Kevin too much credit in the brains category, but let's not forget that if you give a dog a bone, even if it has been in the trash, the dog will still take it. You are just lucky that I didn't want the asshole back after he was with you. Whether or not you want to believe it, if I did want him, he'd be mine, but I have enough respect for myself not to be with a cheating bastard. I can see how you wouldn't understand that because you have no respect for yourself. So, enjoy Kevin. He is all yours. Thank you for helping me see that he isn't worth my time.

"You know what else? You were my friend. You were one of my best friends. So, what does that say about you, other than you are a wretched person? I mean, really, what kind of friend goes after her friend's boyfriend? I hate to ruin the end of your story, but you have no happy ending in your future. Your kind of evil doesn't get one. *Now, get the fuck out of my house!*"

"You just refuse to admit the truth, don't you? Come on, Roxy. Tell everyone what we both know. The perfect Roxanne Daniels couldn't keep her boyfriend happy. That's why he's with me. I didn't steal him. He loves me, and he would never leave me for you. Who wants to be with a stuck-up rich bitch like you anyway? I guess what they say is true. The apple doesn't fall far from the tree. No wonder your father was never around. You really are just like your mother. Thank God she is dead."

The world slowed at her words. I didn't care what had happened between Kevin and me. That bitch had no right to say anything about my mom.

I lunged at Sara, grabbing on to her hair and shoving her to the ground. I was on top of her, punching her face over and over. She screamed and tried to push me off. Arms wrapped around my waist and lifted me into the air. I was still swinging my arms as I was carried away from Sara. I briefly saw Tonya jump on top of Sara before she had a chance to get up.

Jordan was yelling for anyone to get Tonya off Sara. His arms tightened around me. The cold air bit at my skin as he carried me outside. I didn't remember it being this cold before.

"Put me down!" I screamed. I wanted to go back in the house and kill the STD-infested whore.

"Rox, you need to calm down." Jordan set my feet on the ground but still held on to me with my back against his chest. He had a tight grip on my arms, and he wasn't letting go.

"Jordan, let me go." All I could see was red. I had no qualms about committing murder tonight. I would gladly spend the rest of my life in prison as long as the bitch was dead.

Travis was carrying Tonya's top half while Scott had a hold of her thrashing legs. Ethan was standing in front of the door, keeping everyone inside. The handful of people outside didn't dare ask what was going on. Instead of putting Tonya down, like I'd assumed the brothers would, they kept walking to the pool and threw her in.

"Why did you do that?" I screamed.

Tonya came up, gasping for air. "Assholes!" she screeched.

Scott just shrugged. "She needed to cool down."

Tonya pulled herself out of the pool. "I should kill both of you for that."

Tonya might have been tall, but she was no match for Travis, who did nothing but laugh.

Scott was already across the yard shouting, "Sorry!"

Tonya stomped in Travis's direction.

He pointed at her. "You come any closer, and you're going back in the pool," he warned.

Tonya changed her direction and came over to Jordan and me, who still had a vise grip on me.

"Let her go!" she shouted at him.

"I will once she calms down," Jordan assured her.

"I'm calm," I said through clenched teeth.

I was lying, and they knew it.

Ethan came outside. "She's gone," he informed Jordan.

"Why did you let her leave?" I yelled.

Ethan put his hands up and walked back inside. Everyone outside might have been keeping their distance, but all eyes were on us.

Great. Just fucking great.

I looked down in embarrassment. I noticed there was blood all over the front of my dress.

Am I bleeding?

The blackness started closing in.

"Jordan…" My voice was weak, and I was having a hard time remembering to breathe.

"Fuck, Rox. Close your eyes."

But it was too late.

I cracked open my eyes. I knew I was no longer outside. It was too bright.

"I can't believe I forgot about her problem with blood. I'm a terrible best friend," Tonya scolded herself.

"You're not the only one who forgot. Just make sure you are cleaned up, too."

I shivered and realized that I wasn't wearing my dress anymore. I started to sit up.

"Whoa. Wait a sec, Rox. I need you to keep your eyes shut. I haven't cleaned your hands yet."

I was about to look at my hands, but then I comprehended what he had said, and I squeezed my eyes shut. "I'm cold."

I felt a blanket cover me. At least, I wasn't lying in just my bra and underwear anymore.

"Hey, dollface. I just thought you should know that you are the most badass chick I know."

"Yeah, she is a regular Mighty Mouse," Jordan said, sounding anything but impressed.

I felt his hand grip my upper arms as he pulled me up to a sitting position. A warm washcloth moved over my hands and arms.

"Just keep your eyes shut, Rox," Jordan reminded me.

"God, Roxy, I wish I'd gotten a picture of the bitch's face when you hauled her to the ground. I don't know what the fuck she was expecting by coming here, but it wasn't that."

I could hear the pride in Tonya's voice, and I almost wanted to smile.

I still couldn't believe Sara had had the audacity to come into my home, and then she'd talked crap about my mom. Just thinking about what she'd said made me want to kill her all over again. She could have continued to say anything she wanted about Kevin not wanting me. I could have handled that. But the moment she'd brought my mom into it, I had gone to a different world—a world of hate, a world where I didn't care if I killed her because that was exactly what I wanted to do.

"Am I bleeding?" I asked.

I couldn't believe how much blood had been all over me. The memory of looking at my dress made me feel dizzy. I didn't remember getting hit, but I didn't remember much of the actual fight either.

"No, hon. All the blood was Sara's. You busted her nose with the first hit. She never got a hit in on you. Stacy tried to jump on you, but I knocked the bitch down. Then, Mr. Referee here pulled you off Sara, and I jumped in."

Tonya was way too happy about Sara and I getting into a fight.

"Is it safe to open my eyes?" I asked.

"Yeah, you're good," Jordan answered.

I opened my eyes to see Jordan's face. His worried look made me feel guilty, and I didn't like it. I looked away from him and focused on Tonya's happy face.

"I don't know about you, but I'm sober. I think it's time to restart the party." She pumped her arms in the air, looking completely ridiculous.

I agreed with her. I had lost my happy buzz and wanted it back.

"I think you both have had more than enough to drink," Jordan stated.

I didn't know what his deal was, but I was sick of it. I was still mad at the fact that he had been chatting it up with Hookerella to begin with.

Who the hell does he think he is, telling me how much to drink?

"Yeah, okay, Downer Dave. You might want a bit of the happy juice, too." Tonya smirked.

"Drinks sound perfect." I smiled at Tonya, who was holding out a black dress for me to put on.

"Roxy, I'm serious. You should take it easy for the rest of the night."

I got up from my bed and pulled on the dress. "I don't remember asking you what you thought, but if you want to go find slutface, I'm sure she would love to know."

"Where the hell did that come from?" he asked, bewildered.

I took a step closer to him and jabbed my finger into his chest. "I saw you talking to her. You knew who she was. Don't act like I have no right to be mad." I didn't care that he wasn't my boyfriend. As my so-called friend, he shouldn't have been talking to her.

He gripped my wrist, pulling my hand down. "I didn't place her, Rox. I knew that I had seen her before, but I couldn't remember from where."

I pulled my wrist out of his hold. "I doubt that," I scoffed. "Come on, Ton. There is fun to be had and vodka to drink." I dragged her from the room, not giving Jordan a second look.

I didn't care if he had cleaned me up or even if he had told me the truth. He had still been talking to her, and he should have remembered the girl who took part in destroying my perfect life.

Once we got downstairs, the dozen or so people who hadn't left earlier hooted and hollered for Tonya and me. She curtsied and called for shots. I put on a fake smile and pretended that I was as happy as everyone else.

The truth was, I missed the days of seclusion when the most drama I'd had in my life was hearing about Brent's or Ryan's. The aching pain in my chest was inching its way back. Everyone had heard what Sara had to say about Kevin. She had been right. Kevin had left me, and even though I had told her that I could get him back if I wanted, I'd known it wasn't the truth. He'd left me. He didn't want me.

Three shots later, and the pain was still there. I took the bottle of Belvedere Vodka off the table and swallowed gulping mouthfuls. I didn't want the pain back. Tonya was in the corner, kissing Gavin. I guessed her grand plan of sharing the brothers had dissolved in the pool.

Travis and Scott were playing a game of quarters while Jordan sat and observed. Well, he was actually studying me more than their game. I was pissed off at him, and I couldn't stand the way he was watching me.

I staggered into the living room where I found Ethan and three other guys playing Xbox. I made my way to Ethan.

He looked up at me and handed his friend the controller. "You okay there, Roxy? You look a bit drunk."

I could still feel the pain trying to push its way to the surface. I shrugged. "Not drunk enough. Come drink with me!"

Ethan stood up as I took another swig from the bottle. He grabbed on to my waist to steady me, which was good. For a second, I'd felt like I was going to fall.

I wrapped my arms around his neck. "My hero," I purred.

"Let's get you sitting down." Ethan guided me to the couch.

He sat down next to me as I chugged another drink. My body didn't shake at all this time.

"Um…Roxy, why don't you share?" Ethan smiled.

I giggled and handed Ethan the bottle. The warming effect was starting to come back, and I welcomed it.

Ethan set the bottle down without taking a drink.

I leaned into him. "I thought you wanted a drink?" I squinted my eyes accusingly and then smiled.

"Eh…maybe later." He shrugged. "Hey, Roxy, where is your boyfriend?" he asked.

The mere word made all the pain I had been working on pushing down shoot right back up.

"Didn't you hear? He's not my boyfriend anymore. My guess is, he's with Hookerella and her rearranged face." I could feel the tears forming. I bent forward and dug my nails into my palm. I couldn't start crying.

Ethan rubbed my back and leaned down with me. "No, Roxy, not Kevin. I'm talking about your boyfriend who's here tonight."

I shot up and looked at Ethan. "Jordan? He's not my boyfriend, and I don't care where he is."

Ethan was still rubbing my back. It felt really nice, but the pain wasn't gone.

"Sorry, Roxy. I just assumed he was your boyfriend."

"Can you hand me the bottle again?" I put my hand on his upper thigh, hoping it would get me what I wanted.

"I think you've had enough for the night." He grinned.

Earlier, I hadn't wanted to ruin my friendship with Ethan, but right now, I couldn't stop looking at his lips. Maybe kissing him would take away the ache just like kissing Jordan had. I crawled on top of him and straddled his lap. His eyes widened.

"I haven't had that much to drink." I pouted.

"Yeah, you kind of have." His face was too adorable for me to get upset.

I slid my hips from side to side, trying to entice him. He placed his hands on my hips, but instead of getting into it like I had expected he would, he stilled my body.

"Roxy, you're making it difficult for me to do the right thing here and tell you no," he warned me.

That's the point.

I pressed my hands on his firm chest and looked into his deep blue eyes. "So, don't tell me no." I leaned in to kiss him.

Before my lips ever touched Ethan's, I heard Jordan roar from across the room, "Roxy, what are you doing?"

Hearing him yell almost made me crack up. *Why is he upset?*

He'd had no problem chatting it up with Hookerella earlier.

"Why does it matter to you?" I snapped.

"Out!" he shouted, pointing toward Ethan and the guys on the couch. "All of you need to get the fuck out. Party is over."

I got off Ethan and stumbled. Ethan again steadied me.

"You guys don't have to leave," I tried to assure them.

Ethan was holding on to me to keep me from falling. The whole room seemed to be spinning.

Jordan had made his way across the room. "Get your hands off of her!" he shouted at Ethan.

Ethan held me steady with one hand while putting the other up in innocence. "Look, man, I would never hurt Roxy. This isn't what it looks like. I wouldn't take advantage of her."

Jordan shook his head. "Just get everyone out of here," he said to Ethan.

I grabbed on to Ethan's arm. "You don't have to leave!"

"It's late, Roxy. We should be heading out anyway. I'll see you again soon." He gave me a quick hug.

Rage came over me as Ethan let go of me, and he started herding everyone out of my house.

"Who do you think you are?" I pushed against Jordan's chest.

It didn't have the desired effect I had been going for. He hadn't even budged.

"Tell them they don't have to leave!" I shouted.

He took a deep breath. "Roxy, the party is over. You need to go to bed."

"Don't tell me what to do! You don't get to order me around. If anyone should leave, it's you! Get out!" I was furious.

"Roxy, you're drunk. Go to bed!" he ordered.

I hated that he was standing there, telling me what to do. My brother was gone this weekend. I didn't need another man trying to be my warden. I defiantly crossed my arms. This almost caused me to fall.

I steadied myself and looked up at Jordan. "No! I'm not done having fun." I used the couch for balance and made my way to the bottle of vodka.

Jordan snatched it up before I could even reach for it.

"You're done having fun. Go to bed." His voice was more forceful this time.

I sat down on the couch. "No! You don't get to tell me what to do."

"Roxy, take yourself to bed, or I will carry your ass up there," he threatened.

How dare he think he can order me around! He has no say in what I do. He's not my boyfriend. He's not my anything.

I looked away from him. "I want you to leave."

"Trust me, Roxy. I want to leave as badly as you want me gone, but I'm not going anywhere until you are in bed."

Having him tell me that he wanted to get out of here tore at my chest. He didn't want me any more than Kevin had. I was on the verge of crying. I couldn't stand the pain. I got up, shoved my way past Jordan, and staggered into the kitchen. I sat down on Scott's lap and smiled before I gripped the open bottle of Jack Daniel's. I started chugging.

"Goddamn it, Roxy." Jordan ripped the bottle from my hands, spilling it all over Scott and me.

Scott claimed his innocence, "She sat on my lap, bro."

Jordan threw the bottle against the wall. "You're done!" he screamed in my face.

Had I not been used to my brother doing the same thing, I might have flinched.

Tonya was now shouting, "What the fuck, Jordan? Don't scream at her that way."

Jordan pointed at her. "You either help me get her to bed, or get the fuck out of my way." He scooped me up and tossed me over his shoulders, carrying me fireman-style up to my room.

I pounded on his back with my fists and called him every name I could think of.

He finally tossed me on my bed. "Go to sleep!" he demanded.

"What makes you think you can order me around?" I shouted back. I tried to move off my bed, but everything was spinning, and I was feeling woozy.

"You're a terrible drunk, you know that? The last thing I wanted to do tonight was take care of your drunken ass!" he yelled back.

Once again, his words ripped at me. He didn't want me. No one wanted me.

The tears started before I could rein them in. The room didn't seem to have enough oxygen. I felt the stabbing pain in my chest and stomach. No one wanted me. I couldn't breathe.

Jordan was saying something, but I couldn't understand him.

All I knew was that I was going to be sick. I shot off my bed and ran past Jordan to my bathroom. I barely made it to the toilet before I was puking up everything. I cried and puked and cried some more.

Jordan was right there with me. I felt him lay a wet washcloth on my neck. I tried to focus on the cool feeling, and I laid my head on the cold tile, begging my stomach to stop churning. I closed my eyes. I just wanted to disappear.

I felt like I was floating. Maybe I was disappearing, not that anyone would even notice. Jordan didn't want me. Kevin hadn't wanted me either. My dad didn't love me. All I was to Ryan was someone who needed to be constantly watched. He probably hated me. The only person who had ever loved me was my mom. She was dead, and no one wanted me. No one loved me. It was good that I was disappearing.

I thought of my mom. Maybe I could disappear and be with her.

Is disappearing just like dying?

At that moment, I wasn't scared to die. I felt my bed beneath me. I wasn't disappearing.

But I want to go away. I don't want to be here. I don't want to be without her anymore.

I willed my body to move. I needed to reach the pills. I wanted to die. I just couldn't make my body move. I didn't have the strength.

"Just let me die," I mumbled.

Then, I felt nothing.

My body was tender, and my head pounded like it was being smashed between concrete blocks. Even blinking was painful. My mouth was completely dry. I had what Tonya and I referred to as cow tongue.

Ugh, I forgot how much hangovers suck.

Last night's events were hazy, but I remembered most of what had happened.

How did everything get that screwed up?

Oh, right. Hookerella once again brought havoc into my life. God, I hate her.

I closed my eyes, wanting to go back to yesterday and stop myself before I'd screwed everything up with Jordan.

What is wrong with me?

I rolled off my bed, and the whole room began spinning. I stood up and steadied myself. I had to get to the bathroom. My foot kicked the edge of something with my first step. I looked down to see that it was Jordan.

He stayed? He slept on my floor?

I slowly stepped over him and tried not to fall. I made my way into my bathroom. I closed the door and slid down it. I begged my head to stop pounding. I hugged my knees to my chest.

What am I supposed to say to him? Why is he even still here?

My body reminded me why I had headed into the bathroom to begin with. I got up and did what I had come in here to do.

As I washed my hands, I cringed at my appearance. My eyes were red and puffy. Black streaks of mascara had run down my face. I looked hideous.

Is this what I looked like last night? God, I hope not.

I took a washcloth and washed my face. I brushed my teeth and took off my dress. Disgustingly enough, it had leftover vomit splattered on the front.

Ew!

I hardly remembered throwing up. I pulled on my robe and then took in a few deep breaths.

I can do this.

As I walked out of the bathroom, I found a very tired-looking Jordan sitting on my bed. He glanced up at me. I wanted to run away and hide, but I forced myself to walk over to him. I sat down next to him. We were silent for what seemed like an eternity.

"We need to talk." His voice was scarily calm.

I felt that sick feeling in the pit of my stomach, the one that came when I got caught doing something wrong. I swallowed hard.

I opened my mouth, but I didn't even know what to say. I closed my mouth and nodded instead.

"Are you happy?" he asked.

What? Is he asking if I'm happy with him or just in general?

I took a moment to think about his question. I knew what happiness was. I had been the happiest girl in the world, but that was before.

Am I happy now? No.

I was nowhere close to happy. I hadn't been happy since the night I found my mother's body. I had, however, had moments of happiness, but that feeling had never lasted.

"Are you going to answer me?"

"Yes, of course, I'm happy," I lied.

"I thought we didn't lie to one another, Rox. Full disclosure, remember?"

What does he want me to tell him?

He already knew that I was broken. I'd told him that I had to hold myself together.

Why is he bothering to ask if I am happy?

I faked happy. It made everyone else feel better.

Isn't that enough?

"You want honesty. I honestly don't know what you want me to say."

"That's the thing, Rox. I don't want you to say anything. I want you to tell me if you are happy, and I want the truth."

I stood up. I didn't want to have this conversation.

"Look, if this is about last night, I'm sorry. I'm a dreadful drunk, but being a sloppy drunk doesn't mean that I'm not happy." I tried to fake a smile, but it was more of a grimace.

"Don't do that. Don't lie to me."

"This is dumb. Can we please just file last night into the let's-never-discuss-it-again folder and move on?"

"No, we can't. You said you wanted to die last night. Is that how you feel, Rox?"

Horror washed over me. *Oh God, I didn't say that. How could I have let that slip?* Those were my demons, and I didn't want to share them with him or anyone else.

"Roxanne, answer me," he ordered.

I was getting extremely sick of him telling me what to do. I didn't want to talk about this. *Why is he pushing it?*

"Why does it matter to you how I feel? I'm not your girlfriend. This"—I motioned between him and me—"is just supposed to be fun."

"Are you freaking kidding me right now? Are you seriously telling me that's all you want? Because things have changed on my end, Roxy."

"I don't care if things have changed for you. They haven't changed for me. I don't want or need you to care about me." That wasn't entirely true, but I was too angry to say otherwise.

He stood up. "Now, I see why Brent only calls you Princess. It couldn't be a more fitting nickname."

"What the fuck does that mean?" I yelled.

Brent had been calling me that since I was ten. I didn't see how it related to right now. This conversation was going in every way but the one I wanted.

"It means that you are a selfish brat, and it has to be your way or the highway. You don't give a fuck how anyone else feels. You just demand to have things your way and expect it to be like that. All hail Princess Roxy." His voice rose in irritation.

My throat tightened as tears started building. I wouldn't cry in front of him. I dug my nails into my palm and crossed my arms.

Jordan looked me up and down. "Damn it, Rox. I'm sorry. I'm an asshole." He pulled me into him.

I tried to push him away, but he wouldn't have it. I dug my nails deeper. I would not cry.

"Baby, I'm sorry."

"Let me go." My voice was weak, and the words came out more like I was begging than demanding.

Jordan released me. "Roxy, I'm sorry. You just make me crazy at times. You are constantly reminding me that we're just friends with benefits and just supposed to be having fun. I was worried sick about you last night, and you won't talk to me. You won't let me in."

I sat down on my bed. "You want full disclosure? I'm a shadow of a whole person. I'm a completely broken mess. So, when you ask if I am happy, the answer is no. How can someone as broken as I am be happy? There you go, Jordan. You know the truth now. Is it everything you hoped it would be?"

"Baby, you—"

"Don't *baby* me. I am not your baby! I want you to leave." I pointed at the door.

"Roxy, please stop pushing me away. Let me in. Let me help you."

"I don't need your help. I want you out."

"I'm only going to ask you one more time. Don't do this. Don't push me away. I want to be with you, Roxy. Let me in. No more holding back. I want all of you."

It took everything I had to stand up and look at him. "This was a mistake. You were a mistake. I don't want a boyfriend, and if I did, it sure as hell wouldn't be you," I seethed.

Jordan's face fell as he took a step back. "I won't stand here and continue to beg you to be with me. If you want to push me away, fine. You wanna tell me I'm nothing but a mistake? Fine. This won't change who you are. You can continue to hide behind those fake smiles, but anyone who cares enough to look is going to see right through them to the sad girl you really are. I don't think you are broken, Roxy—at least not beyond repair in the way you believe. But you are never going to be happy if you don't stop running away. If you want me gone, I'm out." Jordan stormed out of my room and down the stairs.

I didn't allow the tears to start falling until after I heard the front door slam.

I was in full self-loathing mode. *What have I been thinking? How did I let everything get screwed up?*

The pain went from raw throbbing to excruciatingly pounding. It was too much to handle. As much as I'd said I wasn't getting attached, I had gotten attached. I didn't want to feel any more pain.

I took out the bottle of pills that I hadn't touched in over a week and slid three out.

I walked into my bathroom and filled up a glass I had in there with water. I couldn't even look at myself. I just needed the pain to go away. I brought the glass back to my bed and took the pills. Then, I lay down on my bed. Here I was, back to being the girl who cried all the time and popped pills.

What's the point of even trying to survive all the pain?

I sat up and grabbed the bottle of pills again. I took four more.

If I died, all the pain would finally end.

There were only two pills left in the bottle. I slid them into my hand.

I don't want to survive the pain.

I took the last two pills.

I closed my eyes, waiting for the numb feeling to come. I hoped that would then lead to eternal darkness.

I saw my mom's face in my mind. I placed my shaking hands on my stomach. The guilt of disappointing my mom rushed over me like a wave, and I was drowning in it. I hated myself for being weak. She'd raised me to be better than this pathetic pill-popping suicidal idiot.

I didn't have to deal with my pain in this way. I was stronger than this. I'd lost my mother, boyfriend, and perfect future, and I'd survived. It might have been painful, but it was the pain that reminded me I was alive.

I am alive.

My mother hadn't been this lucky. Jordan was right to call me out. I was selfish.

I got up and ran back into the bathroom. I knelt in front of the toilet. I stuck my fingers as deep down my throat as they would go. Then, I puked. I made myself get sick like that over and over until the only thing coming up was stomach acid.

This moment was a low and disgusting point in my life. It was even worse than not showering for days, and that had been pretty awful.

I never wanted to feel this way again. It would be an uphill battle, and I'd be fighting the hurt, but I couldn't keep running from it. I would fight my personal demons one day at a time, no matter how painful it was going to be. As much as I wanted to die, I couldn't. I had to live—not just for my mom, but also for me.

12

Tonya made her way into my bed later that morning. I was too ashamed to tell her what I had done with the pills, but I did tell her about Jordan no longer being a part of my life. She said she was glad. I guessed he had gone pretty crazy last night.

She gave me a day to cry about him before she put her foot down. I was forbidden to sulk or hide out again.

We spent the next day at the spa. She claimed it was a preemptive intervention. I thought that was a bit of an exaggeration, but it was a welcomed distraction.

I wished spa day would never end, but it did.

As soon as I got home, I was sad again. Although I had told Tonya that I was fine and over Jordan, I was far from it. I was furious at him, but more than that, I was angry with myself. I had pushed him away, and I was frustrated that I cared that I'd pushed him away. I was irritated that I'd cared for him at all. That was never supposed to happen.

Annoyingly enough, I couldn't stop thinking about him. I couldn't understand why he had even said he wanted me. He was perfect while I was an emotional disaster. He had seen how damaged I was.

How could he actually want to be with me?

I concluded that he hadn't and that he had just had a moment of misjudgment.

The next day, Brent and Ryan returned from Los Angeles. They told me that the interview had gone extremely well. Ryan said they'd be heading back down to Los Angeles on Sunday. They were going to be gone for four weeks. This should have made me happy, but I didn't feel excited.

I moped around the house for most of the day. This whole living-life-and-fighting-the-hurt thing fucking sucked. I retired to my room early that night and silently cried myself to sleep.

The next morning, I sat at the kitchen island. I pressed my forehead down onto the cold granite countertop. It had been four horribly long and depressing days since I kicked Jordan out of my house and out of my life.

Jordan never tried to contact me, and if I didn't have a picture of him on my phone, I would have started to think that he didn't exist. I contemplated calling him and begging him to talk to me.

Pathetic, party of one? Right here.

If I miss him this much, he probably misses me, too, right?

No, dum-dum. You pushed him away. You kicked him out. He made it crystal clear that he was done.

I chastised myself for even considering calling him. I knew better. If Jordan actually did miss me, I would have heard from him by now.

So, why the hell can't I just forget about him?

I opened up the photo of him on my phone and stared. I had been staring at a fucking picture for the last few days.

Stupid, stupid Jordan and his stupid perfect face.

I tossed my phone onto the counter and sighed loudly.

I eyed the last banana in the fruit bowl in front of me. It was covered in brown spots. Those brown spots stared back at me as proof that it was unwanted. Just because the banana had a few spots didn't mean it was inedible, but for me, that was exactly what it meant. It was damaged and unwanted. I had a lot in common with that banana, and I didn't want to look at it. I grabbed it, walked over to the trash can, and threw it away. Sadly, the disgust I felt with myself hadn't disappeared along with the unwanted banana.

"I would have eaten that," Brent informed me as he eyed me from the kitchen table.

"No, you wouldn't. It wasn't any good. It had too many bruises," I told Brent.

"Bruises don't mean it's not good, Princess. It's just sweeter."

I squished my nose in disgust—not because he wanted the gross banana, but because he'd called me Princess. I now loathed being called Princess. It reminded me of Jordan's harsh words.

"Please don't call me that," I said.

"Like I keep telling you, old habits die hard. You'll always be Princess to me."

I groaned and sat at the table with him. "Why the hell do you call me that anyway? Is it because you think I'm some spoiled bitch?"

Confusion crossed his face. "No! Why would you ever think that?" he asked.

I hunched my shoulders. "Then, why? I mean, I used to think it was because of my continuous Disney-inspired Halloween costumes, but I don't get why you haven't stopped."

"If it bothers you that much, I will do my best to stop calling you that." He placed his hand over mine. "Please realize that it has only ever been a compliment."

"A compliment?" I questioned.

"Yes. You have always been this beautiful but untouchable person. You walk into a room, and everyone notices you. When we were kids, I would watch you dance. You were the definition of graceful. If I had to describe what a true princess was, it would be you. You are magnificent. Why would you ever think I meant it as a bad thing?"

At that moment, I wanted to smash Jordan's face in for blemishing the meaning of my nickname. I also felt a tickle in my stomach at Brent's words. He thought I was magnificent. I had been called a lot of things but never that. I felt my cheeks warm.

Brent cleared his throat and pulled his hand away from mine.

"There you two are," Ryan said, causing me to jump.

Brent gave Ryan a nod.

"Are you feeling any better, sis?" He squeezed my shoulders.

"Yeah, I am feeling much better." It was the truth.

"Good," he said, walking toward the counter. "Are you still planning on coming out to the lake tomorrow?"

I had already told Tonya that we would go, so there was no getting out of it. "Yeah, Ton's gonna come, too," I informed him.

Ryan frowned. "You two had better behave yourselves," he warned.

"Really, Ry? We probably won't even be around you and your stupid friends."

"I'd rather you were around. That way I can keep an eye on you."

I flipped him off, causing Brent to snicker.

Then, I stood up. "If you will both excuse me"—I curtsied—"this Princess"—I looked at Brent, letting him know that I was okay with my nickname, and his grin widened—"has a best friend to call and trouble to plan."

"Why are you being weird?" Ryan asked.

I smiled and shrugged. Then, I headed to the stairs.

"No scheming. Do you hear me, Roxanne?" Ryan hollered after me as I made my way to my room.

The next morning, Tonya and I stood at the end of the dock, waiting for Brent and Ryan to bring the boat over. It was at least ninety degrees out. Of course, this would have been fine if we were actually in the water and not standing on the dock. Right now, it was just hot and uncomfortable.

"You okay, Rox? You look tired," Tonya said.

I was tired. I felt like I hadn't slept in a week. Ever since my fight with Jordan, nighttime had become my enemy. My nightmares had returned, and when I was awake, fighting sleep, Jordan would invade my thoughts. I was having a hard time getting him out of my head.

Fucking mind ninja.

In fact, the amount of time I had spent thinking of him could be considered borderline obsessive.

"Yeah, Ton. I'm fine," I lied.

She incredulously looked at me. She knew I was full of crap.

"Yeah, okay," she stated sarcastically. "You're still hung up on him, aren't you?"

I didn't have to answer. She already knew.

"Rox, you're supposed to forget about him. Boy toys only and painless good-byes, remember?"

"I know. I don't know what's wrong with me, Ton. I want to be mad at him. I want to forget him. I just can't."

"Well, there is your problem." She snorted.

"What?"

"You can't be angry with someone and forget him, Roxy. You have to stop being angry first."

"But that's the thing. I'm not angry. I just want to be," I informed her. "I miss him, Ton. I know it's stupid and that I haven't known him that long. It's just that"—I took a deep breath—"he made everything not...I don't know...not suck so badly." I sighed.

"Oh, dollface. That was exactly what he was for. Now, you need to find another boy to fill his spot. He's not the only guy who will be able to make you feel better."

That was the problem. He was the only guy who could make me feel better. He'd made me smile and laugh when I hadn't thought I could. I wasn't sold on the fact that some other guy would be able to make me feel the way Jordan had.

I didn't feel like arguing about this with Tonya, so I just shrugged.

"I think you should hook up with someone today," Tonya stated.

"What?" I gasped. That was completely out of the blue.

"Don't what me. It will be good for you. You're in an unnecessary funk. We need to snap you out of it. I think today should be a you're-hot-and-you-have-a-penis-so-you-should-come-over-here kind of day. Seriously, just grab the first sexy guy you see and start kissing him."

I exploded with laughter. "You're nuts, Ton."

"No, I'm not. A new pair of nuts is exactly what you should focus on finding today."

"Absolutely ridiculous." I shook my head. "Besides, today is more of a look-don't-touch kind of day. All the guys that we're hanging with today will be friends with Ryan, and I'm so not crossing that line again."

I looked out at the water to see Brent's white-black-and-green signature Four Winns in the distance. He had gotten the boat from his parents for his twenty-first birthday. It was one gift he hadn't had a problem accepting.

Tonya started repeatedly nudging me. "Holy sex god, Batman. Please tell me your brother doesn't know him."

I turned to see a group of guys by an expensive-looking red-and-black pontoon. I had assumed she was talking about the tall guy tying down the boat. Holy sex god was extremely exaggerated. I'd had the sex god, and that guy was not one. Okay, Jordan was never mine, but I now knew the difference.

Fuck, here I am, thinking about Jordan again. Seriously, he's a mind ninja.

Tonya continued nudging me.

"Stop. You're going to bruise me," I said, slapping her elbow away. "And I don't know who he is. I've never seen him."

Tonya was practically drooling. I wasn't saying that the guy wasn't cute, but he just didn't spark anything in me. Tonya's object of lust looked athletic with large sculpted arms. He was wearing gray board shorts that hung low on his waist. When he walked to the other side of the pontoon, I saw that he had a tribal tattoo running from shoulder to shoulder on his back.

One of the other guys standing with Tonya's sex god gestured our way. He must have noticed that Tonya and I were looking their way. Tonya waved as Brent and Ryan pulled the boat up to the dock. Ryan jumped off the boat to tie it down.

"Hey, Ry. Do you know them?" I asked.

Ryan looked over at the guys. "No. Why?"

"Because I'm about to be the greatest best friend ever," I sang.

I smiled at Tonya before skipping over to the group of guys. I looked over my shoulder to see Tonya standing there, openmouthed and stunned.

"Hi," I said to Tonya's crush of the moment.

"Hey." He grinned.

Okay, the boy has a nice smile. Maybe Tonya isn't crazy.

"See that hot girl over there?" I pointed at Tonya. "She's my best friend. She thinks you are hella cute, and I wouldn't be doing my job as a bestie if I didn't get your digits." I beamed at him and prayed that he wouldn't shoot me down.

Thankfully, he didn't. He gave me his number and asked for my friend's name.

"Tonya," I answered.

"Tell Tonya that I'm Shawn, and I can't wait to hear from her." He smirked.

Seriously great smile.

"I will. Thanks."

His buddies started to hoot, and it reminded me how dumb guys could be.

The one who had noticed us checking out Shawn was now looking me up and down. "What about you, sexy? Are you looking for someone to get to know better?"

Why are guys such pigs?

I turned on my heel. "No, thanks. I have a boyfriend."

I went back to Brent's boat. I didn't want anything to do with that guy, but I wasn't sure why I'd told him that I had a boyfriend. I didn't, and I didn't want one.

Do I?

Tonya engulfed me in a hug, shaking me out of my overthinking state of mind.

"What was that, Roxanne?" Ryan grilled me.

"I told you. That was me being the greatest best friend ever."

I then gave Shawn's name and number to Tonya. She was beaming as she put it in her phone.

"Should I text him right now?" she asked.

"Totally," I encouraged her.

Tonya smiled down at her phone. I was glad that she was happy.

"Don't run off and talk to random guys anymore, Roxy. It's not safe," Ryan reprimanded me.

"Shut up, Ryan. You don't always have to be a buzzkill," I sneered.

"Are you ready for a day of kick-ass fun, Princess?" Brent questioned, holding out his hand to help me board the boat.

He has no idea.

"Yes." I nodded enthusiastically. Maybe today would be full of distractions, and I could finally forget about Jordan.

Tonya and I rode in the bow of the boat. It was always my favorite spot. I loved the light spray from the water as it misted my skin, reminding me that this was what summer should feel like.

Brent turned up the music. With Hot Chelle Rae blasting, I tried to get lost in the beat of the music. Tonya and I loudly sang along to "I Like It Like That," and I found myself without the ache. I laughed. It was the first time all week I hadn't been shoving down pain. It felt amazing. I quickly braided my hair into a fishtail French braid. I didn't want to deal with frizzy hair after being in the water.

"Oh, oh! Do mine," Tonya begged.

I loved how excited she was. Today, she was rocking black streaks in her hair. I parted her hair in a zigzag and braided it into two French braids.

The black streaks popped and looked amazing. When I was done with her hair, I looked up, and I saw the beach area where we were headed. Actually, I couldn't see the beach, but I did see the hoard of boats anchored by it.

Let the craziness begin.

Tonya pulled off her sundress and started rubbing on sunscreen. I followed her lead. Looking down at my string bikini made my chest tighten as the memory of Jordan came at me full force.

Damn it!

I'd originally bought the suit for Jordan to enjoy. Tonya had found it and demanded that I wear it today. I hadn't wanted to explain why I didn't want to. So, I'd sucked it up and put it on. It had a low-rise Brazilian-cut white bottom with flirty ruby-red ruffles on the backside and matching red strings that tied at the hips. The triangle bikini top was also white with the same ruby-red strings. It was so sexy. Although I looked great on the outside, I still felt like shit on the inside.

At least, I was excellent at faking.

Tonya handed me the sunblock and turned around. I started rubbing it on her back. She had on a bow-shaped strapless bikini that tied in the back, and she'd paired it with low-rise black booty shorts.

Today might be a look-don't-touch day, but at least, we wouldn't be the only ones looking.

I turned around to face Brent as Tonya rubbed the sunblock on my back. I playfully stuck my tongue out at him. I expected him to be playful in return, but he just stared at me.

Did I not rub the sunblock in on my face?

I touched my fingers to my face, trying to feel for sunscreen that I might have missed.

"Uh…Princess," Brent stammered.

"Yes?"

He studied my body. It wasn't like he hadn't seen me in a bikini before, but even I knew, this one was the most scandalous I'd ever dared to wear around the wardens. My bikini was all about the whole less-is-more theory.

"I…I…" Brent seemed to be at a loss for words, and that made me warm from the inside out.

"Cat got your tongue?" Tonya teased Brent.

"Oh no! Not happening. Put your dress back on, Roxanne!" Ryan thundered, coming toward us from the stern of the boat.

"What? No! You don't get to tell me what I can and can't wear," I announced.

"When you are around my friends, I do. Put your dress back on. You, too, Tonya. The both of you are not walking around, looking like that—not on my watch," Ryan ordered.

Crazy man say what? Why can't I have a nice, normal brother?

"You are insane. There is nothing wrong with what we are wearing. We won't be the only girls in bikinis. Are you going to cover up every girl today?" I shot back.

"I don't give a fuck about what other girls are wearing. Those girls are not my sister and her best friend. I will not have you getting off this boat, dressed like that, especially not around all the guys who will be there. Have a little respect for yourself, Roxy."

His words infuriated me. "Respect? I respect myself just fine, Ryan. Maybe you should try giving me some. I'm old enough to choose what I want to wear, and there is nothing wrong with what I have on. It's not like I'm walking around in a thong. I know for a fact that other girls there will be wearing much less than this. I will actually be surprised if some aren't completely naked. I won't be the one the guys are looking at!" I yelled.

"Roxy's right. How about you lose the fun police badge and chill out?" Tonya added.

I had a strong urge to high-five her, but I refrained.

"Shut it, Tonya!" Ryan aimed his finger at her before pointing it at me. "Roxanne, I don't give a flying fuck what anyone else will be wearing. You are not getting off this boat in that."

Ryan and I glared at one another. It was always the same with him. He had to be the one in control. I was beyond sick of it.

"Ah!" I screamed in frustration as I stomped my foot.

"Throwing a fit won't help you, sis. Put your dress back on, or I'll have Brent turn the boat around, and I'll take your ass home. That goes for you, too, Tonya."

Tonya leaned in and whispered in my ear, "Let's just put our dresses back on. We won't be around your brother all day, so we can just appease him for now."

She was right. There was a crap-ton of people on the beach. Ryan couldn't keep tabs on us all day.

I gave him an evil stare and then pulled my white sundress over my head.

"When are you going to get that stick removed from your ass, Ry?" Tonya asked after her dress was back on.

"When are you going to stop dressing like a slut?"

"Fuck you, Ryan!" Tonya spit.

Brent turned up the music. It was his way of trying to end their fight. I marched to the back of the boat and took two beers from the ice chest. I handed one to Tonya and sank into the seat next to her.

"Princess, do you really think you should be drinking?" Brent asked.

"If I can't wear what I want, I'm sure as hell going to drink what I want. Pick your battle. It's the beer or the dress. You and Ryan can't have your way on both."

Ryan snorted. "Let her drink. With our luck, after a few beers, she will pass out. Then, we can put her back on the boat and not have to worry about keeping an eye on her."

I rolled my eyes. "You can't control my life forever."

"That's what you think." Ryan smirked.

"Fuck off." I popped the tab on my beer and took a long drink.

At this point, I didn't care if he took me back home. It would be better than having to deal with his crap all day. *So much for mindless fun.*

Ryan was more than determined to make this day suck.

Brent pulled in front of a roped-off section of the beach.

Of course he would have a roped-off spot.

I bet that he'd had some girls show up early just to block a spot for him.

Brent beached the boat, and Tonya and I stood. We were eager to get away from the fashion police. I looked out at the crowded beach. A massive amount of people were there. I should have expected as much. When Brent and Ryan hosted a party, they always pulled in a crowd.

Tonya elbowed me.

I really wish she would stop doing that.

"This is extreme—I mean, even for Ryan." She gawked at the crowd.

It was extreme. There was a giant inflatable trampoline floating on the edge of the lake. In the distance, a stage had been set up, and a band was playing. Today was supposed to be fun and carefree.

Why do I have to have a brother who doesn't believe I should enjoy the same experiences as him?

I shrugged. "The more people, the better. We can get lost in the crowd."

We clicked cans.

"To getting away." She laughed.

We chugged our beers and tossed the cans in the corner.

"Princess, you could throw those in the trash," Brent informed me.

"I could," I agreed even though it wasn't going to happen.

If he wanted the cans in the trash, he could pick them up his damn self.

He looked at me, waiting for me to pick up the cans.

"Let's go," I told Tonya.

She giggled as we climbed off the boat.

"Roxy!" Ryan called after me.

My jaw clenched. He was not going to ruin any more of this day. I stuck my hand in the air and flipped Ryan off as we walked away.

Tonya and I made our way through the crowd. After being bumped into and our feet stepped on more times than we could count, we were both over trying to party in the crowd of people. Walking along the shore, we went farther down the beach.

"This is crap," she said as she dropped down onto the sand. She pulled out her phone, checked her texts, and started beaming. "Okay, maybe not crap. Shawn invited us to hang out with him and his buddies."

I lay back on the sand. The hot sun wasn't as bad with the cool breeze blowing off the water. "Sounds like a blast. Tell him to pick you up. I'll cover for you."

"What do you mean, you will cover for me? Aren't you coming?"

I leaned forward, propped up on my elbows. "Ton, you know Ryan will flip if he finds out that I left and didn't tell him. You should go and have fun. Make out with the sex god. There is no reason that today should suck for both of us," I teased.

"I'm not going to leave you. Besides, I don't even know the guy. This might not be the brightest idea we've ever had."

I thought about that for a minute. "True. Total dummy moment. How about you just ask him to come over here and hang?"

"See? Now, that is brilliant."

She went back to texting as I lay back and soaked in the sun's rays. I pulled my dress up to my waist. It was unbelievable that I was worried about my brother catching me with it off.

Tonya lay down next to me. "He said they would try to make their way over later. They're wakeboarding." She sounded bummed.

I sat up. "This is lame. We're at the lake, and we should be having fun. Let's grab some tubes, some beers, and float. That will be fun and get us away from the gyrating crowd."

"Sounds perfect." She seemed more excited.

If she was happy, I was happy.

We got up and headed back. After we finally made it through the toe-stepping, body-bumping evil crowd to the boat. I was surprised to see Brent was still on board, talking on his phone. I untied the tubes and tossed them onto the sand. I filled a plastic bag with a dozen beers from the ice chest and handed the bag to Tonya.

If we manage to finish those off, we will be happy and drunk.

It was hard not to notice that Brent was having a heated discussion with someone in hushed tones. It was wrong, but I pretended to be looking for something under the seat as I listened.

I wondered if Jordan had told him about me. *Maybe Brent's talking to Jordan.*

I am seriously pathetic.

"I told you that already. I don't see why you keep bringing it up. It's not a big deal." Brent eyed me and then turned his body away from me. "I'm not having this conversation with you anymore. If you want to break up with me, then do it." He hung up the phone.

Wait—what? Break up? As in, Brent has a girlfriend? When did that happen?

It wasn't like I hadn't seen him with other girls. I had seen him with a lot of girls, but I didn't remember him ever having a girlfriend.

Why didn't I know about her?

I knew I should just keep my mouth shut, but I couldn't. I looked at him. "You have a girlfriend?"

His eyes widened as he realized that I had been listening in. He cleared his throat. "Um…yeah, Princess, I do." He sighed, looking away. "Or I did. I'm not sure at this moment."

Tonya coughed, trying to get my attention. She knew what Brent had meant to me in the past. She must have seen how surprised I was by this information.

Way to keep a straight face, Roxy.

"I think we got everything. Let's go float." Tonya tried to pull me away from the conversation she knew I was about to start with Brent.

I ignored her and pulled my arm from her grasp. "How did I not know about her? What is her name? Why haven't I ever met her? How long have you been together?" I bombarded Brent with questions.

He turned. "Don't worry about it, Princess."

"Why won't you tell me?"

He scratched the back of his head. "I have never lied to you. I don't want to start now. My relationship is complicated, and I don't want you to judge me for it."

What the hell is that supposed to mean?

"I don't understand how telling me her name would cause me to judge you." I eyed him.

"You're right. Her name is Emily."

Emily. I didn't know her, but I hated her name, not that I was jealous. I just didn't like the name. "How long have you been with her?"

"I really don't want to talk about this with you, Princess. Let's just drop it, okay?"

What is his deal? It was a simple question.

"Brent, it's not rocket science. It's just a question of time. You said you've never lied to me. Isn't hiding something kind of the same thing? I mean, we live in the same house, and I've never met her. I'm just kind of curious."

"Fine. You want the truth?"

"Doesn't everyone?"

"Two years," he said, staring at me.

My eyes widened, and I thought they just might pop out of my head. I must have heard him wrong. There was no way that he'd just said he had been with this girl, who I'd never even heard of before, for two years. So many thoughts were racing through my head.

Two years? Two fucking years? That can't be right. I've seen him with tons of other girls in the last two years. How could he have had a steady girlfriend? Wait—has Brent been cheating on her? No, he wouldn't. He would never be that type of person. He's too good, too sweet. He's Brent.

"Princess, are you okay?"

All I could do was nod my head. I wanted to ask. I needed to ask. I just couldn't get the words out of my mouth. I swallowed the disgusting taste that had risen from my throat.

Brent closely watched me. Without him saying a word, the look of guilt on his face answered my questions.

"You didn't," I barely whispered.

"That look on your face right now is why I never told you," he admitted.

I pushed down the nausea I was feeling. I just wanted to get away from him. "It's not any of my business anyway. Sorry I even started asking questions." I could do this. I could act like everything was fine. I just needed to get away from him.

"Princess?" He looked at me with troubled eyes.

I was already shaking my head at him. I couldn't believe that he would do something so terrible to another person. I couldn't talk to him anymore. I didn't even want to look at him.

I turned to Tonya. "Let's go have fun." I plastered on a fake smile.

She was looking more than a little uncomfortable. "Let's do it."

She forced a smile of her own, and we climbed off the boat.

13

My head was still reeling from the information I had just received. Brent stayed on the boat and didn't dare try to talk to me about his girlfriend. He knew I wasn't in a place to discuss it anymore. I wasn't sure I would ever be.

Tonya pulled off her sundress. "Roxy, we are getting in the water. Take off your damn dress. If your brother wants to bitch, let him bitch. It's not like you are prancing yourself around his friends."

She was right. I pulled my dress up and over my head, and then I tossed it back on the boat. Brent's eyes locked on to my body. Before, Brent looking at me like that would have caused my body to flush and my mind to go to restricted places. Right now, it just made me feel sick.

Two fucking years!

Tonya and I pushed the tubes out onto the water and climbed on. Tonya latched our tubes together and handed me a beer.

"Do you wanna talk about what happened back there?" she asked.

I gave her one last look before pulling my sunglasses down. "Not even a little bit."

Turning over, I lay on my stomach. I wanted to forget everything that Brent had just told me. My ideal perfect man was no more. He was now just a lying, cheating dickhead who belonged in shark-infested waters with Kevin and Sara.

Okay, so I didn't know the whole story. Maybe he wasn't that bad. Then again, maybe he was worse. If I'd learned anything today, it was that he wasn't the Brent I'd thought I knew. That Brent was a big fat lie.

Tonya and I talked about anything and everything not related to Brent. I mostly listened to her gush about how she couldn't wait to see Shawn and run her tongue over his tattoo.

I continued to down beer after beer.

After my fifth beer, I fell asleep.

I awoke to water being sprayed all over my body. I sat up to find two guys on Sea-Doos. Of course, they were none other than Luke and Chase.

Why didn't I even think about Chase being here?

He was a part of my brother's fraternity, and they all had been invited.

Chase brought his Sea-Doo up close enough to me that it caused my tube to rock.

"What's up, sexy lady?" He worked his eyes up and down my body.

I wished I had just listened to my brother and kept my damn dress on. I glanced over at Tonya, hoping for some help with the situation. She was passed out, so she wasn't going to be any help.

I smirked. "Well, I was asleep, but then someone got me all wet." The moment the words were out of my mouth, I regretted them.

"I got you all wet, huh? I would love to feel for myself," Chase flirted.

Yep, that's exactly what I deserve for being dumb. New approach—be rude.

I laughed. "Oh, well, that won't ever happen. If you don't mind, I was enjoying my rest."

"Are you playing hard to get? I have to say, I love a good chase. It is my name after all." Once again, he was laughing at his own joke. He seemed to do that a lot.

Why is this guy so lame? Lame should be his new name.

"I'm not playing hard to get. I'm impossible for you to get. I'm not interested. Sorry."

"You mean, you're not interested unless you get something out of it, like that night at the bar. I promise you, you will be getting something from me." He licked his lips.

Ew…I think I just threw up in my mouth a bit.

"Princess!"

Even though I knew it was Brent calling me, I still looked over my shoulder. He wasn't exactly the person I wanted to talk to, but he would have to do.

I shook Tonya's tube. I could feel Chase's eyes still on me.

"Ton, wake up. We need to head in."

She popped up her head and took in the situation before quickly sitting up. Luke was now by Chase.

"What up?" Luke gave Tonya a nod.

"Hi," she said to him.

"I never heard back from you. I thought you might have disappeared," Luke said to Tonya.

"Nope. I'm still around. I've just been busy," she replied.

I didn't even know that Tonya had been avoiding him. I hoped it wasn't because of me, but deep down, I knew that it probably was.

"I think these two are playing hard to get." Chase laughed even though nothing he'd said was remotely funny.

"Princess!" Brent yelled again.

"I'm coming!" I yelled back.

"Princess, huh?" Luke snickered. "What did you do to get that nickname?"

I glared at him. Then, I eyed Tonya, and she could tell I would rather deal with Brent than Chase and Luke.

"We should head in," she said.

"We should," I agreed.

"Oh, come on, ladies. You don't have to leave just because of Brent," Chase protested.

I slipped off the tube, landing in the waist-high water, and headed toward the shore. I looked back to find Chase staring. Luke was leaning toward him, saying something. When I turned around I could still feel Chase's eyes on me, and it sent a creepy chill down my spine.

Tonya and I pulled the tubes onto the shore. Brent was holding out our dresses. His body was rigid, and his jaw was clenched.

Why the hell is he mad?

"Are you trying to piss your brother off?" He scowled at me.

I snatched the dresses from him. "No." *How dumb is he?* I hadn't asked Chase to come talk to me.

I handed Tonya her dress, and she put it on.

"If your brother saw you talking to them, that is exactly what would have happened. Don't act like you don't know that."

I hadn't done anything wrong, and I wasn't about to let Brent treat me like I had. "He shouldn't have invited them then. Chase came up to me, Brent. I didn't start that. I was passed out, minding my own fucking business. I was out there, trying to stay away from all of Ryan's and your friends. God forbid one of them dares to talk to me or look at me as anything other than Ryan's little sister!" I shouted.

Brent started talking, but I couldn't hear him. My heart stopped as I saw Jordan walking over from the other side of the boat. My mouth dropped open, and I had to quickly snap it shut.

What is he doing here?

Use your brain, Roxanne. He's Brent's cousin after all. Brent probably invited him.

But why did Jordan come? He had to know I would be here—or at least assumed that much.

Did he want to see me?

I was terrible to him the day I'd kicked him out, so there was no way he was here for me. In fact, he probably hated me. I would hate me if I were him.

"Are you even listening to me?" Brent interrupted my inner ramblings.

"Huh?" I couldn't tear my eyes off of Jordan. *Why does he have to be so damn beautiful?*

Tonya elbowed me once again.

I'm going to remove her freaking arm.

"What? I mean, yes, I'm listening," I said, finally tearing my gaze away from Jordan.

Jordan stood behind Brent and cleared his throat. Brent looked over his shoulder at Jordan. Jordan moved, so he was now standing beside him and directly in front of me.

My heart still wasn't beating correctly. I forced myself to look away.

I could feel Jordan's eyes moving up and down my body. This made my decision to not put my dress back on one hundred percent worth it. I wasn't even worried that Ryan could come up at any moment and freak out. I had bought this suit for Jordan, so he might as well see me in it.

I wanted to look at him so badly that it hurt. Instead, I compromised with myself, saying I could look at his feet.

Fuck me. Even those are perfect.

Tonya started with the elbowing again. I looked up at her. I was about ready to scream at her to stop, but the look on her face was priceless. She was full-on gawking at Jordan as if he couldn't be real. This time, I elbowed her back, and it worked. She stopped staring and began rubbing her side.

Doesn't feel too good, does it, Ton?

"Sorry about that, man. I had to deal with these two," Brent told Jordan.

I stared angrily at Brent. *These two? That's how he's going to address us?*

Brent was giving me all kinds of reasons to loathe him today.

These two? I mean, seriously?

Asshole.

"We have names," I snapped.

Brent looked down and then back up. His gaze went from me to Jordan. He then let out a long sigh. "Seeing as you will meet at some point"—he looked at Jordan—"I would like you to meet Princess. You, however, can call her Roxy, and this is her best friend and partner in all crimes, Tonya." He then slung his arm over Jordan's shoulder. "This is my cousin, Jordan," Brent introduced us.

I just stood there, looking at them. I didn't know what to say. He really hadn't mentioned me to Brent. *Has he even thought about me all week?*

Tonya finally broke the silence, "It's nice to meet you." She stuck out her hand toward Jordan.

He shook it. "You, too."

Wow! Really? We're really going to pretend not to know each other? Fine.

I put on my award-winning fake smile and did as Tonya had. "It's so nice to meet you."

Jordan took my hand, and electricity shot through my body, awakening every thought and desire I had ever had for him. My knees felt weak.

"It is really nice to meet you, too. I have heard a lot about you." He smiled.

My heart beat faster. "That's scary. Hopefully, it was all good things." I tried to joke, but it came out stiff. I realized I hadn't let go of Jordan's hand, so I quickly did so.

"You need to put your dress on. I'm going to find your brother and tell him that I'm taking you two back home."

"What?" I asked, stunned.

"I don't want your brother to have to deal with his friends being all over you. I know you said you didn't initiate it, but you don't have to do anything to make guys want you. You just being you is enough. Everyone is starting to get drunk. The last thing we need today is your brother getting into a fight. And please put your damn dress back on," he snapped.

"I don't know why you are making her cover up, coz. I think she looks great." Jordan grinned.

I loved the way he was looking at me. Maybe he didn't hate me after all.

Brent glared at him. If looks could kill, Jordan would be dead. I tightly pressed my lips together and tried not to find the situation funny.

"Don't. You know what you are doing. Don't even think about it," Brent said, unclenching and clenching his hands into fists.

I was worried Brent might start throwing punches, but it wasn't because I thought Jordan couldn't hold his own. Brent and Jordan were pretty evenly matched. I just didn't want Jordan to get hit at all.

I pulled my dress back on and changed the subject. "This is ridiculous. Why did Ryan even insist on me coming?"

"You've been sad all week. He didn't want you to be alone," Brent informed me.

I couldn't even look at Jordan. I didn't want him to know that I had been sulking over him.

"You don't have to take us home. You are just being paranoid. I guess that comes with the territory when you spend years lying to people." I gave Brent my most hateful look.

"Roxanne, I never lied to you!" he yelled.

Great. Now, I've really pissed him off.

At least he was mad at me and not at Jordan anymore.

"I'm not talking about me—even though you kind of did. I'm talking about Emily. Does she know about all the other girls? Does she know what a lying, cheating lowlife piece of shit you are?"

Tonya tugged on my arm. I knew I had crossed a line. Brent gave me a sinister look. I had never seen him that upset with me before. I was starting to regret what I'd said.

"I can't deal with you right now. Jordan, do me a favor and stand here with them while I go find Ryan."

I wanted to apologize. I had taken it too far. "Brent—"

"Save it. I don't want to hear it," he snapped before stalking off into the crowd and disappearing.

"Rox, what was that about?" Jordan asked.

"That was nothing. Brent is a lying ass, and I called him out on it. It might have been the wrong place, but oh well."

Tonya laughed. "You didn't just call him out, dollface. You destroyed him."

"What did he lie about?" Jordan asked.

Did he not get enough information from my rant?

"Brent has a girlfriend and never told her," Tonya informed him.

"You're mad because my cousin has a girlfriend?" he asked.

I could clearly see that it bothered him. I had to make him understand. "No, I'm not mad because he has a girlfriend. I don't care if he's with someone. I'm mad because he has been with her for the last two years, and in those years, I have seen Brent with more girls than I could ever keep track of. I'm mad at him because he's a cheater. You know how I feel about that."

Jordan nodded in understanding.

I nudged Tonya. "Come on, let's go."

"Wait, Rox. Where are you going?" Jordan inquired.

I started walking backward. "To have fun. Are you coming?"

Jordan quickly caught up with Tonya and me as we made our way into the cluster of people.

We finally found a keg and filled up some cups. After downing three cups full of beer, I was feeling warm and tingly again. That feeling only intensified when Jordan wrapped his arms around my waist from behind.

He whispered into my ear, "I've missed you."

I spun around in shock from his words. I wasn't sure if it was Jordan or how quickly I'd turned that made me feel dizzy. He had no idea how much I had missed him. Well, he might have some idea, seeing as Brent had said that I was sad all week. I still had no words to express what I felt.

Instead, I chose to use my mouth in a different way. I wrapped my arms around Jordan and pressed my lips to his. Jordan returned my kiss with just as much passion as I was giving him.

After I didn't know how long, Tonya interrupted us, "Not to rain on your kissing party, but watching you two is kind of getting me all hot and bothered. I'm pulling the third-wheel card and telling you to knock it off."

I laughed a real laugh. "Don't watch, you perv."

"Easy for you to say. You haven't watched the two of you kiss. It's hot," she joked.

Jordan slid his hand into mine, interlocking our fingers. "Let's go do something fun."

I mock-pouted. "But that was fun."

"It was, but Tonya has spoken." Jordan gave me a devilish grin.

"Tonya? Tonya who?" I teased.

Tonya playfully punched me on the arm. I stuck out my tongue at her, and then I turned and claimed Jordan's mouth once again.

A few short moments later, he pulled away. Jordan took his phone out of his pocket. He laughed and then showed me a text message.

I asked you to watch the girls and you disappeared?

"He has no idea how convincing you can be, does he?" Jordan kissed me again.

Reluctantly, I pulled away. "I guess we should head back." I didn't want Jordan catching crap from Ryan or Brent because I'd taken off.

"I would rather be home anyway. Shawn just texted me and asked if he could take me to a movie tonight," Tonya informed us.

"Yay!" I cheered. "Let's go."

We made our way to the boat through the hoard of people. Halfway through, someone clutched my arm, stopping me.

"Hey, sexy. I didn't think I would run into you again," Chase said.

I really didn't want to deal with him right now—or ever again. "Chase, twice in one day. Who woulda thunk it?"

"Come over here and dance with me." He pulled me into him.

I pulled my arm out of his grasp and stepped away. "I'm actually leaving."

Jordan took my hand in his again and stepped closer to me.

"Don't be like that. One dance won't hurt you." Chase laughed, reaching out for my arm again. He was trying way too hard.

Get a clue already.

I felt Jordan's grip on my other hand tighten. Then, he stepped in front of me.

Once again, my hero.

"She told you no," he informed Chase.

"Just who the fuck are you?" Chase sized Jordan up.

"Her boyfriend," he stated.

I gasped at the words but didn't correct him.

Chase looked around Jordan to me. "You have a boyfriend?" Chase asked in disbelief.

I smiled and stood next to Jordan's side. "I do."

Tonya was standing behind us, choking back laughter.

"What a fucking waste of time," Chase said before turning and stomping away.

I felt Jordan's body stiffen. "Who was that clown?" he asked.

"Just one of Roxy's many admirers." Tonya chuckled.

"He was no one," I told Jordan.

He looked at me like he knew there was a story to be told, but he didn't push it, and I was grateful. I stood on my tippy toes to kiss him.

"Just thinking out loud here, but you two might want to cool it on the PDA. Brent already looked like he wanted to kill you, Jordan, but Ryan will straight up end you."

Tonya was right. Plus, I didn't want Brent or Ryan to know about what was going on with Jordan. They would just ruin whatever it was we had. I didn't know exactly what that was right now, but I didn't want to give him up—not yet.

I stopped Jordan before we exited the crowd. "My brother is going to yell at me, and I need you not to react. You might want to, but I am begging you not to. Just let him yell."

I really needed Jordan not to go off on my brother. It wasn't like Jordan had never yelled at me. He knew firsthand how much I could piss someone off.

He gave me a quick kiss and then stepped away. "Let's get this over with, so we can leave."

We made our way over to the boat. I hated not being able to touch him. It was all I wanted to do, but it was for the best. I held on to Tonya's hand instead. She gave me a sympathetic look. She knew we were walking into hell.

Before we even got to the boat, Ryan saw me.

He thundered, "Where the hell did you go?"

If he wasn't my brother, I would have been terrified. I saw Jordan's body stiffen at the way my brother was yelling at me. I hoped Jordan wouldn't try to play hero. Ryan was all bark and no bite.

"I had to pee. Brent put his cousin on babysitting duty, so he came with."

"You didn't think to use the bathroom on the boat?" Ryan roared.

"What? No way. There's a bathroom on the boat?" I feigned surprise.

"Don't you play dumb with me, Roxanne!"

He should win an award for best overreaction.

Jordan stepped forward.

Before he could say anything, I cut him off and said to Ryan, "Okay, you caught me. I didn't want to leave. Tonya and I walked off. Jordan came after us, telling us we needed to come back. You should thank him. You could have lost me forever."

I knew how much Ryan hated my sarcasm. Luckily, his anger with me made him oblivious to Jordan squeezing his hands into fists.

"Get on the boat. You're going home," he commanded.

"Aye, aye, captain!" I shouted in my best British accent, which was terrible, as I saluted Ryan.

Maybe the beer had gone to my head.

Tonya and I laughed all the way back to the boat. As we climbed up, I saw Brent walking out of the crowd. I didn't miss the relief that crossed his face when he saw me. I used to find it endearing that he worried about me, but right now, it was hard to see past the vileness of what he had done to his girlfriend.

How did I ever think he could have been the one?

I fell back into the seat next to Tonya.

Today was full of crap moments, but it had gone way better than I could have ever imagined. Jordan and I were talking—and kissing—again. At some point, we would have to talk about what had happened between us and the whole boyfriend comment with Chase, but none of that mattered. He was here, and I wasn't faking being happy anymore. I just was. The realization made me smile.

I also noticed that I hadn't felt any tightness in my chest. Even with the drama with Ryan and Brent, I was good. I adored Jordan and his pain-blocking, happiness-giving magical powers. My body tingled at the thought, and the butterflies in my stomach started dancing again.

Oh, butterflies, how I have missed you.

I watched Brent walk over to where Ryan was still talking to Jordan. They chatted for a moment longer before making their way back to the boat.

I was relieved to see Jordan getting on the boat with them. I didn't know whom he'd come here with, but I was glad he would be leaving with me. He smiled at me as he walked past. He sat on the bench seat across from Ryan.

I turned, looking at Jordan, when Brent startled me.

"Jordan is going to drive you two home," Brent said firmly.

"He is?" I smiled.

Tonya elbowed me—hard.

Seriously, I'm going to have a bruise.

"Yes, Princess. My cousin is going to take you both home."

I heard it in his voice. He was making it a point that Jordan was his cousin, so he was off-limits to me.

I shrugged nonchalantly. "How nice of him." I then sank back into my seat and rested my head on Tonya's shoulder.

What Brent didn't know was I'd already crossed that line, so there was no going back.

It took everything I had not to turn and look at Jordan again. The boat ride took forever. Brent finally pulled up to the dock, and Ryan jumped out to tie the boat in place. Jordan got out next. He and Ryan held out their hands to help Tonya and me off the boat.

"No matter what they say, take them both straight home. They've been drinking, and the last thing they need is to be out in public," Brent told Jordan.

"I've got it covered," Jordan reassured him.

"Don't forget what I told you." Ryan eyed Jordan.

"I won't, man. They're safe with me," Jordan replied.

"I don't want you two causing any kind of trouble. Just go home, order in dinner, and watch girlie movies tonight," Ryan told Tonya and me.

What is he? Fifty?

"Shut up, Ry," I sneered.

Tonya just started laughing. "Hate to burst your dictator bubble, Ryan, but I have plans that do not involve staying in tonight. I have a date. Nice try with the brotherly act, but you're not my brother," Tonya stated.

"Whatever you say, Tonya. Just don't drag my sister out with you. Do you understand?"

I groaned in frustration. *This is so demeaning.* I turned and stomped off down the deck.

"I'm serious, Roxanne. You'd better stay home!" Ryan yelled.

For the second time that day, I stuck my hand in the air and flipped off my brother.

14

"You wanna talk about it?" Jordan asked, pulling me closer to him on the couch.

It didn't take a genius to see that I was in a bad mood.

On the car ride back, I'd tried really hard to keep up the small talk. It had been pretty easy, considering Tonya wouldn't shut up about Shawn. But after we'd dropped her off, I'd had a hard time holding a normal conversation with Jordan. Too much had been going through my head. Plus, I had still felt embarrassed about Ryan's behavior. Also, there was that pesky fact that I had felt a little bit nervous that Jordan might go away again after tonight.

I shrugged. "It's a long list."

"Good thing we have all night." He kissed me on my forehead.

That kiss alone warmed my body. Here I was, trying to have a pity party, and he was a fireball of comfort.

I snuggled into him. "Can I ask you something?"

"You just did." He chuckled.

"Ha-ha." I tightened my lips to hold back my smile.

Jordan rubbed his hand up and down my arm. "Ask me anything, babe."

I didn't think I would ever tire of hearing him call me babe. "What did Ry and Brent say to you after Ton and I got on the boat?"

"Your brother thanked me for going after you."

"That's it?"

"Not exactly. He asked me why I went after you. I told him it was because Brent had asked me to watch you both while going off to find him. I couldn't do that if I didn't go with you. I also said I was in a hurry to get home. He asked if I would mind taking you and Tonya back. We were about to go to the boat when Brent walked over and told me to stay away from you."

"What?" *Why did Brent want Jordan to stay away from me so badly? He's as bad as my brother.*

"Ryan was confused, and Brent said that he didn't want me around you. Ryan informed him I was taking you both home. Brent didn't want me to at first, but I lied and stated to him that as fine as you were, I had a hotter piece of ass waiting for me tonight. I don't know if he believed me, but he didn't push the topic anymore. Ryan then warned me that if anything bad happened to you while I was with you, he would have no problem killing me."

I laughed. "So, you have a hot piece of ass waiting for you?"

He pulled me onto his lap. "A very hot piece of ass."

His look was full of desire. My body felt hot, and my pulse quickened. I wanted him, but we still had many other things to talk about.

I kissed him on his nose. I tried to ignore my intense need for him. "What should we order for dinner?"

"You are the only thing I want to eat." He kissed up my neck.

My body betrayed me as I melted under his kisses. I let out a moan. I felt like I was vibrating between my legs.

Wait—I am vibrating between my legs.

I inched back. "As good as that feels, do you want to get that?"

Jordan pulled his phone out of his pocket. "That feels good, huh?"

He pressed his vibrating phone between my legs. I started to throb harder just as the vibrating stopped. I bit down on my lip. I wasn't planning on having sex with Jordan tonight, but there was nothing in the world I wanted more.

He pulled me back into him and kissed me with more passion than I'd ever felt. His phone started to vibrate on the couch. I tried to ignore it. I really did, but when it went off for the fifth time, I was just annoyed.

I pulled away from Jordan. "Will you get that, please?"

Someone was obviously desperate to reach him.

He looked at his phone and then tossed it back on the couch. "It's my cousin again. I will call Brent back later."

Big warning signs flashed in my head. *Oh no!*

I slid off Jordan and dug through my purse for my phone. I saw that I had twenty-four missed calls from Ryan and Brent. *Absolute psychos.*

"Shit!" I yelled.

Jordan raised an eyebrow at me, and I showed him my phone.

"Are they always like this with you?" He seemed irritated.

"Sadly, this is nothing." I called my brother back.

It didn't even take Ryan a full ring to answer. All I could hear was the noise coming from people around him.

"Hold on!" he shouted into the phone.

The loudness faded, and I assumed Ryan was walking to a less crowded spot. Jordan's phone vibrated on the couch once again. He reached over to get it. I gestured for him not to pick it up. He gave me a nod and let it be.

"Roxy, can you hear me?" he shouted again.

I almost shouted back, but I remembered that I didn't need to. "Yeah, I hear you," I answered.

"Why haven't you been picking up?" He sounded genuinely worried.

Why does he have to be so protective of me? It's not like I'm breakable. Oh, wait—I am. But seeing as I'm already broken, he should ease up.

"I was in the shower. I didn't even have my phone upstairs," I lied. I wished my relationship with Ryan didn't have to be like this.

"Brent's cousin is not there, right?" Ryan asked.

I looked at Jordan smiling at me from the couch. He looked so yummy, and I just wanted to get back to kissing him. "What? Why would he be here?" *And the Golden Globe goes to…*

"Roxanne?" He was using his parental voice, trying to make sure he was getting the truth.

Too bad for you, Ryan.

"God! No, Ry, he's not here. He left right after I was in the door."

Jordan shook his head in amusement.

"Just making sure. I believe you."

Okay, I might have felt a little guilty for lying to my brother, but he only had himself to blame.

"I'll be home in the morning. Brent and I are leaving for Los Angeles after five. That way, we don't have to deal with traffic. Make sure you're home. We'll do an early dinner before I head out, all right?"

I prayed Brent wasn't planning on going to lunch with us. I was still extremely upset with him.

"Uh-huh. I'll be here," I mumbled unenthusiastically.

"Roxy, look, I'm sorry I yelled at you today. I should have handled the situation with your bathing suit differently. I just worry about you getting hurt. Guys only have one thing on their mind, and I don't want you to catch the attention of some dude who doesn't care what he has to do to get what he wants. I guess I was freaking out about that when I didn't know where you were. But I also shouldn't have shouted at you when you came back to the boat either."

My brother had been apologizing a lot lately.

He must really believe I'm fragile.

"Sure, Ry. Whatever you say."

"I know you're mad. We will talk about it tomorrow, okay?"

"Uh-huh."

"All right. I love you."

I knew my brother only wanted to keep me safe, but he was wrong. I didn't need protecting. I needed to be able to live my life.

"You, too." I hung up the phone and then texted Brent.

Talked to Ryan. Don't have anything to say to you. Don't bother calling me again.

I tossed my phone back into my purse. "Now, where were we?" I smiled at Jordan.

Jordan stood up. He took my dress by the hem and pulled it up over my head. My body shivered with excitement.

"I really love this suit on you, but I was glad Brent had you put your dress back on. I saw the way other guys were looking at you, and I didn't like it."

Aw, he's jealous. I liked it.

I playfully pushed him back down on the couch and crawled on top of him. "I bought the suit for you. I'm glad you like it." I kissed him. With that kiss, I wanted to let him know that I didn't care who else had looked at me. The only eyes I wanted on me were his. I finally pulled back. I untied the string around my neck, exposing my breasts. "I want you," I breathed. My stomach fluttered nervously.

Jordan's mouth was on mine again. His kiss was full of all the passion I'd needed. His hands went to my ass, squeezing it. He pressed me against him as he stood up, never taking his mouth from mine. I wrapped my legs around his waist.

I broke the kiss and giggled as he carried me to the stairs. "You don't have to take me upstairs to have your way with me, silly."

"You're sandy. I thought I would wash you off. I mean, if that's okay with you?" His eyes glistened with the same need I felt inside of me.

Desire coursed through my body. *Damn, I want him.* I bit down on my lip and nodded as he continued carrying me upstairs.

My naked body was twisted up with Jordan's, my head lying on his chest. We had been silent for several minutes, but it was a comfortable silence, a peaceful one. As he twirled my hair around his fingers, I thought about tonight's events.

Once we'd come into my room, I had been certain that we would just have sex, but he'd stuck to what he'd said, and he'd carried me into the bathroom. We'd showered together, and he'd washed me and then some.

I bit down on my lip, thinking about how he'd sent my body to places I hadn't even known it could go. Then, he'd brought me, dripping wet, to the bed.

After the awkward condom convo, we'd decided that since I was on birth control, we would go without one. Jordan had made sure that I understood what a big deal that was for him. He'd never had sex without one. It might not have mattered to someone else, but knowing that had made me feel incredibly special.

Even after everything we had done in the shower, I had still felt extremely nervous. He had way more experience than I did. Thankfully, Jordan had kissed away my self-doubt. He had been sweet and gentle with me—well, the first time at least.

Now lying in bed, we were still recuperating from round three.

Good Lord. I had seriously been missing out.

Sex was way more amazing than I had ever known, and I'd thought I loved it before.

Wowzers! I suddenly understood how people could become sex addicts. There was a huge chance I would be joining that group of sex-crazed people.

"That…" He didn't continue.

That what? I turned my head to see his face. He had the most glorious grin I had ever seen on him.

"Yeah?" I was dying to know what he had wanted to say.

"I don't even have words, Rox." He squeezed me tighter. "But whatever the right words are, it was that times a million."

I was smiling so hard that my cheeks hurt. I buried my face in his chest, so he couldn't see my ridiculous grin.

Jordan kissed the top of my head. "You hungry, babe?"

I sat up, holding the sheet against my chest. I didn't know why I was being shy. He had already seen everything.

"Starved," I breathed.

Jordan rolled off the bed and walked his beautiful naked ass into my bathroom.

Damn, his body is insanely perfect.

He returned a moment later, wearing only his boxer briefs. He tossed me his shirt.

"You know that we're in my room, right?" I snickered.

"And?" He licked his lips, making my body tingle.

"And…I have an obscene amount of clothing."

"I know, but I don't want you in anything but my shirt." He smirked.

The request seemed oddly possessive, and it turned me on like nothing else. I pulled on the blue Billabong T-shirt and then got up. His shirt hung mid-thigh on me, and the look on his face said he approved.

I giggled. "Come on, lover boy. I want pancakes."

"Mind-blowing sex, and now, you're going to cook for me? I don't know, Rox. I might have to keep you forever." He grinned amorously.

I knew he was just being playful, but his words made me feel uneasy. We still had a lot to talk about.

Jordan came from behind me and scooped me up into his arms before carrying me downstairs.

"You are sensational." He gave me a sweet kiss before setting me down in the kitchen.

I was no longer worrying about what we needed to talk about. I just wanted to enjoy this time and make him some sinfully delicious pancakes.

"You're not too shabby yourself."

He was far from shabby. He was drop-dead gorgeous.

But he has to know that, right?

"Nah, when people see me with you, they'll be like, 'How the hell did that guy get her?'"

I stood on my tippy toes to kiss him.

"Look at you—not only hot, but modest, too." I laughed and started taking out the ingredients for the pancakes.

It was my mom's recipe. She used to claim that she had spent years perfecting it. Whether or not that was true didn't matter. They were hands-down the best pancakes in the world.

It was strange to think about my mom and not feel like I was going to burst into tears. Even stranger, the painful ache that usually resided in my chest was nowhere to be felt. It was almost like magic. I smiled at Jordan.

Just as I'd known he would, Jordan loved the pancakes. Soon after we were done eating, we enjoyed rounds four and five downstairs, and then we made our way back upstairs. After round six, I was spent. I curled up against Jordan and quickly fell asleep.

I awoke to Jordan kissing my forehead. "Mmm...I'm tired. Just a few more hours of sleep, and I'll be ready to go again," I grumbled.

"Baby, I was just kissing you good-bye."

I shot up, now wide-awake. "Good-bye?" I looked at my clock. It was four in the morning. *Wow, I've been asleep for hours already.* "Where are you going?"

"I wanted to make sure I'm not here when your brother comes home."

Gah, how I wish I were an only child. I stuck out my lip and pouted. "You're right, but I wish you didn't have to go." I wanted to go back to sleep, wrapped in his arms, and stay there forever.

Well, not forever. Nothing is forever. I knew better than to even think such things.

"I know." He kissed me again.

I wrapped my arms around his neck and passionately kissed him.

"You know, I don't have to go. I will gladly let your brother hit me. I won't even try to stop him." He gave me a playful grin.

"Don't be silly. I like your face the way it is." I squished his lips together to give him a fishy face before affording him one last kiss. "I just wanted to give you something to think about until I see you again."

"Even if you hadn't kissed me like that, you would still be on my mind. You always are. I really missed you, Rox."

He had no idea how much I'd missed him. Those days without him had been horrid.

I tightly hugged him. "I missed you, too, more than you could imagine. I know we have things we need to talk about, but—"

He kissed me, shutting me up. "We don't have to talk about any of that right now. Lie down, and I will tuck you in before I go."

"Will you lie with me until I fall back asleep?"

Jordan lay down next to me, and I curled back into him.

"Sweet dreams, baby," he said.

15

I woke up hours later to Tonya bouncing on the side of my bed. I cracked my eyes open to take in her way too bubbly expression.

What did she do? Rob a Starbucks?

"Stop bouncing," I muttered. I pulled my sheet up, and I rolled onto my back. My body tensed at how sore I felt from last night's sexcapades. *Ouch.*

"Why are you naked?" Her voice was as bouncy as she appeared.

"My clothes and I decided to start seeing other people. My blankets were comforting, and I made them my rebound," I joked.

She laughed. "Oh my God, you did it. You had sex last night. I knew that's why you weren't returning my texts. Yay!" she squealed. She scooted me over and lay down next to me on her side, propping herself up with her elbow. "Tell me everything." She wasn't wasting any time.

I yawned. "I have no idea what you are talking about."

"Stop stalling. I want all the juicy details."

How does she have this much energy right now?

"Did you see Ryan downstairs?" I asked, stalling the conversation a bit longer. It was fun to see her squirm.

"No. Now, tell me what happened," she whined.

I twisted my hair around my finger. "Kevin is no longer the only guy I've had sex with." I chuckled.

"Eek. Was it good?" she squealed.

I let out a dreamy sigh. "Oh, Ton, good doesn't even come close to describing it. It was…it was absolutely perfect. I had no idea sex could feel like that. I mean, I've had orgasms before, but…oh, wow…" I sighed again.

I looked at her, waiting for more gushing, but she confused me with her perplexed look.

"What's wrong?"

"Are you falling for him?" Her tone was serious.

I had only known him for a few weeks—one of which was when he had been in Oregon, and another one was when we hadn't talked. I was not falling in love. Hell, I was still on the fence about even having a boyfriend. "No, I'm not falling for him. Why would you even think that?" I protested.

"Because of all this." She waved her hand at me.

"This is just what someone looks like after she has been properly fucked," I explained.

"Yeah…okay, dollface. For the record, whatever it is, it looks good on you. I mean, I know I wasn't all Team Jordan before, but if he can make you smile like that…" She grinned.

I rolled my eyes. "All right, enough about me. I want to hear about how last night went with Shawn." I just wanted to change the subject. The last thing I needed to think about was my feelings for Jordan—not that I had feelings for him. Well, it wasn't the kind she had referred to.

"I didn't have incredible sex like you did, but I can report that he was a superior kisser. He—"

"Sorry, Ton. I have to pee." I crawled off the end of my bed. "Keep talking." I rushed into the bathroom.

"He picked me up, and we went out for pizza. He's from Santa Barbara. He came up here with some friends for the weekend," she continued as I went to the bathroom.

I washed my hands and inspected myself in the mirror. I didn't look like the sad girl who had stood here weeks ago. I still felt broken inside, but no one could tell how damaged I really was just by looking at me. I had come a long way. I smiled at my reflection.

I pulled my toothbrush out of its holder and started brushing my teeth.

Tonya continued telling me about Shawn, "He just turned twenty-one. He's a psych major. He is Phi Psi, but don't worry. He doesn't know Ryan, not that it matters. Ryan's not my brother. But I asked Shawn if he did know Ryan just in case he had a hot friend you might, you know, want to hook up with."

I rolled my eyes at Tonya's comment. "How sweet of you." I laughed and went back to brushing my teeth.

"Don't act like I'm not the greatest best friend ever. Oh, best part—he's the perfect height."

I could hear the happiness oozing out of her. I was glad last night had worked out for her. "I'm happy for you, Ton."

"He's headed back to Santa Barbara today, but he told me he wanted to see me again. He is coming back up next weekend just to spend time with me."

"Aw, Ton, he sounds like a keeper."

She snorted. "Let's not go too far. You know me. I don't get attached, but with that said, he does have possibility."

She was hopeful, and I was happy for her.

"I'm gonna jump in the shower. Do you wanna go get breakfast when I get out?" I asked.

"Sounds like a plan. I'll be raiding your closet. I feel like making you my life-sized doll today."

I chuckled. "When am I not your personal doll?"

"You love me dressing you. Don't act like you don't."

"No, I just love you, so I don't complain," I corrected her. Although truth be told, I didn't mind her dressing me. It was fun, and she always put together fabulous outfits.

"That's because you're a good doll," she praised me as if I were a dog.

I was laughing hard as I got in the shower. Something had changed in me. I didn't know what it was, but something just felt different. Maybe it was the peaceful night of sleep, maybe it was the sex, or maybe it was just being around Jordan again. Whatever it was, I liked it.

Tonya collapsed on the couch. "Too much food," she groaned.

I giggled at her dramatics. Today was turning out to be a fantastic day. I liked being this girl, the one who went out to brunch with her BFF and talked about boys. I might be all discombobulated on the inside, but today, I wasn't worried about falling apart. All my shattered pieces were staying put. It was nice not to fake being normal but to actually just be normal.

"Gah," she whined, holding up her phone. "The parentals want a family night."

Her aversion to spending time with her parents rubbed me the wrong way. I loved Tonya to death, but she was clueless as to how freaking lucky she was.

I sat down next to her. "Ton, don't be like that. Your parents love you," I pressed.

She leaned over and placed her head in my lap. "Come with. You're family." She smiled.

"Yeah, I don't think so, Ton. Rain check?"

Our moms had been close friends. They were a lot alike. I was having a good day, and I knew there was no way I would stay emotionally intact if I spent time with the loving Miller family. It would just be a reminder of what I didn't have anymore—my mom.

"You know my mom loves you just like a daughter, Roxy. I have no problem sharing her," Tonya stated.

I was fully aware of how much Mrs. Miller cared about me, but she wasn't my mom, and I didn't want a surrogate.

"Thanks, Ton, but I'm not looking to replace my mom." It came out colder than I'd meant for it to.

"I didn't mean that. I just meant…oh, Rox." Tonya engulfed me in a hug.

I felt bad for snapping at her. I reassuringly patted her back. "It's fine. I know your heart was in the right place."

"Okay. I guess I should head out."

She got up, and I went with her to her car. I could tell she was still feeling bad for what she had said, and I hated that I'd made her feel that way.

"Love you, bitch," I teased, trying to make her smile again.

It worked.

She turned before getting in her car, and she gave me the biggest smile. "Love you more, slut."

With that, I knew we were okay.

As Tonya was pulling out, Brent and Ryan pulled up.

Ryan jumped out of the truck. "Hey, sis. Where is the devil running off to?"

I hated that he was such a dick to Tonya. She didn't deserve his asshole ways.

"If you are referring to the wonderful person who is my best friend, she is off to family night at the Miller household. They are a regular family, so they do that kind of stuff."

"Are you insinuating that we are not a normal family?" he quipped.

"Sorry, Ry. We stopped being a normal family a while ago." *You know, the night Mom died?*

Brent got out of the truck and headed toward the house. "Hey, Princess." He stood in front of me.

I looked past him and didn't respond.

"I see Jordan got you girls home safely."

I didn't know if I would ever be able to look at Brent in the same way as I had before. I continued to ignore him.

"You're really going to ignore me, Princess?"

I could hear the hurt in his voice that he was trying hard not to show. I almost felt bad—almost.

I peered around Brent to see my brother. "Ryan, I'll be in my room if you need me."

Ryan was oblivious to me and just continued unloading the truck. I turned away from Brent and headed inside.

Brent pushed the door back open before it had shut, but I continued walking away.

"Princess…"

I took the steps two at a time. Once in my room, I fell onto my bed.

How am I supposed to talk to him when he did the one thing I believe to be unforgivable? How could he stand there and think I would ever be okay with what he did to that poor girl?

I didn't care if I wasn't the one he had been cheating on. What he had done was wrong. There was no way around that.

For the first time all day, my chest started to ache.

Stupid, stupid Brent.

I wanted to call and talk to Jordan, but I had left my phone downstairs, and I wasn't about to go get it. I tried to get lost in my thoughts of him, hoping the ache would just disappear. I wondered what he was doing and if he was thinking about me as much as I was thinking about him. The way he could make me feel was unreal. I started to think about what Tonya had said.

Is it even possible to love someone I barely know?

But I do know Jordan.

The week that he had been in Oregon, we'd spent getting to know each other. We'd talked about everything. I actually knew him better than I knew other people in my life—case in point, Brent.

Evidently, I know nothing about that cheating, lying—

There was a knock on my door, interrupting my thoughts.

"What?" I called. *So help me God, it'd better not be Brent.* I wasn't in the mood.

Ryan opened the door and came in. "What's up with you? Why are you giving Brent the cold shoulder?" he questioned.

"Why do you care?" I snapped.

"He's my best friend, you're my sister, and we all live in the same house. I'd say it concerns me."

"Did you know he has a girlfriend?" I asked, hoping that my brother would not be okay with his buddy being a douche bag.

"Yeah, I did. Why does that bother you?"

Way to suck, Ryan. Now, you are no better than Cheater McGee.

"Seriously, you knew? Do you not see the problem with that?" I was yelling now.

"Roxy, are you jealous? 'Cause if that is what your bitch act is about—"

I cut him off, "No, you moron. I'm mad because he's a cheating asshole." *How could my own brother be okay with this when he saw firsthand how much Kevin hurt me?*

"Uh, Roxy…what Brent chooses to do with the girls in his life isn't our business. It doesn't concern you. Why get upset?" he probed.

He acted like what Brent had done was no big deal. It was a huge deal.

"He's been with her for two years!" I couldn't believe that my brother didn't get it.

"I know, Roxy. I've met her," he told me.

What?

What?

He'd met this poor girl, and he was still okay with how she had been treated.

How sick are these two?

"How can you be his friend? How can you not feel that what he is doing to that girl is terrible?"

My chest was full-on throbbing now. Of all people, I'd expected much more from Ryan. He wasn't the heartless prick that he was coming across as.

"It's his life, Rox. Who am I to judge? He's not affecting my life in a negative way," Ryan stated.

"I don't get you, Ryan. You witnessed firsthand the effects Kevin's cheating has had on me. How can you not care?"

"You're my sister, and if I ever see that piece of shit again, I'll kill him for what he did to you. But Brent's girlfriend is nothing to me. I'm not going to ruin a friendship over someone I don't care about. He's my friend, Roxanne. I'm not here to tell him how to live his life."

"What about the girl he's lying to? It affects her life."

"Again, that doesn't affect mine. What is going on with their relationship is between him and her."

"You have a warped view on life then, Ry, because it should bother you that your friend is a lying worthless piece of shit," I barked.

Ryan rubbed his forehead. I was clearly starting to annoy him.

"I'm not the one he's lying to, Roxy. Why should I care?"

"He's not lying to you that you know of. I mean, facts are facts. He's a fucking liar," I rebuffed.

"I think you need to hear the whole story before you judge him. The world isn't all black and white, wrong and right. There are many gray areas, too."

Is he seriously trying to convince me that there could actually be some reason that makes what Brent's doing okay?

I don't freaking think so.

"Whatever, Ry. You are no better than him if you are condoning his behavior."

Ryan shrugged. "Eh, I'll survive. Now, what do you want to do for dinner? I'm starving."

"I'm not hungry," I stated.

"Too bad. You are coming with anyway. I want to spend time with you before I leave. I need to lay down some rules for you while I'm gone." He smirked.

"Seriously, you're such a moron. Now, I'm definitely not going."

"Yeah, you are. I'm going to finish unpacking the truck and then pack for Los Angeles. You have plenty of time to get past your issues with Brent before we head to dinner."

"You're a terrible brother," I jeered.

He kissed the top of my head. "The fact that you think that proves I'm a great brother." He smiled.

"Again, you're a moron."

He stood at the door. "You're going to dinner, Roxanne. Be ready."

When Ryan called me downstairs a few hours later, I unenthusiastically made my way down.

"Hey, Princess," Brent greeted me as I came into the living room.

I walked by him as if he wasn't there.

"How long are you planning on ignoring me?" Brent asked.

I was not going to give in. I kept my eyes focused on the fireplace as if it were the most fascinating thing I'd ever seen.

"All right." Ryan got up from the couch. "Are you two ready to go?"

Brent and I both stayed quiet.

"Don't answer all at once." Ryan laughed at his own statement, disregarding the fact that nothing he'd said was remotely funny.

I walked out of the house first and made my way to Ryan's Audi S5 Cabriolet. I might have to attend dinner, but I sure as hell didn't have to talk to either one of those assholes. After tonight, they would be on their way to Los Angeles, and I wouldn't have to fucking see them for a month. I couldn't wait to get this dinner over with.

The car ride over to AJ's Steak House was filled with Ryan talking mostly to himself. Brent gave a few unintelligible grunts here and there.

Once at the restaurant, I continued to remain silent, except for when I ordered my food, but that didn't count. I was actually impressed with my own willpower.

Ryan caught my eyes as he took a drink of his soda. "All right, Roxy. I just want to make sure you remember the rules while I'm gone."

I rolled my eyes. It didn't matter what he said. I wasn't planning on following any of them.

"No parties, no drugs, no hooking up with guys, no letting Tonya talk you into some ridiculous scheme," he listed.

I would never understand his need to always blame Tonya for any trouble I got into. She and I were a duo. We split the bonehead ideas equally.

"Roxanne, I'm serious. I can't rush back from Los Angeles if you get into trouble."

I rolled my eyes but stayed silent. *He's an idiot.*

Ryan grunted, "This is a bad idea. I shouldn't even go. You're obviously not responsible enough to be alone for a few weeks. I was wrong to tell Dad that I thought you would be okay by yourself."

Wait—what? This got me to look at him. He'd better go. I was not only looking forward to them being gone, but I was also counting on it. "Are you freaking kidding me? I am plenty responsible," I hissed.

This caused Ryan to snicker. "It's nice to know that you are listening."

"Yes, Ryan, I heard you—no sex, no drugs, no parties. Did I miss anything?"

"Yeah, the part where you never talk about having sex again. I don't want to hear that crap come out of your mouth." He gave me a disgusted look.

"Oh, sorry, I forgot. I mean, it's okay for me to watch you take floozy after floozy to your room, but God forbid your little sister has a sexual bone in her body," I sniped.

I had raised my voice, and people from other tables were now watching us.

Great. Just freaking great.

Ryan pinched the bridge of his nose in frustration.

I let out a deep sigh. "Nothing bad is going to happen. I wish you would just give me a break and not be so overprotective."

"You don't make it very easy, Roxy, but seeing as I don't really have a choice in the matter, I can only hope for the best. Oh, and Dad will be home next weekend. Try to play nice."

"Why he is even coming home? It's not like you will be there, and we both know he doesn't give a damn about me."

"Roxanne!" he warned through clenched teeth.

"What?"

Thankfully, our food came at that moment, forcing us to take a breather and be pleasant. Ryan didn't bother to continue that conversation after our waiter had left. He focused on eating his food as if it were the last meal he would ever have.

For the first time since we'd gotten there, I looked at Brent. He was on his phone, texting. His forehead wrinkled in frustration.

"What's wrong, Brent? Typing out another lie to your girlfriend?" I should have kept my mouth shut, but I was being me, so it hadn't happened.

His eyes shot up at me. I saw the hurt that crossed his face, but I refused to let it get to me. He was the bad guy, not me.

"Roxanne, stop being a—"

I could only guess what the next word out of Ryan's mouth would be.

Brent interrupted, "It's fine, Ryan. And no, Princess, I was texting Jordan. I was letting him know that I'd be out of town for the next few weeks."

"Oh," I said. I didn't want to let on that Jordan had already known that Brent would be gone—or the fact that Jordan was looking forward to it. I poked at my dinner.

"You should ask Jordan to check in on Rox while we're gone, man," Ryan suggested.

Brent's eyes widened. "I didn't think you would want Jordan around her."

"Nah, man. He seemed cool. I think you were overreacting. When he and I talked, he didn't seem like someone I would have to worry about. In fact, it was relief to see a guy with no interest in my sister."

"Um…said sister right here. Stop talking about me like I'm not around. Besides, I will be just fine. I don't need or want a babysitter." I wasn't about to tell them that I was planning on having Jordan in my bed every night.

"I don't know if that is entirely true. I do know that I would feel better if someone kept an eye on you—preferably, someone I didn't have to worry about. Seeing as Brent's gonna be in Los Angeles with me, that leaves Brent's cousin," Ryan declared.

I couldn't believe that Ryan actually thought Jordan wasn't interested in me. Jordan most certainly deserved the Oscar for pulling that off. It took everything I had not to start laughing.

If Ryan only knew the truth…

"I don't think you should be that trusting of my cousin. I know the kid, and believe me, Princess has him interested. I saw the way he looked at her at the lake," Brent chimed in.

"Really, man? Because he just seemed to have other—"

"Ry, trust me. He fed you a load of bullshit," Brent interrupted him. "She isn't someone Jordan would ever overlook. With that said, I've already handled it. I told him to stay away."

"Hello? How can you two continue to talk about me like I'm not here? I hate when you guys do that," I snapped.

"Roxy, unbunch your panties, and I guess stay away from Brent's cousin," Ryan warned.

I had gone beyond crossing the lines, and I wasn't about to uncross them. I'd known Jordan before I'd known who he was.

"Seriously, the guy brought me home. I don't see what makes you think I would ever be around him again." A little lie to keep them in the dark wouldn't hurt anyone.

"Because, Roxanne, I know you, and I know you're upset with Brent right now. I wouldn't put it past you to pull some dumb stunt. Just don't, okay?" Ryan snapped.

Ouch! That's harsh. How could Ryan think I would go out of my way just to piss Brent off? Sure, I was mad at him, but I wasn't vindictive.

"It's not like he's one of your friends, Ryan. He isn't on the do-not-touch list."

"He's Brent's family, and if Brent thinks you should stay away from him, then you will stay away from him. I don't want to hear about you being disrespectful and going against Brent's wishes. He said the kid's no good. Stay the hell away from him."

"You're a dick, and in case you haven't noticed, I don't give a damn what Brent wants." I got up from the table.

Ryan stood up. "Where do you think you're going? Did you forget I drove here?"

"Don't worry. I'll find my own way home. Or you could give me Jordan's number. Maybe he'll pick me up. You don't mind him chauffeuring me around when it suits you."

"Roxanne," Ryan hissed.

"Have fun in Los Angeles," I said before walking away.

I couldn't wait for my brother to leave.

I left the restaurant and started walking down the street. I called Tonya to pick me up, but she didn't answer.

Great.

I was going to call Jordan, but I knew that would only cause more drama if Ryan or Brent somehow saw him with me. My threat back there had been just that. I didn't need to give Ryan any real reason not to leave for Los Angeles. He was crazy enough that he might just stay if he saw me with Jordan.

I chose to call Ethan instead. Like always, he was dependable. He picked me up and took me home. When he dropped me off, we made plans to have dinner in a few days. I missed Ethan, and I was glad that my crazy drunken night at my party hadn't destroyed our friendship.

16

Once I was in the house, I called Jordan. I had missed him, and I was tired of fighting the urge to talk to him.

"Hi ya, baby!" he answered.

"Hey."

Just hearing Jordan's happy voice made me smile. It didn't matter how irritated I was with Brent and Ryan. Jordan had a way of making all that just disappear.

He and his flipping magical ways.

"I miss you."

"Would you like to come over for dinner tonight?"

"Weren't you just at dinner?" he questioned.

Brent must have mentioned it when texting him. "Yes, I was at dinner, but I didn't eat. So, are you coming over tonight or not?"

"A deranged serial killer couldn't keep me away."

I could hear him smiling again, and it made my stomach flutter in anticipation of seeing him.

I giggled. He had a way of turning me into a giggling goof.

"Good. Be here at eight. That way, Ryan and Brent will already be out of town."

"See you at eight, babe."

"See you then."

After hanging up, I hugged my phone to my chest. I was extremely excited about seeing him later. I rushed upstairs to figure out what I was going to wear.

When Ryan and Brent came back home, I had every intention of ignoring them until they left, but Ryan wasn't about to let that happen. He marched into my room, chewed me out for leaving dinner the way I had.

Sure, Ryan was an overbearing ass most of the time, but it was easy to overlook his flaws when he was the only person I had left who loved me unconditionally despite the fact that I was completely broken and mildly crazy at times.

After I knew they were gone, I ran upstairs to change into the dress I had picked out earlier. It was a sky-blue strapless A-line dress that hung mid-thigh. The skirt had layered ruffles that accented my curves. The color made my blue eyes pop. I knew Jordan would love it. I was a ball of excitement while getting dressed.

While making dinner, I was extremely nervous about having Jordan over tonight. Jordan and I still needed to talk about some things, but after the perfection of last night, I didn't want to think about what everything meant. I was scared that if we had the conversation about what was going on with us and what it all meant, then whatever this was would end.

The doorbell rang, making me jump. Ready or not, he was here.

I opened the door to see Jordan's smiling beautiful face. All my nervous feelings faded with that smile.

Oh, Jordan and his magic.

He offered me a bouquet of lilies, and another piece of the wall guarding my heart crumbled. While Jordan had been in Oregon, I had mentioned in a text that lilies were my favorite flower.

I thought of my mom's words after an old lady from down the street had brought her a bouquet of roses.

"Roxanne, honey," she said, putting the flowers in a vase, "roses are the slut of flowers. They are given to everyone. You want to be given a flower that shows someone cared enough about you to remember your favorite. So, choose one wisely."

I had been with Kevin for four years, and no matter how many times I'd told him that I hated roses, it was what he'd always brought me. Lilies, on the other hand, were special. Proving that my mother had been right, the fact that Jordan had remembered made me feel special.

"Whoa, Rox! You...you look unbelievably gorgeous." His eyes drifted over my body.

I was no longer thinking about Kevin or my mother. I accepted the flowers from Jordan with a huge smile on my face.

"You're pretty unbelievable, too."

And he was. He was dressed in dark blue jeans with a white long-sleeved button-up shirt. It was a simple combination, but on him, it equaled stunning. After giving him a quick peck on the cheek, I gestured for him to come in, and I headed back into the kitchen to put my flowers in a vase. My body warmed in the way only Jordan could make it. I mentally compromised with myself that I would stay calm through dinner before I went all sex-crazed attacker on him.

Jordan wrapped his arms around my waist and brushed kisses from my right shoulder up to the side of my neck.

Okay, is he trying to kill me here? How am I supposed to keep my composure with him making me melt?

"I'm trying to cook you dinner, and if you don't stop that, I won't be able to finish it. Then, we won't have anything to eat, and I will be sad because you didn't get to taste the amazing dinner you were supposed to have."

Jordan slowly moved his left hand down my waist and then to my ass where he gave a small squeeze before taking a step back. "You're right. I'm sorry. I couldn't resist."

When I turned around, the smile on his face was almost enough to make me throw my resolve out the window, but I really wanted tonight to be perfect. I gave him another quick kiss and then finished preparing dinner.

Considering how much he'd enjoyed the meal, I felt it was worth all the extra effort it had taken to keep my clothes on and finish it.

"Baby, you are an amazing cook. That was delicious." He rubbed his stomach in appreciation.

I stifled a laugh. "Thanks. My mom taught me how to cook. Her cooking was always phenomenal, but she was known and worshiped for her baking." I was happy to share parts of my mom with Jordan. Once again, I was able to talk about her without the throbbing pain taking over. This still amazed me.

"Are you telling me that you can bake, too? If you can make snickerdoodles half as good as this meal was, I might just have to marry you."

I started to clear the table with a smile that I didn't feel right giving him. It made my stomach contort in discomfort to hear Jordan talk about marrying me, even as a joke. I didn't have some delusional idea that he and I would run off into the sunset and live happily ever after. I didn't even believe in that shit. I knew it didn't exist. People could hurt and betray you. In the rare chance that a couple did find real death-do-you-part love, then death would fucking part them. I only had to look at my dad to know that happily ever afters were a myth.

I took a breath and shook off my uneasiness. There was no sense in getting caught up in thinking about stuff that would never happen.

I put the dish in the sink "I do bake, but don't go running out to buy a ring. I only bake for extremely important people.

I turned and leaned against the counter. Jordan made his way over to me. He was now standing in front of me. His fingers pushed away the few curls that had fallen from my clip and into my face.

"You just wait and see, Rox. I'll make that list one day."

His words made my breath hitch. I swallowed hard before biting down on my bottom lip. His thumb eased my lip from between my teeth before he closed the space between us and kissed me. His kiss was tender but loaded with passion. If I hadn't wrapped my arms around his neck, I would have collapsed from how weak my knees felt.

Jordan's eyes were hungry. "I'm ready for dessert."

"Um…I actually didn't plan any. I'm sorry. I ran out of time. I think we might have some ice cream?"

I dropped my arms from around his neck, and in that same moment, he swept me up into his arms.

"If you didn't bake it, I don't want it. I just want you." He carried me to the stairs.

I didn't know why the boy always wanted to carry me, but I wasn't about to have him put me down.

Part of me knew that I should stop him and that we should have the conversation about what this was between us. But that part was very, very small. The other part of me just wanted to go up to my room and enjoy every bit of Jordan. So, that was exactly what I did.

As we both lay naked in my bed, Jordan traced his fingers up and down the curve of my waist.

"I will never get tired of seeing this." Jordan's breath was hot against my neck.

"Uh-huh. Sure you won't," I teased.

"You don't believe me?" he asked as he propped himself up on his elbow.

"That is the beauty of this." I motioned between us. "I don't have to believe you because this is temporary, remember?"

Jordan sat up. "You're still on that, Rox? I thought after yesterday and tonight you would understand how I feel about you."

Why couldn't I just keep my big mouth shut? I didn't want to have this conversation right now. I wanted to go back to happy-after-sex land.

"Forget I even said that. Just lie back down. I'll make it worth your while." I wiggled my eyebrows.

"We said we would talk about everything later. It's later. What is this to you, Roxy?"

I pulled the blanket up to my chest. *Good-bye, happy-after-sex land.* "The day we met, I told you that I didn't want a boyfriend. That hasn't changed."

"Is this about your rules? Because I hate to point out that you haven't exactly been abiding by them."

"That doesn't mean they don't exist. I might not have followed any of those rules, but I have reasons for making them." I wouldn't be able to handle the heart-shattering pain that came from loving someone and then losing him. I was already broken. *How am I supposed to put my heart on the line and chance that he won't break it?* I couldn't. I knew I wouldn't survive that kind of heartbreak again.

"Oh, of course. That way, you can hide behind them, so you don't have to commit to someone. Well, aren't you the smart one?" He tapped his finger to his forehead in a mocking way.

I hated the tone he had used with me. He had known what this was from the beginning. We'd both said that we didn't want anything serious.

"What the heck happened to you not looking for anything serious either?" I didn't mean to be snappy, but he was starting to piss me off.

"*You.* You happened. You came into my life like a whirlwind and kissed me, remember?"

"Jordan, why can't this just be what it is? We don't have to ruin it with mushy talk."

"You are the strangest girl I have ever known. Do you have any idea how many girls have begged me to give them more than just one night? And here you are, telling me you don't want me for any more than sex."

Wow. Way to ruin whatever we might have had.

"First of all, I really don't want to hear about the horde of girls you've fucked before me right after you've fucked me. Second, I told you that I didn't want a boyfriend the day we met." *How many times do I have to keep reminding him of that?*

Jordan stood up and began to get dressed. "Then, I don't see why it matters to you who I was with before."

"I can't give you any more than this," I told him.

"Can't or won't, Rox? From what I have noticed, you are capable of anything. I don't see why you won't try."

The look on his face hurt me.

"Why can't you just be okay with what this is and let it be?" I pleaded.

"You know what, Rox? You're right. It is what it is." He started moving out of the room.

"Wait—where are you going? Why are you still leaving?" I yelled after him.

"No sleepovers, remember, Rox? Besides, I'm not your boyfriend. I don't have to tell you where I'm going."

"Jordan!" I wrapped the sheet around me and followed him downstairs. "Jordan, don't go like this," I called after him.

"I'll call you later, Roxy." He walked out the front door.

"Jordan!" I ran after him. *How the hell did I become the girl chasing after a guy? Damn it! I thought not having a boyfriend meant avoiding this fighting crap.* "Jordan, please wait!"

Jordan turned around "What, Roxy?"

"I don't want you to go."

"Why do you want me to stay? Doesn't that go against your ridiculous rules?"

"You're right. Those rules are ridiculous. Please understand that I made up those rules in the moment to try to make sure we wouldn't get too close. We were never supposed to be anything. I can't handle getting hurt again. That's all I'm doing. I'm trying to keep myself from getting hurt."

"I'm not going to hurt you, Rox."

"You might not want to, but that doesn't mean you won't. I can't tell you what we're doing, Jordan, because I don't know. I have never been in this situation before. I don't know what this is or where it might or might not go. All I know is that I don't want you to leave."

"I want more from you."

I could see how much he meant that.

"I know, and I wish I could give that to you, but I can't—not right now, maybe not ever. Right now though, I'm naked underneath a sheet, standing outside in the middle of the night, and I'm asking you not to leave. Don't you see that if I didn't care about you, I wouldn't have chased after you? This is kind of huge for me. Please try to be patient with me. Please stay."

Jordan walked over to me and traced his hand down the side of my face. "You did chase after me."

"I did." I smiled. I wanted him to stay. Part of me even felt that I needed him to stay.

"I'm not gonna stop wanting more," he reminded me.

"I know. But can we take it one day at a time?"

"One day at a time." He kissed me.

That kiss was full of all the emotion I felt. It said everything I wanted to say but couldn't. That kiss was perfect. That kiss was the beginning of something new, something I wasn't sure I would be able to survive.

In the morning, I awoke to Jordan lying on his side, staring at me. He had chosen to stay, and it had changed things between us. I wasn't willing to put a label on what this was, but all the emotions were there. As much as it scared me, I knew I was way past just liking Jordan.

Looking at him, lying there and staring at me, made me want to start crying, and it surprised me. I didn't feel like crying in the normal gut-wrenching and sad way. My emotions were of pure happiness.

"I have plans for us today. Time to get up, babe." He grinned.

"What kind of plans?"

"The date kind. I wanna take you out. We have never had a real date, and I want one."

"Hey, I made you dinner last night and gave you amazing sex. What do you call that?"

"Everything about last night was sensational, but I have a special day planned, and you are going to love it." He kissed me.

"I don't know. I don't think you can top this." I ran my hand down his chest. "We should just stay in bed all day." I smiled against his lips.

He kissed my nose and then rolled off the bed. "Nope. Today, I am taking you out."

I crossed my arms and mock-pouted. "But…but…but I'm naked, and I want you."

He pulled the blanket with me on it toward the edge of the bed. "You can have me." He scooped me up, causing me to squeal. "But you will have to have me in the shower. We're on a schedule. We have a long day ahead of us."

I kissed his mouth. "Well, I guess that's okay—as long as I get you in the shower first."

17

Jordan and I had breakfast at a small café not far from the beach where we'd met. During breakfast, I couldn't stop thinking about how crazy it was that I had parked behind him that day. If it wasn't fate, maybe it was something better, like a gift.

I looked at Jordan and smiled. Maybe he was a gift from my mom. I knew how crazy the thought was, but it didn't stop me from wanting to believe it. Everything was better since Jordan had come into my life. There was also the fact that, for whatever reason, he could make the pain go away.

"What are you thinking about, babe?"

"Nothing much."

He raised an eyebrow at me. "I doubt that."

"So, what are we doing today?" I asked, changing the subject.

Jordan reached down and picked up the bag he'd brought in with us. "After you eat, I need you to change." He handed me the bag.

I pulled out a pink one-piece bathing suit. "This is why you ran into the surf shop before coming here?"

"Yes."

"You know, I have, like, thirty different bikinis at home, right? You didn't have to buy me a bathing suit. And a one-piece? Really?"

"I can only imagine how many bikinis you have, but I didn't want you in one today. I want you in that. It's a small, so it should fit."

The bathing suit had a high neckline and thick shoulder straps. The most revealing part of the suit was from the crisscross lines on the back. It was something I normally wouldn't be caught dead in.

"It's, um…" I tried to find the right words.

"It's pink." He smiled.

"It is." I smiled weakly. "It's also, um…"

"You hate it," he stated.

"Sorry, but yeah." I gave a small laugh.

"That's fine. I didn't think you would like it, but it is what you're going to wear."

"Wait—what? You got me a bathing suit that you knew I wouldn't like?"

"No, I said that I didn't think you would like it, not that I didn't want you to."

"So, why did you get it?"

"Because, Rox, I'm taking you down to the beach today, and guys are going to stare at you no matter what you're in. I don't want them to have more of a reason to stare than necessary. I want today to be perfect, and if I have to fight off guys, it won't be."

"So, you thought an ugly pink bathing suit would help make today perfect?"

"Are you mad?" He looked genuinely worried.

"No, I'm not mad." I chuckled. "I just think you're crazy. You're in luck. I have a lot of experience with crazy."

"I can accept that you think I'm crazy. You make me feel that way," he admitted.

I pushed away from the table. "I'm going to put on this monstrosity, but just so you know, I could rock a black plastic bag if I needed to. You should stop worrying about who is looking at me, and remember that I'm spending the day with you." I kissed his cheek.

"Easier said than done, babe." He sighed.

I walked away to find the ladies' room.

After I put on the swimsuit, I looked at myself in the mirror. The swimsuit looked as atrocious on as I'd thought it would, but I wasn't about to let Jordan know that he was right about not calling attention to myself. The suit was anything but sexy. I didn't care if anyone else was looking at me, but I did want to look good for Jordan.

Oh well. It's his loss.

Once we were outside, Jordan laced his fingers through mine and kissed the side of my head. "I don't even get to see what it looks like?"

"You will be lucky if I ever take my dress off," I huffed.

"I thought you said you could rock a plastic bag."

"I could work with a plastic bag. There is no altering this pink nightmare you bought."

He took my hand. "Do you really hate it that much?" His eyes showed his disappointment.

I forced a chuckle. "It's fine. I know your heart was in the right place even if your heart is a tiny bit jealous. Let's have fun, okay?" I squeezed his hand three times, and then I quickly pulled my hand out of his as if it were on fire. *Oh my God. I did not just do that.*

"Whoa. What's wrong?" He was clearly concerned.

"Hand spasm," I lied. I held up my hand as if to prove something was wrong with it. There had to be something wrong with it. Three squeezes were saved for certain individuals—those I loved.

I swallowed hard. Right now was not a time to think it over. I would just enjoy the day. I could go crazy with what it all meant later even though I was pretty sure I already knew the answer.

"You know, I am kind of surprised you picked the beach as part of our date today." I pulled my hair into a high messy bun. I checked my reflection in the window of his truck. At least it wasn't a giant frizzy mess.

Jordan stood behind me. "You have no idea how sexy you look with your hair up." He wrapped his arms around my waist and nibbled on the back of my neck. "This part right here"—he kissed the nape of my neck—"drives me absolutely insane."

He pulled me closer against him, so I could feel through his shorts just how crazy I was making him. I felt my cheeks heat, and a familiar warm feeling began pooling below my waist. My body went weak in his arms. He pecked the side of my neck once before stepping back. I was amazed that I hadn't fallen back on my ass when he had done that.

"Okay, baby, are you ready for a day of fun?" His mouth pulled into an excited smile.

"Again, I'm not sure why you picked the beach." I grinned.

He pulled two boards from his truck. One was way longer than the other. "Where else am I supposed to take you surfing?"

Jordan effortlessly carried both boards as we made our way down to the sand.

"I just feel like we haven't had the best of luck on beaches. So, if I drown today, I'm holding you completely responsible."

"Are you kidding me? We have had great luck with beaches. I won't let you drown."

"Great luck? How do you figure?" I gave him a cynical look.

"Well, I met you not far from here. Then, I found you again on this beach in that hot-pink bikini, and in case you have forgotten, our first kiss—our first *real* kiss—involved this beach, too. Actually, it's kind of our spot, and I can't think of a better place to spend the day."

"Funny, I seem to remember things very differently. I remember feeling humiliated because I had to kiss you, a complete stranger, to save face in front of my ex. Then, let's not forget the night we were on this beach, and you called me a whore. Oh, and there was that amazing glass-in-my-foot incident not too far from here, which was followed by me passing out. Once again, that was completely humiliating. But you are right about one thing. It is kind of our spot. I just don't know if it's a good one."

"I jumped to a conclusion, but I never called you a whore, Rox." He sounded defeated.

"Oh, you implied it." I smiled, trying to push the mood back to playful.

"Do you always just remember the bad stuff?" Jordan asked.

I shrugged. "What can I say? I'm a pessimist."

Jordan shook his head and smiled at me. "Life is made up of moments—good moments, bad moments, and so-so moments. Some moments make enough of a mark on your soul that they become memories. Bad moments have an easier time of becoming memories because they rock us and shake us out of our happy little bubble, making a deep mark. Too many people take being happy for granted, like it's something they are owed, so it has less meaning when it happens. Those good moments don't get to make their mark because we just let them pass us by.

"I say, you start enjoying the good and the happy moments, and don't ever let them slip away. They are easy to take for granted, but that's why you must hold on to them with all you have. If you don't, then the bad moments will be all you remember. If you begin making deeper marks with all your good moments instead of just letting them pass you by, only then will the good memories become more powerful and memorable than the bad."

Who would have guessed that Jordan was so deep?

As for actually buying the beautiful words he'd said, I wasn't completely sold. My eyes rolled back before I could stop them.

"I feel like you don't believe me."

"No, it's not that. It's a beautiful sentiment, but I don't think any amount of good moments could ever overpower the bad ones."

"Okay, humor me for a minute then." He laid the boards down on the sand. "Your first love was Kevin, right?"

Really? He is bringing up Kevin? Seriously? "Um...yeah. Your point?" I was slightly frustrated.

"My point is, he was also your first heartbreak."

I shook my head in annoyance and turned to walk away. *Way to ruin the day, Jordan.*

"Hold on." He caught my wrist. "Before you go and turn into Mighty Mouse, just hear me out."

I pulled my wrist from his hold and crossed my arms over my chest.

"Would you erase the memory of the moment you fell in love with him just to avoid the pain he caused you?"

"Yes," I answered quickly.

"Really? You would go back and delete that moment from your life?" He was completely serious.

I took the time to really think about it instead of quickly answering. "No, I guess I wouldn't because I would lose something essential if I did," I reluctantly admitted.

"Exactly. The moment you realized you loved Kevin, that happy moment, left a deep mark. That mark led to other marks, and they outweigh the painful memory that losing him left. If they didn't, you would have answered yes. You would have wanted to go back and not fall in love. But undoing that good moment seemed worse than living through the pain he caused. The good moments were more powerful than the bad."

I shrugged. He might be right, but the last thing I wanted was to think about Kevin right now. Thinking of Kevin made me feel more like shutting down than opening up to letting memories in.

"Okay, I can tell that you're still skeptical. How about a different example? This one will probably hurt, too, but please know that I'm not trying to hurt you."

"Are you trying to make me leave?" I gave a small laugh.

"No, baby. I'm trying to make sure you truly understand."

I was scared about what he was going to say.

"Think about your mom," Jordan said.

My heart ached with how much I missed her. Without a doubt, I knew I wouldn't erase one moment I'd ever had with my mom even if it meant that I wouldn't have to feel this hurt.

Jordan wrapped his arms around me. "After my dad died, there were so many times that I prayed I could just forget him altogether. I thought that if I did, the pain I was feeling would finally end. Then, one morning, I realized I couldn't remember what his laugh sounded like. I sat in my living room, watching old recorded videos we had for hours and hours. Over and over, I would rewind the parts where he laughed. That was when I realized how important it was not to let the good moments in my life just pass me by."

A single tear slid down my cheek. Once again, another small piece of the wall guarding my heart fell and disappeared.

"I understand completely. I will try not to take my happy moments for granted, but I have to admit that this moment right now is not making that list." I pulled away and gave him a sad smirk.

He ran the back of his hand down the side of my face. "Don't worry, Rox. I plan on filling your life with tons of happy moments. I just wanted to make sure you wouldn't take them for granted along the way."

"Oh, really?" I smiled. I was glad it was a real smile.

"Yes, we are going to have moments that will be burned into your soul, the kind you never forget, and we're going to make as many as we can," he said, picking up one surfboard.

"And you expect surfing to be one of those moments? I don't see how drowning me is going to make a good mark. Bad mark? Maybe. But good?" I was a bit skeptical.

"You told me you have never been surfing. First times of anything are the easiest ways to make deep marks and great happy memories." He grinned.

He was excited about this, and it was hard not to become excited with him.

"You know, I kind of think you're perfect." I blushed at my honesty.

"Good. Keep thinking that. That way, I get to keep you."

"Whoa! Who said I'm up for keeps?" I teased.

"I'm just hoping the beach continues to be my lucky spot because I have every intention of keeping you."

"Well, when you put it that way, for today and today only, I'm all yours." I couldn't stop the ridiculous grin crossing my face.

"I'm not going to want to go back to you not being all mine." His eyes were serious.

"I'm sure you won't. No one ever does." I sighed humorously. "It's a hazard of hanging out with me. I'm kind of addictive, but I'm sure we can find you an RA meeting after today. Stick to the steps, and you will be on the road to recovery in no time," I joshed.

Jordan raised a questioning eyebrow. "RA?"

I mocked surprise. "You've never heard of Roxanne Anonymous? It's where all the guys who have fallen for my charming ways get together to discuss how horrible their lives are without me. They developed a step-by-step method to help them cope with life after me. I hate to tell you, but there is no cure for getting over the amazing Roxanne Daniels, only ways of coping with the pain." I giggled.

Jordan laughed. "All right, you. How about you and your ginormous head step off of your overly confident box, or I'm going to start saying things just to deflate that ego of yours?"

"Aw, don't lie. What you really want to tell me is that I'm beautiful, stunning, sexy." I vogued with each adjective.

"You're impossible." He shook his head. "How about I tell you that you look like a dead seal on a board? Would that help?" he jabbed.

I covered my mouth in utter shock. Okay, it was mostly to hide my smile. "Are you calling me fat?" I feigned disbelief.

Jordan's eyes widened. "No, not at all. I was just—"

I busted out laughing and interrupted Jordan's attempts to assure me that he was just kidding.

"Jordan, you are going to have to try much harder if you want to deflate my ego because, babe, you suck," I stated.

"Hey, hey, I'm not the one who needs my ego to be deflated." He acted hurt.

I danced in circles with a huge grin on my face. "Sorry, my bad. Come on, loser. Teach this seal how to surf."

He laughed at me. "You're going to be using the longboard."

I went to pick it up, and I couldn't believe how heavy it was. *Good Lord. How did he carry both of these boards down here and make it look like nothing?*

"Before you go dragging the board into the water, you should know that your lesson begins right here on the sand." He grinned.

"You're going to teach me how to surf on the sand?" I asked. That was the dumbest thing I'd ever heard.

"Yep. Lie down with your stomach on the board and try not to break it, fatty." He chuckled.

"Aw, I'm so proud. That was much better. If my ego wasn't so big, I might have even been a little hurt." I lay with my chest on the board.

"I'm going easy on you and playing it safe. I know that a hurt you equals a mad you. Then, Mighty Mouse comes out, and all hell breaks loose."

"Yeah, you'd better play it safe. This Mighty Mouse will kick your ass," I threatened playfully.

"Now, that's something I just might enjoy." He devilishly smiled down at me.

Jordan spent the next couple of hours, teaching me how to pop up and land my stance while still on the sand. He told me all about feeling for the right wave. None of the water talk was making much sense since I couldn't imagine the water below me.

This is ridiculous.

After plenty of complaining from me and mostly begging to just get in the water, Jordan finally gave in. We made our way into the ocean.

18

The next few days with Jordan were picture-perfect, like chick-flick worthy. He'd spent every night at my house. We'd watched movies and played games. He'd even attempted to cook for me. I'd distracted him by kissing him, which had led to him kissing me back. That had turned into us making out, hot and heavy, and dinner had ended up getting burned, but it was the thought that had counted. This week had been so incredible that I hadn't even been annoyed with my brother's daily calls and texts. I had felt too happy to even care.

I was putting the popcorn in the microwave when Tonya came barreling through the front door.

"Roxy," she called.

I hit Start on the microwave, and then I met her in the living room. "Hey, chica, what's up?"

"What's up is that you haven't been returning my calls. All I have gotten from you over the past few days are vague text messages. I'm in a funk, and I need my best friend."

Jordan snickered on the couch. "You couldn't just call?"

"Like I said, I have been calling." She glared at him. "Roxy has obviously been too busy with you to pick up. I'm pulling out the BFF card. Whatever plans you had, Romeo, you're SOL. She's mine tonight."

I gave Jordan an apologetic look. Tonya collapsed on the couch opposite of the one Jordan was sitting on.

I sat down next to her. "What's going on, girlie?"

"I think I am falling in love with Shawn, and I don't know how to freaking stop it," she whined.

Jordan choked back a laugh. That got him death glares from Tonya and me.

"I'm going to go check on the popcorn. I think I heard the microwave beep," he said, getting up and heading to the kitchen.

"What's wrong with falling for Shawn? From everything you've told me, he seems like a nice guy."

"Rox, are you not hearing me? You are supposed to be the one with all the brains. How can you think the way I feel for Shawn is okay?" She was freaking out.

"So…it's not okay?" I didn't know what she wanted me to say.

"No! No! No! It's not okay, Roxy. I have known him for less than a week. I should not be feeling this way. It's beyond wrong."

"Just because it's fast doesn't make it any less real."

"Less than a fucking week, Roxy. That is beyond fast. I mean, come on. Who are you? And what have you done with my cynical best friend? I want her back," she demanded.

Jordan snickered in the kitchen.

"Don't make me come in there and cut your balls off!" Tonya yelled. She was in grouch mode.

Apparently, this is a very serious matter.

"Breathe, Ton. Most likely, you aren't falling in love with him. It is probably just extreme infatuation."

She snuggled into me. "You think?"

"Yes, the only part of you in love with him is below your waist. You are confusing lust with love. That's all this is."

"Promise?" She looked up at me with sad puppy-dog eyes. She looked adorably pathetic.

"Well, I can't promise you that. I'm not you. But whatever you're feeling, I promise to be here, no matter the outcome."

"Good to know if I go crazy over some guy, you'll still be my friend."

I laughed. "Always."

Jordan came in with a bowl of popcorn. "Is it safe?"

"Keep asking questions like that, and it won't be," Tonya sneered.

Jordan made himself comfortable on the other couch. I hated that he was sitting by himself when tonight was supposed to be our night, but Tonya needed me, and he had gotten me to himself all week.

"Did you ever have dinner with Ethan?" Tonya asked.

Jordan shot me a look.

"Um...no. I have been busy this week. I sent him a text, telling him I couldn't make it. We rescheduled for next week."

Jordan's eyes were still on me and full of questions.

Great.

It wasn't that I had been hiding this from Jordan. It just wasn't that important to talk about.

"Just making sure you're on good terms because he is having a party tomorrow. Shawn is coming up on Saturday, and it seems like the perfect way to get rid of this anxious feeling. Do you wanna go?"

I really wished she hadn't mentioned the party in front of Jordan. He was leaving tomorrow to go home to see his mom. I didn't want him to think I was waiting for him to leave to go party—not that I had to explain myself or what I would be doing. He and I hadn't put a title on our relationship.

"Yeah, he sent me an invite today."

Jordan's whole body visually tensed at my words.

"But I'm not sure if I want to go."

That didn't help ease his tension.

"Please, Rox. I need something to get my mind off Shawn, or I'll go crazy. What if I say the wrong thing to him and it makes him run away from the psycho girl? Please…" she begged.

"I'll think about it, Ton."

"Fine." She sighed. "What movie are we watching?"

Jordan stood up and handed me the remote and Tonya the popcorn.

"Where are you going?" I asked.

"Bed. Early flight, remember?" His words were flat.

I hated that he was upset, but he had no right to be upset. I hadn't done anything wrong.

"Okay, I will be up in a bit."

He walked away without another word.

Seriously? This was not how I'd wanted his last night here to go.

Stupid, stupid Tonya and her big stupid, stupid mouth.

Tonya got a call from Shawn five minutes into the movie. She ignored it. Then, five minutes later, she got up, saying that she should get home and get some rest. I knew she was lying, but I wasn't about to call her out on it. She wanted to talk with Shawn, and I wanted to salvage my evening with Jordan.

After seeing her out, I made my way upstairs. I slipped off my clothes, except for my panties, and I crawled into bed. I started kissing up Jordan's chest, hoping that would change his mood into a much happier one.

"I'm tired, Rox."

Jordan's statement not only shocked me, but it stung.

Is he really that upset about a dinner with a friend that I didn't even go to? I mean, what guy fucking turns down sex? Oh, right. This guy does.

"You're kidding me, right? You're leaving tomorrow. You don't want to enjoy the time we have before you go?"

"Not in the mood, Rox. Maybe you can call Ethan. I'm sure he would love to help you out."

"Oh no, you don't get to do that. Ethan is my friend," I stated.

"You seem to have forgotten that I've seen the way the guy looks at you. Trust me. He doesn't want to be your friend, Rox."

"I have been friends with Ethan since kindergarten. You can't tell me how you think he feels. I won't let you sit here and play the jealous-boyfriend card. Let's not forget, you're not even my boyfriend."

Jordan shot up. "And whose choice is that?"

"Mine. And this is why. I don't want to be with someone who thinks he can tell me who I can or can't hang out with. I had enough of that with Kevin, and look what that got me—a big Fuck You, I'm Sleeping with Your Friend."

"I'm not him, Roxy. Stop pushing me away because of what he did to you," he pleaded.

"I'm not pushing you away. I just don't want a boyfriend. What is wrong with what we have? It's been perfect all week long." I rubbed his forearm, trying to reassure him that things were great just as they were.

"Perfect for whom? You think I want to leave? I know you can run off and fuck whomever you want the moment I'm gone," he snapped.

"First of all, I have no plans of running off and fucking anyone. Second, if I did want that, I wouldn't have to wait for you to leave." His accusations were pissing me off.

He stood up and started pacing in front of the bed, rubbing his hand through his hair. "Roxy, you are making me crazy. I can't keep doing this."

I didn't know what else to tell him. I had already told him what I was capable of. I couldn't give him any more. I wasn't ready. I didn't understand why he couldn't just be okay with what we had. I also couldn't stand him telling me that he couldn't do this with me.

If that's how he feels, then why the hell is he still here?

"You know what? Then, don't. If you can't handle what I am offering, then leave because I'm not ready to give you anything else."

"I told you that I wasn't going to stop wanting more, but here you go again, pushing me away when I remind you what I want. You are always pushing me away." He dropped his arm, defeated.

"Do you not remember that I ran after you the last time you walked away from me? I do not always push you away. I cannot give you any more than this. I don't know how to, and I'm not ready. If this isn't good enough for you, then you should leave, but if you choose to leave, I won't run after you this time. Don't expect me to."

"I wouldn't expect you to do anything that takes work, Roxy, and that's what relationships are. They are work, give and take. I was delusional to think you would ever want to have one with me."

His words sliced through me. My teeth clenched, and I was holding back tears. I dug my nails into my palms. I wouldn't let him see me fall apart.

He wasn't all the way wrong. I wasn't ready to jump into another relationship. I didn't know if I ever would be, but it wasn't just with him. It was with anyone.

Jordan put on his shoes and left my room. There was no more yelling or slamming of doors. He just left.

With him, he took a piece of my heart that I had been trying hard to protect.

So much for being strong.

I curled up on my side, wrapped my arms around myself, and let my tears fall. The tears didn't help to lessen the ache. It was still there as I cried all night.

Finally, I cried myself to sleep.

19

"Thank you, thank you, thank you for this." Tonya linked her arm through mine.

"It's not like I had anything better to do." I smiled at her.

"I'm sorry Jordan was an ass to you. He shouldn't have said what he did."

"Yeah, well…he wasn't all wrong either."

"That doesn't matter. You told him what you were willing to give. He should have dropped it there. Besides, any time with you is a gift. He's a douche not to see that."

"Thanks, Ton, but the last thing I want to do tonight is talk or think about Jordan."

I knew the not-thinking-about-him part was going to be pretty impossible, but I sure as hell didn't have to talk about him. After he'd walked out last night, I'd half-expected a call from him today, saying he was sorry. That call never came. By now, he was in Oregon and probably not thinking about me at all.

I need a drink.

Tonya and I walked up the stone staircase to the front door. I had always considered my family in the above-average range when it came to wealth. Ethan's family, however, was more like Brent's—obscenely wealthy and then some. While I'd gotten a BMW M3 for my sixteenth birthday, Ethan had received a brand-spanking-new Maserati GranTurismo Convertible.

Ethan never acted like a spoiled rich kid, and I honestly adored him for that. Ethan's father, a famous Hollywood director, was in Los Angeles directing top box-office movies while Ethan, his mother, and younger brother lived here on the Central Coast in San Luis Obispo. We'd bonded over having absentee fathers when we were in elementary school. It was something a person had to experience to really understand.

Not only was his family's property on twenty acres, but it also looked like something straight out of the movies. I guessed that was expected since his father was a movie director. Their ginormous house had indoor and outdoor pools, a full-scale indoor professional basketball court, a home gym, tennis courts outside, and a stadium-sized baseball field. Ethan's father had hired people to build the field when Ethan started playing little league.

I missed coming here and spending time with everyone. As much as I might have missed it, my chest still tightened as we walked through the front door.

Hello, racing heart. How I haven't missed you.

Music was blasting, and Tonya's hips instantly started to swing. From the amount of cars parked outside, more than a hundred people had to be here, not that anyone could tell. They were all spread out over the large floor plan. I watched Tonya twist and spin as she tried to get me to dance with her. Usually, I would be all over it, but I wasn't really in a dancing mood right then. I needed a drink, and maybe then I would change my mind.

We made our way to the outside bar in the backyard. Only Ethan's mom would hire a bartender for her teenage son's party. I was used to Mrs. Frost's inappropriate parental behavior. I remembered how much my mom had absolutely despised her for it, but she never told me I wasn't allowed to hang out with Ethan.

She'd reminded me that it would be unfair to judge him for his mother's shortcomings. As she had said, "You should never judge anyone based on his or her parents."

With that said, my mother always asked me not to drink, but peer pressure and my enjoyment of drinking had usually won out. After a party at Ethan's, Tonya and I had stumbled into my house, drunk. That was the last time she'd trusted me to abstain from drinking. Since she'd no longer thought I was responsible, my mom had begun dropping me off and picking me up from parties.

Thinking about my mom made the ache intensify. *God, I miss her.*

I ordered a double shot of Patrón from the bartender, and as soon as he handed it to me, I threw it back.

"I like the way you think, sister." Tonya ordered two more double shots of Patrón. "Here is to forgetting about stupid boys who make you feel crazy."

Two arms hugged me from behind and lifted me off the ground. "Damn, Roxy. What did I tell you about eating? You need to get on that." Ethan chuckled into my hair before setting me back down. He gave Tonya a not-as-overly-affectionate hug. "Hey, Ton."

"Great turnout." Tonya beamed.

I ordered a strawberry margarita. I tapped my fingernails on the bar as I waited for it to be made. When I got the margarita, I took a sip and involuntarily shook. *Fucking mixed drinks.*

I turned and smiled at Ethan. "Thanks for the invite."

Ethan smiled, his brilliant blue eyes sparkling. "You are always invited to any party I'm throwing. You know that. It wouldn't be a party without you here." He cleared his throat and quickly looked away from me. "Without the both of you, I mean."

"Uh-huh. Sure, that's what you meant," Tonya teased.

I smiled at the slight reddening of Ethan's cheeks. He was adorable when he blushed.

"I have to make my way around one more time, but after I'm back, we're"—he pointed in the air and then made a circling motion between the three of us—"gonna hang."

"Sounds like a plan." I was already feeling the warming effects of the tequila. The ache in my chest was still there though.

I tried gulping my margarita, but all that did was give me brain freeze. *Note to self: Don't try that again.*

"Fuck." I pressed the palm of my free hand to my forehead, and I started rubbing my tongue on the roof of my mouth, hoping it would help my head to stop hurting.

After about thirty seconds, I was all better.

Ethan had turned and made his way back to me. "Try to take it easy there, Roxy." He rubbed his hand down my arm.

He was sweet for worrying, but I knew what I was doing, and I knew what I didn't want to think about or feel.

I kissed Ethan on the cheek. "Don't get lost. There is tons of fun to be had."

I realized I had surprised him with the kiss. I guessed it was a bit forward. *Oh, who cares?* I was done overthinking everything. Apparently, that just made people go away—case in point, Jordan. *Ugh! I have to stop thinking about him.*

Tonya bumped her hip into mine and laughed. I started to move my hips with the music. Tonight could be fun. I just had to be careful with my thoughts.

"Oh, trust me, Roxy. I will be back in a jiff." Ethan winked at me.

"Who the hell says jiff?" Tonya spouted, almost spitting out her margarita.

"Duh, Ethan does, Ton. Didn't you know that word was coming back?" I stuck up for Ethan whose cheeks were coloring again.

"Exactly." He sounded more sure than I thought he felt.

Once again, it was adorable.

Ethan walked off. Tonya and I made our way to a set of empty pool lounges.

We watched two guys who each had a girl on their shoulders. The girls' hands were interlocked as they playfully fought to knock one another off the shoulders of the guy they were on. It was amusing if I could get over the fact that the girls who were playing the game were also topless. I didn't understand why there always seemed to be naked girls in the pool at parties. But as I looked around at all the guys hooting and cheering them on, I understood how it could make them feel more important in that moment. Maybe the tequila was getting to me, but the thought of taking my shirt off for attention didn't seem as disgusting as I'd once considered it.

I looked at Tonya, who was smiling down at her phone. I could only guess who was responsible for that goofy grin on her face. I wondered if that was how I'd looked when I thought about Jordan.

Again with the Jordan thoughts. Fucking mind ninja.

"How is Shawn?" I asked her.

"He's good. He was just telling me how excited he is for tomorrow." She grinned before her eyes widened with shock, and she covered her mouth. "Damn it! What am I doing?" She threw her phone back into her bag.

"Ton, don't be so hard on yourself. You clearly like him. I don't think there is anything wrong with that, especially when he makes you smile like that."

"You think?" She pouted.

I nodded.

"I don't know, Roxy. This is abnormal for me. I am not this girl. I am more of the that-was-fun-don't-let-the-door-hit-you-on-the-way-out kind of girl."

"That's just because you were hurting. That doesn't mean you have to be that girl forever. It's okay to like him, Ton. I mean, he must like you, too, if he is coming all the way up from Santa Barbara to see you. Think about it."

"I guess." She downed the rest of her drink. "You're out, too. Let's get refills."

We were drinking too much, too fast, but seeing as the ache was finally gone and I was feeling warm and tingly, I didn't really care. We ordered two more margaritas and a round of shots.

"All right, I'm calling in a bestie favor," Tonya announced as we waited for our drinks.

"What is this favor you need?"

She held out her pinkie toward me. "Pinkie swear that you will do it."

I shook my head. "I don't even know what you want. You could be asking me to kill someone for all I know."

She shook her hand at me. "You will just have to trust me. Now, pinkie swear."

If anyone else had asked me to trust blindly like this, I would have laughed in the person's face and walked away. She was my best friend though, and I highly doubted she would ask anything of me that was all that bad.

"Fine." I looped my pinkie around hers. "What am I swearing to?" I asked while our pinkies were still intertwined.

"You just have to go to dinner with Shawn and me tomorrow night." She shrugged.

I instantly knew there was more to what she was asking than that.

"And?"

"And maybe keep his friend Jared company." She smiled like she'd just told me I won a prize, not that she wanted me to go on a double date. Tonya pulled her hand back. "No take backs. You already promised."

God, she's being childish. Then again, I guess pinkie swears are kind of childish to begin with.

"I don't know, Ton," I whined.

"You already promised." She crossed her arms. "Besides, it will help keep your mind off of Jordan."

I considered what she was saying, but I decided if the alcohol I was drinking tonight couldn't do it, then neither would this Jared guy. *Jordan is a mind ninja, for Christ's sake.*

"Fine, I will go because I promised, but just know, it'll be completely against my will."

"You can file your grievance with the I Don't Give a Fuck department down at the You're the Greatest Best Friend Ever office." She chuckled.

Our drinks were placed in front of us, and I couldn't help but notice how cute the bartender was. But the way he'd looked at Ethan earlier more than had me questioning his sexual preference.

After tossing back the shots, I took a drink of my margarita. I found the familiar shiver wasn't as prominent, so that must have meant I was feeling good—that was, until Danny and Brendon made their way over to the bar.

When it came to guys in high school, these two had been the epitome of scum. Sure, their parents had a lot of money, but considering the private school we'd attended, that wasn't unusual. These two were lacking class of any kind. If there was a girl they could use and verbally abuse, they would make sure they did just that.

Just seeing them made my skin crawl. *Why the hell did Ethan invite them?* I was pretty sure he hated these two.

"If it isn't Foxy Roxy…" Danny slithered way too close for comfort, making me take a step back.

"And Tonya Bo-Bom-Ba," Brendon added, thrusting his hips at her.

Gross. I think I just threw up in my mouth a little.

I looked at Tonya, who had the same look of repulsion as I did.

We turned to walk away when Danny caught my arm. "Where are you going, sweet cheeks?"

I yanked my arm from his grasp. "Wherever you're not."

"Aw, don't be like that. You know you want some of this." He gripped the crotch of his pants. "Let me show you what Kevin never could."

Yep, there's definitely a bit of throw up this time.

"Are you on something? Roxy wouldn't be caught dead with you," Tonya stated.

"Don't be a bitch. Let your friend talk for herself. Everyone knows Kevin dropped her for that slut, Sara. That says a lot about your friend here. Her value has dropped," Brendon stated.

My stomach turned.

Tonya's hand shot up and smacked him hard across the face. "Don't you ever say that kind of shit about Roxy again, you bastard."

"You fucking bitch." Brendon moved toward Tonya, and I thought he might hit her.

As he raised his hand, he was pulled back and thrown on the ground. I saw Jordan, and the shock of seeing him caused me to drop my drink. The glass shattered, and liquid splashed onto Tonya's and my legs. We both flinched as we watched Danny turn to punch Jordan. Jordan ducked and punched Danny hard in the stomach, causing him to double over. Brendon got back on his feet and went after Jordan. Jordan socked Brendon in the face, knocking him back to the ground.

Ethan came running over. "What are you two doing in my house?" he yelled.

I knew Ethan was better than to give those two scumbags an invite.

My shock at Jordan's arrival was still in full force.

Danny helped Brendon up.

Brendon pointed at Tonya and me. "This isn't over."

Jordan lunged for them again. Ethan and his buddy Adam held him back. I was completely amazed that they were capable of restraining him. Jordan looked like he was out for blood. Two other guys from the high school water polo team made sure Brendon and Danny found their way out of the house.

"Are you okay?" Jordan asked Tonya before turning to me. "They didn't hurt you, did they?" He pulled me into a hug.

I got lost in his warmth, and I let him hug me before realizing that he shouldn't even be here. I pushed away from him. *What is he doing here? Shouldn't he be in Oregon?*

"We're fine," I answered.

Tonya started cracking up. It was her way of dealing with stressful situations.

"You sure you're okay, Ton?" Ethan eyed her.

Tonya continued to laugh. Having Brendon raise his fist at her must have really startled her.

"She'll be fine," I told them.

I asked the bartender for two more double shots of Patrón. Tonya stopped giggling just before she swallowed hers. After I downed my shot, I felt my gums starting to numb.

"That was eventful." She smiled.

Jordan's eyes were burning into me. But I couldn't just fold whenever he came around. He had been wrong. He'd walked away, not me.

"I guess it's time to start having fun." Ethan smiled at me.

Jordan's jaw clenched, and he stepped forward. "Roxy, can we talk?"

"What else is there to talk about? I'm pretty sure you said all you had to say last night. So, if you will excuse me, I want to hang out with my friends."

"Roxy?"

"Shouldn't you be in Oregon?" I spit. I walked away from him, motioning for Tonya to follow. I called over my shoulder to Ethan. "Grab a bottle of Patrón, and get your ass over here, Ethan."

Jordan stared at me and shook his head. We both knew I was drunk. This night was not the night for a heart-to-heart. I had absolutely nothing nice to say to him.

"Did you invite him?" I asked Ethan.

He poured us shots. I gazed around the backyard, trying to find Jordan. He must have left because I couldn't locate him.

"Yeah, I ran into him at the gas station this morning and told him to drop in if he wasn't busy," Ethan answered. "I thought you two were together now."

I snorted. "Whatever we were, it wasn't together, and it's completely over."

"What the hell is he doing?" Tonya gestured across the pool to where Jordan was sitting in front of the fireplace.

I looked over to see a big-breasted topless blonde offering him a beer.

Are you fucking kidding me? My stomach turned.

Why the hell is he here anyway? Does he find this entertaining? Is he enjoying ruining my life by making me jealous?

You know what? Two can play this game.

I threw back another shot. If I had any more, I would be puking. I'd had just enough to make me fearless.

I stood up and peeled off my top, exposing my pink lace bra. "I want to go swimming. Who's in?"

Tonya stood up. "I'm in." She unbuttoned her skinny jeans and pulled them down, revealing her yellow thong.

"Do you girls want me to find you a shirt to wear?" Ethan offered.

I kicked off my heels and stood in front of him. Then, I turned around, giving him a close-up of my ass as I pulled off my shorts. I looked over my shoulder while I was bent over. "Are you trying to tell me you have a problem with the view?" I teased.

Ethan cleared his throat and readjusted in his seat. "The sight is phenomenal, Roxy, but you're kind of drunk. I don't want you to be full of regrets tomorrow."

I glanced over my shoulder to see Jordan glaring my way. The blonde bimbo was still pining for his attention. I swallowed hard. If he didn't want me the way I was and with what I was willing to offer, then I would find someone else.

I smiled at Ethan and straddled his lap. "I would never regret you," I purred. *Okay, that came out more slurred than sexy, but he has to know what I'm going for.*

Ethan put his hands on my hips. "Roxy." His eyes were unsure, but his lower half was obviously turned on.

I moved his hands from my hips to my ass. "No regrets." I bit down on my bottom lip as I swayed my hips to the music.

"Bitch, pool now!" Tonya ordered me.

I flipped her off and leaned in to kiss Ethan. My lips brushed across his. As much as I wanted to get lost in him, I was already feeling bad. Ethan was right. I would regret this. I pushed the truth away and pressed my lips against his, trying to feel anything but doubt.

"We need to talk—now!" Jordan growled from behind Ethan.

I pulled away from Ethan and glared at Jordan. "We have nothing to talk about, but I'm sure your bimbo would love to chat."

I moved in to kiss Ethan again, but he stiffened beneath me. He knew I was using him, and I was a bitch for treating my friend this way.

Way to suck, Roxanne.

I moved off of Ethan's lap, hoping the apologetic look I was giving him would be enough. I walked over to Jordan and pulled him off to the side of the yard. "What? What do you want? Why are you even here?"

"You, Rox! I want you. I am here for you."

"We already had this conversation. I can't give you what you want."

"You thought you would hook up with another guy to prove that you can't give me what I want? Why won't you just try?"

"I don't want to try." I pushed my hands against his chest. "And I can kiss whomever I want. I'm not your girlfriend. Why don't you find Miss Big Boobs and see if she can give you what you want?"

"You are making a fool of yourself. This isn't you, Rox. Don't turn into the slut everyone talks bad about the next day just to make me jealous."

How did he know I was trying to make him jealous? Wait—did he just fucking call me a slut?

"Slut? Slut!" I screamed. "This is not me being a slut. You want to see slut?" I unhooked my bra and pulled it off. Then, I turned around and waved my hands in the air. "Who wants to screw me?" I shouted.

An echo of hoots and catcalls started. Jordan spun me around and picked me up before throwing me over his shoulder.

"Put me down, you Neanderthal." I pounded on his back.

Jordan called out to Ethan and demanded for him to make sure Tonya, who was in the pool, stayed put until he got back. Jordan carried me out of the house as I beat on his back.

"You can't do this. Let go of me!" I hollered.

"No."

I called out to the people we passed, "I don't want to go. Someone stop him."

I found it disconcerting that no one was coming to my rescue.

What the hell is wrong with people?

At his truck, Jordan opened the driver's side door and put me inside before getting in after me.

"You can't just carry me out of there like that. You don't get to tell me what to do, where to be, or how to dress."

"I am not going to stand by and let you act this way. I care about you too much for that shit to be okay."

"Stop caring about me!" I screamed.

Jordan took off his shirt and threw it at me. Then, he peeled out of the driveway. "Put the shirt on, Roxy!"

Realizing I was only in my thong, embarrassment started to wash over me. I wasn't about to admit to him that I wasn't proud of my behavior. I scooted all the way over to the passenger door. I pulled the shirt on and crossed my arms, refusing to look at him.

The drive from Ethan's house back to the city was long, and I felt my eyes getting heavy, but I tried to stay awake. Eventually, the alcohol won, and I passed out.

When I woke up, I was in my own bed. At first, I was confused, but the night's events quickly rushed back—well, all of it up to being carried out of the party by Jordan. I didn't remember much after that.

I made my way to the bathroom. I pulled Jordan's shirt off and turned on the shower. A note was taped to the mirror.

BROUGHT BACK YOUR CAR. TONYA IS IN YOUR BROTHER'S BED. YOUR PURSE AND KEYS ARE ON THE TABLE.
I KNOW YOU WANT ME TO STOP CARING ABOUT YOU, BUT I JUST DON'T KNOW HOW TO. PLEASE DON'T HATE ME.

XO,

JORDAN

After reading that, my heart ached for him. I had been terrible to him last night. I couldn't believe how stupid I'd acted. My head was pounding, and my stomach turned at the memory of my actions last night.

I also thought of Ethan. I would be lucky if he ever talked to me again. I'd really tested his friendship with my horrible drunken behavior.

As for Jordan, I couldn't even think about the crap I'd made him deal with last night. I seriously sucked.

I got in the shower and tried to wash away the disgust I felt with myself. I had some serious apologizing to do today.

20

I pulled on my pink-and-white Abercrombie & Fitch tee and put on my favorite pair of faded jean shorts. I grabbed my white-and-pink ballet flats from my closet and put them on. After I was dressed, I French-braided my hair and put on some light makeup. My eyes still looked tired and puffy.

That's what Patrón will do to a girl.

I made my way to my brother's room to find Tonya passed out and snoring. It was not a glamorous picture.

I lay down next to her and nudged her shoulder.

"Five more minutes, Mom," she grumbled before rolling over and giving me her backside.

I started to poke her butt cheeks. "I'm not your mom. Wake up, stinky butt."

Tonya's sleepy eyes looked over her shoulder. "Oh, I'll give you stinky butt." She pressed her butt closer to me and let one rip.

"Ton!" I whined.

Laughing, she rolled over to face me. "That's what you get for waking me up when I still feel drunk."

"I felt the same way when I woke up. A hot shower will work wonders, I promise."

Her stench hit my nose, making me gag.

"Good God, what died in your ass, woman?" I asked with my hand clasped over my nose.

"You're the one who started with the Patrón last night. You know what tequila does to my stomach." She fanned the smell toward my face, continuing the torture.

I rolled off the bed. "I have to go talk to Jordan. You will be okay by yourself, right?"

"Yeah, I'm going to take a shower and head home. I'm supposed to meet Shawn at one. You're still coming to dinner tonight, right?"

"I don't know, Ton."

"No, no, no, Roxy. You pinkie swore," she reminded me.

I wanted to claim drunken insanity, but I knew it wasn't going to get me off the hook. I would be going to dinner tonight whether I wanted to or not. A pinkie swear was sacred. "Ugh, fine. I will be there. Text me the info."

"Yay!"

"Yeah, yeah. You owe me." I walked out the door.

"I love you, bitch," she called after me.

"Love you, slut. I will see you tonight. Don't slip in the shower!" I yelled back.

I sat in front of Brent's condo, debating whether or not to get out of my car. I owed Jordan an apology. I just wasn't sure that I was ready to admit to him that I was not only wrong, but also thankful that he'd dragged me out of there. I had acted extremely dumb last night.

I refolded his shirt for what seemed like the hundredth time. I probably should have washed it first.

My phone started singing, causing me to jump. It was Ryan. He had been calling all morning. He hadn't left a message, which was a very bad sign. It meant that he was too upset to even yell at my phone.

I took a deep breath. It was time to talk to the warden. *Is it bad that being chewed out by Ryan seems like a better alternative than apologizing to Jordan? Yep, I'm pathetic.*

"Hello, brother that I love so much."

"I have only been gone a week, Roxanne. One week."

Ryan wasn't yelling like I had expected him to. In fact, his voice was scarily calm.

"And I have missed you very much." I tried to suck up to him.

"Goddamn it, Roxanne!" he screamed. The cool and collected approach had left. "Are you really going to make me come home? Do you have any idea how important this internship is to me?"

"I don't even know why you are upset, Ryan. So, how about we start there?"

"You have got to be kidding me! You are really going to play stupid with me?"

I had been worried this might happen. Plenty of people who knew my brother had been at Ethan's last night. I wasn't surprised that Ryan had already heard about my drunken behavior. But I had no idea how much he knew about last night, and I wasn't about to offer any extra information.

"Ryan, how about you just tell me why you're mad, so I can apologize and get this convo over with?"

"That's it, Roxanne! I'm calling Dad. You might think he doesn't care about you, but he will show you just how much he cares when he takes away your car and credit cards. I swear, Roxy. What the hell were you thinking, getting wasted like that? I mean, the drinking is one thing. But stripping? Really?"

I swallowed hard. *Crap, he knows way more than I wanted him to ever know.*

"I know, Ryan. I was dumb, and trust me, I am more disappointed in myself than you or Daddy could ever be. Please don't call him. I swear, it will never happen again."

"And I am supposed to believe you? What about when you are off at school? Is this how you are going to behave? I swear to God, Roxy, if it is, I will make sure Dad pulls you out and makes you go to school with me. Is that what you want?"

"Again, Ryan, I am sorry. It won't ever happen again."

"It'd better not. You need to get your act together, Roxanne. What if someone took pictures of you or recorded you? That kind of shit could ruin your life."

I knew he was right, but there was nothing I could do about last night. It was already done and gone.

"Ry, I swear, it will never happen again. It was stupid. I was stupid."

"Who was the guy who carried you out of the party?"

"What?"

"Who was the guy, Roxanne? Did he hurt you?"

"No, Ryan, he didn't hurt me. He covered me up and took me home. Then, he made sure Tonya got home safely, too."

"I should have known she was there with you, Roxy. You get in more trouble with that girl—"

"Shut up, Ryan! What I did last night was not her fault. Stop trying to find someone to blame for my bad behavior, and face the fact that your sister isn't perfect because I'm not, Ryan. I'm not perfect."

"Roxanne, you know what I mean."

"You know what, Ryan? I don't care what you mean. I am done talking to you. I said I was sorry, and I meant it, but you will not talk badly about my best friend." I hung up on him and turned off my phone.

He could yell at me later. I was beyond pissed at my brother. I was sick of him painting Tonya as some kind of villain, so he could explain my stupidity. I was eighteen. I was going to screw up with or without her. I was just glad she was always there when I did. We were only making sure we would have amazingly funny stories to laugh about when we were old and gray.

I found the courage I had been lacking earlier, and I got out of the car and headed to the condo.

I pounded on the door. When no one came, I rang the doorbell. There was no turning back now.

Jordan answered the door, seeming half-awake. His hair was disheveled, but it still managed to look movie-star perfect. He was in a pair of blue basketball shorts with no shirt.

My mouth went dry, and I forgot why I had come here to begin with. All I could feel was need. I wanted him, and I wanted him now. *Damn it, why is he so hot?*

"Rox?" he said, surprised. "What are you doing here?"

I threw my arms around his neck and pressed my mouth to his. Without missing a beat, he wrapped his arms around me. His hands moved down my body. He hitched up my leg and pulled me up. I wrapped my legs around his hips. He shut the door with his foot before pressing me up against it, and then he kissed me deeper. A primal growl came from the back of his throat as his lips moved down my neck. He leaned away from me as he took off my shirt.

My head fell back against the door as he worked his mouth over my chest and back up my neck. My hands fisted his hair and pulled, bringing him back to my mouth.

"I'm sorry about last night," I said against his mouth.

He carried me away from the door, not taking his mouth from mine, and he laid me down on the couch. He undid the button on my shorts. "Shh...baby. You're here, and that's all that matters," he said as he unzipped them.

I lifted my hips, so he could take them off. He made sure to bring down my thong with the shorts.

He was right. Yesterday was gone, and right now was all that mattered. I let myself be consumed by Jordan, and I was going to enjoy every second without regrets.

Jordan smiled down at me and kissed my nose before he rolled off of me. Every inch of my body was tingling.

"Come here, baby," Jordan said as he pulled me into him.

I smiled and tried not to start giggling as he held me. I curled my body into his with my head on his shoulder. I placed my hand over his heart. I looked up at his perfectly sculpted face. I had never seen a man whose beauty was so pure from the inside out.

His fingers traced my lower back, sending shivers up my spine. Sex with him was hands-down beyond incredible, but lying naked in his arms in a happy comfortable silence filled my heart with a contentment I'd thought I would never feel again.

My eyes drifted down his body. *Absolute perfection, every single part.*

As I stared at his lower half of flawlessness, I started to feel the throbbing between my thighs again. I had to calm my sex drive. Jordan and I had already been at this—I glanced at his clock. *Wow...*—for over four hours.

My face heated as I thought about every surface downstairs where he'd had his way with me before carrying me upstairs and continuing our fun in his bed. I didn't understand why my body couldn't get enough of him.

I imagined him running away in horror as I chased after him, begging for sex. I giggled at the ridiculous thought.

"What's so funny?" Jordan smiled down at me.

I felt my cheeks warm even more. Maybe he would just think it was an after-great-sex glow. I was in no way about to stroke his ego by telling him that he was the best sex I'd ever had. He had been with tons of other girls. I didn't want to know where I ranked or chance having him lie to me. I was blissfully happy, and for now, I wanted it to stay that way.

I rubbed my hand down over his goods. "I think I should be able to name it." I couldn't believe that was what I'd come up with, but it was out of my mouth before I could take it back.

A laugh vibrated through his chest. "You wanna name my cock?" he asked, stunned.

I grinned, and I held my own laughter back. "Yep."

He was starting to grow in my hand. I sat up and crawled over until I was on top of him. I felt his erection beneath me. My throbbing intensified. I didn't want him to see me as some sex-crazed girl, so I forced myself to think about names.

"Do you already have a name for him? I mean, I know guys sometimes do that."

He laughed hard. It shook through my body and rubbed me in all the right places. He placed his hands on my hips. I smiled down at him. He stared into my eyes, and I could see that his were burning with lust.

"I can't get over how beautiful you are. I don't think I ever will."

"Yeah, yeah," I teased. "Let's get back to naming the penis!" I grinned.

He pulled his hands back and placed them behind his head as he smirked at me. "Hit me with what you think it should be named."

"So, you don't already have a name?" I asked.

His smile grew. "I sometimes call it Buddy."

Now, it was my turn to shake with laughter. "It's not a dog."

He chuckled. "You asked."

I watched him while I thought of good names. *Man, he's distracting.*

His abs screamed for me to run my tongue up and down them. I licked my lips. Then, I bit down on my bottom one. *Think, think, think! Not about abs! Names!*

"Oh, I know. What about Princess Buttercup?" I exclaimed.

He shook his head and voiced his amusement, "You cannot name my dick Princess Buttercup."

I pouted and then smiled. "Fine, but for the record, it's an awesome name."

"Yeah, sure it is," he stated sarcastically. "Next!"

"What about Lucy? Then, I can be like, 'Lucy, I'm home,'" I said in a terrible Ricky Ricardo voice.

Jordan laughed long and hard, causing me to chuckle with him. He sat up and wrapped his arms around my waist. He kissed me and then flipped me over, so I was under him.

"You have officially lost your naming privileges after trying to give my dick another girl name."

I pouted again. Jordan sucked on my stuck-out bottom lip and then nibbled on it. I let out a moan.

"How about we just stick with calling him Buddy?" He smiled down at me.

I guffawed. "Fine, but whenever I want sex, I'm saying, 'Hey, Buddy. How you doin'?'" This time, I impersonated Joey from *Friends*.

Jordan's body shook with hilarity again.

After he caught his breath, he looked me in the eyes. "Buddy will always be ready."

I couldn't help but grin. I wrapped my legs around him and challenged him. "Prove it."

The kiss he gave me next took my breath away. I no longer cared what we called his flawless cock. I just cared that he and all his perfection wanted me. I pushed away the small part of me that knew I was getting way too attached, and I let myself get lost in him once again.

I rolled over and cracked open my eyes. The first thing I saw was Jordan's sexy naked body. Then, I noticed it was getting dark outside. I looked at the alarm clock and shot up.

Fuck! I'm going to be late.

I scrambled out of bed and tripped over my own legs. "Son of a fuck bitch!" I screamed, crashing to the floor.

Jordan sat up.

Damn it! I didn't want to wake him.

"You okay, babe?" He smiled.

I was so glad I could amuse him with my klutziness. *Not!* "Yeah, I'm fine. I just have to get going."

He grimaced "Go? I was kind of hoping you would stay the night."

"I can't. Sorry," I said before rushing downstairs.

He was right behind me. "What do you mean, you can't?" He was pulling on his boxer briefs.

I found my shorts and pulled them on as I looked for my bra.

Jordan picked up something from the side of the couch. He held up my pink thong. "Missing something?" He was trying to hold back a laugh.

"Lucky you. You can keep it." I didn't have time to undress for panties. I'd survive without them.

If I were late tonight, Tonya would, without a doubt, think I was bailing. I didn't want that. After all, I'd pinkie sworn to be there. I found my T-shirt but still couldn't find my bra.

Ugh, fuck it.

I threw my pink-and-white Abercrombie & Fitch T-shirt on and prayed I had a hoodie or something in my car.

Now, shoes. I found one and slid it on.

"Will you be coming back for your bra and thong later?" Jordan teased, swinging my thong around his finger.

"Um…" I said, looking for my other ballet flat. "I'll get them tomorrow or whenever."

How in the world did we make such a mess in this living room? How could I have lost only one shoe? It should have been right by the other.

"Do you see where my other shoe is?" I asked.

I looked up to see an amused Jordan. "Nope, and I'd help you look, but I'm in no hurry for you to leave. I think you should just get undressed and stay. Whatever you have to do, it can wait." He wrapped his arms around me and nibbled on my neck.

I was in no mood for games. I pushed away from him. "Seriously, I need to go."

"What? Are you late for a date or something?" he asked with laughter in his voice.

Now, I was fully annoyed with him. "Actually, yes, and I needed to be gone fifteen minutes ago."

I couldn't believe I'd let myself fall asleep. Then again, after the sexcapades, I couldn't really blame myself. I was exhausted.

"Seriously! Where the hell is my shoe?" I shouted.

Jordan picked up his shorts and pulled them on.

Nice to know he knew where his crap was.

He picked up a couch pillow by the wall and found my lost shoe.

"Thank God! You found it," I said, reaching for it.

Jordan picked up my shoe but didn't hand it over.

"Give it to me," I ordered.

"Let me get this straight. You're telling me that you spent all day having sex with me, knowing you were going out on a date tonight?"

Jordan was upset with me. I didn't like it, but I also didn't have time to talk about it. He wasn't my boyfriend.

"Just give me my shoe, please." I wasn't above begging for it, but I didn't want to.

"Not until you answer me!" He was not backing down.

This was not what I needed right now. I let out an exasperated sigh. "I didn't come over today with plans to have sex. I came over to give your shirt back and thank you for last night." I shook my hand at him, wanting my shoe.

"You still knew you had plans with some other guy tonight?" he yelled.

"I'm going out with Tonya and Shawn. I promised to keep Shawn's friend company!" I shouted. "Give me my freaking shoe."

"You're going on a double date? You spent the day in my bed, knowing you would be with someone else tonight! You don't think there is something wrong with that?"

The way he was speaking to me made me cringe. I knew it sounded bad, but it wasn't like I'd planned to have sex with him today. It'd just happened. As for tonight, I didn't even know this guy. I was going because I'd made a promise to Tonya. It was a double date, but I didn't even want to go. I shouldn't have to explain myself to him anymore. We weren't a couple.

"What I do when I'm not with you is none of your damn business. Give me my shoe!" I screamed.

"Nice, Roxy. Real nice. You want your shoe? Here." He threw my shoe hard, and it hit the wall across the room.

I picked it up and put it on. "Fuck you, Jordan!" I seethed.

Jordan flopped down onto the couch. "You already did that, remember? Oh, wait—I'm just one of the many. You might have forgotten," he said scathingly.

His words hurt worse than if he'd actually had hit me. "Go to hell, asshole!" I screamed. I walked out the door before slamming it behind me.

"Already there!" I heard him yell through the door.

I couldn't believe that he'd just acted that way.

I was furious with Jordan, but more than that, I was hurt. My chest burned, and my eyes filled with tears. I'd messed up by getting too close to him. I cursed myself for letting my guard down.

How am I supposed to keep myself from getting hurt if I can't keep people out? Why the hell does it seem like all Jordan I ever do is have sex—granted, amazing sex—and fight?

I got into my car and refused to let myself cry. I would not shed one tear for him. I dug my nails into my palm. I didn't care how amazing today had been. He wasn't my boyfriend, and he never would be.

I sent Tonya a text.

On my way.

By the time I got to Benched, a new sports bar and grill downtown, I was already forty-five minutes late. Of course, I'd hit every red light on the way there. I was trying not to read into that part too much. I didn't need any more reasons not to go tonight. I had already picked up my phone over ten times to call Tonya and just cancel. The last time was when I'd realized I didn't have a hoodie of any kind in my car.

I quickly re-braided my hair, trying to look somewhat put-together. I tugged on my tee, feeling uncomfortable about not wearing a bra. I was lucky to have perky breasts, but that luck wouldn't matter if it were cold in there.

I took a deep breath as I walked into the building. Tonya waved me to their table. As soon as I got there, she knew something was wrong. I gave her the we-will-talk-about-it-later look and sat down.

"Roxy, you remember Shawn."

I smiled at Shawn. "And this is his friend Jared," Tonya introduced me.

"Hi." I held out my hand.

Jared shook it. He had a nice strong grip. My mom used to say that one could learn a lot about a man from his handshake. I liked his. He was also very easy on the eyes with his athletic build, blond hair, and tan complexion. And his eyes—*Wow!*—were a honey color with flecks of green.

"Hey." He smiled back at me.

His voice was smooth and deep. It wasn't as sexy as Jordan's, but I completely approved.

Ugh! I have to stop thinking about Jordan. Damn mind ninja.

"They both go to University of California, Santa Barbara," Tonya informed me. "Roxy is going USC in the fall." She was talking to Jared, but she wasn't talking as much as shouting. The place was packed and tremendously loud.

One thing was sure though. It was not cold in here. In fact, it was overly hot. Every part of me wished I were back in Jordan's bed, naked and sleeping.

No! No! No to Jordan. I'm done with him. Jordan equaled ass.

I took a long drink of my water.

"USC? That's a great school. Do you know what you're going to major in?" Jared asked me.

Forget about Jordan!

"Oh, um…sort of." I gave a small smile. "I want to major in public relations and maybe minor in dance."

I thought of how terrible next year would be while going to the same school as Jordan. Maybe I would get lucky and just never see him.

I cursed myself for still thinking about Jordan. I was here with a cute guy. I was single, and I needed to enjoy it.

"What about you?" I asked Jared.

"My freshman year, my major was history. I wanted to be a high school history teacher. But last year, I had this killer economics professor. He changed my way of thinking. As of now, I'm undecided, but I'm leaning more and more toward majoring in economics and maybe getting a government job. Who knows? Politics might even be in my future."

"That's cool. So, you will be a junior next year?" I asked.

"That he will, and my man here is also our new fraternity president," Shawn chimed in.

Tonya squeezed my hand. "I told you they were Phi Kappa Psi, right?"

I nodded my head.

"Tonya was telling me that your brother is also a Phi Psi at Cal Poly? What's his name again?" Jared asked.

"Ryan Daniels." I hated that I had to shout. I was already getting a headache from this place.

"Trust me, you would know if you knew him. He is impossible to forget," Tonya added. "But lucky for Jared, you don't because Roxy isn't allowed to date any of Ryan's friends."

I shot Tonya a look. *Why the hell is she talking about dating?*

I looked away and felt myself blush. I stood up and bumped the edge of the table, almost knocking over the drinks. "Sorry," I apologized. *Ugh, why am I such a klutz today?* "Tonya, you coming?"

She got up. "Sorry, boys. Girl time." She blew Shawn a kiss and then linked her arm through mine.

"Spill it," Tonya said as we walked through the restroom doors.

A few girls were in line for the restrooms, and they gave us a funny look. Usually, I was the obnoxiously loud one, but tonight, Tonya was giving me a run for my money.

"I spent the whole day with Jordan, and we might have been naked," I told her.

"Shut up! You did not! You little skank," she squealed.

The girls in front of us turned and gave us annoyed looks.

"He kind of flipped when I said I had a date tonight."

"Why did you tell him?"

"I was running late, Ton, and he wanted to know why. It just came out."

"Roxy, do you *like him*, like him?"

I looked at my reflection in the mirror. I knew the answer, but I wasn't willing to admit to her that I was completely falling for him. I shrugged my shoulders. "Yeah…kind of…I guess."

"Oh my God, Roxy. You totally *like him*, like him. You wanna be with him, don't you?"

"It doesn't matter, Ton. We are never going to work. He wants more than I can give. I don't even know how being with him would ever work, and there is also the small problem that we fight a lot!"

Two stalls opened up for Ton and me. We continued our conversation through the thin metal walls.

"Rox, you're not like me. As much as I wanted you to get out there and screw everything that moved so that you could get over Kevin, you went out, found one guy, and stuck with him. You are a relationship girl. I know you are scared to have a boyfriend, but I think it's what you might need. I just wanna see you happy. You know that's all that matters."

I met Tonya at the sink. The crazy looks we were getting from other women in the restroom didn't go unnoticed, and I just did my best to ignore them.

"You and Shawn look sweet together." I grinned.

"Don't we? Seriously, Rox, if you don't want to waste time with Jared, you can leave, and I'll totally cover for you."

I was strong enough to make it through tonight. At least, I hoped I was.

"No, I'll stay."

"Yay!"

Tonya and I pushed through the door and made our way back to the boys.

Dinner was entertaining. Ton was right about Jared. He was captivating. I'd found myself enjoying everything he had to say, which varied from knock-knock jokes to air pollution.

But I never stopped thinking about Jordan.

Tonya invited me to hang out with them after dinner was over, but I was ready to leave.

I got in my car, and made my way home.

I pulled into my driveway to find Jordan sitting on the front step of my house.

Shock coursed through my body as I stepped out of my car. "What are you doing here?"

He held up my bra and thong. "I thought you might want these back."

"Seriously?" I yanked my undergarments from his hand and shoved them into my purse. "Thanks. You can leave now."

He blocked my entrance to the door with his body. "Wait, Rox. I don't wanna fight. Can we just talk?"

"Should I take off my shoe for you to throw?"

"I'm sorry. I shouldn't have acted that way. I just lost it, knowing that you were leaving my bed to be with another guy. It made me crazy."

"I witnessed it, Jordan, and I wasn't just with some other guy. Ton and Shawn were there, too. It was just dinner."

"I don't care what it was. I didn't like it."

"I'm sorry you feel that way, but you don't have a say in whom I spend my time with."

"You're driving me nuts."

"Jordan, I can't give you what you want. I am terrified of being in a relationship again. I don't want to get hurt."

"I don't want to share you, Rox. I was going out of my damn mind tonight. Please, baby, just try this with me?"

Maybe Tonya was right. I needed to rethink my no-relationship hang up. Jordan wanted to be with me. I couldn't deny that I wanted him, too. Tonight with Jared had been fun, but he was no Jordan, and Jordan was what I wanted.

Jordan took my hand. "Baby, please, tell me you're mine."

"Jordan…" I didn't have the words to explain how he made me feel. I wanted him, and I wanted to be his. I was just too scared to admit it.

Why is it so hard for me to just tell him that?

"I'm serious, Rox. I need to hear you say that you're mine, completely mine." His eyes darkened with determination.

He wanted me—broken, messed-up, baggage-carrying me.

I closed my eyes and let out long sigh. "I'm yours."

When I look at him he seemed overjoyed. Just knowing I was the cause of his beautiful smile melted my heart.

"No more dinners with other guys." He was still grinning, but his tone was serious.

"I told you that tonight was a favor for Tonya. It didn't mean anything."

"I don't care, Rox. I hated it."

"I'm yours, but you are going to have to chill the guard-dog act. I have friends who are guys. I'm not going to stop talking to them because you don't want to share."

"I don't want to share."

"And you won't have to in all the ways that count."

He took my face between his palms. "All of it counts with you, Rox."

"I will try to be less of a guard dog if you try not to push the limits. We need to be honest with each other, Roxy. Having any guy talk to you is going to make my skin crawl more than it did before. Don't try to make me jealous, baby. Please just consider my feelings before you do things. Can you do that for me?"

I nodded my head. Jordan kissed me, and just like I always did, I got lost in it. Everything else just faded away, and I was blissfully happy.

I pulled away and looked at him. "Hey, boyfriend, will you stay the night with me?"

"I thought you would never ask."

I opened the front door, but before I could walk through it, Jordan scooped me up into his arms. I couldn't help but giggle as he carried me inside and up to my room.

22

"Roxanne Marie Daniels, what the hell do you think you're doing?"

I shot up, terrified. *I could have sworn that I'd just heard Daddy yelling at me.*

When I focused and saw his red face, it looked as if it was about to turn purple.

This is not happening. This has to be a bad dream.

"Answer me, young lady!" Daddy roared.

Jordan scrambled out of my bed and pulled on his pants.

Oh fuck! This is real—oh-so very real and horrible.

"Mr. Daniels, I am sorry. I didn't mean any disrespect to you," Jordan tried to apologize for what my dad had just walked in on.

Thank God that we had just been sleeping, but I was still shocked silent.

What is he doing home? Why is he in my room? Did Ryan call him after all? I shouldn't have hung up on him. Damn it.

I looked down, feeling grateful that I still had on Jordan's shirt from when I'd made him pancakes last night.

"Roxanne!"

Why am I thinking about pancakes? And why the hell can't I say anything?

I saw the look of panic on Jordan's face. This was not the first impression he'd wanted to make on my father.

I pulled myself together and found my voice. "Daddy, what are you doing home?" I smiled weakly.

My father pointed at Jordan. "You! Get the hell out of my house! Now!" he yelled.

Jordan scrambled to get his things. While he was looking for his shirt, I cleared my throat. His eyes widened as he realized that I was wearing it. He gave me an apologetic look and made his way past my dad. I felt horrible that this is how Jordan had met my father. I wanted to die from the embarrassment of it all.

Why is this happening to me? I thought my life was just starting a new happy and pleasant path. This moment was neither.

I looked at my father. "Daddy, please don't start with the lecture."

"Lecture, Roxanne? You don't want a lecture? What do you think you are doing? Have you forgotten whose house you are in? There are rules, Roxanne. Your brother wasn't kidding when he said you were having trouble staying here alone. I have never been so disappointed in you." He looked away from me as if he were disgusted.

My stomach dropped.

If he had walked in on Ryan, Daddy would have just closed the door and gone on with his day.

Why is there a double standard when it comes to me?

Thinking this made my blood boil. I was furious with my father. I was eighteen. He had no right to treat me this way. It wasn't as if he thought I was a virgin. He was a doctor. My mom had talked about me going on birth control with him. For fuck's sake, he wasn't stupid.

"This is my house, too, you know. I am the one who actually lives here full-time. And that guy you just chased off is my boyfriend. How could you do that? You wouldn't act this way if it were Ryan in this situation."

"You do not get to take that tone with me, young lady. In this home, there are rules, and no boys staying the night is a big one. I might not be here all the time, but you'd better believe that I expect my children to respect my rules. As for your brother, he has enough common sense not to be in a situation like this."

Seriously, you have got to be kidding me. Ryan parades girls in and out of this house all the time.

"You will not be seeing that boy again. Do you understand me?"

"What?"

"You heard me."

"You're crazy. You can't tell me who I can and cannot date."

I was now beginning to understand where Ryan had gotten his crazy. Without a doubt, he was our father's son.

"You will not drink or go out to parties. You will behave yourself." He was counting his list off on his fingers.

"You can't come in here and play dad, not when you have spent so many years not being one," I spit.

"You might not like my rules, Roxanne, but as long as you are living under my roof, you will obey them."

"Then, I won't be under your roof anymore."

"You know where the front door is."

He did not just tell me to get out if I wasn't going to follow his stupid rules. I must have heard him wrong.

"Make sure you leave your keys. My money bought that car, so it belongs to me."

He is seriously going to kick me out.

"I hate you! Mom would never have treated me this way. I wish it were you who died and not her." The words were out before I could stop them.

My dad's face paled, and he looked defeated. I had hurt him in the worst way. I was a horrible daughter.

"That makes two of us," was all he said before he turned and left my room.

The thing about words was that once they were said, you couldn't unsay them. You could say you took them back, you could say you were sorry, but that wouldn't make the person not hear them. It wouldn't take away the pain the words had caused.

I was mad at my father, but I didn't really want him dead. I felt sick with myself for even saying it.

I rolled over and pounded my fist into the bed as I cried.

Hours later, I showered and got dressed. I needed to talk to my dad. I didn't know what I was going to say, but I had to make things right.

I walked down the hall to my parents' bedroom—well, I guessed it was just his room now. The door was cracked, so I pushed it open. I heard my father crying. I walked in and looked for him. He wasn't anywhere in the room. The crying was coming from Mom's closet.

I hated myself for what I'd said to my dad. I hated that I'd caused him pain.

I opened the closet to see my dad sitting against the wall, his hand cupped over his face. This was a version of my dad that I wished I hadn't seen. This man almost seemed more broken than I felt. I wanted to make him feel better, but I knew nothing I could do would ever help. You could never recover from losing someone who had meant everything to you. You just found ways to manage the pain and get through the days.

I sat down next to him and wrapped my arms around my legs to keep from pulling him into a hug. "I'm sorry for what I said. I know my words don't make you feel any better right now, but please understand that I said those things out of anger, not because I meant them. I am a terrible daughter. If you want me out of the house, I understand. I disrespected you by breaking the rules. I am so very sorry."

He wrapped his arms around me and squeezed. It surprised the crap out of me.

"Listen to me, Roxanne, I love you. I love you as much as any father could love his child. Your brother and you are my world. I know that I don't always show that, but everything I do is for you two, so you can have the best future possible.

"You were right. Your mother would never have reacted the way I did. She would have known what to say, but I was acting the way any father would have. You are my baby girl, Roxanne, and that was as hard for me to walk in on as it was for you to have me see. I know you are an adult now, but no matter how old you get, you will never stop being my little girl. Do I make myself clear?"

I was at a loss for words once again. All I could do was nod, and I wasn't really even sure what I was nodding for.

"I want us to forget the conversation we had earlier. We both said things out of anger. I am going to need a while to wrap my head around what I want to say to you. Until then, please remember, I love you. I don't tell you that enough, and I am very sorry about that." He kissed my forehead.

My father got up and left the closet while I was still in a state of shock from what had happened.

Seriously, what the hell just happened?

The next morning, the world seemed to still be spinning like every other day. There was no apocalypse, and zombies weren't taking over. My dad's emotional heart-to-heart with me had thrown me for a loop. In all honesty, I'd thought pigs might appear in the sky. Of course, they hadn't.

After my dad had left the house yesterday, I'd assumed he would come back to tell me that I had just been pranked. That hadn't happened either. Instead, my dad had come home late last night, and he'd gone straight to his room. He hadn't bothered to check on me or even say good night.

I didn't know why I had expected things to be different.

Today, I found a note from him on the table.

ROXANNE,

I DIDN'T WANT TO WAKE YOU. I WILL BE IN SAN FRANCISCO FOR A CONSULTATION. I SHOULD BE BACK HOME IN A FEW DAYS. WHEN I COME HOME, I EXPECT TO MEET YOUR NEW BOYFRIEND. LET HIM KNOW WE WILL BE GOING TO DINNER.

LOVE,

DAD

P.S. NO BOYS IN THE HOUSE WHILE I AM GONE.

I looked out the window, but there were still no flying pigs. Maybe yesterday had changed something. He might not have said good night or even good-bye, but he'd left a note, and that was more than he had ever done before.

A smile crossed my face, and I felt good.

I called Jordan and told him I would be over to see him later on tonight. Just because he couldn't be in my house didn't mean I wouldn't be staying with him.

Tonya and I had plans to go shopping today while Shawn and Jared played golf. It was crazy to see Tonya happy about a guy, but I was happy for her.

I left my house to pick up Tonya.

She was scarily quiet as we made our way downtown. I pulled into a spot in the parking garage.

I turned and looked at Tonya. "Are you okay?" I asked.

"No," was all she said before opening the car door and getting out.

As I got out of the car, Tonya slammed her door shut.

"Hey, be nice to my car. It didn't do anything to you. What is wrong?"

"I hate feeling like this."

"Um...feeling like what?"

"This! I'm becoming some crazy selfish person. I know I'm the one who asked him to bring Jared up with him, but that was when your relationship with Jordan was over, and I wanted you to meet him. But you went and got back together with Jordan, leaving Jared with no one to hang out with, and I'm missing out on time with Shawn."

"I'm confused. Weren't you the one who told them to go play golf?"

"Yeah, but that was only because I felt bad that Jared didn't get to hang out with you like I had originally planned. I didn't expect you and Jordan to get back together, let alone you agree to be his girlfriend. Where the hell did that come from anyway?"

"First of all, you're absurd, Ton, and second, I really like Jordan. I'm tired of pushing him away because I have issues. If he's willing to be with me, baggage and all, then why shouldn't I try?"

She let out a sad sigh, and we continued walking down the street.

"I'm a terrible friend, Roxy. I'm sorry. It's not that I'm not happy for you. I am just bummed to be losing hot-sex time with Shawn."

"As much as I love you, that is your own fault. I never asked you to play matchmaker. I didn't even want to be set up."

"Don't remind me. It was a spur-of-the-moment crap idea. Can we just forget my stupidity and spend money?"

"Sure, but only if you stop being in a shitty mood. You can wallow in your stupidity on your own time."

"Fine, fine. You're right. Change of subject—have you talked to Ryan yet? Did he tell your dad to come home?"

I pulled open the door to Victoria's Secret and took in a deep breath. I loved the way this store smelled. "If I never talk to Ryan again, it will be too soon. Judging from his lack of phone calls, I can only assume he was the reason our dad made a trip home."

"It's not like your dad actually caught you sexing it up."

"True. That would be the only thing in the world that could have been worse. It was still so bad, Ton. Poor Jordan. You should have seen him. That was not the way he'd wanted to meet my dad. He was still upset about it when I called him earlier today."

Tonya shrugged and held up a hot black lace number from the rack. "I'm sure you will make him forget all about the awkwardness of yesterday when you see him tonight."

"That's the plan. And I think you should get that in red."

"You think?" She found a red one in her measurements. "Do you think I'll have time to go get red streaks put in my hair?"

"Definitely buy that outfit. Call Sally and see if she can squeeze you in. We can head over after we're done here."

Tonya's face glowed.

Yep, this is the Tonya I haven't seen in a long time.

I couldn't help but smile with her. As she made the appointment, I went back to trying to find something sexy to surprise Jordan with tonight.

Tonya was bouncing with anticipation as we left the salon and made our way to my car. Her red streaks had turned out incredible. She was going to blow Shawn away tonight.

I tried to shove away the tiny bit of guilt I felt for not being able to help keep Jared entertained, but this was one hole I couldn't dig her out of. Even if Jordan knew the situation, he would never be okay with me hanging out with Jared. Besides, I was sure it wouldn't be Jared's first time hearing his friend have sex. I wouldn't want to take his place. I'd had to suffer through hearing Tonya more than once. She was loud and freaky.

I choked back a giggle at the memory. *Poor Jared.*

Tonya nudged me. "You gonna share what you find funny? It'd better not be my hair. I need tonight to be perfect."

"Oh, nothing. I just remembered something. It's not a big deal."

Tonya skeptically eyed me. "Uh-huh."

"Your hair looks fabulous. Shawn isn't going to know what hit him."

"That's what I'm hoping for because…well, um…I think I'm going to ask Shawn to be exclusive tonight." She brought her thumb to her mouth and started gnawing on her nail. Whenever she felt uncertain, she would do that before the giggles started.

I grabbed her by the shoulders. "That is amazing, Ton. Don't doubt yourself."

After she calmed down from her giggle fit of nervousness, she started to speak again, "Roxy, we haven't even been dating that long. I mean, seriously, I wouldn't be surprised if he just ran out on me." She let out a few more giggles.

I almost started cracking up from her ridiculous way of handling fear, but I maintained a straight face because I knew she needed me to.

"Don't overthink it, Ton. Just follow your heart."

"That's easy for you to say. Your dad might have walked in on you and Jordan in bed, but my parents completely sex-blocked me the last two nights. He probably thinks I'm a complete loser with crazy parents."

"I can't believe your parents just left town this morning." I chuckled as we made our way down the street.

"That's why tonight has to be perfect."

She looked desperate, and I just wanted to put the sparkle back in her eyes.

"Ton, it will be. The fact that he has stayed after your parents crashed your weekend should count for something. And you two had a blast yesterday. I think he wants more from you than just your la *cooch*-aracha."

A smile crossed her face. "We did have fun yesterday. Even with Jared there, we all had a blast. I wish you could have come."

Tonya had invited me to go to the beach with them, but I hadn't wanted to leave my house.

"I was waiting for my dad to come home. A whole lot of good that did." I laughed even though it wasn't funny.

"Yeah, yeah, whatever. I think I'm shredding your BFF card."

"What? I don't think so. I went to that stupid dinner for you even though it completely pissed off my boyfriend." I couldn't get over how much I loved calling Jordan my boyfriend.

"In my defense, he wasn't your boyfriend at the time, and when I asked you to go, the two of you weren't even talking."

"You still don't get to take my card." I stopped before we got to the car, and I stuck out my tongue at her.

"Like I could ever replace you anyway." She stopped and hugged me.

"Yeah, you'd better remember that." I squeezed her harder.

23

I walked through the door and called out to Jordan. There was no reply. I dropped my bags by the door and made my way upstairs.

"Oh, boyfriend?" I called out louder.

There was still nothing. At the top of the stairs, my stomach plummeted back down to the first floor. Jordan's door was cracked, and his music was on. I felt a sick feeling wash over me. It was the same scene the day I'd found Kevin and Sara together. I knew I was going to open that door and see Jordan with another girl. I swallowed back the stomach bile rising in my throat.

This isn't happening.

I turned around and rushed back down the stairs. I wouldn't let this happen to me again. As I pushed off the last stair, I slammed into a solid force and almost fell on my ass, but two strong hands gripped me.

"Whoa, babe. Where is the fire?"

I peered up to see Jordan giving me a bewildered look. He wasn't upstairs. He wasn't with another girl. The tears were falling before I could stop them.

"Baby, what's wrong?"

I flung my arms around him and squeezed him as hard as I could. I had never been so happy to be wrong in my life.

"Rox, you're scaring me. Tell me what's wrong, babe."

I pulled away, smiling. "Nothing is wrong. I haven't been this happy in a long time." I squeezed him again.

I loved that I could tell him that and know I was being one hundred percent honest. I was happy, ridiculously happy. A relationship with Jordan might not have been something I'd thought I wanted, but some greater power had known how much I needed him. Life was better with him. I was better with him. I couldn't help but wonder if maybe, just maybe, my mom had really had something to do with him being in my life. Maybe he was her last gift to me.

It might be crazy, but who knows?

"All right, I'm just going to take this as you having a moment." He kissed the top of my head.

"Yes, I am having a moment—a very, very happy moment. Be happy with me, Jordan. You and I just made a memory and an extremely happy one."

He gave a small chuckle. "I'm glad we just made a memory, Rox, even if I'm not sure what it was." He kissed my left cheek. "Sorry I didn't hear you come in. I was outside on the patio, checking how much charcoal was left. I thought I would grill us some steaks tonight."

"That sounds perfect. After dinner, I have a surprise for you."

"A surprise, huh?"

I walked over toward the front door and grabbed the pink Victoria's Secret bag. "Mmhmm…"

"I don't know about you, but I'm not that hungry anymore."

"Too bad because I'm starved."

"Is that so? Because I'll give you something to eat." He ran my hand down the front of his pants.

Luke Bryan's "That's My Kind of Night" started playing from my phone, and I knew Ryan was calling.

"Hold that thought." I had a few choice words for my brother, and I wasn't about to miss this phone call.

I answered the phone, "Just so you know, you are no longer my brother. I hate you."

"Well, hello to you, too, sis." There was a hint of amusement in his voice.

"Oh no, you don't get to sis me. You no longer have a sister. If you did, you wouldn't have sent our father home to check on me without telling me."

"How could I tell you when you refused to answer any of my calls?"

Okay, he was right. I had ignored his calls, but that wasn't the point. The point was, he'd called Dad and told him I needed to be checked on.

"Had I known he was going to find you in bed with some guy, I would have been there to see it for myself. What the hell is wrong with you, Roxy? First, the stripping, and now, you have Dad finding you in bed with a guy?"

"You don't get to yell at me or judge me. I hate you for sending Dad home and for not warning me. If it wasn't for you, Dad would never have walked in on that situation. Do you have any idea how humiliating that was?"

"Good. A guy shouldn't have been in your bed to begin with. Maybe it won't happen again."

"You do know that I'm not a child, right? I'm going to have sex, Ryan—lots and lots of sex. So, get over it and realize that I'm not a baby."

"Gross, Roxanne. Don't say stuff like that to me. I don't wanna hear that crap come out of your mouth."

"Sex, sex, sex—me naked with a guy."

"Grow up, Roxanne!" Ryan yelled before hanging up the phone.

I sank down into the overstuffed tan leather couch and tossed my phone on the coffee table. I hated fighting with my brother, and he was right. The way I had acted was immature, and it had totally gone against my whole I'm-not-a-child statement. He was just so infuriating.

Jordan sat down next to me. "That sounded like it went well."

I chuckled and leaned into him. "My brother is a douche bag."

"Eh, I don't know. If I had a little sister, I would probably act the same way. He is just trying to look after you."

"No, no, no. You don't get to side with him. I don't care if you are right. As my boyfriend, you have to side with me when it comes to my brother."

He slung his arm around my shoulders. "As your boyfriend, huh? In that case, your brother is the biggest bag of douche ever. In fact, he's douche juice."

"Douche juice?"

"Yeah. You know the stuff that comes out after douching?" he stated nonchalantly.

"That is so beyond gross. I think I'm going to gag. If you wanted to make sure I wasn't hungry, you succeeded."

"Look at that. I managed to be the perfect boyfriend and get you right where I want you. Now, let's get back to talking about that pink bag?" He pulled me onto his lap.

My stomach grumbled, proving that I was still in fact hungry.

"Perfect boyfriend, huh?"

"Am I not?" He nuzzled his mouth against my neck and tenderly kissed me.

"Um…I don't know. I think the perfect boyfriend would cook something for his girlfriend to eat."

"I thought you weren't hungry anymore?"

His breath was hot against my neck and had my body sending out different signals. I knew I was hungry, but I also had a need to get lost in Jordan.

My stomach growled loud enough for Jordan to hear this time, and it was the deciding factor. He lifted me off of him. "I hear you," he said to my stomach.

I laughed. "Sorry. I haven't eaten all day. I skipped breakfast because I thought Tonya and I were going to grab lunch, and we have a tendency to pig out. Then, she wanted to get new red streaks put in."

I was about to mention Chase and Luke, but I stopped myself. I didn't feel like explaining that awkwardness.

"Rox, don't apologize. I want to cook for you. Besides, I get you all night." He kissed me and then pulled away. "I do get you all night, right?"

"Yes, you get me all night." I smiled down at him as I stood up.

He got up off the couch and placed his hands on my hips. "Good. I'm going to go start the grill. Would you mind washing the vegetables for the salad, babe?"

"Oh, I see how it is. Tell me you will make me dinner and then put me to work." I laughed as I turned away from him.

He playfully smacked my ass. "Get your ass in the kitchen, woman."

As I walked into the kitchen, I spun to face him. I pulled up my shirt, flashing him, before spinning back around and heading to the counter with the large bowl of vegetables. Jordan came up behind me, wrapping his arms around my waist.

"You keep that up, and I might just make you starve," he growled in my ear.

I turned into him. "Worse things could happen."

He hoisted me up, and I wrapped my legs around his waist while fiercely kissing him. He set me down on the counter and pulled off my top. His hand fisted my hair as the other unclasped my bra. He pulled off my bra as I tugged up on his shirt. He helped me take it off before his mouth devoured my lips again, his tongue playing with mine. I would never get tired of kissing him.

My stomach decided to ruin the moment as it growled out in starvation. I wasn't even hungry anymore, so I didn't know what its problem was. All I wanted was Jordan.

I continued to kiss him, hoping he hadn't heard it, but my stomach was unrelenting.

Stupid, stupid stomach.

Jordan chuckled against my mouth. He dipped his head down to my stomach. "All right, I'll feed you."

"Just give me a piece of bread. That will shut it up. I swear, I'm not even hungry anymore—at least not for food." I wiggled my eyebrows at him.

"Nah, baby. I'm gonna feed you. I need to make sure you have stamina for tonight, and that requires food." He kissed me again before handing me his shirt.

"Well, when you put it that way..." I pulled on his shirt. It was soft in the well-worn way and smelled of Jordan.

The smile that crossed his face at seeing me in his shirt made my tummy flutter.

He kissed my forehead and then headed outside. Three words were on the tip of my tongue and were dying to come out, but I swallowed them down. It was too soon. I shouldn't be feeling like this.

I hopped off the counter and focused my attention on the salad.

Last night was one for the record books, and that was saying something, considering Jordan and I could never go just one round. Nonetheless, last night was pure perfection.

As we lay in bed, Jordan's arm was slung over my waist. He looked peaceful. I hated to move, but my body had needs, and I couldn't keep ignoring this one.

I carefully eased out of Jordan's hold and made my way to the bathroom. After my bladder was no longer screaming at me, I washed my hands. That was when I saw it. Jordan had put a new toothbrush on the counter. It was pink and had a bow on it.

Can he be any more thoughtful?

The little bit of the wall that was still up and guarding my heart completely disintegrated with the sight of the toothbrush. I *loved* Jordan, and there was no denying it.

I brushed my teeth with a perky smile. It was kind of painful to smile that hard for so long, but I couldn't stop. I wanted to jump on Jordan and kiss him to death when I came out of the bathroom.

But Luke Bryan started blaring out of my phone. I raced over to shut it up before it woke Jordan up.

"What?" I hissed.

"That is no way to answer your phone."

"Sorry. What the hell do you want, Ryan?"

"Come on, Roxy. How about you drop the hostility? I just want to talk to you."

I breathed a sigh of annoyance and decided I was tired of fighting with my brother. I walked back into the bathroom, shut the door, and slid down against it.

"Fine. What would you like to talk about?" All the anger was gone from my voice.

"How have you been?"

Now, it was back. "Seriously?" I couldn't believe he had asked that. He had made my life a living nightmare.

"Okay. Too soon for jokes. I get it."

"What do you want, Ry?"

"I would like for you not to be mad at me. I thought about everything, and I might have gone a bit overboard by telling Dad to stop by the house on his way to San Francisco."

That's great.

My brother had known that Dad was headed to San Francisco. I hadn't found out until after he left.

"Is that supposed to be your way of apologizing?"

"No, not exactly. It might have been the wrong way to handle things, but I'm not sorry that I did it. Dad said that you and he talked. He said he felt like you both took a step in the right direction for once."

I rolled my eyes. Here I was, talking to my brother about how my dad had felt instead of hearing it from him.

Sure, right direction.

"That doesn't change what you did or how much it sucked."

"I get that, Roxy, but put yourself in my shoes. I was worried about you."

"I'm still mad at you."

"I know, and I might even deserve it."

"Oh, you'd better believe you deserve it."

"I'm not apologizing, Roxy."

It was nice to know my brother no longer saw me as fragile anymore.

"I wouldn't expect you to."

"Can we move past the whole Dad mess then?"

I sighed. "I guess."

I really had no choice. He wasn't going to apologize, and I was sick of being mad at him. Fighting with my brother had never been something that I was good at.

"Good. Now, we can move on to our next issue."

"Next issue? What the hell are you talking about?"

"The guy, Roxy. Who was the guy?"

"Oh no, we are not having this conversation." I pressed the back of my head against the door. *Please let it go, Ryan.*

"You promised, you would keep me in the loop. You told Dad that he was your boyfriend. I want a name."

I knew not having to tell Ryan about my boyfriend was just wishful thinking. There was no chance that Ryan would let it go. He was as stubborn as I was.

I couldn't tell Ryan that it was Jordan, not over the phone, so I did what any other person would do. I lied. I said the first name that came to mind, "Ethan. His name is Ethan."

"Ethan? As in Ethan Frost?"

"Is there another Ethan?"

Okay, I hadn't claimed it was that Ethan. I just hadn't denied it either.

"Why didn't you just tell me sooner, Roxy? Ethan is a great guy. I'm glad you are with him."

"What? You are?"

"Yeah, he is a stand-up guy. I approve, Roxy.

"Thanks."

"No problem. Oh, before I let you go, I want to invite you down to Santa Barbara the weekend after next."

"Really. For what?"

"My boss is letting Brent and me use the company's vacation house for the weekend—you know, for all our hard work."

"Um…yeah, sounds fun."

"Great! I've missed you, Roxy. It will be nice to see you."

"Yeah, whatever. You act like you've been gone for years."

"This is where you say, 'Geez, Ryan, I have missed you, too.'"

I laughed. "I have missed you, too, Ry."

"I will talk to you later."

"Yeah, I'll talk to you later."

"I love you."

"Love you, too."

After I hung up with my brother, I realized how excited I was about going to see him. I'd missed the jerk more than I would ever admit. I wasn't thrilled about Brent being there, too, but I would just have to deal with that later.

Thinking about Brent made my heart hurt a little. He and I used to be close. I hated that he'd turned out to be Mr. Slutty Cheater Butt. But no matter how much I hated what he had done, I was kind of missing him, too—even though I would never admit that.

I exited the bathroom to see Jordan sitting up, not looking very happy.

"What's wrong?" I crawled onto the bed.

"Whom were you talking to?" He scratched the back of his head.

"My brother." I grinned and gave Jordan a quick kiss on the lips. "Sorry I woke you up."

"Can I ask why you were talking about Ethan?"

I hadn't expected Jordan to hear the conversation. I could probably lie and get away with it, but Jordan and I were finally in a good place. I wasn't about to start lying to him now.

Besides, full disclosure, right?

"My dad told Ryan that I had a boyfriend. Ryan wanted to know what his name was."

"And you said it was Ethan?"

"Yes, but before you get upset, I only told him that because I want us to tell him that we're together."

"Why do you even care about what your brother thinks? You seem to be pissed off at him most of the time anyway."

"That's not true. I love my brother. We just like to bicker. When all is said and done, I would give my life for him if I had to. I just hope that it never comes to that. I'm pretty happy right now, and I would like to keep, you know, living. But you should know my brother's opinion means a lot to me. He told me before he left that I needed to stay away from you. That was only because he didn't know that we'd met way before I knew you were Brent's cousin. You're kind of supposed to be off-limits to me. I want Ryan to find out about us the right way, not over the phone."

"You're happy, huh? Really happy?"

I smiled a real smile at Jordan. The whole part about him being on the do-not-touch list hadn't even fazed him. All he cared about was that I was happy.

"Yes, I'm really flippin' happy."

Jordan pulled me onto his lap. "I don't like that you told him your boyfriend's name was Ethan, but I understand why you said it. Just don't think you are going to be parading Ethan around to keep up your lie."

"I wouldn't dream of it." I pressed my lips to his, and I kissed him with all the love that I felt for him. I pulled away, and he looked bummed. "I want to talk to you before I get any more distracted."

He nuzzled my neck and started kissing it. "Oh, but I'm trying really hard to distract you."

"I know, and you are doing a fantastic job. That's why you need to stop." I laughed. "Just give me five minutes, and then you can distract the hell out of me."

Jordan reluctantly pulled away and placed his hands behind his head as he leaned back against the headboard of his bed.

"Start talking. The clock's ticking." His devilish smile almost made me forget what I'd wanted to say.

Oh…Santa Barbara. That's right.

"Well, my brother just asked me to go down to Santa Barbara and visit him while he takes the weekend off. His boss is letting him use the company's vacation house for the weekend. Apparently, he kind of misses me. I'm pretty sure he just wants me down there to keep an eye on me, so I can't get into any more trouble. I swear, I don't know what he is going to do when I am at school. Back to my point, I think we should go together."

Jordan sat there, thinking about everything I had just said.

"Brent texted me a few days ago and asked me to head down there, too. I already told him I was busy."

"You just said that because you didn't want to leave me, right? You're not actually busy, are you?"

Jordan was quiet again and was now staring down at his hands, and I started thinking that asking him to go with me was a bad idea. It was obvious that he didn't want to. My shoulders slouched in disappointment. Then, Jordan sat up and pulled me onto his lap.

"I'll text him later and tell him that I have changed my plans and will be there."

I was thrilled and could barely contain myself. I threw my arms around his neck and kissed him hard. "I'm so excited. I think that weekend will be the perfect time to tell them about us. What do you say?"

"You want to tell Brent and your brother that we're together that weekend?" Jordan asked.

I excitedly nodded my head.

"You're sure?"

"Absolutely. I don't want to keep lying. I don't want you to think that I'm keeping you a secret just because of my brother's stupid need to have control over whom I let into my life."

"I can't wait to spend the weekend in Santa Barbara with you. It means a lot to me that you want them to know, but be forewarned, Brent is probably gonna take a swing at me. I'm the last person that he wants you to be with."

"I don't care what Brent thinks. I'm not going to let it bother me. He and Ryan can't continue to dictate whom I am allowed to be with. I don't care that you're Brent's cousin."

He shook his head and smiled at me. "If you only knew..."

"Knew what?" I asked.

He didn't bother to answer me. Instead, he just kissed me long and hard. He laid me back on the bed and leaned over me.

"I adore you, Rox."

My breath hitched at his words. "I adore you, too." Every part of me wanted to say *love*. I knew what I was feeling, but I just couldn't say it.

Once I did, it would be out there, and I wouldn't be able to take it back.

What if he doesn't feel the same?

That would completely crush me. Seeing as we were keeping our relationship from certain people, right now just wasn't the time.

Maybe after we tell my brother?

That would give me time to build up the courage to tell Jordan how much I loved him. I could do it on the beach at sunset. It would be perfect and romantic. I decided that was when I would tell Jordan how I felt. That was when I would make sure we would make another happy memory.

"So, didn't you have something you wanted to distract me with?"

"Are you ready? Because I'm about to distract the hell out of you." He smiled before covering my mouth with his and doing just as he'd said.

The next day, I wanted to call Tonya and gush about how in love with Jordan I was and tell her all about my plans for Santa Barbara, but there was someone else I wanted to tell first.

I went to the cemetery, and I made my way across the grass. The pain I felt from losing my mom never went away. It was an ache that I carried with me everywhere. Some days, it would be more painful than others. Today, that ache was excruciating. It caused every nerve in my body to fill with sadness to the point where I almost felt as though I would drown in it all over again.

But I didn't turn back and run away. I would face the pain, and I would feel the sadness and let it hurt. It was my own reminder that she had been here.

I knelt down in front of my mother's grave. I looked over at the graves on either side of my mother's. They both had bouquets of flowers. I felt guilty for not bringing her any.

"I guess that I should have brought you flowers. I'm sorry that I didn't. I will next time though."

I ran my fingers over the engraving on her headstone. The tiny crystals under her name sparkled in the sunlight. It was a small thing, but my mother would have loved the crystals.

I wiped away the tears. "I should have come back sooner. It's just that the last time I was here, it was hard. I guess I was scared to come back because of how painful it was. That was selfish of me though. You're gone, and I shouldn't stay away because of how much it hurts. I'm sorry I did."

I sat down and crossed my legs. Talking to her seemed as strange as it had the last time, but I didn't stop.

"Ryan and Brent are down in Los Angeles right now. They landed an internship with a great company. Between you and me, the only reason they got it was because of Dad, but I'm still happy for them."

I wanted her to know that we were all somehow surviving without her. I was trying to stay upbeat for her, but I couldn't.

I wrapped my arms around myself. The pain was winning. I dug my nails deeper into my palms, but it was no use. All I could do was feel hurt and pray that it wouldn't consume me.

I sat there, quiet, as the tears continued to fall like raindrops.

The clouds covered the sun, darkening the sky. I looked up to see the color of the sky had changed to a gloomy gray as if it were hurting as badly as I was.

"There will never be a day that goes by when I won't miss you and pray that you could come back to us. I'm not hiding out or trying to rid myself of the pain with pills anymore. I'm sorry that I ever did that. I can't imagine how upset that must have made you."

I pulled my knees up to my chest and squeezed them. The pain in my heart was increasing. I held my breath and tried to ease it. I thought of Jordan's face and remembered why I had come here to begin with. I let out a deep breath, and the ache in my chest stopped threatening to consume me.

Jordan and his magic.

Just thinking about Jordan made me feel better. The clouds moved, and I felt the warmth of the sun as it shone down on me. The sky was still a deep gray, but it no longer reminded me of sadness.

"Thank you, Mom. Thank you so much for him. I know it was you who brought us together. Thank you for sending him to me. I love him. I've tried to fight it and pretend that I don't, but I do. I just wanted you to be the first person that I told. I love you, Mom. I miss you."

I stood up. I blinked back the new tears forming. I didn't want to cry anymore today. I wanted my mom to see me staying strong. I wanted her to know that I was happy.

As I walked away, hope flowed through my body. For the first time, I thought that I might actually be okay one day—or at least, not as broken. I hoped it was possible for all my broken pieces to mend themselves. I wasn't delusional. I knew that I would never be whole again, not without my mother, but that didn't mean I was destined to fall completely apart.

This new feeling of hope had me thinking that maybe I wasn't as screwed up as I had thought. It would just take time, lots and lots of time, but I would somehow come out stronger in the end.

The hope I was feeling made me want to believe that anything was possible.

25

I called Jordan as soon as I got back home.

"Hey, babe."

"Hello, boyfriend." I would seriously never get sick of saying that.

"I will never get tired of hearing you say that."

I loved that I could hear a smile in his voice. My own smile grew even bigger. "Are you still picking up lunch?"

"I was just about to head out and pick it up."

"Good. I'm hungry."

"For me? Because I could stop by and feed you before I pick up lunch."

"As tempting as you are, I'm in need of food."

"But I want you," he whined.

"You just had me—twice in fact—just a few hours ago. I think you will survive until after lunch and a movie."

"I don't know. Wait—what? Now, I have to wait till after a movie, too? You're killing me, Rox," he teased.

"I miss you." Again, I wanted to say *love*, but that would just have to wait.

"I miss you more."

"Then, you should hurry and get our food."

"I'm going. I'm going."

He made kiss noises into the phone, and my heart turned to mush.

"See you soon."

"Yes, you will. I will be the guy with lunch and a hard-on."

"Oh God! I'm hanging up now."

"What? You don't want to talk about Buddy?" He laughed.

I was cracking up. "Hanging up!" I said in a singsong voice.

"He wants you, babe."

"Food," was the last thing I said before hanging up.

God, I love that man.

I tossed my phone onto the couch. I couldn't stop the permanent grin on my face. It felt incredible to feel happy like this again. I hadn't thought that I would ever feel this way after my mom passed.

I ran upstairs to change my clothes. The doorbell chimed as I pulled the dress I had picked over my head. I headed downstairs.

As I reached the bottom of the stairs, the doorbell rang again.

"Coming!" I yelled.

I opened the door, ready to tell some salesperson to buzz off and never come back, only to have all the air vanish from my lungs. My heart stopped.

Did hell just freeze over? What is he doing here?

"Hey, Rocket." Kevin stood there, looking at me with his signature cocky grin.

I used to love that grin. Now, I just hated it and wanted to smack it off his face.

Seriously, what is he doing here? And why can't I find my voice?

"You gonna invite me in?" he said with that smile.

What is he so goddamn happy about?

He brushed back his hair that had kept falling into his eyes.

Oh…those eyes.

Those eyes had hijacked my heart and made his every wish my command. Now, I could barely stand to look at his stupid smug face.

I swallowed hard. "What are you doing here?" I asked in a shaky voice.

I mean, really? He has to be nuts to come to my house. If my brother were here, Kevin would be in serious pain right now.

"I wanted to talk to you. I figured that this would be the best way to do that."

There was no way he was brave enough to chance running into my brother. "You knew Ryan was out of town, didn't you?"

He shrugged as his cocky grin turned into a smirk.

What an asshole.

"Can I come in now?"

"No."

"Come on, Rocket. I just want to talk."

"I told you to stop calling me that!"

"I'll stop. Are you gonna let me in now?"

I knew that I shouldn't, but for some stupid reason, I stepped to the side and motioned for him to come in. Okay, that stupid reason was that I used to love the guy, and a small part of me was curious to hear what he had to say. It shouldn't have mattered to me, but it did.

He walked in like he belonged and made his way over to the couch before falling into his usual spot. My stomach turned as I thought about all the times when we had shared that couch together back when I was blissfully happy and completely in love with him.

He patted the cushion next to him. "Come and sit down, Roxy."

I crossed my arms, walked over to the opposite couch, and sat as far away from him as possible.

He laughed.

Seriously? He is laughing at me?

I glared at him. "You said you wanted to talk, so talk!"

"Don't be like that, Roxy. There is no need to be hostile." He got up and came over to sit on the same couch as me.

I raised my voice as I said, "For the last time, what do you fucking want?"

"Rocket…chill. I wanna talk about us."

"Use that name one more time, and I will take a bat to you! Also, there is no us. In case you've forgotten, you have a girlfriend! We have nothing to talk about!" I stood up and walked away from him.

It was painful having him that close. It wasn't because I wanted him, but having him here was causing me to think of the memories we had made. Now, those memories just led to pain because he'd ruined everything to be with some slut.

"I don't care about Sara. I never did," he announced, making his way next to me.

Did he not see I moved away from him for a reason? If he didn't care about Sara, why was he willing to throw us away for her?

"Then, why, Kevin? Why did you…why did you…" I couldn't even say the words. Tears burned my eyes. I couldn't cry in front of him. I wouldn't cry in front of him. I crossed my arms and dug my nails into my palms.

"What I did was a mistake. I was freaking out, Roxy. You were gonna go to New York. I was having a hard time dealing with that. Then, your mom died. I just didn't know how to handle everything."

Really? That's his excuse for shredding my already broken heart into pieces.

Angry, I threw up my hands in the air. "So, you chose to ignore me and fuck Sara?" I yelled.

"I'm not saying that it was right."

"I would hope not, Kevin, because it wasn't right. I needed you, but you were too busy fucking some whore to care."

"I never meant for you to see that."

"It was a mistake, and you never meant for me to see it? That makes a ton of sense. Oh, and thanks for calling the cops on me. Way to make what you were doing that much better." I turned away from him. I didn't know how much longer I was going to be able to keep the tears at bay.

He turned me to face him and kept his hands on my shoulders. His touch burned my skin with painful memories.

"Roxy, you were freaking out. You went after my car. I didn't know how else to stop you."

I shrugged off his hands and walked toward the door before spinning around to face him. "You shouldn't have been with her to begin with. As for your car, I wish I had a bat right now."

"Roxy, please calm down. I don't want to fight. I'm trying to fix things."

Fix things? Really? "Seriously, Kevin, you might think I went insane, but you are the mental one if you think you can do anything to fix things. I'm talking certifiable."

"We were good together once, Roxy. Who says we can't be good again?"

"Me! I say we can't! I don't feel like repeating the past. I already know how that story ends."

"We could change the ending, Roxy. We could make it work."

"See, that's where you're wrong. We had the perfect story. You changed our happily ever after, Kevin. I wanted forever with you. The whole reason why you're here, trying to fix things, is because you broke them. You ruined it all. I loved you."

"Are you telling me you don't love me anymore? I still love you, Roxy."

"You don't love me, Kevin. I'm not even sure you ever did. When you love someone, you don't hurt that person the way you hurt me. You don't break that person, and that's what you did to me, Kevin. You broke me. So, no, I don't love you anymore. I'll never forget you, but I won't live in the past with you either. Someday, I hope I can forgive you, but that is not happening today. When I do forgive you, it will be for my benefit, not yours."

"Rocket, come on. We had plans. We had our future ahead of us. You were supposed to be Mrs. Kevin Styles."

"Well, you should have thought about that before you stuck your dick inside Sara. I am sure she would love to be your future wife because that will never be me." I opened the front door for him. It was way past time for him to leave.

"Roxy, please?" he begged, looking beyond pathetic.

I saw Jordan pulling into the driveway, and my heart fluttered. I was doing the right thing. I had a great guy in my life, and I wasn't about to throw that away.

"No, Kevin, I wasn't enough for you, and now, you're not enough for me."

He looked absolutely taken aback by my words, and I was glad. I could see he was about to protest leaving, but Jordan walked through the door. He looked at Kevin and gave me a peck on the lips.

"Hey, babe. You didn't tell me that we were having company?" Jordan smiled at me.

"That's because Kevin was just leaving," I informed him.

Kevin walked toward the door as Jordan carried the bag of food over to the dining room table.

Kevin's eyes were sad when they met mine. I was glad that he was feeling pain. He deserved it.

"You're making a mistake, Roxy."

"No, Kev, that was you who made the mistake."

Kevin walked out the door to his car without looking back. I'd meant it when I said I wasn't in love with him anymore. As he drove away, I said a last good-bye to what Kevin and I had been.

I closed the door and smiled at Jordan. "I don't know about you, but I'm starving."

"Are we gonna talk about what just happened, Rox?" Jordan's voice was full of concern, but he had nothing to be worried about.

I'd just let my past walk out the door, so I could enjoy my life with my future.

"Nope. I don't want to waste time talking about things that no longer matter."

26

I invited Tonya over for some girl time.

Jordan was spending the day with Travis and Scott. He'd tried to tell me what they were doing, but I'd tuned him out after he'd mentioned dune buggies. It wasn't that I hadn't cared what my boyfriend was up to. I just had no interest in dune buggies.

That doesn't make me a bad girlfriend, does it?

I pondered this as I made Tonya and me mojitos. Britney Spears boomed from the outdoor stereo system. Apparently, we were having a girls' power day.

Tonya sashayed out of the pool house, shaking her hips. I couldn't help but laugh at my bestie's goofiness. A day of carefree relaxation was exactly what I'd needed. Kevin stopping by yesterday had done more for my psyche than I cared to admit.

Then, there was that infuriating email from my father, telling me that he would not be coming back home tomorrow and that we would see each other in a few weeks. That email had had me seeing red.

I poured more Bacardi into my drink. I sucked down half of it before topping it off again. Honestly, part of me wondered how far away I was from hiding vodka bottles under my bed.

Okay, I'm not that bad. Am I?

I shook off the thought.

I was hoping that a day of fun with my best friend would make the frustration and sad feelings disappear.

"This was a fantastic idea, Rox. No boys—just you, me, and the pool."

I spun around and held up the drinks. "Oh, let's not forget about the guest of honor."

Tonya squealed and skipped over to get her drink. "Mmm...minty-fresh goodness with a kick. I'm telling you, dollface. You could have a future in bartending."

"Oh God! Let's hope not."

"When are Jordan and the guys planning on returning?"

I tossed the lounger rafts into the pool. "Um...not until later tonight. He said something about them getting dinner before they come back."

"Is there trouble in paradise?" Tonya eyed me suspiciously.

"Oh no, nothing like that. In fact, everything with Jordan is going great. I'm actually in love with him."

The slew of excited oh-my-gods that came from Tonya shocked the hell out of me. Until now, I hadn't been sure if she was one hundred percent on board with Jordan and me dating.

"Have you told him yet?"

"No…not even close. I mean, what if he doesn't even feel the same way?"

"You are kidding me! How could you even think that he wouldn't feel the same way? Rox, the guy is crazy about you. It's written all over his face every time he looks at you."

"Well, I hope so."

I sank into the pool. The water was perfect. I pulled myself onto my lounger. I paddled my way over to the poolside to pick up my drink.

"If it's not love problems, then what's got you in a funk?"

"Am I that transparent?"

Tonya giggled. "Maybe not to most, but I'm your best friend, and I know when something is off with you."

"I know that we already talked about it, but Kevin's surprise visit is still bothering me. Why the hell couldn't he just stay away and let me continue to hate him from afar?"

"Do you miss him?"

"No, it's not that I miss Kevin. I still want to kill him for what he did to me. I guess seeing him in my house, sitting in his old spot, kind of made me nostalgic for all the happy times that we had. I don't miss Kevin. I miss what I thought Kevin and I had. That's what makes me wanna break down all over again. I hate that I will never be able to blindly trust a guy and fall blissfully in love. He ruined that for me, and I hate him every time I think about it. Then, I just get furious because I want to forget him, but there he is, ruining every other relationship that I will ever be in. It's not fair."

Tonya settled onto her raft with her drink in hand and smiled at me. "I told you before, Rox. You can't be mad with someone and let him go. You have to stop being mad first. That is the only way he no longer has any hold on you. With that said, even when you do one day forgive him, every relationship after him won't be the same as it was with him. You were hurt. That kind of emotional damage doesn't ever go away. Trust me, I have tried to have a relationship without thinking about Blaine. It's impossible. He is the one who I compare every other guy to—but not when it comes to looks or anything. I always wonder if the guy that I'm with will hurt me in the same way that he did. It sucks, and I hate it. All I can tell you is that when you find the one you want to make it work with, you just have to jump in with both feet. If you don't, the doubts and what-ifs will tear the relationship apart before it even starts."

"You still compare every guy to Blaine? What about the guys you were with after him? Do you compare anyone to them?"

"Nope. It all goes back to Blaine. He wrecked me, but on a happier note, Shawn doesn't seem to mind that I'm slightly emotionally damaged."

I gulped my mojito and felt the shiver. "I'm happy for you, Tonya. I think you two look adorable together."

"I know that it might seem like everything with Shawn and me is happening quickly, but it kind of keeps me from overthinking anything, and I think that is exactly what I've always needed. You did say that the guys wouldn't be home till later, right?"

"Yeah. Why?"

My question was answered as I looked over to see Tonya taking off her bathing suit top.

"I should have known." I laughed.

"What? You know how much I hate tan lines."

"Yeah, yeah." I slipped off the raft and made my way out of the pool.

"Where are you going?" Tonya whined.

"I'm just going to make sure the front door is locked, and I am in need of a refill."

"Oh, refill mine, too, please?" she paddled to the edge of the pool.

I took her glass. "Yes, your highness."

I set the glasses on the outside bar, grabbed a towel, and made my way through the house. I was surprised to see that the front door was wide open. Tonya must not have made sure it was shut. I closed and locked it. That way, I would know when Jordan was back, and I could keep him and his buddies from seeing us topless.

I untied my top and laid it on the couch before making my way back outside. There was something sexy and freeing about walking around topless. I wondered what a day in a nudist colony would feel like. Then again, I would have to see everyone else's naked bodies, too, and wrinkly old butts didn't make me think sexy and free. It was just gross.

"Hot mama!" Tonya catcalled from the pool.

I went to the bar, made our drinks, and got back into the pool.

We spent the afternoon floating while rotating from our backs to our tummies. Today was exactly what my ghostly skin had needed.

I was lying on my stomach, starting to doze off, when I swore, I saw someone dashing across the far part of the backyard. I pushed up so fast that I rolled off the raft before landing in the water.

Tonya was laughing as I surfaced.

"Way to go, klutzo. Why the spaz move?" She continued her laughter.

"You didn't see that?" My heart was racing.

Tonya sat up and looked around the yard. "See what? You falling into the water? Yep, I caught the whole thing."

I searched the yard for some kind of proof that I hadn't been seeing things. "Not that, you jerk. I could have sworn that I saw someone running across the yard."

"I think you have had one drink too many. It was probably just a bird or something."

"I'm not dumb, Ton, and a bird looks nothing like a person."

"Rox, we would have heard if someone were back here."

I swam to the edge of the pool and climbed out. "You're right. I'm probably just imagining things. I'm going to change the music. I've had enough of your Britney playlist."

"Oh, put on some Rihanna."

"That I can do." I made my way into the pool house and changed the music. Out of the window, I saw another moving shadow. *Okay, there is no way that I am just seeing things now.* I grabbed Tonya's iPod and left the pool house.

"Hello? You were supposed to change the music, not turn it off," Tonya stated.

I got close to the pool. "Tonya, can you get out? I need to see you in the house for a second."

"What? I just got comfortable again."

Damn, she's whiny.

"Tonya, please."

Tonya rolled off her raft and made her way over to the edge of the pool. "What's up, Rox?"

I picked up her top and crouched down. "Tonya, I think someone is in the backyard."

She turned to look.

"Don't look, you moron. Just get out of the pool and come inside with me," I hissed through clenched teeth.

Tonya quickly got out of the pool.

"Laugh, and act like we are joking while we head in."

Tonya and I faked laughter until we were inside the house. Then, I locked the door behind us. Tonya's face showed that she was as scared as I was. She continued giggling. She couldn't stop.

"Do you really think someone is back there? I'm feeling all sorts of creeped out right now." She was trying to hold back her laughter.

"I don't know, Ton. I just didn't have a good feeling, and I swear that I saw someone."

"Should we call the cops?"

"Um…no. I'm just gonna call Jordan. Make sure all the doors and windows are locked, okay?"

I called Jordan and told him what I thought I had seen. He repeated over and over to lock the doors and not to answer the door for anyone but him.

I'm not a complete dummy. I know that much.

After checking all the upstairs windows, Tonya made her way back downstairs. I was on my hands and knees, searching for my bikini top.

"What are you doing?" She laughed.

"I'm looking for my top. I took it off and put it on the couch. Now, I can't find it."

"Are you sure you didn't bring it outside?"

I stood up, put my hands on my hips, and contemplated the thought. "I am pretty sure that I put it on the couch, but maybe you're right. I might have brought it outside."

"Well, I don't see you getting it until Jordan gets here."

"Nope. I guess not. Why don't you find something to watch on TV while I go throw on a dress?"

"I feel like we should be huddled together and holding knives, not watching TV." She chuckled.

"The house isn't under attack. We are just taking precautions." I sounded more reassuring than I felt.

"With that said, reruns of *America's Next Top Model* will have to be our entertainment." Tonya smiled.

At least she wasn't still laughing. "Sounds perfect."

I made my way upstairs. Once in my room, I found a light-yellow sundress and pulled it on. I couldn't shake the eerie feeling I had. I was so sure that I'd left my top on the couch. I looked around my room to see if anything looked out of place, but everything seemed to be exactly where it should be.

Maybe I did just have too much to drink? Maybe the sun was getting to me?

I'd probably made a big deal out of nothing.

I went back downstairs to watch *America's Next Top Model* with Tonya until Jordan got here. I loved the fact that he was going to come back to check on me.

An hour later, the boys arrived. Jordan, Travis, and Scott were making their way through my house and backyard, making sure no one was there.

"I'm sorry that I crashed your guys' outing." I pouted, hugging Jordan.

"Don't be, baby. If you felt uncomfortable, then you did the right thing. I'm glad that you called me."

"I really think I saw someone, Jordan."

"You might have, Rox, but no one is out there now."

I walked outside and looked for my swimsuit top.

"What are you searching for, babe?"

"My bikini top. I thought that I took it off inside, but I couldn't find it in there, and now, I can't find it out here."

"You girls were topless?" Jordan gave me his disapproving look.

"Damn, we should have just stayed here," joked Scott.

Jordan shot him a death glare.

"She bit me, bro. You can't blame me for being hooked ever since."

Travis pulled his brother into a headlock and gave him a noogie. "You don't get to have those kinds of thoughts about his girlfriend," Travis reprimanded his little brother.

"That's easy for you to say. You're not the one who she bit."

Scott was going to hold on to that moment forever. The memory of me biting him would forever make me blush now.

Travis shoved his brother into the pool, causing everyone to crack up.

"What was that for, you dick?" Scott shouted at Travis when he surfaced.

"I didn't feel like throwing you under a cold shower."

Scott pulled himself out of the pool. I almost felt bad for him. He looked ridiculous in his waterlogged clothing.

I went into the house and found some sweats and an old T-shirt in Brent's room. Being in his room made me miss him more than I'd expected. I hadn't talked to Brent since he and Ryan left, but I found myself wanting to work things out with him. Part of me was kind of excited to see him next weekend. Maybe we could find a way to get past what had happened and move on. No matter how much I tried to pretend, I was not okay with Brent not being in my life. I couldn't fathom it being a forever thing. He meant way too much to me. I couldn't possibly lose him forever.

I pushed down my sadness concerning Brent and went back outside.

"Stop thinking about getting me naked, and you can have these." I held out the dry clothes as a peace offering.

"I should just stay in the wet clothes then, Roxy. My brain doesn't always do what it should."

Jordan playfully punched Scott on the shoulder. "Keep my girlfriend out of your dirty mind."

Scott held up his hands in innocence. "Okay, okay. I will do my best."

He then winked at me before taking the clothes and going inside to change.

I shook my head in disbelief at his overly flirtatious ways.

"All right, girlie, seeing as no mass murderer is sneaking around your home, I'm gonna head out. I'm leaving tomorrow, and I haven't even started to pack yet," Tonya said.

I pulled her into a strong hug. "I'm sorry if I ruined our afternoon."

"Don't be, dollface. I had a blast, and there was just enough drama to kill my buzz, so I can drive now." She kissed my cheek.

"I'll see you next weekend. Until then, get all the sexy time you can with your man." I wiggled my brows at her.

"I'm planning on keeping him naked for as much of the week as possible." She laughed, but I knew she was completely serious.

"Later, boys." Tonya waved at the guys before turning to leave.

Jordan made his way over to me and wrapped his arms around my waist from behind me.

"Where is she going?" Jordan nuzzled his lips against my neck.

"She is going to spend the week with Shawn in Santa Barbara. I told her that the four of us can do something one of the days when we're down there." I turned in his arms and pecked his lips.

I thought I saw confusion in his eyes for a moment, but it faded quickly, and he smiled back down at me.

"Sounds fun."

"Hey, man. Scott and I are gonna head out," Travis announced.

"Oh, you guys don't have to leave. I feel horrible for crashing your day. At least, let me cook dinner for you?" I offered.

"That's sweet, but our mother actually just called. Scott and I have to move some furniture for her. Dinner another time?" Travis gave me a one-armed hug.

"You just tell me when." I smiled at him. Travis wasn't nearly as scary as he had been the day I met him on the beach. He was just a muscled, tattooed teddy bear.

"Do you guys need me to help you out?" Jordan asked Travis.

"Nah, bro. Stay with your girl. Scott and I can handle it."

Scott came over for a hug of his own. "Thanks for the clothes, Roxy." He squeezed me against his chest and lifted me up off the ground.

As he put me back down, Travis smacked him upside the head. "Get your own girlfriend."

Scott rubbed the back of his head and smiled at me. "But she's perfect."

"Yeah, it's time for you to leave," Jordan told the brothers, glaring at Scott in a way that I didn't think was all that playful anymore.

Jordan and I walk the brothers to the front door. After they left, I took Jordan's hand and pulled him toward the couch. We sat down, and I curled up next to him.

"Thank you for coming to check things out."

"Of course, babe. I would do anything for you." He pulled me in tighter and kissed my forehead.

I knew that I should respect Daddy's rules until he came back home and had a chance to meet Jordan, but since he couldn't make time in his schedule to even call me, I wasn't going to follow his stupid rules.

"Stay the night with me?" I smiled up at Jordan.

"There's nowhere else I would rather be."

I crawled onto his lap and ran my fingers through his soft thick locks. Looking into his eyes, I wanted to tell him that my heart was overflowing with love for him. Instead, I pressed my lips to his and put every ounce of emotion I felt for him into it. I might not have said it, but deep down, he had to know how I really felt about him.

He has to.

27

I was glad that Jordan had stayed the night. I hated to admit it, but the fact that I never found my bikini top had me more than a little freaked out. I tried to tell myself that I hadn't really seen anyone and that it had all been in my head, but I couldn't explain the missing top. I shook my head, trying to stop thinking about the creepiness of yesterday.

Jordan walked out of the bathroom with a white towel wrapped around his waist, looking all sexy. I knew I had to get away from him before we never made it to the movies. I blew him a kiss before making my way downstairs.

I loved how comfortable our relationship was. We had only been together for a short amount of time, but it felt like we had been together forever. Everything was just right with us. We just seemed to fit perfectly together.

We'd even started making plans for school. I was excited that I would be going to the same college as my boyfriend. It was another reason that I was convinced my mother must have sent him to me. Once again, I said a silent prayer and thanked my mother for Jordan.

I was reapplying lip gloss and making sure I was ready to leave when Jordan's phone started belting out "Operate" by Three Days Grace.

"Honey, your phone," I called up to him.

I picked up his phone from the coffee table to take it upstairs to him. A picture of a beautiful blonde making a kissy face lit up his screen. I stared at it, and my stomach seized.

Who the fuck is Amy? And why is her stupid kissy face on my boyfriend's phone?

Jordan came down the stairs, full of smiles for me. He made his way from the stairs over to me as the phone continued to sing. "Thanks, baby." He held out his hand, waiting for me to hand over the phone.

I was stiff, and all I could do was stare dumbly at him. The phone finally went silent.

"Rox, what's wrong?"

I swallowed back the fear rising from the pit of my stomach, and I handed him his phone. "Who's Amy?" I tried to ask casually, but the fear and cracking in my voice came out louder than thunder.

Jordan's face crinkled up and then went blank, like he was uncomfortable but wanted to hide it. His phone started blaring again. He looked down before ignoring the call and powering it off.

Oh my God, this is not happening.

I felt sick. Not trusting my body to hold me up, I walked to the couch and sat down. I wrapped my arms around myself.

This can't be happening again.

Jordan moved quickly to sit next to me on the couch. I couldn't stop my reaction as I cringed away. I stared at him in disgust.

"Rox, don't look at me like that. It's not what you're thinking."

How can he know what I'm thinking unless it is what I am fucking thinking?

Any innocent, rational person wouldn't go to that dark place.

"Who is she?"

"That's Amy, my ex."

"That's your ex? I didn't know you guys were still friends. She seems eager to get a hold of you. You should probably call her back." My voice was as stiff as my body. I was shutting down, trying to remove all my emotions and become stone. It was the only way I would be able to stay together, or this would be the moment that completely destroyed me.

How dumb could I be to let myself get close to someone again? What the hell was I thinking?

I hugged myself tighter.

"I don't care that she calls, Rox. I never pick up."

I wasn't sure if he was just informing me or trying to convince me.

Jordan pulled me into an unwanted hug. I stayed frozen against him and continued to think.

Just stay as hard as stone. You won't fall apart.

I had to put my walls back up. I couldn't let him see me fall apart. I wanted to run away from him. I needed to get away from him. I couldn't hold myself together and be close to him at the same time.

I attempted to push away from him, but Jordan squeezed me tighter.

"Baby, I have you. Remember, I won't let you fall apart. Please believe me. I don't talk to her. She calls, and I ignore her. I'm yours, baby, all yours. I'm not him, Rox."

I felt tears starting to fall. I wanted to believe him. I should believe him. He had never lied to me. I dropped the death grip that I had on myself, wrapped my arms around him, and clung to him as though I might lose him if I didn't hold on tight enough.

"I'm sorry!" I cried.

"You don't have to apologize, baby."

"No, I do. I saw her picture on your phone, and I instantly thought the worst of you. I shouldn't have done that. I'm sorry, Jordan. I'm screwed up, and I have trust issues, but you have never given me a reason not to trust you. I'm very sorry for jumping to that terrible conclusion."

Jordan took my face in his hands. "For as long as you're mine, I will always be yours, only yours. I promise."

I kissed him with more passion than I knew was possible. Every doubt that I'd had was swept away with that one kiss.

He finally pulled away and looked at me. It seemed like he wanted to say something, but he just kissed my forehead instead. With all my doubts destroyed, I realized that I was irrefutably in love with Jordan. I had known this for a while, but in that moment, I wanted to shout it from the rooftop. He'd said he was mine. He must feel the same way, but I didn't want our perfect memory to be tarnished by his ex. Our perfect memory would happen after everyone knew about us.

Wow! I am in love. Just thinking about it made my whole body tingle.

"Are you ready to head to the movies, baby?"

I stood and checked my reflection in the mirror. Even with the smudge of mascara under my eyes, being in love looked great on me. After I fixed my face, I turned to Jordan and gave him a huge smile.

"Yes, boyfriend, I am ready—well, almost ready."

"What's up, Rox? Do you need me to get you something before we go?"

"Not to come off as a jealous girlfriend"—*Okay, I am totally a jealous girlfriend*— "but what is up with the kissy face photo?"

Jordan shook his head at me and smiled. "That's been her contact photo for the last year and a half."

"So, would you be offended if I asked you to delete it?"

Jordan wrapped his arms around my waist. "You know, you're pretty adorable when you're jealous."

Let's see how freaking adorable he thinks I am if he doesn't delete that picture.

I raised an eyebrow. "Is that a yes? You'll delete the picture?"

After messing with his phone for a minute, Jordan handed it to me. "Would you like to do the honors?"

I looked down at his phone. On the screen was a message asking if he was sure he wanted to delete that photo.

I laughed and pressed my finger on Yes. As easy as it was to delete her photo from his phone, that wasn't going to stop her from calling him. I didn't know the girl, but I knew I didn't like her, and I didn't want her talking to my boyfriend. I would have to deal with all that at another time. Besides, I trusted Jordan. It wasn't his fault that she wanted his attention.

I pushed away my anxiety over Amy, and I was determined to have a great day with my amazing boyfriend because that was what he was—mine—and I wasn't about to let him go.

The next few days after the Amy incident had flown by, Jordan and I spent every day together, and it was like we hadn't even experienced that little bump in the road where my insecurity had come to the surface. Tomorrow, we would be going to Santa Barbara, and by tomorrow night, Jordan would know just how much I loved him.

Even though I was ridiculously excited to tell Jordan how I felt, I was also extremely nervous.

The notion of telling Jordan I was in love with him was kind of terrifying. It was a monumental moment in one's life—at least, it was in mine. I considered how people today threw out those words without thinking of the impact it might have on the other person. Those three words were the most life-changing and the most powerful words in the world. It was something that should have been said with care and plenty of thought.

At this point in my life, I was still uncertain about many things, but my love for Jordan was not one. I couldn't get rid of my goofy grin at just the thought of telling him how I felt.

I was singing to myself and dancing around my room. Lost in my own little love spell–filled world, I didn't even notice Jordan standing in the doorframe of my room, watching me. I laughed loudly, trying to cover up my embarrassment, before running over to him and jumping on him. I wrapped my legs around his waist and kissed him, long and hard. I slid down his body and smiled up at him.

"Hey, honey. I'm just finishing up packing. So, here is what I was thinking."

I walked back to my suitcase and loaded it with more clothes. Half of which would probably never be worn, but it was better to be prepared.

"You do all the driving, and I will keep the ride interesting. I'll play DJ, and if you're really lucky, I might even give you a BJ." I blushed as soon as the words were out of my mouth. "Yeah, um…okay, I know that was lame, but it sounded clever in my head. Plus, I'm kind of desperate. I loathe driving long distances, and I despise traffic of any kind. Be a good boyfriend, and say you would love to do all the driving." I pouted and hoped I was coming off as adorable and not the spastic nutcase that I was beginning to feel like.

"Um…Rox, can you sit down for a minute?"

His face was serious, and I instantly felt uneasy.

Nothing good ever comes after the words, "Can you sit down?"

"Jordan, what's wrong? You're worrying me."

"I can't go with you this weekend. I have to fly home."

I sat down on the edge of my bed. I felt like Jordan had just stabbed a pin into my balloon filled with happiness.

"Oh." I tried to hide my disappointment.

Jordan dropped to his knees in front of me and took my hands in his. "Rox, please don't be mad. If I didn't have to go back home, you know I wouldn't cancel on you."

The guilt washed over me. Once again, I was being selfish. I really had to work on that. I knew how much seeing his mom meant to him. He'd already given up one weekend to stay here and fix things with me. I should be happy that he was having another shot to see her so soon.

God, I am a terrible girlfriend.

I squeezed his hand three times. I didn't care if he didn't know why I did that. In this moment, I had to tell him in some way.

"No, it's fine. I know how much time with your mom means to you. I'm glad you get to see her. I'm just going to miss you."

"My mom?" He gave me a quizzical look.

"Yeah, that's why you're headed home, right? Your stepdad is gone again?" I had assumed that would be the only reason he'd cancel our weekend. I was praying that I wasn't wrong.

Jordan ran his fingers through his hair and then smiled up at me, but it was a sad smile. "Uh...that isn't why I have to go home, Rox."

"Wait—what?" I was flabbergasted. *If he's not going home to see his mom, then what in the hell is so important that he has to cancel on me at the last minute?*

"My best friend from Oregon, Adam, is getting married. I was originally supposed to be his best man, but we had a falling-out. He called me and asked if I could still make it. We're not on perfect terms with one another, but he didn't want me to miss out on his wedding. He's like a brother to me, Rox. I have to go. I know how hard it must have been for him."

All I could do was sit there and stare at him. Inside, I was screaming with anger. As I sat there, I knew I had no reason to be upset. Okay, maybe I had a few small reasons, but I saw how important this was to him.

"Rox, please say something," Jordan pleaded with me.

Pushing down my disappointment and selfish reasons for being mad, I smiled a small but real smile. "I understand. This is important to you, and I know that if I had to cancel on you for the same thing, you would understand."

"Oh, baby, you have no idea how much it means to me to hear you say that. I know this weekend was important to you, and if there was any way I could do both, I would. I am sorry, Rox." He laid his head in my lap and held on to me.

I could see how much canceling on me was bothering him. My heart melted for him. I wished he didn't feel bad.

I ran my fingers through his hair. "When will you be back?" I asked.

He looked up at me. "Sunday. We could still drive down to Santa Barbara together today. I will do all the driving there, and then I will just get a flight out of Santa Barbara to Oregon. Then, I can either drop you off at the house with your brother, or you could drop me off at the airport. When I get back, we can drive home together. Again, I will do all the driving."

The fact that he was trying to salvage some part of our weekend made me smile. I decided I would tell him how much I loved him when he picked me up on Sunday. As for right now, I just wanted to show him.

I fisted the hem of his shirt with one hand and pulled him on top of me while shoving my suitcase off the bed with the other. I could repack later. "I want you."

"Oh, you do, huh?" He leaned into me.

I scooted back on the bed while Jordan crawled on top of me. His hands worked up my thighs and kneaded my flesh.

"You bet. A whole weekend without you will be terrible." I nibbled on his bottom lip.

"I'm sure we can have a few no-pants parties to tide you over. I think we should start giving you things to think about while we are apart." He pulled my dress up and off my body before planting slow soft kisses along my stomach.

I tugged on his hair and moaned. "Oh, you'd better believe that we will be having hot long talks at night, but I still don't think that will be enough now that I have had the real thing."

"I guess we should make sure your memory is fresh with sexy details to help you get through the few days we're apart." He smiled at me before thumbing the lace of my panties and pulling them off.

My body shivered as I lay there, completely naked. Jordan's eyes looked up and down my body. I never felt more beautiful than I did when he looked at me this way.

"I-I—"

Jordan pulled off his shirt and looked down at me. "What, Rox?"

I wanted to tell him that I loved him, but I was determined to make sure everything was perfect, so I forced myself to hold it back. I swallowed hard and smiled at him. "I'm gonna really miss you."

He moved off the bed and chuckled as he undid his pants and pulled them down along with his boxer briefs. "I'm planning on harassing you the whole time. You won't even notice that I'm not there."

Seeing him stand there in his full glory made heat pool in my lower stomach. *I need him.*

"Do you still want me to tell Ryan and Brent without you?" It wasn't a conversation that I was looking forward to having without him, but I would if it meant that I would no longer have to lie about Jordan to anyone.

"Baby, if that's what you want to do, then I understand, but I would like to be there when you do it." He kissed his way up my body until he reached my lips.

"We will wait until Sunday then." I gently ran my nails down Jordan's back. I was going to enjoy every inch of him while I could.

"Now, where were we?" His eyes filled with lust.

"We were just about to fill my memory with mind-blowing moments to look back on later."

"Oh, right." He held my stare as he thrust himself deep inside me.

Everything about last night was beyond perfect—well, everything except for the fact that I couldn't tell Jordan just how much I loved him. I'd kept telling myself that it would make the moment when I did tell him that much more perfect.

Once we were in the car and on our way to Santa Barbara, I began to think that maybe I was setting myself up for disaster. I imagined myself confessing my love to Jordan, but before we could share a kiss, I'd slip and fall off a cliff to my death. After that dreadful thought, I reminded myself that nothing bad was going to happen. I was trying hard to stay positive. Staying positive became difficult when I started seeing groups of fire-throwing clowns coming toward us as I was about to tell Jordan how much I loved him.

As if that would happen. Stupid, stupid clowns.

Jordan put his hand on my thigh and gave a gentle squeeze, taking me out of my disastrous thoughts. "You're being quiet. What is on your mind, babe?"

"Oh, um…I was…I was just thinking about how much I'm going to miss you this weekend." It wasn't entirely the truth, but I was going to miss him a bunch.

"I told you, Rox. I'm going to be harassing you so much that you won't even know I'm not there. In fact, you might even get sick of me."

I giggled and laced my fingers through his. "I highly doubt that."

I turned up the music and tried to enjoy the last hour and a half that I had with my boyfriend before he would be off to another state.

As that hour and a half became twenty minutes, I mentally battled with myself not to start begging him to stay.

What the hell is wrong with me? I'm supposed to be the supportive, understanding girlfriend, not this crazy girl who doesn't want to be away from him.

Geez, Roxy, pull it together. You won't see him only on Saturday. It's one day. You will survive one day.

It wasn't just one day though. It was the rest of today, all day tomorrow, and then waiting to finally see him on Sunday.

Yep, I am a nutcase.

"I feel like I've lost you again." Jordan's warm hand massaged my thigh.

"No, you didn't lose me, but you might want to run away from me because I think I'm seriously crazy."

"Crazy, huh? I think you have been saying that about yourself since the day we met, but I'm still here. I don't think you're as crazy as you think you are."

"Okay then, maybe you are crazy, too, because there have been more than enough events to warrant me as being mentally deranged. If you haven't picked up on them, I can only assume that you're as loopy as I am or worse." I laughed.

"Well, I guess we get to be nuts together."

My heart fluttered. *God, I love this man.*

"Promise me, you will hurry back on Sunday. I have something planned for us."

"I have a morning flight, babe. I should be back no later than eleven. What is it that you have planned?" Jordan gave me his movie-star smile.

"Nope. I'm not telling you. It's a surprise. Now, you will have something to look forward to."

"I have you, Rox, and that is all I need."

I held on tight to Jordan's hand for the last little bit of our car ride together. As we were getting closer and closer to the house Ryan and Brent were using, I was still half-hoping the car would just stop working.

I have issues.

When the GPS announced that our destination was on the left side of the street, my heart sank.

"Stop!" I yelled.

Jordan slammed on the brakes. "What?" He looked around, frantic. "Was there something in the road?"

My face heated with embarrassment. "No, I just wanted you to stop."

"Rox, baby, you can't just scream out like that. You scared the hell out of me!"

"I'm sorry. As soon as we pull into that driveway, we have to pretend not to be together. I just wanted to be able to kiss you good-bye while I still can."

Jordan unbuckled his seat belt and then undid mine before pulling me onto his lap.

"We don't have to pretend like we're not together. I told you that we could tell them as soon as we get there." He ran his fingers down my arm, sending a shiver through my body.

"No way. It's not because I don't want them to know. Trust me, I do, but your flight leaves in an hour. I do not want to be left alone with my brother for the weekend after he finds out. I honestly think telling them on Sunday is the best idea."

Jordan just looked at me for a long moment. I saw doubt in his eyes, but he didn't say anything. He leaned into me and kissed me. It was one of his famous tender-but-still-full-of-passion kisses.

Fairy tales were built on kisses like this.

"I'm really going to miss you." I got back into my seat.

"I'm going to miss you more, Rox."

He turned into the driveway and stopped at the massive black iron gate. Jordan rolled down his window and pressed a button on the intercom pad.

"Come on down." Ryan's voice came through the speakers.

I looked out the window, trying to find out how he knew it was us. I then saw two surveillance cameras on either side of the gate. The gate suddenly split into two as it opened to let us in.

I held Jordan's hand as we made our way down the long driveway. I tried to focus on the fact that in less than three days, he would be back.

Jordan pulled up and parked next to Ryan's truck.

Holy mother of awesomeness, this place is beyond brilliant. The luxurious home was built on the side of a cliff overlooking the ocean. I loved being nestled between the mountains and the ocean.

Ryan walked out as soon as Jordan and I got out of the car.

"Wow, Ry, this place is fantastic!"

"Seriously, man, this place is sick," Jordan added.

Ryan picked me up and squeezed me tight. I was too busy taking in the amazing home that my hug lacked the oomph that his had.

"I know, right?" He set me back down and gave Jordan a nod.

"This is ridiculous, Ry. I can't believe you guys get this place all weekend."

"You get to enjoy this place, too." He messed up my hair.

Really, Ryan? I fixed my hair. I was already getting a little annoyed with my brother.

Ryan walked over to Jordan and shook his hand. "It was cool of you to bring my sister here even though you're not staying for the weekend. Roxy hates driving long distances, and I was sure that I would have to go get her. Remind me that I owe you a beer when we are all back in town together."

"Sounds like a plan, but it was no big deal, man. I was headed this way already." Jordan looked over at me and smiled.

"Don't trust him too much, Ryan. I'm sure Jordan got more enjoyment from being around Princess than you think," Brent said as he made his way over to us.

Seeing Brent caused my chest to tighten. I hadn't expected to miss him as much as I had. I had to remind myself that things just weren't the same between us anymore.

Brent leaned against Ryan's truck with his hands shoved into his jeans pockets. I couldn't help but stare for a moment. He didn't look all that thrilled with my arrival. Having him look at me that way stung. But him not scooping me up into his usual hug actually made my heart hurt. Fighting with Brent was awful.

Sadness washed over me like a tidal wave, but it still wasn't enough to make me forget what he had done to his girlfriend. I might have missed him like crazy, but I wasn't going to fold. What he had done to her was beyond wrong.

I pushed down my sadness for the loss of our friendship and held on to why I was mad as I forced myself to look away from him.

"Besides," Brent said to Jordan, "I thought I told you to stay away from Princess."

Jordan's face twisted in annoyance. "Since when have I ever listened to you? Besides, you invited me this weekend. How did you expect me to stay away from her?"

Brent stepped away from the truck. "I asked you to come when I thought Ryan wasn't inviting Princess. And you opted out. So, why are you here? And why are you with her?"

"I actually called him," Ryan interjected.

Brent looked at Ryan, waiting for an explanation.

"Roxy was whining about driving down here, and I knew you had also invited Jordan. I didn't know he wasn't planning on coming. I asked him to bring her with him."

"I am sure he was all too happy to help you out," Brent huffed.

Jordan's jaw clenched, and he was shaking his head. He was pissed, and I couldn't figure out what the hell was up with him and Brent today.

"I surely hope that you didn't try anything with my sister." Ryan looked Jordan down.

I didn't like the way this conversation was going.

"I have a boyfriend, remember?" I tried to steer the conversation away from Jordan and me.

"Yeah, she has a boyfriend," was all Jordan said back to Brent.

There was a look that crossed Jordan's face that made my breath hitch. It was almost as if he was trying to tell Brent something more. Okay, maybe I was being paranoid, but I wasn't ready to tell my brother that Jordan and I were together.

"All right." I clapped my hands together. "Jordan, thanks for the ride, but you should probably go. Don't want you to miss your flight." I smiled a very fake smile, but I was hoping that he would get the hint and just leave.

I didn't expect the look of confusion and then hurt that I saw.

Jordan went and pulled my bags out from the backseat. "Yeah, you're right. I should go. I'll pick you up on Sunday. Later, everyone." Jordan acknowledged Ryan and Brent in his good-bye but didn't look at me again. He just got back into the car and drove away.

I was beyond confused about what had just happened. I thought that we'd both agreed that we would tell them on Sunday.

Why is he mad at me? All I'd wanted to do was race off and call him, but I couldn't even do that.

Ryan picked up my bags and then looked between Brent and me. When I looked over at Brent to see why Ryan was staring at us, I saw that Brent was glaring at me. Brent had never looked at me with such anger in his eyes.

Ryan huffed, "Will you two get over your stupid fight already?"

Brent stepped forward and started to say something, but I cut him off, "So, where is my room?"

I couldn't handle talking to him, not yet. I wasn't ready, and I didn't know when I would be. As much as I had missed him, I needed to stay strong. It was not the time for a heart-to-heart.

Ryan shook his head and rolled his eyes. I knew he wasn't happy with my inability to patch things up with Brent.

Oh well, Ryan will have to get over it.

I was there to spend time with him, not his best friend. I urged Ryan with a look to answer my question.

"Upstairs. Pick whatever one you want. Brent and I took the rooms downstairs," Ryan informed me.

I walked past Brent and made a point not to look at him again. I couldn't crumble just because I had missed him. He had to understand that what he was doing to that poor girl wasn't okay. I took the stairs two at a time and walked all the way down the hall, trying to put as much space between Brent and me as possible. I wished that space would stop the sadness attempting to navigate its way back up.

Without bothering to check out any of the other bedrooms, I chose the last room on the right. All that I wanted to do was hide out and get a hold of myself. Looking around the room, I was certain that there couldn't be a better room than this one anyway. Not only was it double the size of my room at home, which was far from small, one entire wall also had a floor-to-ceiling window. The other three walls were painted seafoam green. The furniture was all white. On the opposite wall of the windows, a four-poster bed was dressed in a fluffy white comforter with a tiny-seashell black pattern.

I dropped my purse on the floor and collapsed onto the bed. It was as soft and fluffy as it looked. I gazed out the window and then got up. I walked over to stand in front of the window. Jordan would have loved the view. Thinking about how special beaches had become for Jordan and me made me miss him more than ever. I turned my back to the window and examined the room that I would be staying in for the next few days.

A black shaggy rug was placed under the bed. A white leather couch was positioned in front of the window. It was a perfect spot to sit and stare out at the ocean. To my right, there was a fireplace and a large flat screen TV mounted on the wall above it.

I opened the door on that side of the room to find a gigantic bathroom that had an enormous spa tub and an equally large shower that looked very high-tech. Like in the bedroom, the bathroom also had a floor-to-ceiling window on one wall.

I ran my fingers over the tub.

I will definitely be enjoying this later.

I smiled and went back into the bedroom before lying down on the couch.

The place was amazing, and the room was more glamorous than some of the five-star hotels I had stayed in. I could lock myself in here all weekend and be completely content, but I was sure that staying in this room all weekend was the last thing Ryan would let happen. I sighed and tried to come up with a list of reasons why I couldn't leave this room. Then, I could enjoy a peaceful weekend here and never have to deal with Brent.

I looked out at the ocean. *I wish Jordan were here to enjoy this with me.*

I missed him so incredibly much.

I got up and went over to get my purse. I retrieved my phone and send Jordan a text.

I miss you so much. XOXO

There was a light tap on the door.

"Come in." I thought it was going to be Ryan bringing up my bags. I was surprised that it was Cheater McGee himself. "Oh, it's you."

"That's quite the welcome, Princess." He gave a halfhearted smile.

"What do you want?"

He walked into the room and held up my bags that he had carried up. "Ryan asked me to bring these up to you."

Thanks, Ryan. Way to help out your sister.

Brent set my bags down by the dresser. "I was hoping we could talk."

"About?" I made my way back to the couch and sat down. I knew what he thought we needed to talk about, but I just wasn't ready.

"Everything, Princess." He walked across the room and sat down on the couch. "I hate when you're upset with me. Please tell me what I can do to make things better between us."

Better? How are things ever going to be better? It's not like he can go back and not lie to me or not cheat on his girlfriend.

I looked out the window. "I don't know if things can ever be better." It hurt to even say the words, but they were the truth.

I didn't know how things could ever be good between Brent and me. He was doing something that I found unforgivable even if it wasn't being done to me.

"Princess, please. I will do anything."

I eyed Brent. "Stop, okay? You can't change the past. Nothing is going to change the way I feel about what you have done to your girlfriend."

"She's not my girlfriend anymore, Roxanne."

His eyes were pleading with me, but I wasn't going to cave.

"What? Did she finally find out what an ass you are and dump you?"

"No. I ended things with her the night of the lake party."

"Are you serious?" I stood up. I couldn't stand to even be close to him. "It's bad enough that you fucking cheated on the girl. But you couldn't at least give her the opportunity to dump you? Does she even know what you were doing? Did you tell her the truth? Fuck, Brent, did you care about the girl at all?" I was so enraged with him that it was becoming hard to breathe.

How could I have been wrong about someone that I thought I knew so well?

It made me want to rethink everything I knew about everyone.

"Please calm down. I know that look. Just breathe and try to listen. Yes, I did care about her. I just didn't care about her in the way that I should have, but I never cheated on her, Princess. You need to know that."

He was not going to stand there and lie to my face.

"You fucking liar. Don't you dare try to fucking say that you didn't. You were with a new girl every week. I doubt you two broke up on a weekly basis. You didn't, did you?" I was beyond upset, and I felt tears forming. I didn't want to talk to him anymore, let alone look at him.

"No, we didn't. Please just sit down and let me explain everything without you interrupting. I will answer all your questions and tell you the truth. Please, Princess. I have never lied to you, and I'm not going to start now."

I walked over to the bed and sat, facing away from Brent. "I don't really want to hear what you have to say. I don't believe you, Brent, and that is not going to change. Just because you say you're not going to lie doesn't mean that it's true."

"Wow, Roxy. Kevin really did a number on you, didn't he?" Brent made his way over to the bed.

I gave him my most hateful glare. "Seriously? Go to hell!" *How dare he bring up Kevin! Kevin wasn't the one who made Brent cheat and lie to his girlfriend.*

Ryan walked into the room. "Okay, you two, time to play nice. I want lunch, so let's go."

I pushed off the bed, stalked past Brent, and headed downstairs. I might have to stay in the same house as Brent, but this weekend was about seeing my brother. I didn't have to say another word to that lying, cheating asshole. I thought I had missed Brent, but really, I just missed the person that I'd thought he was. The real Brent only filled me with anger.

29

The car ride was silent—at least on my part. I hated that Brent was already ruining my weekend with my brother. I sent a text message to Jordan, trying to get out of my bad mood.

Have you boarded?

Why hasn't he texted me back?

I had tuned most of Ryan and Brent's conversation out up until Jordan's name caught my attention.

"I really didn't think it would be a problem," Ryan said.

"He already told me that he wasn't coming down. He had plans to go back home for a wedding. Then, you asked him to bring Princess down, and he is suddenly here."

What? I thought Jordan was just re-invited to the wedding. Did he know he wasn't going to come with me the whole time?

"He didn't say anything to me when I called him and asked him to bring her."

"That's my point. Why did he go out of his way to bring Princess down if he'd never planned on being here? I'm telling you, man. I know how Jordan works. There is no way he was going to skip going to that wedding. I don't think you should trust him with her. I know he is up to something. I'll drive her back home myself if I have to."

"I honestly haven't gotten a bad vibe from him, but I trust you, man."

Seriously?

"Excuse me. I'm right here. I think I have a say in who takes me home," I told the watchdogs from hell.

"Don't start, Roxy. If you wanted that choice, you should have driven down yourself, but you got all whiny. Now, Brent is going to take you back home on Sunday," Ryan answered.

I had been overly whiny because I didn't want it to be odd that Jordan was bringing me down. I thought it had made the perfect cover story. I hadn't expected for Ryan to feel so bad for me that he had also asked Jordan.

I was pissed that Ryan and Brent thought they could decide who would take me anywhere without my consent. But it wasn't the first time they'd pulled this crap.

"Uh, no, he's not! I already have a ride home. Besides, there is no way I'm going to let that liar take me anywhere."

"Roxy!" Ryan snapped. "It's not up for discussion."

"That's what you fucking think," I shot back. "You can't make me leave with him."

"Watch me." Ryan stared at me from the rearview mirror.

Brent turned in his seat to look at me. "Princess…"

I glared at Brent and crossed my arms. I never thought I would feel this way, but I hated him right now.

"Brent, don't even bother. Just let her pout."

Brent turned back around in his seat.

I wanted to shout that I wasn't pouting, but I didn't trust myself not to start crying. I looked down at my phone. Jordan still hadn't texted. I needed him.

I sent him another text.

We have to talk!

After five minutes, Jordan's lack of replying only made me feel more frustrated. I told myself that he must have already boarded his flight. He should be taking off soon. That had to be why he wasn't replying, but then I started thinking about how he hadn't even looked at me when he left.

How could he leave things that way?

I was starting to feel depressed, and I felt myself pushing back tears. I began to think about what Brent had said about Jordan not coming because of the wedding.

Why didn't Jordan tell me about the wedding the day I told him about wanting to come down here with him?

This weekend was turning into complete crap.

I knew Tonya was still here with Shawn. I hated to bother her while she was with her boyfriend, but I was desperate and needed her.

Hey, I'm in SB and hating life! Save me!

> *Oh no! Tell all. Better yet, meet me downtown. Shawn and I are about to go to lunch.*

Where?

Some place called Fish Fist. We're almost there.

I hated that I would have to talk to my brother right now, but I had no other choice. "Um…Ry, do you know where Fish Fist is?"

"Are you actually talking to me? It's a miracle! I thought I would have to spend the whole weekend with you ignoring me."

"Do you know where it is or not?" I said flatly. I hated that he thought because I was talking to him meant that he'd somehow won the augment we were very much still having.

"Yeah, its downtown. It's a killer dive bar. Hands-down, it's the best place to eat seafood. Why?"

"Because that's where I want to eat." I smiled into the rearview mirror.

"We can do that. It's not too far from where I was planning on going. See? You get your way sometimes." He smiled back.

I rolled my eyes.

On my way.

Awesome! See you soon. Xoxo

I sank into my seat, feeling a bit better than I had since I arrived in Santa Barbara. As I continued checking my phone to see if Jordan had texted back yet, that glimmer of happiness faded away. I powered off my phone and threw it into my purse. I was starting to get mad at Jordan, and I hated it. I was sure that there was a perfect reason for why he hadn't texted me. My anger at Brent and Ryan was seeping into the rest of my emotions.

I glared at the back of Brent's head. *Stupid, stupid Brent.*

Ryan slung his arm over my shoulders. "You're going to love this place, Roxy. They have mermaids in a tank."

We walked into Fish Fist. Ryan was right. This place was definitely a place that I loved. It was decorated with wacky ocean décor and had live mermaids swimming in giant fish tanks at the back of the place.

Okay, so they weren't real mermaids. They were real girls dressed up as mermaids.

I couldn't help thinking about how much I would love to have that job. *Then again, being a mermaid would probably get boring after a few hours.*

I watched the girls swim around, do flips, and twirl in the water. They were so splendid that I hardly even noticed when they surfaced for air. I was still watching in amazement when Tonya crashed into me, flung her arms around me, and almost knocked me down.

"Rox!" she squealed.

I tightly held on to her as I felt a calming wave of relief wash over me. Just having her here made every crappy thing about today seem bearable.

"I'm sorry if I'm crashing your time with Shawn," I whispered before pulling away.

"Dollface, are you kidding me? I have been with the guy all week. I'm surprised that I'm not sick of him by now, but seeing you is far from crashing anything. I've missed you."

I could tell she wasn't just saying that for my benefit.

"Really, Roxanne? This is why you wanted to come here?" Ryan sneered at Tonya.

"I've missed you, too, Ryan." Tonya smiled at Ryan, ignoring his rudeness.

Shawn came over to us. "Our table is ready." He kissed Tonya on the cheek. "Hey, Roxy." He gave me a nod.

"Hi, Shawn." I offered him a genuine smile, which felt good.

"Shawn, this is Ryan and Brent." Tonya gestured toward my brother and the evil lying cheat. "Ryan is Roxy's brother, and Brent—"

"Is an asshole," I interrupted her introduction.

"Roxanne," Ryan scolded me.

Brent, on the other hand, just laughed and stuck out his hand toward Shawn. "I'm Brent, or as Princess here has told you, The Asshole."

Shawn laughed and shook his hand. I hated that Brent was actually making jokes and enjoying himself.

Ryan was finding no humor in the situation at all. He grabbed my upper arm and excused us before practically dragging me outside.

"What the fuck, Roxanne? I invited you down here to spend time with you, and you're terrorizing Brent and making plans to hang out with Tonya?"

Terrorizing Brent? Is Ryan kidding me?

"Please tell me that you're joking right now? How can you possibly still defend him?" I felt the tears building again, and the last thing I wanted to do was cry. I wrapped my arms around myself and dug my nails into my palms.

"Roxy, you don't know the whole story, and you won't even give him a chance to explain it to you. You're being an immature brat. I invited you down here because I missed you, but now, I am starting to regret ever asking you to come."

Anger coursed through my body. "You regret inviting me? Well, I fucking regret coming!" I raised my voice. "I can't believe you are siding with him over me. You are the worst brother in history. Seeing as you think

I'm such an immature brat, let me make this easy for you. I will not be spending the weekend with you. In fact, brother of mine, I no longer want to talk to you at all!" I was full on yelling. "As for Brent, there is nothing he could say to me that would ever, ever make cheating okay. So, fuck you, Ryan, and fuck him, too."

I turned and stomped away from him. I didn't know where I was going. I just couldn't be around him anymore.

"Roxy! Roxanne," Ryan called after me. He didn't attempt to chase me though.

I wasn't surprised. He was a terrible brother.

Of course, he didn't want Jordan to drive me home, but he would let me walk off in Santa Barbara all by myself.

Asshole.

After five minutes of walking, I pulled out my phone. When I saw the missed calls, my heart froze as I hoped that they were from Jordan. Of course, they weren't. I was bummed. This day had fully sucked. I was dumb to think that would change.

I called Tonya back.

"Where the hell did you go?" She sounded panicked.

I felt guilty for making her worry, but there was no way I would go back in there with Ryan.

"Sorry, Ton. I just had to leave. I couldn't stand to be around Ryan or Brent. I'm just going to call a cab, head back to the house, and then head back to the beach house."

"Rox, I know this isn't what you want to hear right now, but as your best friend, I'm here to tell you the truth and not just say what you want to hear. I know you don't want to listen to Brent's side of things, but I think you should even if it is just to say that you tried. You don't have to forgive him or even talk to him ever again. I just think that you are spending too much energy being mad at him. You have to talk to him. Hell, scream at him if you have to, but it's obvious that what is going on between you two is affecting your life in a negative way."

"It's not just him, Ton. It's everything right now. I mean, what he did is bad enough. I get sick from just thinking about it. What infuriates me is the fact that I thought I knew him. I cared about him. How could I have not realized what a horrible person he really was? To make matters worse, my own brother is taking Brent's side over mine. Then, there is the whole part of my life that concerns Jordan. He not only canceled on coming with me this weekend, but after he dropped me off, he left in the worst way. I don't know if he is ignoring me or just on his flight. As much as I don't want to be this crazy girl, I am being the crazy girl."

"Oh, dollface, get back here, so I can hug you. You shouldn't be this stressed out. It's not good for you. Please come back, and we will work everything out, okay?"

"I can't go back."

"Roxy, you're letting your stubbornness make this harder than it should be."

I let out a deep sigh as a few tears slid down my cheeks. "You're probably right, but I just can't go back. I need time to think. I need time to be alone. Tell Ryan that I am going back to the house, okay?"

"Roxy, I—"

I cut her off, "I know, but I need to do this my way even if it's the wrong way. Please just tell him that I'm heading to the house. Please."

Tonya huffed into the phone, and I knew she was anything but happy with me.

"Fine, but if you haven't worked things out by tomorrow, then I am hunting your ass down and making you do things my way."

"Deal."

"Love you. Be safe."

"I'll be fine. Love you, too."

I hung up the phone and called for a cab. *Thank God for smartphones.*

I headed back to the house and prayed that Ryan and Brent wouldn't come back too soon. I needed time to decompress and figure out my feelings.

While riding in the cab, I sent Jordan another text message. I knew that I was coming off as the insane girlfriend, but at this point, I didn't care anymore. He wasn't being that great of a boyfriend by ignoring me.

Genius plan, Roxanne.

I stared up the iron gate. I contemplated calling my brother and asking for the code, but I knew he would just enjoy that conversation too much. I walked up to the gate and tried to fit my body through the bars, but they were too close together. I looked around and noticed a tree close to the stone wall surrounding the front of the property. I was probably going to break a leg or something else, but that would still be better than groveling to my brother. I used the tree to help me get over the wall.

Thank God I wore jeans today.

When I was on the other side I picked up my purse and dusted it off. I made my way down the rest of the driveway with a huge smile on my face.

"Seriously!" I shouted up to the sky after I'd tried to open the front door.

I was locked out.

I walked around the house and checked all the doors. Of course, Ryan wouldn't leave anything unlocked.

Since I was locked out, I decided that I might as well work on my tan.

I walked down the gray stone pathway leading out to the pool. The house had a spectacular pool that overlooked the ocean. I was going to sunbathe on a lounge chair, but instead, I walked over to the diving board and stepped out to the end. I gave a little bounce, trying to choose whether or not to just jump in. I decided against that idea, and I rolled up the hem of my shirt and backed up some before lying facedown on the diving board. Resting my head on my arms, I let my thoughts and feelings overcome my mind.

I started with thinking about Jordan. He had no right to leave the way that he had and not contact me before his flight took off. I was undeniably pissed off at him. I mentally checked off the Jordan issue. As of now, he was a prick, and I was going to yell at him when we finally did talk.

I then moved on to my Brent dilemma. I didn't feel as though my actions or feelings toward Brent were unjustified. My stomach twisted up in the familiar way it did whenever I thought about what Brent had done. I felt bad for his girlfriend—or I guessed it was now his ex-girlfriend. Even the fact that he'd broken up with her pissed me off. He should have at least had the decency to let her dump him.

All of this contemplating caused my head to hurt.

I pushed up and walked off the diving board, making my way over to a lounge chair. I lay down and tried to completely clear my head. Thinking wasn't working, so it was better to just not do it at all.

I closed my eyes and focused on the warmth of the sun on my skin. The memory of my mom and me lying out by our pool last April flooded my mind.

I was laughing. "Mom, seriously, I don't understand why you bother trying to tan."

"What do you mean?" She laughed. "I tan." Her eyes sparkled with happiness as she rubbed more sunscreen on her skin.

"No, you burn and then peel. Then, you complain about how you never tan." I giggled some more.

She blew her bangs out of her eyes and chuckled. "What can I say? The sun and I have been stuck in a vicious cycle for most of my life. I should have learned that by now, but I still want the sun to like me as much as I like it."

"That's funny. If you asked me, I would say that you don't like the sun as much as you pretend to."

"Maybe that's why I burn. Maybe it knows how much I hate it. You, my daughter, could be on to something."

The memory of her laughing and smiling made my heart hurt. I hated that it hurt me to remember her.

I wiped away the tears that came with the memory of my mother. "I wish you were here. You would know what I should do with Brent. I miss you, and I feel lost without you."

I wrapped my arms around myself, and I let myself cry for a while longer before once again pushing the pain down. I felt like I could fall apart. I couldn't help but wonder if there would ever be a day when I didn't feel this ache.

I thought of Jordan. Jordan always helped me survive the pain. When he was around, I was able to enjoy life, and talking or even thinking about my mom didn't hurt so badly. He made everything better. I missed him. I needed him.

"Princess?"

I looked up to see Brent coming toward me with a concerned look on his face.

I sat up. I wanted to tell him to go away. I wanted to scream at him and tell him that I hated him, but that would be a lie. I didn't hate Brent. I just hated what he had done.

He made his way to me and sat. He pulled me into him, and I didn't resist. I didn't have the energy to push him away—or maybe I just didn't really want to.

"Please tell me that I'm not the reason you were crying."

His breath was hot on my neck, and it sent a shiver down my spine.

I took a deep breath before pulling away from him. "I could tell you that, but it wouldn't be the truth. You aren't the only reason that I was crying though. Mostly, I just miss my mom. She would tell me what to do and explain why I'm feeling the way that I am. My life has changed so much in the last few months, and I hate not being able to talk to her about it."

"You can talk to me."

I looked up at him as if he'd just grown two heads. He was crazy if he thought that I would talk to him about things.

"Ha! That's funny. No, I can't. I'm still mad at you."

He pulled back from me as he let out a sad sigh and took my hand into his. "Don't be mad at me, please. At least give me a chance to explain."

"I know that I should, but I'm scared that it will just make things even worse. I don't see how anything you say could make what you have done okay. I can't handle being madder at you than I already am."

His eyes were full of sadness. "Emily and I had an open relationship."

"What? What does that even mean?"

"We were free to see other people."

I swallowed down the lump in my throat. "No, I know what it means. I just didn't think it was a real thing. I mean, how can you be with someone who is okay with you being with other people?"

"It's complicated."

I needed him to explain it to me. I honestly never thought Brent could say something to make what he had done okay, but I never thought he would say what he'd just said. I felt a flutter of hope that my relationship with Brent could be saved. I needed more than anything to know everything.

I squeezed his hand. "Good thing that I'm good with complicated."

Brent smiled at me. "We met on spring break during our freshman year. We had a great week together, but then we had to go back to reality. At first, we just kept in touch, and that turned into us talking every night. I missed her all the time. I flew out to New York City to see her. When we were together, it just felt right." Brent took a deep breath. "Do you really want the full story?"

"Yes."

"All right. After that weekend in New York, I knew I wanted her in my life. I just didn't know how it was going to work, but I spent the next few months flying there to see her every other weekend. Finally, I asked her to be my girlfriend."

I thought back and remembered when Brent had been gone all those weekends. I had been too preoccupied with my life to ask where he was. I wish I had asked him about it back then, but at least I knew he was telling the truth.

Brent continued, "It was almost summer break. I was planning on spending it with her, but she had plans with her family to visit Europe. When she came back from her trip, she told me that she had been with other people while she was gone."

I cupped my hand over my mouth at what he had just told me. Emily had cheated on him. My heart broke for him. I knew what that felt like. I didn't know Emily, but once again, I found myself not liking her or her stupid name.

"At first, I was furious. I couldn't believe that she'd cheated on me. I told her that we were done. Then, she asked how I would feel if we had an open relationship. I told her that she was nuts, and I broke up with her. That night, I found a random chick and used her, trying to forget all about Emily, but it didn't work. I still missed her. I missed the late-night phone calls and random texts throughout the day. I missed having someone to call mine. I called her back and told her how I felt. We agreed that long-distance relationships were impossible. We decided to try having an open one. That way, our physical needs would be fulfilled while we kept the emotional connection that we had. You know, the long nightly talks and girlfriend-boyfriend stuff?"

I nodded my head to let him know that I absorbed what he meant.

"When we were together, we were together. We thought the open relationship would just get us through college. After college, we planned to be together exclusively."

As he spoke, I understood how they had come to their conclusion, but at the same time, it made no sense.

How can you be okay with having the person you love be with someone else?

"Do you love her? Or did you?" I felt bad for interrupting him, but I had to know.

"Yes, I did—or at least, I thought I did."

"What do you mean?"

"I mean, I'm not sure if I've ever been in love. I thought I loved her, but I don't know, Princess. I was more upset about you being mad at me than I ever was about her screwing other guys. Knowing that makes me wonder if I ever really loved her."

"I don't understand how you don't know."

"Whatever I felt for Emily in the beginning of our relationship didn't last. I realized I stopped feeling that way about her a long time ago."

"Well, not to knock you down, but I say, you never loved her. When you truly love someone, you never want that person to be with another person, and you would never really be okay with it. I mean, you can pretend that you are, but you wouldn't be. You would only be lying to yourself."

"You're right, and I think I've been lying to myself for a long time."

"So, what happened with you and Emily? Why did you suddenly decide to break up with her?"

"You happened."

"You broke up with her because of me? Why would you do that?"

"Honestly, the disgust on your face when you found out I had a girlfriend was what made my decision easy. I never want to see you look at me like that again."

"I was wrong. You weren't lying or cheating. You weren't doing anything bad."

I hated that I had made him feel terrible enough that he'd dumped his girlfriend. Even if I didn't agree with what they had been doing, it was their choice, their relationship.

"Except I was. I was lying to myself. Besides, I don't want to be the kind of person you look at like that for any reason."

"I'm sorry that I have been such a hateful bitch toward you."

"You had every right to act the way you did. You thought I was cheating on Emily. I understand why you were upset. I'm just thankful that you let me explain everything to you. I'm sorry that I never told you about Emily. If I had, I might never have gotten into that mess to begin with."

"You'd better remember that. I'm a great judge of character. I would have told you that she was a dumb slut to ever not be happy with just having you."

"We all put up blinders for people we care about."

"You're right. I dropped the ball with both Sara and Kevin. I must have had my oblivious shades on with those two."

Brent chuckled, and I could not stop myself from engulfing him into a bear hug. He hugged me back just as tightly.

I rested my head on his shoulder. "Just so you know, I'm glad that we're not fighting anymore. I've missed you."

"I missed you, Princess, more than I even knew was possible."

My phone rang, ending the heart-to-heart conversation with Brent. I dug my phone out of my purse and saw Tonya's name flashing on the screen. At least Tonya would be glad to hear that I'd talked to Brent, so we were no longer fighting.

One problem in my life is solved.

"Hey," I answered.

"How are you doing?" Concern was thick in her voice.

"Better. Brent and I talked, and you were right. He needed a chance to explain everything. We're good now," I said, smiling at Brent.

I was beyond happy that things with him could go back to the way they had been.

"Well, that's good. What about Jordan? Has he called?"

My heart and face both dropped.

I stood up and walked away from Brent, so he couldn't hear what I was saying.

"No, he hasn't, but his plane doesn't land for another half hour. I don't know what I'm going to do if he doesn't call though. I'm already freaking out."

"No freaking out."

"I just don't get it, Ton. Everything was great—or I thought it was. But I didn't like the way he was acting when he left."

"I don't know what his deal was, but if you want me to break his face for you, I will."

Just hearing the determination in Tonya's voice made me smile. "Thanks, Ton. I'll have to get back to you on that one."

I smiled back at Brent, who was closely watching me, and I hoped that he couldn't understand too much of the conversation.

"How are you and Ryan?" she asked.

"He's still an ass. I'm still mad at him even if he was right about me not knowing the whole story."

Tonya laughed. "Ry is an ass, but seeing as he was right about you needing to talk to Brent, maybe you should just suck it up and patch things up with him."

"You're probably right. Hey, can I call you back later? I am still talking to Brent."

"Totally."

I loved her for taking the time to make sure I was okay. After we said good-bye, I made my way back over to Brent.

Brent eyed me skeptically as I sat back down. I could see the wheels turning in his head. I knew what he wanted to know. I knew what he was about to ask. I just wasn't sure if I was going to tell him the truth. Then again, he had just been so honest with me that it wouldn't seem fair to turn around and straight up lie to him.

"Princess?"

"Yes?" I smiled back.

"Is there something you would like to tell me?"

"There are lots of things I would like to tell you." *Avoidance isn't lying, right?*

I was suddenly extremely nervous about telling him about Jordan. What made it worse was that I didn't even know what was going on with Jordan right now.

Maybe he doesn't even want to be my boyfriend.

Maybe I'm going to the extreme, but I have issues these days.

"You know what I'm talking about. Would you like to tell me about your boyfriend?"

Damn. That's a straightforward question.

I didn't want to lie to him, so I held my breath and closed my eyes. "Yes."

I opened one eye to see Brent watching me. I let out the breath that I had been holding. I knew the string of questions was about to begin. I wasn't happy that Brent was going to ask them, but I was glad that it wasn't my brother.

I swallowed hard. "My boyfriend isn't Ethan Frost. It's Jordan."

I saw anger cross Brent's face before he stood up. He laced his fingers together and then pressed them to the back of this head as he paced back and forth in front of me. He dropped his hands and balled them into fists as he continued to pace.

"Are you joking? I'm gonna kill that little shit. I told him to stay away from you. I knew introducing you to him that day at the lake would lead to this. Roxy, you need to stay away from him. He's no good. He will only hurt you."

"Brent, you need to stop freaking out. The lake wasn't the first time that I met him. Jordan's the guy that I met on the Fourth."

Taking in what I had just said, Brent stopped and looked at me. "He's your mystery guy?"

I smiled and tried to let him see that I was happy with Jordan. I might not be at this moment, but in the grand scheme of things, I loved him. I wanted Brent to be happy for us. "Yeah, he's amazing."

Brent sat back down next to me and took my hands in his. "No, Princess, trust me. You need to walk away before you get hurt."

"He's not going to hurt me." I pulled my hands from his. Even as I said that to Brent, I wanted to believe it, but a small part of me was screaming that Jordan had hurt me today even if he didn't know it.

"Roxanne, you're wrong. You just need to trust me."

I shook off what Brent was saying.

It didn't matter that Jordan and I were having a misunderstanding. At least, I hoped that was all it was. We were going to be fine. I loved him, and even if I was upset with him right now, I would get over it, and we would be perfect.

I looked at Brent. He had to understand that Jordan and I were permanent.

"I know you said Jordan was off-limits, but I met him before I knew who he was to you."

"It's not about that. Will you please just trust me? He's not who you want to be with."

I was starting to get upset with Brent again, which was the last thing I wanted. "You don't get to tell me what I want. I know what I want, and trust me, it's him."

"Roxy, it's not. I know you. I know what you deserve. He will only hurt you."

"Why do you keep saying that? Why can't you just be happy for us?"

"Damn it, Roxy. Because I know him! I know why he didn't stay here this weekend. I know where he is and whom he is with. I know how he treats girls, how he tosses them away like trash. You mean too much to me for me to allow him to hurt you."

"You think I don't know who Jordan is? You're wrong. I know him. I know about his past. I know about the girls. I also know where he is this weekend. I understood that he couldn't be here. So, there you go, Mr. Protector. You have nothing to worry about, so just be happy for us."

"He told you he was going to Oregon, and you're okay with it?"

"Yes, he told me. Why wouldn't he? There is no reason to lie about going to a friend's wedding."

"He told you he was going to Adam's wedding? Did he also tell you about Amy?"

"His ex?"

"Yes, Princess, his ex, who also happens to be Adam's little sister."

"What?"

Brent shook his head. "He didn't tell you, did he?"

I stood up. Now, I was the one pacing. "It doesn't matter. I mean, I know who Amy is. He didn't try to hide her from me. He just didn't tell me that she was Adam's sister. But it doesn't really matter. I have nothing to worry about." I didn't know if I was trying to convince Brent or myself. My heart was racing, and my stomach felt as though I had eaten a truck full of rocks.

Brent caught my wrist, stopping me. "This is why I wanted him to stay away from you. He will hurt you. Amy isn't just an ex. She is *the* ex, the only girl he has ever had an actual relationship with. He will drop anything and anyone for that girl. No matter how many times she has screwed him over, he always goes back to her. I told you, Princess, he will only hurt you."

I pulled my arm from his grip. "No! I don't believe you."

"I have no reason to lie to you. Call him, and ask him."

My heart was thudding in my chest. He was wrong. Jordan wasn't that guy. I loved him. He wouldn't do that to me.

"You're wrong. I know Jordan. He's not going to leave me."

I saw the anger Brent was holding in.

"I told him to stay away from you because I know how he treats girls in his life. Do you really believe that nothing will happen with them? Trust me, if she wants something to happen, it will. He can't say no to that girl."

I felt dizzy. My insides seemed like they were being pulled out with a hook.

No, he wouldn't lie to me. He wouldn't cheat on me. He wouldn't do that to me. Brent has to be wrong.

I felt like I was going to throw up. I dropped to my knees.

Brent knelt down next to me and pulled me into him. "The last thing I ever wanted to do was upset you."

I cringed away and tried to remember how to breathe. "Don't touch me. Please...I need space."

Damn it. Breathing shouldn't be this hard.

Brent stood and took a step back.

"I need you to go away. Please go away." I was now begging to be left alone.

"I don't want to leave you like this."

"If you care about me at all, you will go away."

In through the nose and out through the mouth. My body was having a hard time with the simple action of breathing.

"Princess—"

"Please!" I shouted. I was having enough trouble trying to breathe. I didn't want an audience watching me fall apart.

Brent turned and headed back to the house.

I wrapped my arms around myself. I couldn't fall apart. I couldn't let Ryan see me like this. He would flip out on so many different levels. I focused on calming down.

Brent could be wrong, right? There had to be a chance.

After I had somewhat calmed down, I tried calling Jordan. Once again, I got his voice mail. I was going to give him a chance to explain, a chance to tell me that Brent was wrong. Until Jordan could do that, I was playing the denial card.

He should have landed by now. There was no reason for him not to answer my calls. I needed to talk to him.

I headed into the house.

Brent met me at the door. "I'm sorry. I never wanted to make you upset, but you deserved the truth about him."

I knew Brent would never hurt me on purpose, but he had to be wrong about Jordan. He just had to be.

"I know you were trying to do the right thing, but I just need time to figure things out. Please just keep all of this between us. I can't handle Ryan being worried or mad."

"I don't understand what you need to figure out."

"Brent, I need to talk to him."

"Unless that talk you want to have with me is an apology, I don't want to hear it," Ryan said as he walked out of the entertainment room and into the entryway.

Hearing Ryan's voice made me jump, but I felt relief when I realized that he thought I was talking about needing to talk to him. I gave Brent a pleading look and then smiled sweetly at my brother.

"It's a huge apology. I was wrong about everything." Just saying those words made my chest tighten and my stomach twist. I couldn't have been wrong about Jordan. *Could I?* "I was being selfish and treated Brent terribly. I'm sorry for not listening to either of you and for being a pain in the ass. I shouldn't have run off the way that I had today." I felt awful about how I had acted, but at the moment, I was hoping Ryan would just accept my apology, so I could escape to my room.

"Are you two good?" He eyed Brent and me.

"We're great." I plastered on my biggest fakest smile. It wasn't because Brent and I weren't okay. We were. It was just me who wasn't okay. Then again, if Brent had just lied to me about my boyfriend, we weren't going to be okay. I just needed Ryan to be satisfied with the situation, so I could walk away.

"We're good," Brent answered, looking at me, not at Ryan.

I knew Brent was upset, but I couldn't deal with that right now.

Ryan clapped his hands together and smiled. "Awesome. Then, let's figure out what to do this weekend."

"Catch My Breath" blared from my purse, making my heart go into a frenzy.

Jordan is calling.

My mind was racing, and I found myself wanting to burst into tears. I pulled the phone out and headed for the stairs.

"Hello?" I answered.

"What? You're just going to walk off?" Ryan asked.

I didn't have time to deal with Ryan anymore.

"Hold on a second," I told Jordan.

I turned on the stairs to look at my brother, who was clearly annoyed with me. "I'm sorry, Ryan. I have to take this call. I promise that I will be back down, and we can all figure out what to do this weekend."

I didn't wait for his reply, nor did I miss the intense look on Brent's face.

I turned and ran up the stairs. "Are you there?"

"Rox, are you still there?" Jordan was shouting. "I can't talk. I was just calling to let you know that I landed. I will call you later."

"Okay. We really need to talk," I told him.

The phone was silent.

What just happened? I looked at my phone. *Maybe the call dropped. He didn't really just hang up on me.*

I called Jordan back. The call went straight to voice mail.

"Are you fucking kidding me?" I shouted.

"What's wrong?" Ryan called out from the bottom of the stairs.

"I'm fine. I'll be down later!" I yelled down to him.

I rushed down the hall to the room I was using. I shut and locked the door behind me.

I tried to call Jordan again. Once again, it went straight to voice mail.

My stomach twisted into hard knots as the tears formed and slid down my cheeks.

I looked down at my phone, willing it to ring. I kept lighting up the screen after it'd blacked out.

Twenty minutes later, my phone chimed. Jordan had sent me a text message.

In need of a shower. I'll call you when I get out. ;)

I sat there, stunned, as I reread his text message over and over.

This is stupid. He is going to talk to me now.

I called Jordan again. This time, his phone actually rang.

"Hello? Jordan's personal answering service," a woman answered.

"Who the hell is this? Where is Jordan?" I snapped.

The woman laughed. "I'm his girlfriend, and Jordan is in the shower and about to be very busy. Who's this?"

I dropped my phone. I froze. *This is not happening.*

"Hello? Hello?"

I heard the woman's voice coming from my phone. I looked down at it. I picked up my phone and pressed the End button on the screen.

I went to the couch in my room and sat down. My whole body felt heavy. I pulled my knees up to my chest. I wished that my biggest problems were that Jordan had ignored me today or that he hadn't told me about the wedding right away. We could get past that and be okay. I just wanted to go back into my bubble of happiness and pretend everything was perfect, like it had been this morning, but that bubble was busted now.

My phone started to sing "Catch My Breath" again. I pressed Ignore as tears fell down my face.

Kelly Clarkson's voice was singing again. I took a deep breath. I had to be strong. No matter how badly it hurt, I had to know the truth. I accepted his call.

"Did I mean anything to you?" I asked.

"Whoa, Rox. What did Amy say? When she tossed me my phone, I knew something was up, and then I saw your calls." He sounded worried.

What is he worried about? That his charade is up, and I know the truth?

"She told me. She told me the truth." I dug my nails into my free hand and tried to stop the tears.

"Rox, you're freaking me out."

"She told me that she was your girlfriend."

"Rox! You are my girlfriend, baby. There's no one else."

"Stop lying. I just want to know if I meant anything to you. Was it all a game to you? Why, Jordan? Why?" I couldn't hold back the tears.

"Roxy, you need to listen to me."

Brent was right.

"Were you cheating on her with me? Or did you just go back to her?"

"Goddamn it, Roxy. Listen to me! I am with you. You are my girlfriend! Just you!" he shouted into the phone.

My sadness had transformed into anger. "Then, tell me why you never told me that she was Adam's sister. Tell me why you didn't text me before you boarded. Tell me why you couldn't talk to me when you landed. Tell me why she answered your fucking phone and told me she was your girlfriend!" I shouted back at him.

"Rox, you are my girlfriend. I didn't text you before I boarded because I was mad at you. I felt like you'd rushed me off, and I didn't like it. I knew

I should have texted you. I'm sorry that I didn't. As for why I couldn't talk to you after I landed—well, that is pretty simple. I was covered in throw up."

"What?"

"Yes, it was as sickening as it sounds. I was seated next to this little boy. He started crying at the beginning of the flight. Then, his mom started giving him candy to keep him quiet. He was literally bouncing in his seat halfway through the flight. But a bouncing kid was better than a screaming kid. His mom continued to give him candy to keep him happy. The flight landed, and just before I stood up to get my bag, the kid turned to me and puked all over me. It was hands-down the most disgusting thing that has ever happened to me. I had puke on me from my head down to my shoes. If you could have only seen me, it was awful, baby."

"Stop. Don't baby me. I don't care about you being puked on. I want to know why she said she was your girlfriend. Why would she say that if it wasn't true? Why didn't you tell me that she was going to be there?"

"Rox, I need you to calm down."

"If you want me calm, answer my fucking questions!" I yelled.

"I didn't tell you because I didn't want you to freak out. After the way you reacted when you saw she had been calling me, I felt like I couldn't tell you. I didn't want you to obsess over the fact that she was going to be here."

I don't obsess over things, do I?

"So, what you're saying is, you thought I would act crazy. What happened to you not thinking that I'm crazy?"

"I don't think you're crazy. I have seen crazy, and you're far from it. I didn't want you to worry, babe."

"You mean, you didn't want me to think that you were going back home to be with your ex. Because that is what you do, right? Brent told me, Jordan. He told me how you drop everyone and everything for her."

I waited for him to answer. I wanted him to tell me that Brent was wrong. I wanted him to make everything better and repair our happy bubble, but all I got was silence, and that silence was deafening.

I couldn't tell if my chest was being ripped apart or crushed. "You did, didn't you?"

"Roxy, you don't understand. It's a long story, and it shouldn't be explained over the phone." His voice was low and sad.

I hated how all I wanted to do was hug him and make him feel better. *What the hell is wrong with me?* I was hurting, and it was because of him. I shouldn't want to make him feel better.

"I don't understand? Please tell me what I don't understand."

"Roxy, you need to trust me. I'm not the same person I used to be. I didn't come here to be with her. Please, baby, I'm not lying to you."

"I don't trust you. Whatever happened to full disclosure? You knew you were going to Oregon before I asked you to come here with me, but you never told me. You knew she would be there, and you never told me. I don't care what your reasons for not telling me were. She told me she was your girlfriend. Maybe you chose not to tell me about that, too."

The memories I had made with Jordan flooded my mind. Every one of them I wanted to forget. I didn't care if it meant I would forget the good memories, too. I didn't want to remember him at all.

"Rox, you know that's not true. I would never hurt you like that. I would never cheat on you."

"All I know is, I can't do this with you anymore."

"Roxy!"

"I'm done." I hung up the phone.

So much for happy endings.

I fell onto my side and cried. It was the kind of crying where I had to hold my breath to keep in all the pain.

I wrapped my arms around myself. I knew it was useless. Everything that I'd feared would happen if I let myself care about Jordan was happening. I was falling apart.

I was still crying when there was a knock on my door. I wiped my eyes and looked out the window to see the sun was starting to set. I had been up here for hours.

"Roxy, did you fall asleep in there?" Ryan asked.

I sat up. I didn't want my brother to see me this way. He would want answers, and I couldn't handle giving them to him right now. In fact, I never wanted to tell him about Jordan. Maybe I could just pretend that part of my life had never happened. I wanted to forget him.

Ryan knocked again. "Roxy?"

Who am I kidding? I would never forget Jordan. The pain that I was feeling was proof of how much I loved him.

"Roxy, wake up!" Ryan yelled, rattling the door handle.

Thankfully, I had locked it.

"I'm not sleeping, Ryan!" I yelled back.

"Then, open the door."

"Um…I'm just about to get in the shower. I'll be down after."

"Are you serious, Roxanne? Make it fast. Oh, and call Tonya. She called me, trying to get a hold of you."

I let out a deep sigh. I didn't even want to talk to my best friend. That would mean I had to admit to her that Jordan and I were over. My stomach twisted at the thought, and the tears began to fall again.

I stood up. "I'll call her later." I made my way into the bathroom.

I wanted to block out the world, block out the pain. I found myself wishing that I had my mom's pills.

Awesome. I am back to being that person.

I looked at my reflection in the mirror. My face was blotchy from crying.

How is it possible that the girl looking back at me is so different from the one I saw this morning?

I got in the shower and cried the last tears I would let myself cry until I got back into this room. I was falling to pieces on the inside, but I couldn't let my brother know. I'd sworn that I would never let him see me sad like this again.

After my shower, I got dressed in a pair of low-rise blue jeans and a white lacy crop top. I pulled my hair up into a high ponytail. I smiled a phony smile into the mirror. This was about to be my greatest performance ever. All I had to do was get through the rest of the weekend. I could fake being happy and pretend that I didn't feel like part of me was missing. My chest tightened as my heart rate picked up. It was a familiar feeling, one that I hated. I knew I could do this.

I survived losing my mom. I survived losing Kevin. I would survive losing—

I couldn't even finish the thought.

I looked at my phone. I knew that I should call Tonya, but it was taking everything I had not to break down again. Talking to her would just have to wait. I left my phone where it was and headed out of the room.

I made my way downstairs. I found Brent and Ryan watching TV.

"Finally." Ryan stood up. "Do you have any idea how much of my life has been wasted while waiting on you?" He was in a joking mood.

I put on my fake smile and laughed. "Don't pretend like you even have a life," I teased back.

"Ha. Since you chose not to come back downstairs, I get to decide where we eat tonight." He smiled at me and made his way to the door.

I looked at Brent and smiled. His gaze inspected me. I felt as though he could see right through my happy act. His look turned to one of concern, confirming that he knew the truth.

I swallowed down the lump in my throat and smiled bigger at Brent. "Come on, slowpoke. If we don't hurry, Ryan is likely to eat us for dinner."

Brent stood and closed the space between us. "Are you okay, Princess?"

I wrapped my arms around myself and shrugged. "I will be once you convince Ryan to let me get drunk."

He gave me a half smile. "I'll see what I can do." Brent slung his arm around my shoulders. "Let's try to have some fun tonight."

I knew having any kind of real fun wasn't going to happen, but that didn't stop me from smiling at Brent and pretending like it was possible. "Let's do it."

"Who is up for a game of miniature golf after we eat?" Ryan beamed with excitement.

I groaned. The last thing I wanted to do was pretend to be happy and play miniature golf. I didn't know how long I would be able to keep up the façade. I was a ticking time bomb of pain and tears that could explode at any moment. I needed to be alone.

"Aw, come on, Princess. It will be fun." Brent nudged me.

I let out a defeated sigh. "I'll play, but you're buying me a few beers first." I pointed at Ryan.

"In your dreams," Ryan shot back.

"Come on, man, let the girl drink. At least she is with you, and you can watch her."

Ryan raised an eyebrow at Brent and me. I thought he knew that Brent was playing sides.

"Fine. You can drink, but if you get caught, I don't know you. Got it?"

I sat up straighter and saluted him. "Yes, sir."

"You keep that up, and you're not getting crap." Ryan laughed.

I was amazed when a small laugh actually came out of me. It looked like I was getting so good at faking happy that I was even fooling myself.

After we ordered, Ryan and Brent took off to play arcade games. That small bit of surprising happiness I'd felt disappeared with them. I was about to go after them in hopes that I could find it again, but the sadness was pulling me down, and it was heavy.

I couldn't get Jordan off my mind. I was taking apart what had happened today. I kept trying to make up excuses for him. I was trying to find a way to make it all not hurt so badly. All I was successfully doing was torturing myself.

I dug my nails into my palms. I had to hold it together.

I looked up to see Ryan walking over to our table. He looked pissed while he was on the phone. My first thought was that Jordan had called him to get a hold of me and told him everything. My heart was racing then.

When Ryan got to the table, I felt as if it had completely stopped. I held my breath.

"Talk to your damn friend, so she will stop blowing up my phone. Why the hell is she calling me anyway?" Ryan held out his phone.

I let out my breath and took his phone. "Sorry. I left mine at the house."

He shook his head in annoyance as he walked off.

"Hello?"

"Seriously? All you have to say is hello? I have been going crazy all day, trying to get a hold of you. How could you leave me hanging like that?" Tonya was screaming.

I'd known she would be irritated because I had been avoiding her, but I hadn't planned for hysteria.

"Breathe, Ton."

"Oh no, you don't get to tell me to breathe. You get to tell me what the hell happened with you today."

"Look, I'm at dinner. I don't really feel like talking about it right now."

"Did you talk to Jordan yet?"

"I really don't want to talk about it." I let out a sad sigh.

My chest was starting to throb. I took the pitcher of beer and refilled my glass. I gulped it down as Tonya rattled on in my ear. By the end of the conversation, Tonya decided that she needed to see me, and she was on her way.

I went over to where Ryan was playing basketball and returned his phone to him. I had no idea how I was going to hold myself together when Tonya got here and started in with the interrogation.

"Pizza there yet?" he asked.

"No. Here's your phone though. Oh, and Tonya might be on her way."

"You have got to be joking! Don't we see enough of her at home? Why is she coming here?"

"Because she is my best friend, and she thought miniature golf sounded fun. Play nice, or I'll just head back home."

"Keep bringing Tonya around, and I might just send you home," Ryan sneered. He shot another basketball and sank it without even looking.

Show-off. I rolled my eyes and walked back to the table.

Brent was there, chatting up the waitress who had brought another pitcher of beer. I slid into the booth on the opposite side of Brent and refilled my glass again. I was waiting for the tingly warm feeling to run through my body and help me relax, but the beer was slow-acting.

Brent smiled at me. "The pizza should be up soon."

The waitressed eyed me as she continued to flirt with Brent.

"You should go tell Ryan." I took a long drink of my beer.

Brent shrugged. "He will figure it out."

A small smile pulled at the corner of my mouth. Maybe Brent was my new happy magic—or maybe the beer was finally kicking in.

Our waitress cleared her throat, trying to get Brent's attention again.

He looked at her. "Would you mind getting us another pitcher?"

Her flirty smile disappeared. "Oh…yeah. I'll be, like, right back." Her voice was squeaky.

It took everything in me not to start laughing at her right then. But guffaw I did when she walked off.

"What is wrong with her voice?" I chuckled.

Brent laughed with me. "You'd better watch it, Princess. She is the one bringing you the beer." He smiled.

"Well, in that case, I'm pimping you out to keep her happy. I apologize in advance for your eardrums."

"That's nice. Just throw me under the bus, why don't you?" He smirked.

I was starting to feel warm and tingly. Finally, the alcohol was working. I drank the rest of my glass. Now, I just needed to get rid of the throbbing ache coming from the memory of Jordan, and I would be great.

Ryan made his way back over to the table as the pizza arrived.

As we ate, Brent and Ryan told dumb jokes and talked about their internship. I smiled and laughed in all the right places. We polished off two more pitchers of beer, and I was feeling good. I was happy drunk by the time Tonya arrived.

"Oh, look at that. The devil is here." Ryan chuckled.

"Keep pretending, Ryan, but everyone knows how bad you want me," Tonya shot back before sliding into the booth, sitting next to me.

Ryan finished off his beer. "You wish." He stood up. "Air hockey?" he asked Brent.

"Sure, man." Brent slid out after him.

Ryan pointed at me. "Miniature golf in half an hour."

"We will be ready." I smiled weakly.

"Can't wait to kick your ass like always." Tonya smirked at Ryan.

"Still praying you will get leprosy." Ryan walked off with Brent.

For the life of me, I would never understand why Tonya and Ryan couldn't just get along.

Tonya played the not-so-mature card and stuck out her tongue to Ryan's back before turning to me.

"I don't know how he is your brother," she huffed.

"He has his moments." I tore at a napkin.

"Enough about him. You have some explaining to do. Spill."

All the pain that I had pushed down shoved its way back up, and my chest throbbed in agony. I wrapped my arms around myself and squeezed.

"Jordan not calling me back was the least of our problems. In fact, he and I broke up today. It turns out that he didn't think it was important to tell me that he would be hanging out with his ex this weekend. That's the whole story. Please don't ask any more questions. I really can't handle talking about it—at least, not right now." I honestly didn't know if I would ever be able to talk about it again, but I didn't feel like it was going to happen.

I waited for her to suffocate me with more questions. I was trying to think of every trick I had developed for keeping myself together. I was shaking with fear that nothing would work. I knew if I started crying now, that would be it—end of story. I wouldn't be able to stop. I would break down, and everyone would see.

"That asshat. I'm going to break his face," she said before engulfing me in an unexpected hug.

I was waiting for her to ask more about what had happened, but she just held me and said nothing else.

I pulled away from Tonya, and I picked up my empty glass. "I need more beer."

"You? I'm the one who has to tolerate your brother for the next few hours. If anyone needs a beer, it's me."

Tonya laughed, and I found myself able to laugh with her.

Maybe I could survive this.

I was handling it better than I'd thought I was capable of. Maybe if I just didn't talk about Jordan, the pain would just fade away. My heart hurt just at the thought of him, proving that nothing would be fading anytime soon.

32

I woke up with a pounding headache and felt like I was on the verge of getting sick.

Tonya had had the bright idea of bribing Ryan with her silence if he would order us stronger drinks than beer. Ryan had jumped on the offer, and Tonya had remained silent for the first game of miniature golf. I honestly hadn't even thought it was possible. Sadly, Ryan had lost and demanded another game. I had always been amazed at Tonya's skill with a putter. With a real golf club, she couldn't even hit the ball, but with a putter, she was a magician.

Brent and I had equally sucked at it, and we'd kicked the ball in the hole more than putting it.

Ryan had kept the drinks coming as we started game two. That game, unlike the first, hadn't had the silence truce, and I'd thought Ryan's head would blow up by the end. Thankfully, Tonya had been drunk most of the game and played more like I had than her normal self. Ryan had won, and Tonya hadn't needed to die. I wasn't sure how things would have gone if she had beaten him again.

After we'd dropped Tonya off at Shawn's house, Ryan, Brent, and I had come back to our place. I had all been for keeping the party going. I had been having a great night, and I had successfully pushed Jordan out of my mind. That happy, giddy feeling had gone away the moment I hit the couch downstairs and passed out.

I looked out the window. Apparently, someone had carried me to bed. Most people would love to wake up to a beautiful view of the ocean. Right now, all I could think was, *Why the hell would someone build a house with so many windows?*

It was too bright. I rolled over and covered my head. I was at war with myself. I wanted to put my head under the covers, get lost in the darkness, and fall back to sleep, but I felt like I was suffocating.

So, head out of the covers won. I rolled over to find my phone to see what time it was.

My phone stared back at me like a black mark of death. I still hadn't turned it on, and the feelings swirling inside me made me wonder if I would ever be able to turn it on again. Maybe it was time for a new number altogether.

I got out of bed and made my way to the bathroom. My reflection was not one I particularly enjoyed seeing. My face was puffy from drinking, and I looked tired. On the plus side, at least I wasn't red and blotchy from crying. I felt as though that was some small victory.

I wanted to laugh and say, *Take that, Jordan. I'm going to be just fine.*

But all I managed to do was look at the sad expression now on my face and try not to start crying.

As I got in the shower, I contemplated how I had fallen in love with someone so quickly and how it had been so easy for him to let me down. Part of me wondered if he felt bad for not telling me the truth. *Was he thinking about me at all? Did he even care about me? I knew I loved him, but was there a chance he loved me, too? No, there couldn't be. If he loved me, he wouldn't have ever lied to me. He knew how important trust was to me.*

I was annoyed with myself when I realized I was once again crying. I wasn't supposed to be crying over him anymore. He didn't deserve my tears. I had to be stronger. I couldn't let him destroy me.

Even as I thought that, a small voice inside my head whispered, *He already did.*

After my crazed shower full of terrible emotions, I pulled myself together and got out. I took out my suitcase and looked at the clothes I'd brought. I wanted something that screamed, *I'm hot and single and in need of a distraction, but I'm not desperate. Okay, maybe I'm a little desperate.*

I went with a pink-and-black polka-dot bikini. I pulled on a pair of black linen shorts.

Today felt like a beach day. As soon as I thought about going to the beach, my stomach cramped up. The beach was just a painful reminder of Jordan. *Nope, today is definitely not a beach day.*

I pushed down the pain of Jordan as thoughts of my mother came back. She would know what to do. She would tell me how I could make myself feel better. The hurt I felt from missing her was too much to hold back. The tears started falling just as there was a knock at the bedroom door.

"Hold on," I called out. I tried to gather my composure, but before I could, Ryan walked through the door.

"What the hell? I said, hold on!" I yelled before turning around and trying to hide my tear-streaked face.

"Whoa…Rox, what's wrong?"

"Nothing. Can you just get out?" I snapped.

Ryan wrapped his arms around me. "Come on, tell me what's wrong, and don't tell me nothing."

I pulled out of his hug. The look on his face was the exact look I'd sworn never again to cause him to have.

Way to fail, Roxanne.

"I just got a little sad. It's nothing really."

"I thought you were doing better. This is my fault. I should have never left. I knew you weren't ready to be alone."

My heart broke that Ryan thought my sadness was his fault.

"No, Ryan. I'm fine. I was just having a girl moment."

"Wait—does this have to do with Ethan? Did he do something to hurt you? I swear, if he did, Roxy—"

"No! Ethan didn't do anything. We're just not, um…together anymore. It was too much, you know?"

I hated that I was lying to my brother once again.

My stomach twisted, and I just wanted to tell Ryan everything, but it was too painful. Seeing as I'd already let him catch me crying, a complete breakdown was not going to happen. It couldn't. I wouldn't let it.

"I promise. Ethan was nothing but nice. I really am just having a moment. I'll be fine."

"You sure?" Ryan looked far from convinced.

But I was determined to have him smiling and not worried. "I promise."

"All right, I just came up to see how you feel about hitting the beach. Since you are already dressed for it, I guess I had a good plan for the day."

I swallowed hard. The beach was the last thing I wanted to do, but if I backed down now, Ryan would go back to worrying.

I smiled big. "The beach sounds perfect. I was just about to head down and ask you if we could go."

"Sweet. Let me just tell Brent that we're ready, and we can head out."

"I'll be right down."

As soon as he closed the door, I collapsed facedown on the bed.

"Earth, it's me, Roxy. If you could open up and swallow me now, that would be super." I rolled over and looked up at the ceiling. "Life sucks."

I gave myself a second to put my game-winning happy face on before heading downstairs.

"Good morning, Princess." Brent beamed up at me from the bottom of the stairs.

My life might have been falling apart, but the Brent part of it was back to being good. I couldn't help but return his smile. It felt good not to even be faking it either.

"Cooler is packed, and the truck is loaded," Ryan informed us as he entered the house.

"You do know this house has stairs that go down to the beach, right?" I asked.

"Yes, sister of mine, but that is a private beach. What fun is a beach without a ton of people?"

"Let's go find some fun on the beach then, and maybe some hot guys will make the day interesting." I gave Ryan a not-so-real smile. I hated that I couldn't just tell him the truth.

"Don't even joke. You are going to stay right where I can see you. You might be single, but you won't be running off with some jackass just because you're looking for something new. In fact, how about you just stay single for the rest of your life? It will be good for you. Plus, I won't have to worry about you. Yes, that's the new plan, Roxanne—stay away from boys."

"I thought you had a boyfriend?" Brent asked with a curious look on his face.

I knew he was trying to figure out what load of BS I'd fed Ryan.

Ryan gave him a look. "She did, but they're over now. She says he doesn't need to have his ass kicked, but I'm not so sure."

"Did she tell you who he was?"

Ryan smacked Brent upside the head. "I already knew who he was. Remember Ethan? I told you about my dad walking in on them."

"Oh my God! For all that is holy, can we please never speak about that moment again? Please." I walked outside and got into the backseat of Ryan's truck.

Brent got into the truck and turned in his seat to eye me. "Ethan, huh?"

"Not talking about it." I crossed my arms and sank into the seat. *This day is going to fucking suck.*

I lay on my towel, the sun warming my body. I was trying to remember why I used to love the beach. My mind kept going back to Jordan and all the reasons I never wanted to be on a beach again.

I rolled over onto my stomach and turned my iPod up as loud as it would go. Paramore blasted into my head. I might go deaf, but at least, I wasn't thinking anymore. I closed my eyes and listened to the lyrics. Maybe Paramore wasn't the best choice for I'm-not-going-to-think-of-Jordan music. The lyrics crashed down upon me and made me feel as though I were being crushed by my sadness. *How the hell am I supposed to hold it together and pretend I'm fine when everything makes me want to break down?*

I pulled out my earbuds and sat up.

Ryan was making his way back from the ocean. He stood in front of me and shook his wet hair like he was a wet dog. It was nice to see that he had been letting it grow out.

I pulled my sunglasses down halfway.

"Nice, Ry. Real nice," I deadpanned.

"You refuse to get in the water, so I brought the water to you. I should get a Brother of the Year award. What do you think?" He sat in the sand next to me and gave me a nudge.

"Oh, you deserve a *Something* of the Year award. I'm not sure it will be brother though. I think ass is more fitting."

"That's really nice of you, sis. But I must tell you, seeing as you're my sister, I don't think it's appropriate for you to give me an award for my amazing ass. Kind of gross, don't you think?" He smiled at how clever he thought he was.

I rolled my eyes behind my glasses. "You're impossible."

Ryan reverted his attention to his phone as I lay back down.

"Are you fucking serious?" he roared.

I shot back up, startled. "What's wrong?"

"Your crazy-ass friend is what's wrong!" he sneered.

I gave him a confused look.

"Tonya has called my phone over a hundred times. What the hell, Roxy? Why isn't she calling you?"

"Um…I left my phone at the house. I forgot to charge it last night, and it was dead." That wasn't the total truth, but it was close enough.

Ryan held out his phone to me. "Call her and tell her to stop blowing up my phone. I swear, if I have to get a new number because of her—"

"Chill. I will call her. Look, Brent is back from the store. Go grab a bag of chips, and calm down."

Ryan was the genius who had packed the cooler with beer but hadn't thought to bring snacks. Brent had been nice enough to make a snack run.

My stomach grumbled as I thought about food, but food could wait. I had to call Tonya before my brother really flipped out.

She began yelling as soon as she answered, "Why the hell is your phone still off? Do you know how long I have been trying to get a hold of you? I have been freaking out. You can't do that to me. I'm pretty sure Shawn thinks I'm crazy now. If he breaks up with me, it's on you."

"Wow, you are crazy. Calm the fuck down."

"You don't get to call me crazy. We haven't even been able to talk about what happened with you and Jordan. How am I supposed to know you're okay?"

"I told you yesterday, I don't want to talk about it."

"Where are you?" she yelled.

"What?"

"Never mind. I see Ryan."

"What? Hello? Hello?" *Did she hang up on me?*

I looked around the beach and found Tonya marching toward Ryan and Brent. I made my way over to them, too.

"You"—Ryan pointed at Tonya—"stop calling my phone."

"Go to hell, Ryan!" Tonya yelled back.

Apparently, she wasn't in a joking mood.

Ryan chose to keep his mouth shut. I thought he was as shocked by Tonya's behavior as I was.

I was suddenly kind of scared of my best friend. She marched up to me, and I thought that she might actually hit me. I didn't think I deserved it, but she looked crazy.

Tonya threw her arms around my neck and squeezed. "Don't you ever do that to me again!"

She was crying.

Why is she crying?

Ryan and Brent looked over at us.

I did the only thing I knew to do. I wrapped my arms around Tonya and squeezed her back. "I'm sorry I upset you."

"You didn't upset me. You scared me."

I pulled back and gave her a confused look.

She grabbed my hand and led me away from hearing range of Ryan and Brent. "You were just starting to get better. I was scared that because things had ended with Jordan, you would…" She couldn't even finish her sentence, but she didn't need to.

She looked away from me, but I knew what she was thinking. She thought I would go back to being the pill-popping zombie. My heart broke. I wrapped my arms around her.

"I won't lie to you. I'm dying inside. But I won't ever be that person again. I promise. I'm sorry I haven't turned on my phone. I'm scared, and I can't deal with all that right now. I'm sorry I worried you."

She pulled back and wiped away her tears. "I'm sorry I sort of went crazy."

We both laughed.

"It happens to the best of us."

"Would you mind if I joined you for the rest of the day?"

She looked like an abandoned puppy. It was pathetically adorable.

"Like you even have to ask." I linked my arm through hers, and we headed back to where my brother and Brent were. "But I am dying to know, how did you find us?"

Tonya laughed. "Well, after calling your brother I don't know how many times, I finally called Brent. He told me where you were."

I pulled out a beer from the cooler and handed it to Tonya. She was definitely in need of one.

"You're crazy," Ryan told Tonya.

Tonya smirked at Ryan. "Don't you ever forget it! Ignore my calls again, and I'll cut you."

Brent and I laughed while Ryan looked shocked again.

Then, a small smile crossed his face. "Whatever." He tried to act unaffected by Tonya.

The rest of the day went better than I'd expected it to. I'd found myself laughing more than I'd thought possible. I hadn't even thought about Jordan.

Okay, that's a lie.

I'd thought about him. But the only time it was close to unbearable was when I'd looked out at the ocean to see the surfers. Those damn surfers had almost been my undoing. But Ryan's bad jokes, Brent's caring words, and Tonya's amazing friendship had gotten me through the day.

33

I was glad I survived the day but by the time we got back to the house I felt the sadness forcing its way to the surface. Once in the room, I crawled into bed without even bothering to wash my face or brush my teeth. All I wanted to do was go to sleep and stop feeling this gut-wrenching pain. I cried silently into my pillow until I fell asleep.

I awoke in the darkness of my room to the sound of shouting. I knew I wasn't dreaming, but I just didn't understand why Brent and Ryan were fighting. I hurried out of bed and quickly grabbed some clothes.

My heart was racing as I pulled on my pants and then my T-shirt over my head. I raced out the door and down the stairs.

"You have done enough damage. I told you to stay away from her, and this was why!" Brent yelled.

"I'm not leaving until I see her."

"Jordan?" I knew that it was him, but for some reason, I was having trouble believing what I could see right in front of me. *What is he doing here?*

"Rox...baby, please talk to me." He stepped toward me, but Brent blocked his way.

"I asked you to leave. I won't ask you again." Brent's hand was on Jordan's chest, stopping him from coming closer.

Jordan shoved Brent's hand away and got in his face. "Get out of my way."

The last thing I wanted was to see Brent and Jordan fighting. It didn't matter how mad I was at Jordan. I loved him and wanted to talk to him— or scream at him and maybe even hit him. The only thing I knew for sure was that I didn't want him to leave.

I rushed between the two of them. "Stop! It's a miracle that Ryan isn't up, but I will kill you both if you wake him."

Brent stepped back, glaring at Jordan, with his teeth clenched. "I was handling it." He growled. "Jordan was just leaving."

Jordan stepped closer to me as he spoke to Brent, "You're out of your damn mind if you think I'm going anywhere."

"Please, stop it," I pleaded with both of them. I looked at Brent. "I'm fine. You don't have to protect me."

"Roxy..."

Brent was hurt, and I understood why. But no matter what Jordan had done to me or the lies he'd told, I still loved him, and I wasn't about to let him leave without talking to him. I wasn't strong enough to do that.

"Just let me talk to him, please. I need this." I tried to make Brent understand.

"Fine. Talk to him. If you need me, you know where I will be," he said to me before shooting Jordan a murderous glare. He then walked off, shaking his head in annoyance.

I turned to Jordan, and he quickly closed the little space left between us, pulling me into him and wrapping his arms around me.

"Baby, I've been going nuts. You turned off your phone and wouldn't talk to me. Roxy, you had me freaking out."

I stayed stiff against him. Everything about him holding me felt so right, but I knew everything about me being up against him was all wrong. I shouldn't feel happy to be in his arms. I was hurt and angry with him.

"Rox, please say something," he begged, squeezing me tighter.

I pushed away from him and stepped back. I pointed to the door to let him know that I wanted to go outside. Again, I was still scared to wake up my brother.

We made our way outside, and I was at a loss for words.

Jordan brought me into his arms again, but I gently pulled away from him and shook my head. I couldn't have him touching me and still maintain my thoughts. He had really hurt me, and I was mad at him. His hugging me was making it hard for me to remember why I had broken up with him.

Jordan stepped back. The pain I saw in his eyes was heartbreaking. Every part of me just wanted to comfort him.

What the hell is wrong with me?

I tried to mentally check off the reasons why I was upset with him. Okay, so those reasons were not coming to me at the moment. Having him just feet away from me was messing with my head.

"Please turn around," I said.

"What?" He looked as confused as I felt.

"I can't think with you standing there, looking at me. I need you to turn around."

"Rox, you're being ridiculous."

Oh, he is about to see ridiculous.

"Either turn around, or leave. If you want me to talk to you, you will do as I ask. And don't you dare call me ridiculous again."

I was glad my anger had returned. It was helping me remember why I'd ended things with Jordan in the first place.

Jordan shoved his hands into his pockets and huffed, but he turned around.

I wasn't sure that it would work, but not seeing his face helped a little. I crossed my arms, hoping I could say everything I needed to say without falling apart.

"First of all, you shouldn't have shown up like this."

Jordan started to turn around to object, but I stopped him.

"If you turn around, I will go back into the house and never speak to you again. You're the reason that we are in this situation, so shut up and listen."

Jordan remained quiet and went back to facing away from me.

"Yesterday, my whole world was rocked. I was shaken out of my happy bubble that I had with you. It sucked. I trusted you. I let you in, even when I knew I shouldn't have. I didn't want a boyfriend. I didn't want to care about someone. You knew how scared I was to get hurt again." My voice shook.

I saw Jordan's body tense, and I knew it was taking everything in him not to turn around.

I wasn't sure how much longer he would stay that way, so I quickly continued, "You should have told me the truth about Amy being at the wedding." The tears were building, and I wasn't going to be able to stop them from falling. "You had to know there was a chance that I would find out about her, but it was more important for you to keep your secret than it was for you to keep my trust. You didn't care that you might wind up hurting me."

Jordan turned around. "Roxy, that is not true. Baby, I was too scared to lose you. I care about you way too much, and I couldn't fathom having you push me away. If you knew Amy was going to be there, you would have flipped. I knew you wouldn't just walk away from me, Roxy. You would run. But, baby, I never meant to hurt you."

He closed the space between us, but I stepped back.

"You never meant to? How could you think that I wouldn't be hurt, knowing you chose to lie to me?"

"Rox, baby, please…it was a horrible mistake. I shouldn't have lied to you. But you can trust me. I would never cheat on you. You know me. You have to trust me." His eyes were pleading, and his hands were shaking as he took my hands in his.

But I was furious.

I pulled away from him. "Trust is a big word, and your act of lying speaks volumes. How can you expect me to trust you when you fucking lied? You didn't have to lie. You could have told me that she was going to be there. I wouldn't have freaked out. It's not like I knew the entire truth about her anyway. Once again, you didn't think I deserved to know it."

"You would have freaked, Rox, and you know it. I lied but not really. I just left out some information that I thought would make you start worrying about something you didn't have to worry about."

"Oh my God, Jordan, not telling someone something is the same as lying."

"Fine, you're right. I did something stupid. But I did it for you. She means nothing to me. I didn't want you to even think about her being there."

"How could she possibly mean nothing to you when you have always given up everything else for her? She used to mean everything to you. How do you expect me to believe that you wouldn't leave me if she asked you to?"

"Because I haven't. She has been calling me nonstop since she found out that I had a girlfriend. I told you, Rox. I didn't do serious. Everyone knew that about me. Before you, I probably would have gone back to her if she asked me to. But not now, not ever. I love you, Roxanne. I love you."

My heart stopped as soon as the words came out of his mouth.

No, no, no. He is not telling me he loves me right now.

"No, shut up. Don't say that to me. I don't want to hear any more of your lies."

"Rox, baby, I'm not lying."

I dropped to my knees and wrapped my arms around myself. It was more out of habit than anything else. I was infuriated and in pain. I didn't want this to be my life. I didn't want the man I was in love with to tell me that he loved me like this. We were supposed to have a perfect moment when we exchanged those words. This was so far from happy.

I began sobbing.

Jordan sat down, pulled me onto his lap, and held me. "I've got you. I'll keep you together," he whispered in my ear as he rocked me while holding me tightly.

I wanted to push him away, but I just couldn't. Instead, I let him hold me while I listened to him tell me over and over that he loved me.

When I finally calmed down, I took his face in my hands. As always, he looked perfect while I was sure that I looked like a blubbering wretched mess.

"I hate that you chose to lie to me. I hate that I'm sitting here, wanting to kiss you, but I mostly hate that I don't hate you. I love you."

Jordan's eyes widened in surprise and then shimmered with happiness. As mad as I was with him, it warmed my heart to see that smile crossing his face.

"You love me?" he asked.

"Yes, I love you."

Jordan leaned into me and kissed me, long and hard. I kissed him back as the tears began to fall again. I wasn't sure if they were happy or sad tears. Maybe they were a mix of both. When I pulled away from Jordan, I saw that he was crying, too. I wiped away his tears.

"Why are you crying?"

"I was terrified that I lost you."

I wanted to reassure him that he hadn't and that I was his forever, but I couldn't. I loved Jordan, but the pain that I had originally felt hadn't just disappeared. I was pushing it down, but it was very much still there. I wanted Jordan and me to be okay and for our love to be enough, but deep down, I wasn't sure if it was.

For tonight, I would pretend like it was. I didn't have the strength to do much else. The weekend had turned out to be emotionally exhausting, and I wished I could just pretend like it never happened.

"Let's go to bed. I don't want you to be tired for the drive home tomorrow."

Jordan kissed my nose before I stood up. He got up and then swooped me into his arms.

"I love you, Roxanne Daniels."

My chest tightened, but I smiled at him. "I love you, Jordan Carter."

Thankfully, when Jordan and I went back into the house, Brent was nowhere to be seen.

I directed Jordan to my room where he finally laid me down on the bed. He pulled me into his chest and held me. This was where he should have been all weekend. We belonged together.

I closed my eyes and breathed in the scent of Jordan, trying to lose myself in it and fall asleep the way I used to, but the nagging voice in the back of my mind kept whispering things I didn't want to hear.

What else has he lied about?

How will I ever be able to trust him?

I tried to push away the despicable thoughts, but it was no use. I wouldn't be getting any sleep tonight.

34

No sleep was exactly what I'd gotten. As exhausted as I had been, I couldn't fall asleep. Instead, I had been lying awake, perfectly still, pretending to be asleep for hours now. I hated the fact that I was now a person who pretended to sleep. But seeing as I was trying to forgive Jordan and get over what he had done, I pushed down the pain and decided that I might as well get up.

I packed up all my things as quietly as possible, trying not to wake up Jordan. I wasn't ready for another heart-to-heart or whatever kind of conversation would come this morning.

I changed my clothes and got ready for the day before I headed downstairs to make some much-needed coffee to get me through the ride home.

As I entered the kitchen, I was startled to find Brent sitting at the table. The sun was barely even up.

Why is he awake?

"Good morning," I half-whispered.

Brent turned to look at me. He looked sad, and I hated the feeling that washed over me. I knew I was the reason for the look on his face.

"Morning. I had a feeling you would be getting up early today. I also figured you would try to slip out early without saying good-bye."

Brent knew me better than I was comfortable with sometimes, and this was one of those times. I had planned on getting Jordan up and out of here before Ryan or Brent woke up.

"I just figured we would get an early start home. It's been a long weekend, and I'm not feeling all that great."

"I take it that you and Jordan worked everything out?"

I nodded. "We did."

"Then, why aren't you waiting for your brother to wake up, so you can rave all about your boyfriend?"

I swallowed hard.

It wasn't that I didn't want to tell Ryan about Jordan. I just didn't want to tell Ryan about Jordan yet. Ryan was going to realize that I had lied to him. He was going to know that it was Jordan who had made me cry. Ryan was going to know that it was Jordan who Dad had found me in bed with.

Telling Ryan was no longer something I was excited about. He wasn't going to like my boyfriend. He was going to be pissed, and I wasn't ready to deal with that just yet. It wasn't lost on me that, just a few days ago, I hadn't cared that Ryan was going to be mad about Jordan and the fact that I had lied about him.

But that had been when I was happily in love. I was still in love with Jordan, but I wasn't as happy as I had been.

I pushed the thought from my mind.

"I will tell him but just not today, and I would really appreciate it if you kept my business to yourself."

"Don't worry. I'm not about to spill your secrets to your brother, but I'm also not going to sit here and tell you that I'm happy for you and Jordan. I stand by what I said before. You shouldn't trust him. He's not right for you." Brent stood and walked toward me. "You deserve better, way better."

"Thanks for looking out for me, but you can stop with the brotherly act. I get enough of that from Ryan, and that is what I'm trying to avoid right now."

"Just promise me that you will be careful."

"I will." I was able to give him a real smile this time. That smile grew even bigger when an honest smile appeared on Brent's face, too.

"What is the story you would like me to share with your brother?" Brent asked, walking over to the counter and pouring another cup of coffee.

I shrugged. "Just tell him that I was sick and called Tonya to pick me up and take me home. He will be annoyed that I didn't say good-bye to him, but he'll also be happy that he doesn't have to be around me while I am sick." I was trying to make light of the situation, but it didn't get the laugh I was hoping for from Brent.

The fact that I was still lying to my brother bothered me like nothing else. I was also upset with myself for being mad at Jordan for lying when I lied to people all the time.

Hypocrite party of one, your table is ready.

Brent handed me the cup of coffee he'd just poured. "I'll make sure he gets the message." He gave me a hug and then went to leave the kitchen.

I hated the awkwardness I felt as he walked away.

"Brent?" I called after him.

"Yeah?" he answered, turning around.

"I hated when we weren't talking. I don't ever want that to happen again. You mean way too much to me."

Brent smiled. "Those were some of the worst weeks of my life."

"We're okay now, right? I mean, you're not mad at me or anything?" I was scared of his answer, but I had to make sure.

"You and I are great. Don't worry about us, okay?"

"Okay, good." I set my coffee down and went to give him another hug.

I held on tight to him. I'd almost forgotten how safe I could feel in Brent's arms. I was grateful we were back to being us.

Brent rested his chin on my head. "Be smart, Princess. Trust your brain when it comes to Jordan." He gave me a final squeeze before letting me go and heading to his room.

I stood in the kitchen for a moment, contemplating what he had just said. I grabbed my coffee and made my way back upstairs. I sat on the edge of the bed and watched Jordan as he slept.

The love I felt for him was as strong as ever, but I couldn't deny the doubt that had crept into my mind and heart. I wanted to trust him. I just didn't know how to.

It wasn't even all his fault. I was the one who was the broken mess with emotional issues. I kept thinking that if I was just a normal girl, none of this would have ever been a problem. I would have found out what Jordan had failed to tell me out of fear. I would have been upset for a bit and then moved on.

I was anything but normal. I thought again about how Brent had told me to follow my brain. My brain was warning me to be cautious, to maybe even get out, but my heart was fighting with everything it had, telling me not to give up and run away. My heart had been wrong when it came to Kevin. I said a silent prayer that it wasn't wrong this time, too.

I set my coffee down and gently shook Jordan, waking him up.

He cracked his eyes open. "Baby, it's too early. Why are you up?"

"I thought we could get an early start back home." I lay down and snuggled into him.

Jordan pulled me from beside him to on top of him in one swift movement. "Or we could stay in bed all day and leave tonight." He ran his hands up my shirt.

"As tempting as that sounds, I think I would rather just go home. It's been a long weekend." I got off of him and then lay back on the bed. "All my stuff is ready to go, so whenever you are ready, we can leave."

Jordan sat up. "You okay, Rox?"

"Yeah, I'm fine. I just really want to go home. I promise, we can stay in bed for the rest of the day as soon as we get back."

I was trying to leave before Ryan woke up, but I also really did want to go home. I wanted to be in the last place where Jordan and I had been blissfully happy. I was hoping it would just make everything else fall back into its perfect place.

"That sounds like a plan." Jordan got out of bed and made his way to the bathroom. Before closing the door, he stopped. "Hey, Rox?"

"Yes?"

"I love you." He smiled.

My heart fluttered at his words, and the butterflies went crazy in my stomach. *The fact that he can still give me butterflies has to count for something, right?*

"I love you, too."

It had been a week since Jordan and I returned home from Santa Barbara.

As much as I wished that I could say things were better than ever between Jordan and me, that wouldn't be the truth.

The first night back, the nightmares had started. I would walk into the room where Jordan was supposed to be waiting for me, and there she would be, kissy-face Amy, laughing at me while straddling Jordan.

Then, he would look at me and say, *"You didn't really think I could ever love someone as screwed up as you, did you?"*

On top of the terrible nightmares, I was also getting paranoid when it came to Jordan.

The other day, I'd walked into the room just as he was getting off the phone. I'd asked him whom he was talking to, and he'd said Scott. I'd had a normal reaction and said okay, but later that night, while he'd been sleeping, I'd found myself going through his phone like a nutcase, seeing if he had lied to me. It had turned out that he wasn't.

I hated that I had become that person.

Last night was the first night I'd made up an excuse not to stay with Jordan. I had felt relieved when he'd bought my story of needing to spend time with my dad.

As if my nerves weren't already fried, my dad was home, but preferring time with him over Jordan said more than I was willing to even think about.

I got ready for the day and made my way downstairs. Dad was sitting at the table, drinking coffee, as I entered the kitchen.

"Good morning, Roxanne."

"Good morning," I replied as I opened the fridge and looked for something to eat.

"Before you get anything out, I was thinking you and I could have breakfast at the club."

I stared at the orange juice. I was certain that I must have just imagined what my father had just said.

"Roxy, did you hear me?" he asked.

So many things were going through my head, and I had no time to pick apart and think about any of them.

I closed the fridge. "Sorry. Yes. I mean, sure, that sounds great."

"Good. I also wanted to quickly talk to you about college."

Oh, I knew there was a catch. Dad never goes out of his way to spend time with me.

"What about it? I mean, if you are still trying to get me to change my mind, I'm not going to. I know you're disappointed that I chose not to attend Juilliard, but I don't want to go there anymore."

"Roxanne, I paid your school tuition to USC last week. What I wanted to talk to you about was the fact that there wasn't a bill for the dorm. Did you sign up to live there?"

He was so calm that I felt like an ass for jumping to conclusions.

But I wasn't sure how much longer his calm attitude was going to last.

"Um…not exactly. I'm not planning on staying in the dorms."

His eyebrow quirked with confusion. "Where do you plan on staying?"

"I found an apartment off-campus. I will be rooming with a girl named Megan." I smiled, and even though I hoped that would be the end of it, I knew better.

"Roxanne, I wish you had consulted me about this first. How do you even know if this is a legitimate person and not a scam?" He started rubbing his forehead in the way he always did when I disappointed or irritated him.

I was beginning to doubt that breakfast was still on.

"I was smart about it. I checked everything out. I have talked to her on Skype. And I also had Uncle Zack run her name. Her only offense was a parking ticket two years ago. She's nice, Dad. She is also a sophomore, so she can help me out."

He stood. "I don't like it. I prefer that you stay in the dorms."

"Dad, I already paid my deposit and first month's rent," I argued.

"I don't care. I want you in the dorms."

"You didn't make Ryan stay in the dorms."

"Roxanne, that's because he was living at home."

"Dad, I don't want to live in the dorms. They are cramped and coed. Therefore, they are full of horny college guys. Why would you want me there instead of at a large apartment where I will have my own room? Plus, come on, communal restrooms. Ew." I knew it wasn't the best sales pitch, but it was all true.

"Roxanne—"

I doubted that it would even work, but I wasn't above begging. "Daddy, please. This way, I won't have to deal with being stuck in a small room with someone I might not like. It will be better for my education, too, because Megan was very stern on not wanting some party girl. I was smart about this. The apartment is in a gated community and within walking distance to school. Please."

He let out a deep sigh. "You can stay there for the first semester. If your grades don't impress me, you will move into a dorm. Do you understand?" His voice was proof enough that I was not to push it.

"Yes," I answered quickly.

"I will put extra money in your account. Seeing as you have an apartment, I expect you to buy groceries and eat healthy."

"I will, Daddy." I couldn't contain my smile.

"Did you and Ryan decide what day he is taking you down?"

"I don't need Ryan to take me. I was just planning on loading up my car."

"Actually, you will need Ryan to take you."

"Why?"

"Los Angeles is a different place. I know that you might not understand this, but I don't want you to take your car with you. We will buy you another car for school. You don't need to have a BMW and subject yourself to getting carjacked or worse."

My Cheshire Cat grin disappeared with his words. "Are you kidding me? You can't take away my car."

"I'm not taking away your car. It will be here when you come home. Your uncle suggested getting you a less expensive car. It's a safety measure."

"You have got to be kidding me!"

"Roxanne, I'm allowing you to stay off-campus. The car is not up for discussion."

I opened my mouth to object but quickly shut it. I was already pushing my luck with living off-campus. I would survive with a piece-of-crap car if I had to. I plastered on another fake smile and nodded my head.

"I guess we should head to the club."

I was still shocked by the conversation my father and I had just had, but the fact that he still wanted to spend time with me surprised me the most. Again, all I could do was nod, but at least I was able to smile a real smile.

During breakfast, conversation flowed easily. It was surprising but a welcomed change—well, except for the part when he'd brought up the boyfriend he was expecting to properly meet soon. Without even thinking about it, I'd told him that we weren't together anymore. For him, that had been enough, end of discussion. Our conversation had moved on. For me, the fact that I had been so quick to say that Jordan and I weren't together weighed heavily on my heart.

By the time I got back home, I couldn't stop the unpleasant thoughts from flowing into my mind. Every part of me wanted to push them down and just let it be done. But I knew myself, and the things I pushed down and tried to forget always resurfaced.

For the first time in months, I found myself walking across the backyard to my dance studio. As I stood in front of the door, my chest tightened. The last time I had been in here, I had been with my mom. My hand was on the doorknob, and that was all it took to cause the painful throbbing to start. This pain was like no other.

Hello, pain. Have you missed hurting me?

I knew the hurt was only going to continue if I went inside, but I couldn't turn back. Inside this room, I needed to dance my way through my demons, through my problems, and through my pain. I hadn't been strong enough to come in here before, but I was stronger now.

I entered the room. I questioned if I really had the strength to get through this. Just being in here without her here made every nerve in my body burn with pain.

I took a deep breath and wrapped my arms around myself. I could do this. I might not be going to Juilliard anymore, but I could still dance.

I docked my iPod and selected Secondhand Serenade. I warmed up to "Good-bye." Two verses into the song, and I was already bawling. The lyrics hit me in a way they never had before.

I guess you can't truly understand that kind of heartbreaking pain until you've experienced it. I now understood it more than I wanted to.

I danced through the entire *A Twist in My Story* album twice. I put all my emotions into my movements and left it all on the floor.

It hurt to dance again for many reasons.

One, my body was not prepared for it. I had been lazy for months, and I could feel every muscle screaming at me.

Two, it made me miss my mom more than ever. I hated knowing that she would never watch me dance again. I would never hear her cheering me on. Mostly, I hated that it was just another reminder that she was gone.

Three, I had a hard choice to make, and even though I hated to even admit it to myself, I'd known what my decision was with the first song.

With all my pain, fears, and heartache poured out onto the floor, I finally collapsed, drenched in sweat and still crying.

As I lay in a heap of despair, I thought about how much I hated Kevin. I wanted more than anything to be able to fall foolishly in love again. I wanted the hopeful feeling and to believe in happily ever after again. I wanted my world to once again be full of happiness and possibilities.

I hated that I'd lost all that, and no matter what, I would never get it back. The sad truth about my life now was that it was full of sadness and betrayal, and anything was no longer possible. My mom was never coming back. I could never *un*-break my heart. I was never going to be the whole person I once had been. I was just a fragmented shadow of my former self, and more and more pieces fell off every day.

I stood up and looked at my reflection. I had no more reasons to keep holding myself together. I was broken. I would forever be broken. I grabbed the chair from the corner and threw it into the mirror, shattering them into pieces. It seemed fitting to see myself in the shattered pieces. I could finally see how I felt inside.

As I looked at myself in the wrecked mirror, I remembered the last time I'd felt defeated while my mom was still alive.

"Mom, I'm not sure I want to go to Juilliard," I told her as I bent forward and stretched.

"What do you mean, you're not sure? You have been working for this most of your life. Of course you want to go."

"I'm scared. New York is so far away. I know I should be excited with my senior year almost done, but I'm not. I'm just worried. I'm scared that Kevin and I won't stay together. I'm scared that Sara and Tonya are going to go and find new best friends. I feel like I will lose everything I love after I leave."

Mom chuckled. "Oh, honey. That's what growing up is. It is knowing that things are going to change. But that is how things are supposed to be. I can't tell you if you and Kevin will stay together or if you will always be best friends with Sara and Tonya. But I can tell you that there is nothing wrong with the way you are feeling. You are strong and amazing. I know you have a brilliant future to look forward to."

"How can you be so certain? I feel like my life is spinning out of control."

"Stand up for me."

I stood.

"Now, spin," she ordered.

"What?"

"Spin around."

I turned in a circle and then stopped, giving her a look of confusion.

"No. Spin around in circles until I tell you to stop."

I began spinning around in circles.

As I started to get dizzy, I slowed down.

"Don't slow down. Spin faster, and don't stop."

"Mom, I am going to fall." I laughed and continued to spin.

"Don't stop," she instructed.

I continued to spin faster. I felt sick, and I knew I was going to fall over soon. As I was spinning, I bumped into a chair and heard it fall over.

"Don't stop," she said again.

I knew I was all over the room, and I couldn't figure out why she didn't want me to stop. I ran into a table and heard items from the table crash to the ground. I lost my balance and also fell onto the hardwood floor.

I rolled onto my back and closed my eyes, willing myself not to puke.

I opened my eyes to see my mom's smiling face. She reached out her hand and helped me up.

"If you wanted me to feel like throwing up, you succeeded." I gave her a weak smile.

"No, Roxy, I wanted you to feel what not having control really felt like. After you were spinning for a while, you had no control over where your feet took you. You couldn't stop yourself from knocking things over and making a bit of a mess. You fell. But what I wanted you to focus on the most was that you got back up. You survived spinning out of control."

"Mom, you're weird. You could have just given me an encouraging speech."

"I could have, but that was much more fun to watch."

"I wouldn't have gotten up if you didn't help me."

"Yes, you would have. Maybe not as quickly, but you would have."

"How are you so sure?"

"Because you are my daughter. I know you. You weren't going to just lie there and do nothing."

"I could have."

"You also could have stopped at any time. You chose not to. You chose to trust me."

"You say that like it's a bad thing."

"It's not. Just try not to give up control of your life so easily. With that said, your life lessons are finished." She smiled. "Go back to stretching."

"What if I don't want to?" I teased.

"Don't try to take control now, honey. I have a small amount of time left to order you around."

"Mom, I feel like you will still be telling me what to do when I'm as old as you are." I laughed.

"You're probably right. But do you think you will still listen?"

"I doubt it." I sat back down and started stretching again.

The memory hurt. I hated that it hurt to remember her.

I was no longer in tears when I walked out. I was just angry. I was mad at the world, and I just wanted to forget. Once I was inside, I avoided my dad and went straight upstairs. I pulled the bottle of vodka I had shoved in my closet and headed into the bathroom. I started running the water for a bath. Maybe I could drown my pain and hate with some vodka. By the time I got out of the tub, maybe my life wouldn't be such a hellhole.

I unscrewed the top of the vodka and took gulping drinks before shaking violently. *Just maybe.*

I woke up with another pounding headache. I seriously had to stop waking up this way, but on the plus side, I had gone to bed without the aching pain in my chest. I wanted to argue that the pounding headache was a fair trade, but I was having trouble seeing straight, so I just lay there and begged the room to stop spinning.

I drifted off to sleep again and woke up hours later to a knocking at my door.

"Roxanne, are you up?" my dad asked through the door.

I rolled over and looked at my clock. It was almost twelve. I shot up. I didn't want my dad to come in and see that I was hungover.

"Yeah, I was just about to get in the shower. Is everything okay?"

"Everything is fine. I just need to head back to LA, and I just wanted to say good-bye before I left."

Okay, what the hell has happened to my father?

I was flabbergasted that he was actually taking the time to say good-bye. I was also pissed off with myself for not being able to tell him good-bye properly because I was embarrassed about being hungover.

"Well, thanks for letting me know you're leaving. I love you. Drive safe."

"I will call you and set up a day to go car shopping once you're in LA. I-I love you, too."

I could tell this whole supportive-and-loving-father thing was still hard for him, but I felt joy building at the fact that he was actually trying.

"Bye, Daddy."

The joy I was feeling dissipated when I looked at my phone and saw all the missed calls from Jordan. I couldn't keep ignoring him. I had to stop running away from my problems and trying to drown them out. I reluctantly rolled out of bed.

Time to face life, Roxy.

I gave myself a pep talk the whole way over to Jordan's.

As I sat in front of the condo, I was having an extremely hard time convincing myself that I could actually go in and tell Jordan that things were over.

How could I say good-bye to someone I love?

As much as I wanted to, I couldn't trust him, and that wasn't fair to either one of us.

I blinked back the tears that were about to spill over. I could cry later.

I made my way to the door and knocked. A moment later, Jordan was standing in front of me in all his glory.

"Baby, I've been calling you all morning. I was going nuts, missing you." He pulled me into a hug and placed kisses down my face to my mouth.

When he was done, he pulled back and gave me a concerned look. "Rox, are you okay? Were things bad with your dad?"

"Um…no. Things with my dad are fine. It's just I was…I, um…I was hoping we could talk."

"Damn. I was hoping I would be the one to tell you. But I should have known he would tell you first. Baby, don't worry. It's not a big deal. Travis and Scott are heading back to school early anyway. We are just going to move into the house and enjoy the last few days of summer before school starts."

"What?" I asked, completely confused.

"Isn't that what you wanted to talk about? I'm sorry. I just assumed Brent called you and told you he'd kicked me out."

"He what? Why?"

"He didn't tell you? What was it you wanted to talk about then?"

"That can wait. Why did he kick you out?"

"I think the reason is pretty obvious, Rox. I was actually supposed to be out last week, but seeing as he won't be back until tomorrow, I was taking my time. It's not that big of a deal." He pulled me back into him and kissed the top of my head.

I had no clue how to tell Jordan what I had originally wanted to say. It was a terrible time to do this to him. I felt sick about it.

"Rox, it's really going to be okay. The only thing that is going to suck is waiting for you to get to school. But it will only be a few days. Then, we will be back together." He lifted my chin, so he could look into my eyes. "I love you."

Those words were almost my undoing. *How am I supposed to walk away from him when he is standing right in front of me, telling me he loves me?*

I should have just taken the chicken way out and sent a breakup text. But I'd thought he deserved more.

That was the point though. He did deserve more. He deserved someone without baggage who could love him without fear, someone who could trust him and not question everything he said. As much as I wanted that person to be me and as much as I loved him, it just wasn't enough. I was too screwed up, and I couldn't trust him.

Jordan noticed how I hadn't said the words back to him. I was about to step away from him when he took my face in his hands. He closed the small gap between us and kissed me with the kind of passion I hadn't felt since before we left for Santa Barbara.

I knew why I had come here, but my body had no intention of stopping this kiss. I wrapped my arms around his neck and fisted his hair while parting my lips. His tongue plunged into my mouth and danced with mine. His hands moved down my body and squeezed the back of my thighs before hoisting me up to wrap my legs around his waist. He spun us around and pressed me up against the wall.

He looked deeply into my eyes. "I love you so much, baby."

His mouth engulfed mine again without even giving me a chance to respond—not that I could have. My mind and body were completely consumed with him. I couldn't get enough, and I wasn't sure I even wanted to. His lips left mine, only to go to work on my ear and neck. A moan of need came from my mouth. He had my entire body buzzing with passion.

Jordan pressed himself into the place where my body was throbbing for him.

"I need you," I practically begged.

Jordan pulled me off the wall and carried me to the couch. I was working at his pants as soon as he laid me down. He pulled off my shirt and started kissing down my shoulder.

I clasped his face in my hands. "Jordan, I need you now."

He saw the urgency in my eyes and smiled. He quickly stood, undid his pants, and dropped them to his ankles.

"Tell me how bad you need me, baby," he growled, pulling my legs toward him and pushing up my skirt.

"I need you like I've never needed anything else before," I answered honestly.

He pulled my panties to the side before pressing his fingers into my wetness. I almost came apart right then. He was all I needed, all I wanted.

"I love knowing what I do to you. I love feeling how much you want me."

"More," I pleaded.

He pressed his fingers in me again, giving me what I craved.

"Yes!" I cried out.

He pulled out his fingers. "Tell me what you want, Rox."

"I want you. I need you."

Jordan placed himself between my legs, teasing me. I needed him to thrust himself inside me. I needed the release I had become used to getting from him.

"Tell me you love me, baby." His voice turned almost primal, and his eyes were full of need.

I was brought back from my high and remembered why I had come here in the first place.

I swallowed hard as I took in the beautiful man above me. I did love him. I loved him more than I'd ever known I could love someone. But I also knew love wasn't enough. Relationships were hard and took work, but they also needed trust.

"Tell me you love me, Roxy," he repeated.

I knew right then that this would be good-bye for me. This would be the last time I ever let Jordan touch me this way. It would be the last time I got to tell him that I loved him and to see his face light up. So, that was what I did.

I looked Jordan in the eyes and told him the absolute truth, "I love you. I love you so much that it hurts."

Jordan's eyes never left mine as he pushed himself into me. I was overcome with emotion, and I had to blink back tears.

Does he know? He has to know this is good-bye.

I pushed the questions out of my mind and let myself just be with Jordan for the last time.

My body came apart with his. He lay down next to me and pulled me into him.

"I love you, Roxanne. I love you with all that I am. I love you with all my heart. I will love you forever."

The tears I had been pushing back began to fall.

Jordan sat up. "Baby, what's wrong? Why are you crying?"

I sat up and put my shirt back on. I couldn't even look at him. "I'm sorry. I can't. I came here to tell you that. I-I just can't."

He took my face in his palms and forced me to look at him. "Tell me you're not saying what I think you're saying, Roxanne—not after all we've been through."

"I just can't do this anymore. We won't work."

"Roxy, we will work. You just have to want it, too."

"I wish it were that easy, and all I had to do was want us to work, but life doesn't work that way. No matter how much I want you or how much I love you, I don't trust you. Because of that, I can't stay with you."

"Are you kidding me, Roxy? You just had sex with me and told me you loved me, knowing you were going to break up with me?"

"I broke up with you when I found out you were a liar. As far as loving you, I do. But what just happened was good-bye."

I stood up.

"Don't do this, Rox. Don't push me away because you're scared."

"I am scared. I'm scared of what will happen if we stay together, and I'm scared of what will happen when I walk out of that door. But you lied to me, and as much as I want to get over it so that we can be okay, I can't. I don't trust you, and it's driving me insane."

"Don't push me away because of what some other guy did to you. I'm not him. I will never hurt you that way."

"I can't stay with you and spend my days hoping that you won't cheat on me or hurt me in some other terrible way. I'm insecure, and it's only going to get worse if I don't walk away now." I dug my nails into my palms. I couldn't cry.

He sucked in a deep breath, and I could see the pain I was causing him.

"You could do this, Roxy. You're just choosing not to. You're pushing me away because you're scared. I promise you, you have nothing to be scared about."

I looked down at the ground.

"Roxy, I love you."

"I'm a mess, Jordan. Trust me. By tomorrow, you will be thankful that I'm out of your life."

I turned and walked toward the door, but Jordan grabbed my wrist, stopping me.

"Roxy, don't do this. You might be a mess, but you're my mess, and I love you."

No matter how much it hurt, I forced myself to look at him again. "I never wanted to be in a relationship. I told you that from the beginning, and this is why. In case you forgot, I also told you not to fall in love with me."

"Roxy, you say that like I ever had a choice. I've loved you since day one. You are the most incredible woman I've ever known." He brushed my hair off my shoulder. "I love you in a way I never knew was possible. But, Rox, if you are looking for why this won't work, then those reasons are all you are going to find.

"I'm not proud of my past or the person I became over the last few years. I've made a lot of mistakes. But I'm not my past. That is who I was. I will forever regret lying to you, but I promise, it won't ever happen again.

"Baby, please, I'm asking you not to run away. I'm asking you to trust me. I'm asking you to believe in us and give this a chance. I know you are scared, and I understand the fact that my lie doesn't ease your fears. But you're not the only one who is scared. I'm scared to lose you. So, please don't push me away. Don't run. Let me love you."

Every part of me ached for him. He thought he would always love me, but I knew for a fact that love didn't last, and at some point, he would hurt me.

"I can't. I'm not just ending this for me. I'm ending it for you, too. You deserve better. You deserve someone who can love you without wondering when it's all going to fall apart. You deserve someone who doesn't come with a life's worth of emotional baggage at only eighteen years old. I need to know that I can get through all of my hurt without you and your magical ways of making it disappear. I need to be on my own. I need to heal. And I need to do it without you."

"Rox, I'm not going to go away."

"Yeah, you will. One day, you will wake up and realize that you're sick of me and all my issues. When that day comes, you're going to go away, and I won't be able to handle that. It will destroy me, and there is nothing in this world that will be able to fix me. But if I let you go now, I might be able to survive this."

"Roxy, don't do this. Don't run away from this. Let me love you, and I promise, I will spend every day of my life reminding you that you are all I could ever want."

"Until the day you don't."

"Roxy"—his face turned hard—"I've begged you to stay with me. I've laid my heart on the line and told you how I feel. If you care that little about me and want to walk out of my life, I'll hold the fucking door for you."

His anger startled me, but I had hurt him, and I deserved it.

"I'm sorry, Jordan." I wanted to hug him, but I couldn't. I turned and opened the door.

He huffed as I walked out.

"You talk about how scared you are of me hurting you, but you don't even care that you are always the one with the power to hurt me. Sad thing is, I won't even be the last guy whose heart you tear out. You will continue to push people away and blame it on your fears of getting hurt all because one guy was too stupid to know what he had," he sneered.

"That's not fair. I was happy. You messed that up by lying to me. I can't just get over it and trust you, and I'm sorry that hurts you, but I wasn't the one who lied."

"Yeah, you were, Roxy. You lied when you said you loved me. You don't walk away from the people you love. You don't just give up and run away because things get rough. At least I know the truth, and it's that you don't love me, you never did."

I felt like he had just slapped me. My stomach twisted painfully.

"What?" I snapped.

"I said you—"

"No, I heard you just fine," I interrupted. "I was giving you a chance to change what you had just said to me."

"I'm not going to. If you ever really loved me, you wouldn't be doing this," Jordan said.

"Fuck you, Jordan. You don't get to say how I feel about you!" I turned and walked out the door.

"You walking away proves that I'm right!" he yelled after me.

"You're not right. You're fucking stupid, and I don't have time to waste on stupid."

I got in my car and slammed the door.

Fucking dumbass!

I was angry, and that had made me strong enough to walk away. But that strength wasn't enough to keep me from watching him in the rearview mirror as I drove off.

The tears streamed down my face. This wasn't supposed to happen. This wasn't supposed to be my life. I had enough pain to last me a lifetime. I wasn't supposed to get more.

Stupid, stupid me and falling in love.

All it had gotten me was hurt, and here I was, still the same broken girl I had been before.

36

The next morning, I was exhausted. Considering that I hadn't slept last night, I wasn't surprised.

Even though I had ended things with Jordan, I was surprised that I was also the one checking my phone every hour to see if he'd called or texted.

There was something seriously wrong with me.

I got dressed and made my way downstairs. I saw him everywhere. The memories flooded my mind and made my heart break. It was even more painful than I'd thought was possible. I should be a pro with pain like this by now, but I had no such luck.

I had to get out of this house. I got into my car and just started driving. When I'd left, I hadn't had a plan of where I was going.

As I pulled up to the cemetery, for the first time all morning, I felt relief. That in itself was a miracle.

I got out of my car and headed to my mother's grave. I walked slower as I got closer to my mother's headstone. The relief I'd originally felt dissipated, and my chest began to tighten. This was never going to get easier.

I sat down in front of her resting place. I looked around the cemetery. For a place that held such pain for people, it was quite peaceful here.

I lay back and looked up to the sky. "Mom, I need your help. I'm lost in this world without you. Everything is all wrong," I told her.

The clouds glided through the blue sky above me. I stared at them, waiting for some kind of answer. If I didn't look away, maybe my mom would magically speak to me and fix everything that was messed up in my life right now. All I ended up hearing was a few chirping birds in a tree not too far from me.

I let out a deep sigh. Coming here wasn't going to fix anything. But it did manage to make me feel guilty for wanting to give up. My mom's life had ended too soon, yet here I was, complaining that life was too hard.

You woke up this morning, Roxanne, when so many other people didn't.

I lay there and contemplated life. The truth was, my life wasn't as terrible as I considered it. Parts of it sucked, but there were still good parts, too. I would be leaving for college soon. I had the world's greatest best friend. And my family somehow still loved me even though I was all kinds of screwed up.

My mom might not have said anything to me, but being here had a way of putting things in perspective. I was still the same damaged girl I had been before, but I would just have to keep pushing through the pain. Giving up wasn't an option.

I stood up and looked down at her headstone. The tiny crystals glistened, and I actually managed to smile. "I love you, and you're always in my heart."

With a smile still on my face, a single tear rolled down my cheek. I turned and headed back to my car. The tightness in my chest lifted. Life was hard, and life without my mother seemed to be impossible at times. But I was walking away with a newfound determination. I would survive.

Broken and all, I would get through whatever life threw my way. I had to—not just for her, but for me. I got into my car, ready for the next chapter in my life. But I was also hoping that it would be a less painful chapter than the others.

That hope was smashed when I read a text from Tonya.

Where are you?

With all the Jordan drama, I had completely forgotten that I was supposed to be helping Tonya finish packing for college. She was leaving today.

Time for another good-bye.

"I'm gonna miss you." I took the picture of Tonya and me off her nightstand and lay down on her bed as I looked at it.

She lay next to me. "Not as much as I'm gonna miss you."

I let out a sad sigh while looking at the photo of Tonya and me making funny faces in our cheerleading uniforms. We'd lost that game, but from the picture, no one would ever know. We were both way too happy.

She nudged me. "I'm taking that one with me."

I handed her the photo.

She got off the bed. "I know I shouldn't be saying this, but I'm really, really glad that you're not going to Juilliard," she said, looking down.

I raised an eyebrow at her. Her statement had caught me off guard.

She refused to look at me though. She instead looked up and stared out her window. "It's not that I don't think you're an amazing dancer or even that you shouldn't change your mind and actually go. It's...it's..." Tonya stuttering rarely happened.

She finally looked at me, her eyes brimming with tears. "New York is just so fucking far away. At least Los Angeles is only an hour flight from me. I mean, as selfish as it is, I wish you would go to school in San Francisco. If I could put you in my pocket and always keep you with me, I would."

I laughed even though I had tears of my own building. I got up, and I held her hand. "I'm glad I'm not going to Juilliard either. I know how badly my mom wanted me to go, but I think it was more her dream than mine." It hurt to say, but I knew it was the truth. "Besides, it will be nice to go to school where she went. I think it's something that will help me. I'll always dance, but I want to do it my way." I smiled at Tonya.

"She would be so proud of you," she told me.

This sent me over the edge, and I could no longer hold back the tears. After crying for way too long, I helped Tonya pack the rest of her things.

"Okay, you know all my measurements. I want everything you make to be ready to wear for me!" I told her, making her laugh.

"Let's just hope FIDM keeps me long enough that I get to make clothes. I don't know how I'm going to survive without you. You are the only reason I maintained a three-point-oh GPA. You got me through high school." She cracked up.

"Well, don't tell them I'm the one who wrote your application essay, and you'll be fine. Besides, I've always told you how smart you are. You just get easily distracted," I reminded her.

Tonya huffed, "Exactly. What am I going to do without you around to keep me on track?"

I hugged her. "You act like I won't be texting you daily, reminding you to get back to work."

"Promise?" she asked, hugging me back.

"Promise!" It was the easiest promise I'd ever made.

I needed Tonya just as much as she needed me.

We finally got all of Tonya's boxes and bags packed in her car. Her parents had left about five minutes ago to get gas. She was supposed to meet them soon. As much as Tonya complained about them driving to San Francisco to drop her off at school, she had no idea how lucky she was.

I would do anything for my mom to take me to college. I wanted to remind Tonya of that fact, but I wasn't about to make her feel bad.

I hugged her again before she got into her car.

"We will text every day and have phone dates at least once a week." She held out her pinkie, waiting for me to promise.

I looped my finger with hers. "Yes," I promised.

I was about to pull my hand away when she tightened her grip.

"Don't you dare make a new best friend, Roxanne Daniels."

"I would never!" I smiled.

She released my finger and looked at me with sad eyes. "I'm really gonna miss you."

"I'll miss you more! Now, go meet your parents before they start freaking out." I feigned impatience.

"Okay, but one more thing. Since you still have two days until you head off to school and you won't have me to keep you entertained and you will have a lot of alone time—"

"Spit it out, Ton!"

"I really want you to think about whether or not breaking up with Jordan was the right thing to do. I don't want you to regret this decision for the rest of your life."

What kind of best friend is she?

She knew why I had done it. She was supposed to support me, not make me second-guess my decision.

I turned on my heel and looked back at her over my shoulder. "Not gonna happen!" I waved.

She sighed angrily. "Fine, but when you're old and alone, I'm gonna remind you that I tried."

I smiled, knowing she couldn't see it, and got in my car. "I won't be alone. I'll have you. Good-bye, Ton!" I yelled.

I blew her a kiss as she started her car.

"Love you, bitch!" she shouted out her window.

"Love you more, slut!" I started my car as Tonya drove away.

I turned the radio up to try to drown out the new thoughts of Jordan now in my head.

Thanks a lot, Ton.

As I walked into my house, I almost ran into Ryan.

"Whoa! Hey!" I said, alarmed.

He smiled at me as he switched places with me in the doorway.

I was happy that Ryan was home, but crashing into him at the door was more of a hello than anyone needed.

"Hey, yourself. How did seeing off your evil side go?" He laughed even though nothing he'd said was remotely funny.

"Shut up! She's not evil, and if you must know, it sucked. She's probably not even out of the county, and I already miss her."

"If you ask me, it will be good for you two to have some time apart. With her gone, maybe you won't get in as much trouble."

Whether Ryan wanted to believe it or not, Tonya was not a bad influence on me at all.

"Huh, I don't remember asking you," I snapped.

"Yeah, yeah. Hey, you wanna come with me? I'm about to meet Brent and some of our brothers for dinner."

"Oh, that sounds like so much fun! Maybe I can make out with one or two or even three frat brothers before I leave. I still have two days left here. I could do a lot of damage in those two days all by myself." My statement oozed sarcasm.

Ryan didn't even crack a smile. "I hope you understand when I tell you that you're no longer welcome."

"Oh, shucks!" I snapped my fingers.

"Make sure you start packing tonight. I don't want you leaving it all for the last day," he reminded me.

I rolled my eyes. "Yeah, I know. Don't worry!"

I turned and walked toward the stairs.

"Rox, a package was left at the door for you. I put it on your bed," Ryan called out after me.

I waved my hand, acknowledging him, before I hit the stairs, but I said nothing.

"Later," he said before shutting the front door.

Kelly Clarkson's voice was singing in my purse. My heart dropped, knowing Jordan was calling. I dug my phone out. We'd said everything we had to say. He'd said he loved me, and I'd told him I couldn't be with him. I thought I'd made myself extremely clear.

I stared at his contact picture and felt my stomach turn. *Why is he calling?*

Finally, my phone went to voice mail.

I wanted to call him back and beg him to forgive me, but I couldn't. The sad fact for us was that love wasn't enough. I was too screwed up anyway, and he deserved better.

I couldn't go to school and be with him. *So what if everything was great for a while?*

If Kevin had taught me anything, it was that love didn't last.

I wouldn't give Jordan the chance to hurt me and ruin my life in Los Angeles. I'd chosen USC for a reason. I couldn't let a guy ruin that. No matter how much I still loved and missed him, I had to remember that happy endings only happened in storybooks.

I sucked in a deep breath, and I pushed down my pain.

After I checked my phone for the fifth time, I accepted that he hadn't left a voice mail. I should probably just delete his number altogether, but I wasn't ready for that—at least not yet. I would do it eventually.

Just not today.

I saw the package on my bed that my brother had brought up. This made me smile. I loved presents. I instantly got giddy. I thought Tonya must have somehow snuck it here because there was no postage on the box. It had definitely been hand-delivered.

I tore off the brown packaging to find a long white box with a black bow. A card was tucked under the ribbon. I opened the card to read text written in red ink.

YOU'VE BEEN A VERY BAD GIRL!

I knew it wasn't from Tonya anymore.

So, who sent it? Maybe it's from Jordan?

I opened the box. Inside laid a dozen red roses, but they were all dead. The dead roses weren't what made me scream. What scared the hell out of me was my missing bikini top folded on top of the rose stems along with many black-and-white pictures of me in the box. Someone had been watching me and taking pictures of me while I'd changed, kissed Jordan, gone swimming while topless, and visited the cemetery.

I was sucking in air like there wasn't enough in the world for me. My chest constricted, and my stomach twisted—not with pain this time, but with pure fear.

What the fuck?

Follow
Roxy, Jordan, Tonya, Ryan, and Brent
as the story continues in *Because of You*.

ACKNOWLEDGMENTS

Whoever thinks writing a book is easy is dead wrong. Writing a book is hard work, and it takes a number of people to get through the entire process.

Without You would never have been created without the support of my loving husband. Thank you, Kris Purdue, for letting me lock myself in the room while leaving you with our three little monsters. Thank you for understanding when, "One more minute," turned into twenty and then turned into an hour. Thank you for letting me sleep in after I spent all hours of the night writing. I will never be able to thank you enough. Just know that I wouldn't have been able to write this book without you. I love you, I love you, I love you.

Next, I have to thank my beautiful children—Krislynn, Ethan and Liam. Thank you for letting Mommy work. I know I said, "Hold on," and "I'll be there in a second," a lot. You three are my little rock stars, and I am so happy to be your mommy. Liam, having you growing inside me while writing this book helped bring out the crazy in my characters. I love writing, but I will always love you three more.

To Mom, who has listened to me talk about my book since the beginning—You were there for me every step of the process, and I am extremely grateful to have such a remarkable woman to call my mom. I love you.

To my best friends:

Sophie, we have been through everything together. Our friendship has lasted throughout times when most others would have failed. You are my family, and I am so thankful for your never-ending support and encouragement. I love you.

Caitlin, you are one-of-a-kind. You're an incredible friend. I love you. Thank you for being as excited about my book as I was. You have always been my personal cheerleader, and I am blessed to have a wonderful person like you in my life.

Not everyone has true friendships that will never falter. I am lucky enough to have two. I love you both beyond words.

But it takes way more than loving friends and family to publish a book.

Thank you to Sarah Hansen at Okay Creations for my absolutely beautiful cover.

Gigantic thanks to Jovana Shirley at Unforeseen Editing for editing and formatting. Because of you, *Without You* became more than just a dream.

Of course, BIG thanks to everyone who added *Without You* to their to-be-read lists and who were interested in this book from the beginning. I will never be able to express how much your interest meant to me and how it inspired me to work hard to finish it.

You all rock!

ABOUT THE AUTHOR

Born and raised in California, Reylynn Purdue lives with her loving husband and three beautiful kids. A lover of books, she reads like crazy. She has always enjoyed writing, but one day, she decided to take it to the next level. She started writing her debut novel in 2013. To say she had no clue about what she was doing is an understatement. As of today, she still has no clue about what she is doing when it comes to publishing a book, but she is learning as she goes. She loves her stories and hopes you will as well. She also finds talking about herself in third person to be very strange, and she kind of hates it.

To find out more about Reylynn, visit:
http://www.facebook.com/ReylynnPurdue
http://twitter.com/PurdueReylynn
http://www.goodreads.com/author/show/6879961.Reylynn_Purdue